BAD

LUCK

CHARM

JULIE JOHNSON

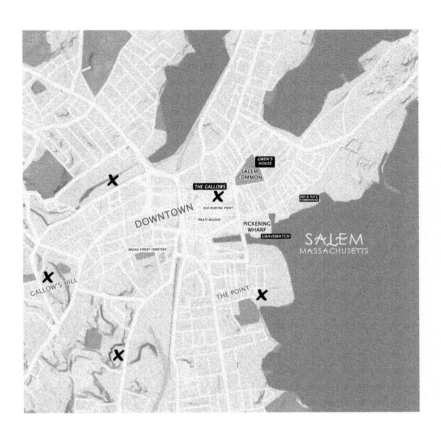

"You've always had the power, my dear. You just had to learn it for yourself."

— GLINDA THE GOOD WITCH, *THE WIZARD OF OZ*

For my family.

As we often say...

"Just let me be a witch!"

PROLOGUE

They say Satan has a sense of humor. That may explain why my life is such a joke.
- Gwen Goode, lamenting recent events

"Whoa. Your aura is so stormy, they're going to put out a Nor'Easter watch for the entire Eastern Seaboard."

The statement greeted me the moment I stepped through the front door of The Gallows, the cafe-slash-bookstore-slash-occult-shop I owned and operated in the heart of downtown Salem, Massachusetts. It was delivered with typical airy nonchalance by Henrietta "Hetti" Charles, the barista-slash-cashier-slash-mystical-hobbyist I'd hired on last spring to help out around the place when the crush of magic-obsessed tourists and latte-nursing locals became too much to handle on my own.

I took her words in stride, unfazed by either the fact that Hetti claimed to see my aura, or that said aura was supposedly

1

the color of dark clouds. It was barely 9AM and already my day had gone to Hell in a hand-basket. Why in a hand-basket instead of something more time efficient, say, a Maglev train or a Maybach, I had no earthly idea. Then again, I wasn't an expert on sub-dimensional travel.

I flipped the CLOSED sign to OPEN before the heavy oak door swung shut at my back with a soft tinkle of bells.

"Good morning to you too, Hetti."

"Oh. Right. *Morning.*"

She grinned at me as she came around the espresso bar, but even an uncharacteristic flash of her mega-white teeth could not erase the crease of worry between her furrowed brows — one of which was pierced with a thick silver bolt. Hetti was a goth girl through and through. Not because it was trendy or because '90s grunge was making a comeback on red carpets and in glossy magazine spreads. She was genuinely cool, the kind of cool that never aspired to be mainstream.

She dressed in killer vintage — mostly black — clothes, changed her hair color every other month, and lined her light brown eyes with a hand so heavy, I was surprised she could keep her lids open. If only she could master basic pleasantries instead of constantly insulting our customers, she'd be the perfect employee. Alas, when asked, she was more likely to give a glare and a hair toss than dispense proper directions to the nearby Witch Museum.

She stopped before me, arms crossed over her chest. Her gaze didn't focus on my face so much as the space around it, as if she could see something in the air invisible to the naked eye.

"I hate to break it to you, boss, but you've got some seriously bad juju swirling."

I heaved a sigh. (A heavy one.) I didn't strictly believe in auras or juju or witchy woo-woo, but the supernatural was so much a part of the daily fabric of life in Salem that even if you weren't a true believer, you didn't let mention of it in casual conversation ruffle your feathers. It was as common to hear about a ghost sighting or otherworldly encounter as it was the daily weather or the score of the most recent Red Sox game.

"Helloooo. Earth to Gwendolyn. This is your captain speaking."

"Sorry." I jolted, realizing I'd spaced out. "What did you say?"

"I asked if you were okay." Hetti gnawed on her bottom lip, smudging her dark purple lipstick. "*Are* you okay?"

Was I okay?

In the past few days, I'd been verbally accosted, physically threatened, kissed, kidnapped, and accused of murder. I'd also been screwed — thoroughly, mind-blowingly, bone-meltingly *screwed* — within an inch of my sanity by a man I was ninety-nine-point-nine-nine percent sure I detested with every fiber of my being. On top of that, one of my other employees had gone AWOL, and my half-grown-out bangs were doing an unforgivable flippy-outty thing at the ends that made me curse the day I'd taken the shears to them. (I blamed girl's night — and the bottle of tequila consumed therein — for hindering my better judgment, along with my best friend Florence, a.k.a. Flo, whose wholly unsound assurances that they'd look quote 'chic as fuck' unquote had been an act of domestic terrorism in the sober light of day.)

So, no.

I was not okay. I was so not okay, I couldn't even summon the words to describe the depths of my not-okayness.

"Not to make your morning worse or anything," Hetti continued in a hesitant voice, tucking a lock of purple hair behind one ear. "But that detective is here again. He's waiting for you in your office. And, boss, he does *not* look happy. His aura is even darker than yours."

At this news, I paled as all the blood drained out of my face. I reached out a hand to steady myself against the espresso bar. "Did he say why he's here?"

Her voice dropped to a whisper. "No. But..."

"But *what,* Hetti?"

"Well... you know that dead body they found? The one with... uh... the knife through the heart?" Her eyes darted away, unable to meet mine as she reluctantly forced out the rest. "I'm pretty sure they think you're the one who stuck it there."

I couldn't see my aura, but I was relatively certain it darkened from Impending Nor'easter to Category Five Hurricane on the stormy scale. Hetti took one look at it and scurried behind the espresso bar to hide.

Hellfire.

If I actually believed in such things, I'd say I was cursed.

TWO
WEEKS
EARLIER

CHAPTER ONE

*Chase my dreams? Honey, I don't even chase my
tequila shots.
— Gwen Goode, ordering another round*

I noticed the man who stepped through the doors of my shop
immediately. Not because he was particularly striking — in fact,
he was exceptionally ordinary in every regard, from his rumpled,
off-the-rack business suit to the slight paunch of middle age
circling his waistline to the scuffs on his season-old loafers. This
was not the kind of man who generally commanded the gazes of
strangers. And yet, my eyes snapped straight to him.

It could've been because he wasn't my typical customer. Not
that we really *had* a typical customer. The Gallows drew in an
eclectic mix of hipsters (who never bought anything, just
hovered in the stacks flipping through our oldest occult texts for
hours on end), tourists (who bought everything, all the witchy

7

trinkets they could get their hands on before they blew out of town), university kids (who parked their asses at my small bistro tables to study and sip free coffee refills) and, of course, the rare true believers (who walked straight past the shiny, tourist-trapping baubles to the vintage apothecary cabinets in the back, where we sold herbs and tinctures and all manner of weird, witchy accoutrements that were less *trinket*, more *double-double-toil-and-trouble*.)

The man who stormed through the front entrance with fury in his eyes fit none of those categories. That might've caught my attention even if he hadn't banged inside with such force, it rattled two books off a nearby shelf and sent my pretty brass door-bells clanging like the report of a machine-gun. A pair of college students who'd cozied up to the curved emerald espresso bar, awaiting their turmeric-ginger lattes, nearly ducked for cover, startled by the sudden intrusion into the otherwise tranquil shop.

Despite its rather macabre name — and incoming irate customer aside — The Gallows was a warm, inviting space. I'd designed it not only to draw you in the door, but urge you to stay awhile. Wander the shelves. Peruse the oddities. The walls not covered by bookshelves or curiosity cabinets I'd painted soothing shades of green. The furnishings were luxe but still comfortable. The high ceilings were a thick, gold patina that matched the expresso machine — which, by the way, had cost a small fortune but looked straight out of an Italian cafe and, thus, was worth every damn penny in my humble opinion. The air smelled like incense and dried herbs and good coffee. Indie music drifted softly from the overhead speakers.

Totally zen.

But the man who darkened my doorstep that morning was decidedly *un*-zen. He did not pause for a pumpkin spice latte or plunk his considerable girth down in one of my comfortable lounge chairs by the window display. He didn't even *look* at the window display — which, frankly, peeved me. It had taken hours to get the books suspended midair with invisible fishing-line so they appeared enchanted. He could've at least spared a glance, after all that effort.

Alas, his eyes scanned the cafe area for mere seconds, quickly dismissing Hetti where she stood scowling behind the expresso machine as well as the clusters of coffee drinkers settled on my cushy armchairs and planted on my lustrous, gold-legged high top stools. They glided right over the selection of incense sticks and sage bundles, then down the two mahogany steps that led into the central part of the shop, which housed an ever-changing supply of mystical curiosities, and, finally, locked on something that made them narrow in a seriously unfriendly way.

That something, regrettably, was little old *me*.

How the very sight of me was enough to trigger such a visceral reaction, I hadn't the faintest idea. As far as I could tell, I wasn't doing anything inherently offensive. I was simply standing behind a display case, restocking crystals. I did this at least once a week, sometimes more frequently during high season — which it currently was, with Halloween fast approaching. No matter how much I ordered, I could never seem to stock enough amethyst to appease the masses.

But I digress.

For a long, suspended moment, the red-faced stranger stood frozen at the threshold, glaring at me across the distance. I entertained a fleeting hope that he was here to see Madame Zelda, my resident psychic — perhaps irked by a reading gone wrong or in need of some emergency psychic counsel. Surely, he didn't seem the type to let a woman in a turban twice as high as her head with penciled-on eyebrows tell him about his future. Then again...

Who was I to judge?

Like I said, The Gallows drew an eclectic crowd, and Madame Zelda catered to many interests. Palm lines. Tarot decks. Hell, I think she even had a crystal ball squirreled away in the small chamber at the very back of the shop where she conducted business.

As soon as the man's gaze locked on me, though, I knew it wasn't Madame Zelda he was after. His eyes were spitting pure fire and, as I watched, the hands at his sides curled into fists. I fought the urge to duck down behind the counter, for the first time in my life lamenting the shop's cavernous, open-plan layout. Before I could even think about running for cover, he charged in my direction like a bull at a flag-waving matador, shoving aside unsuspecting hipsters in his wake, bumping past my table of New Age bestsellers. And I wasn't even wearing red! (I rarely did, rosy hues tended to clash with my dark auburn locks.)

In what seemed like seconds, he'd thundered down the mahogany steps with so much force his bones must've rattled, then proceeded to stomp his way past the medley of spooky souvenirs and strange artifacts arranged in the display cases without even pretending to feign interest. When he careened to a stop in front of me, panting for breath and practically quivering with temper, I didn't even have enough time to greet him with my usual 'How's it hanging?' — admittedly, we enjoyed our gallows humor here at The Gallows — before he leaned in, planted his beefy hands on my freshly-polished display case, and hissed one short but surprisingly venom-laced word directly into my face.

"*You.*"

I blinked slowly. "Me?"

The man's face, already red with rage, seemed to mottle further. This would've concerned me, however, I was slightly preoccupied by his hands. See, I'd only just finished cleaning the glass counter top and he was getting smudgy fingerprints all over it. And as much as I hated being accosted by strange men in my place of employment... I really, *really* hated to Windex.

"You fucking bitch!"

Again, I blinked. And, again, I repeated, "Me?"

I swear, I wasn't trying to irritate him. I was genuinely curious. Because, hand-to-goddess, I was not a bitch. Seriously. Setting aside my slightly sarcastic streak when annoyed and occasional penchant for retail therapy when overwhelmed, I was a good-time girl. It was right there in the name!

Gwendolyn *Goode.*

I saw the best in people. Even the mean ones. I looked for silver linings, no matter how dark the cloud. I laughed my ass off, frequently. I persevered. I stayed upbeat. I never let the bastards grind me down. I kept my head, heels, and standards high, just like Aunt Colette had taught me, just like Coco Chanel had taught her. People liked me, for the most part. And even if they didn't... they certainly never *stormed into my shop* and *yelled in my face* in front of a crowd of paying customers when I hadn't done a single thing to deserve it!

At least, not up to this particular point in my life.

"You've got some nerve, lady," the man told me, every word choked with fury. Spittle actually flew from his lips, sailing past my face (thankfully) and landing (unthankfully) on my once-pristine glass cabinet top. At this rate, I'd be Windexing for the rest of the morning. "Who the fuck do you think you are?"

I kept my voice even, my features composed. "I'm Gwendolyn Goode, the owner of this store. But I'm guessing you know that already, judging by the scene you're causing. Based on the alarming shade of eggplant you're beginning to turn, I'll take another wild leap that I've done something to offend you."

"Don't play dumb!" He leaned farther across the counter, until his pudgy belly was pressed right up against the glass and

11

his face was mere inches from mine. I held my ground, even as he hissed, "You know exactly what you did, bitch."

Again with the *bitch* business. Jeeze, could he at least come up with a new insult? This was getting repetitive.

Distantly, I heard the sound of bells ringing as the front door of the shop opened and closed again — an accompaniment to fleeing customers, no doubt. I didn't blame them. This unfolding unpleasantness didn't really jive with the chill vibes my decor promised.

Not everyone was fleeing, though. Behind the man I could sense a gathering crowd of curious onlookers drawn in by the drama, pretending to browse books on the shelves closest to the stairs. I'd bet my last dollar that Hetti was amongst them, leaving our espresso bar unmanned, but I did not glance over to check for her colorful hair in the crush. I did not shift my focus from the angry man's face. Nor did I raise my voice above the most congenial of pitches as I set down the crystal I belatedly realized I was still holding and clasped my hands together in front of me with a placidness that seemed to piss him off immeasurably.

"The thing is, sir, I can't recall ever, not even once, seeing you before," I informed him. "Nor can I recall dinging your car with my door or stealing a package off your front porch or cutting you in the grocery store line or spitting gum in what little hair you've got left on your head." I allowed my eyes to drift up to his bald spot for a brief interlude before continuing. "As far as I know, my conscience is clear, my karma is good. According to my quasi-psychic barista, even my damn chakras are balanced. So, you're going to have to find some words to explain yourself. Preferably ones that don't involve any more profanity. Because while I personally am not offended by you calling me a *fucking bitch*, repeatedly, at the top of your voice..." My eyes narrowed a shade and my tone cooled significantly. "I'd hate for anyone watching to get the wrong idea and think you're actually succeeding in this adorable little show of intimidation you're putting on here."

What? I said I was a good-time girl. I never said I was a pushover.

"My wife," the man gritted out.

"Someone married you?"

Ignoring my barb, he reached into his suit pocket, pulled out a small bottle, and slammed it down on the counter with such vigor, I was surprised the glass didn't shatter. "You sold her *this!*"

For a moment, we both stared at the bottle. I knew immediately that he wasn't mistaken. It was, in fact, from my shop. From this very section of the shop, in a tall apothecary cabinet just a few steps away.

I tended to stock a little bit of everything, from healing crystals to incense burners to ritualistic ceremonial tools dating back centuries. Glass-doored cabinets held a vast array of bottles. There were tinctures to treat common cuts and scrapes on one shelf. (Surprisingly effective!) Pre-mixed potions to hex a nasty ex on another. (Disappointingly ineffective.) Essential oils and bundled herbs. Vials of strange things like Graveyard Dirt and Eye of Newt and Raven's Feather and Bone Shard that I would've rather hurled myself into the sun than unstopper voluntarily, but nevertheless moved off the shelves and into the hands of eager customers with alarming regularity.

The bottle in question was of this same ilk. On the front, in fine calligraphy, on one of the gorgeous textured labels I had custom-made by a local printer, it said *JILTED JUICE*. I knew, if I looked at the back, it would instruct in much smaller typeface: *To cripple cheating tendencies, apply two drops daily to the undergarments of the unfaithful. Should the occasion to stray ever arise... his staff will not follow suit. [For best results, use at night before bed.]*

Understanding dawned swiftly.

"Oh," I said softly. "That."

"Yes," the man returned not-so-softly. "That!"

My eyes sailed up to meet his. For the first time, I noticed they were red-rimmed. Not with anger. More like he'd been up all night or spent the last few hours weeping.

Huh.

"Sir, I'm still not sure how this concerns me."

"What do you mean?" He tensed visibly. "You sold this to my wife! Do you deny it?"

"No, I don't deny it."

"Then you know why I'm here!"

"On the contrary, I have no earthly idea."

His voice, already shrill, rose to a truly piercing decibel. "You sold my wife this... This... *Jilted Juice!*" His face reddened further, this time from a hint of embarrassment in addition to the coursing anger. "And now, whenever I go to...."

"Perform?" I supplied sweetly.

"Yes! Perform!" He swallowed hard. "I can't."

"Oh."

"Don't just stand there saying '*Oh*', you ruinous whore!" He snapped. At the very least, he'd found a new insult. I was looking on the bight side. "Fix it!"

"I'm not sure how, exactly, you'd like me to fix your marriage." I shrugged. "I might suggest, as a starter course, that you stop cheating on your spouse. Then she likely won't feel the urge to wander into shops like mine in search of... more drastic measures."

"I'm not talking about fixing my marriage!" he snarled. "I'm talking about my..."

"Equipment?" I supplied again, no less sweetly.

His teeth clenched. He did not respond — he didn't seem able to speak at that moment, so thick was his fury — except for a shallow nod of assent.

"I'm afraid I can't fix you, sir." I tilted my head as I eyed him.

"Judging by your anger issues, not to mention your apparent infidelity problems, I'm guessing only a licensed psychiatric professional can do that."

"You're going to fix me. So help me, you will. If you don't..." He leaned over the counter, vengeance in his eyes. "You will regret it."

"Sir, I'd like you to leave now."

"I'm not going anywhere, bitch."

We were back to *bitch* again.

"Well, unless you're here to buy something, you can't stay." I paused a beat. "You wouldn't perchance be interested in a piece of citrine? It's supposed to boost confidence and positivity which, honestly, it seems like you could use right about now."

I wasn't about to squander a potential sale. And, to be candid, I really needed to unload the citrine. Two full boxes had been collecting dust in the storeroom for months. I'd have to find a creative use for them — perhaps passed into the hands of future shoppers with a BOGO promotion. (*Buy-One-Get-One-Urine-Yellow-Rock-Free!* All sales final.)

Shockingly, the man did not seem tempted by my offer. His expression darkened and his voice grew almost desperate. "You've cursed me! This spell of yours has ruined my life. And if you don't undo it, I'm going to ruin yours."

I snorted. I couldn't help it. "*Spell*? Are you serious? I don't cast spells."

"Then what do you call that?"

He jerked his chin toward the bottle. He seemed unwilling to touch it again, as if doing so would somehow unleash even more dastardly consequences upon his manhood. Which was hilarious, seeing as the bottle held nothing but water with a few drops of marjoram essential oil, a sprig of rosemary, and a teeny, tiny shake of itching powder. A concoction that smelled divine — and, okay, I admit, may cause minor crotch-itch in one's cheating spouse — but by no means would keep a man's flag at half-mast.

"Um…" I shrugged lightly and contemplated his question. "A holistic approach to incentivize monogamy?"

"Don't be cute with me."

"You think I'm cute? *Aw!* That's good to hear. I've been really struggling with my bangs, you see, they're still growing out—"

"Shut the fuck up! God! You fucking women. Goddamn fucking *women*. You all think think you can just waltz through life without any consequences. That you can toy with a man's…" He shook his head vigorously. "I'm telling you right now, there will be repercussions for this. I'll make you regret you ever opened up shop. I'll make you regret you ever *breathed*, bitch!"

Despite my outward composure, I did in fact have a threshold for being insulted and threatened — and I was approaching it.

Rapidly.

"Sir, while I do sympathize with your… lack of lift-off… like I said before, there's nothing I can do for you. Seeing as you aren't a paying customer and I've asked you to leave, you are now technically trespassing here. If you don't turn your tail around and walk out that door like the almighty goddess Gloria Gaynor advises… we're going to have a problem."

He absorbed this in silence for a few seconds, holding his breath. His face, already eggplant-purple, went plum. Then his beefy hand lifted and his finger was right in my face, an inch from my nose, waggling with menace. "I want to speak to your manager!"

"I'm the owner. You've already reached the top of the totem pole, I'm afraid."

"Then I'll call the police!"

"And tell them what?" I tried, I really did, but in the end I could not quite contain my bemused smile. "That you cheated on your wife so she went to an occult shop and bought a magical potion to wet your wick?" I waved my hands in the air in what I hoped was a witchy way. "A purchase she made, might I add, of her own free will, from an upstanding, tax-paying business owner — that would be *me* — who you then threatened, unprovoked, in full view of a dozen witnesses, at her place of business?" My lips pursed. "Oh, yes. I'm sure our local PD will be just tripping over themselves to help you, sir."

He blew out a ragged breath. While I spoke, his eyes had glossed over with what looked like real, actual tears. If he were even slightly less of an asshole, I might've felt sorry for him. As things stood, though, I was beginning to think his wife should've gone straight for the *CHEATER'S KARMA* bottle instead of the more mild *JILTED JUICE* she'd opted to begin with.

"Please leave, sir," I requested yet again, my voice as thin as my patience. "Now."

He was silent for another long stretch, then burst out, "You don't understand! Before this, I never had a problem! Never! I was a dynamo! Women begged for it! I had stamina you wouldn't believe! I could go for hours, every time! All night long! I rocked worlds! I brought down the house! But... over the past few weeks.... out of nowhere..." He pressed his eyes tightly closed for a long beat, as if not wanting to even think about what he'd endured. "I thought something was seriously wrong with me. Then, I found this jar in her bedside table. And I knew. *I knew!* It wasn't me, it was *this!* It was *you!*"

My eyes flickered down to his paunch, then slowly traversed back up to his face. Holding his gaze, I allowed my nose to scrunch in disbelief.

"A dynamo, sir? *Really?*"

In retrospect, it likely wasn't my smartest move to throw gasoline on the fire of his already-raging temper. But my smarts apparently took a hike along with my sense of self-preservation right around the time the fourth *bitch* shot out of his snarling mouth.

There was a moment of total silence in the aftermath of my soft, incredulous blow. I simply stood there, smiling the placid customer-service smile I'd perfected years ago, watching my words make impact. He physically flinched back, as if I'd hit him, and then began to breathe so heavily he was almost panting. His face and neck mottled. His eyes narrowed to pinpricks. While actual steam was not yet leaking from his ears, I thought there was a solid chance his head was going to explode.

Unfortunately, in lieu of a Chernobyl-level meltdown, he opted for retribution. He lunged at me across the display case, his beefy hands headed directly for my throat, no doubt with firm intentions to wring it. I sucked in a sharp, startled breath. I had to give him credit — for such a large man, he was rather nimble. Even if I'd been prepared for him to follow through on the violent promise in his eyes, I was penned in behind the counter with nowhere to run. He was twice my size, not to mention twice as angry. When he came at me, the only thought in my head was, '*Thank goodness there are so many people around to witness this ass-whooping, they'll be able to call the ambulance quickly!*'

But the ass-whooping never arrived.

One second, the man was lunging at me across the counter. The next, something tagged him around the collar and yanked him backward with such force, he sailed through the air like a puppet on strings.

What on earth?

It took my reeling mind a moment to realize that the *something* locked around the man's rumpled collar was a large, tanned, masculine hand. And that hand was connected to a thick, equally tanned, muscular forearm. I followed the corded veins of that forearm up past the rolled cuff of a black button-

18

down shirt, over the curves of a bicep straining the fabric, along the broad seam of a shoulder, all the way to the column of a throat that peeked out of a collar with the top two buttons left undone.

As I watched, the Adam's apple in that throat bobbed up and down in a rough swallow. This bob immediately preceded a deep, rasping voice that made my would-be attacker — who, I couldn't help but notice, looked just as bewildered as I did by this sudden shift in circumstances — go paler than the night-gown of a sickly Victorian child.

"I believe the lady asked you to leave."

CHAPTER TWO

*Some people fight their inner demons. Mine mostly
just want to cuddle.
— Gwen Goode, reflecting inwardly*

At the sound of that voice, I went totally still.

Not because he called me a lady — a classification which, even if I'd been wearing my chicest pair of calf leather Louboutin boots with the spiked heel, would require a Gumbi-level stretch of the imagination. Not because he delivered his terse command with such bone-chilling authority, in a rumbling octave that clearly stated, *I-am-not-fucking-around-here-so-don't-test-me-motherfucker.*

No.

I went still because I knew that voice. I'd heard it before and, as it did every time, hearing it set my teeth on edge. Because that voice belonged to the one, the only, the insufferable...

Graham Graves.

A man I disliked with a startling amount of vehemence. A man I'd go so far as to say I despised, if you caught me at the wrong moment. (And *this*, it must be said, was about as wrong a moment as you could catch me.)

"Graves," I managed to bleat after a few seconds of shocked silence.

His green eyes sliced to mine. Goosebumps broke out on my arms as they slid over my face, sharp as a razor blade.

"Miss Goode," he rumbled back.

Hellfire.

My teeth sank into my bottom lip as the effects of those two little words in that rich timbre stole through me. Annoying as I found Graham, there was something about his voice — that damned, deep, rasping voice — that got under my skin. Pushing away the irrational reaction, I focused instead on the simmering dislike that swelled inside me at the sight of his — it must be said — annoyingly attractive face. Freakishly chiseled jaw, high cheekbones, dark brows, straight nose. He looked like he belonged on the cover of Men's Health, not standing in an occult shop with his iron-like grip on the collar of a squirming jerk hell-bent on exacting revenge against me.

It had been a few months since I'd seen him — mostly because I'd been actively avoiding his presence. Not an alto-gether easy feat, I might add, seeing as my best friend Florence was currently head over heels in love with his best friend Desmond. This meant, even if I wanted to avoid Graham completely — and, trust me, I wanted to, I really freaking wanted to — I was strong-armed into spending time with the man far more frequently than was ideal. (The ideal frequency being *never*, for the record.)

Our gazes held for a prolonged beat. I wondered if my eyes were as wide as they felt on my face. I wondered if my expression conveyed my shock at seeing him there, in my store, mere feet away from me. He'd never been here, not in the two years since I started running things, and almost certainly not in the three decades my aunt ran it before me.

"Um," I breathed, swallowing hard. "What are you..."

I trailed off stupidly. I had no idea what to say to him in this situation. Not that I ever had an idea what to say to him in *any* situation, seeing as I avoided situations that included him at all costs. With effort, I smoothed my features into a look of composure I'd spent years honing. My patented Ice Queen look. I'd been using it with the customer while he was causing a scene, but it had slipped a bit at Graham's unexpected interruption.

Graham's face, I noted, was carefully blank. He didn't seem to be exerting any effort at all in holding onto the seething man thrashing against his hold like a misbehaving toddler in need of parental restraint.

"Let go of me!" The man hissed. If he'd been angry before, he was full-on enraged now. Teeth snapping with each word, eye whites flashing like a feral animal that knows its been cornered by a far stronger predator. "I mean it! This is harassment! I'll sue you!"

I opened my mouth to speak, but Graham beat me to it. His tone was level, his annoyance tightly-leashed. "Like I said before, she asked you to leave. She did it nicely. You didn't listen. That means it's my turn and I'm not asking, I'm telling. You may think I'm doing it not-so-nicely but..." He paused and his grip tightened on the suit collar until the man's tie knot was pulled up against his windpipe, constricting his flow of oxygen. The rest of Graham's body stayed stock-still as he did this, but I watched the muscles in his extended forearm flex beneath the skin and knew he was applying considerable pressure.

"Trust me," he continued lowly. "You don't want to see my not-so-nice side."

The customer, already pale, went even paler. I couldn't tell if this was due to the lack of air in his lungs or the fact that this was no idle threat. Graham Graves didn't *do* idle threats. He didn't do idle, period. He was a man of action. He was brawn and brash. (And bothersome, but that was neither here nor there at this particular juncture.)

"Um," I whispered again, thinking I should probably interject.

Graham talked right over me. (See? *Bothersome.*) "You're going to leave this establishment and you aren't going to come back. Not today, not tomorrow, not ever. Am I clear?" he asked. His tone was still level, his control over his emotions as firm as his grip. But I knew, deep down, he was impatient because he gave the man a slight shake when he failed to agree instantly. "Nod if you understand."

The man, who was beginning to panic, did as he was bidden, nodding a frantic assent. As soon as he did, Graham released him. The man fell forward, doubling over with his hands clutching the countertop for support — guaranteeing more Windex in my immediate future.

Fabulous.

I didn't even have time to properly lament this eventuality aloud. The man gulped in three ragged breaths, straightened, shot me one last withering glare, skirted a wide path around Graham, and high-tailed it up the stairs toward the exit without another word.

Leaving me alone with Graham.

Precisely where I did *not* want to be.

Over the past few years, I'd made an art out of avoiding his existence, even when we crossed paths at one of Flo and Des's dinner parties or found ourselves sitting in the same booth during a night out at The Witches Brew. I'd become a certified expert in ignoring him — even when I felt the weight of his piercing green eyes on my face across the table or the heat of his body pressing protectively close to mine in the crowd whenever Flo and I stumbled out onto the dance floor to scream the lyrics of our favorite cover songs after a few too many rounds, his broad frame blocking us from the tidal sweep of gyrating townies. (And trust me, those eyes were not always easy to ignore. The body was even harder, seeing as it had approximately zero percent body fat and more muscles than Michelangelo himself could feasibly sculpt.)

I wasn't blind. Nor was I immune to the fact that Graham Graves was one seriously attractive man. But beneath the chiseled face and sculpted body lay a cruel heart and an even crueler tongue — one I'd felt the biting lash of two years ago, and had no desire to be on the receiving end of ever again, so long as I lived, thank you very much.

Bracing myself, I forced my eyes from the front door as it slammed shut behind the jerk-off, past the gathered crowd of curious onlookers — Hetti amongst them — and, finally, to the glowering man towering before me. Braced or not, it took effort not to physically react when our gazes met. His, as always, hit me like a sucker punch to the gut.

"What are you doing here?" I asked, pleased when my voice came out steady, instead of shaken.

"What am I doing here?"

"That's what I asked."

One dark brow arched upward. "Is there a thank you buried somewhere under all that ice you're blasting my way?"

"Depends. Is there an explanation for your presence buried somewhere under all that entitlement you're cloaked in?"

His eyes flashed. "Two words."

"Pardon?"

"Two words," he repeated, leaning forward an inch. "*Thank*

and *you*. Go on, try them out. You can even tack my name on at the end, if you feel like going for extra credit."

"You're joking."

He said nothing.

"You must be joking."

Still, nothing. After a moment, I realized he was waiting for his thank you. Waiting like it was a foregone conclusion. And the way he was waiting — brow arched, arms crossed, boots planted — dripped with so much arrogance, it made my teeth grind together.

Totally... freaking... bothersome!

"I didn't ask for your help," I declared in a haughty tone, not entirely sure why I was being so haughty but unable to stop myself. Honestly, I should be thanking him. He had saved my ass from the angry jerk. But when it came to Graham, things like logic and manners flew right out the window. "*Therefore,*" I continued, even haughtier than before, "I don't owe you a thank you."

"You don't want to thank me verbally, that's fine. We can work something else out. Clear your debt more creatively."

I tilted my head, totally unsure what that meant. "Pardon?"

"Something wrong with your hearing?"

"No."

"So, you get me."

"Graham," I said with so much fake sweetness, I was thinking of changing my middle name to Aspartame. "I have never, not once, ever *gotten you*."

He studied my face for a long beat. "Uh huh."

"Uh huh, *what*?"

He did not deign to clarify.

I looked at him a bit more closely. His hair was longer than I remembered, the thick dark strands curling around his shirt collar. I

JULIE JOHNSON

doubted he'd had it cut since our paths last crossed several months ago, at the backyard barbecue Flo and Des hosted on the Fourth of July. I'd tried to stay far, far from his vicinity all day, but every time I turned around he seemed to be there — reaching for another beer in the cooler at the same time I did, coming up behind me in the kitchen when I was refilling a bowl of tortilla chips, brushing uncomfortably close to me when I exited the bathroom and found him waiting his turn in the narrow hallway. The harder I tried to escape him, the more the universe seemed to push him in my direction.

How annoying was that?

"Whatever," I muttered, returning my focus to the present. "You're clearly delusional."

Graham shot a pointed look at the bottle of Jilted Juice on the countertop, then smirked. "Yes. That's it. You run a business selling magic potions and *I'm* the delusional one."

"Feel free to leave if my shop offends you." I paused. "Seriously. Go on. *Leave.*"

"Is that any way to treat someone who just saved your ass?"

"I had it well in hand."

"Did you?" His other brow arched to join its mate. "Looked to me like he was about to wring your neck."

"Looks can be deceiving," I bluffed. The man was *totally* about to wring my neck and likely would've without Graham's intervention. Not that I was about to admit it.

"I suppose you were ready to whip out a magic wand to keep him at bay."

"Funny," I snapped.

"Defensive ward?"

I glared at him.

He grinned. It was an annoyingly good grin. "Rune of protection?"

"You know, for someone who claims to hate the supernatural, you sure know a lot about it."

26

He rolled right past that comment. "Let me guess, you were going to jab a crystal in his eye socket."

"That's one way to get rid of the citrine," I said under my breath.

"What was that?"

"Nothing." My eyes narrowed. "Pray tell, is there a reason for this visit?"

"Maybe I just wanted to see you, Glinda."

"*Gwendolyn.*" The correction came out in a low, vicious bite. His nickname for me, inspired by *The Wizard of Oz*, was neither cute nor funny. Especially not the way he always said it. (Read: mockingly.) "My name is Gwendolyn. Or Gwen, to my friends." I paused. "You can call me Gwendolyn."

His grin widened. His teeth were very white against his tan and very, very straight. His amusement seemed to expand in direct proportion to my annoyance. And the more amused he appeared, the more my annoyance grew. Such was the way of our strange, adversarial acquaintance.

"Are you ever going to tell me why you're here or are we going to stand around taking in circles all day?" I crossed my arms over my chest. "I have things to do."

His gaze dropped, tracking my arm movement, and stayed there. Awareness seared through me. I didn't need to look down to know that the silky material of my blouse was now pulled tight against my chest, an unintentional consequence of my uppity posturing. I quickly dropped my hands and curled them into fists at my sides instead.

When Graham's eyes slid — with excruciating slowness — back up to mine, I sucked in a breath at the banked heat in their depths. So much heat, there was not one single trace of the ice I usually saw there.

Um.

What?

He'd never looked at me like that before. It rattled me. Which, I figured, was precisely his intention. A new tactic in our never-ending war of attrition. He was trying to throw me off balance and, damn it to hell, it was working. Digging my fingernails into my palms, I swallowed hard and summoned icy composure.

"Fine. Stand there, I can't stop you. Peruse the crystals. I recommend the citrine, if you're in the market." My voice dropped to a low mutter he couldn't hear. "Shove it up your ass for maximum potency."

I turned my back on him, directing my attention at the open box of amethyst I'd been restocking before my morning went completely off the rails. This was a mistake, I learned half a heartbeat later. Because as soon as I looked away from him, Graham used the opportunity to close the distance between us, walking right around the display case to my side — as in, the *staff-only* side — and leaning a hip against it. His forearm came down to rest on the countertop. His strong fingers splayed out on the glass surface.

I blinked down at them.

His hands, I couldn't help but notice, were large, the skin bronze from time spent outdoors and, I'd bet my last dollar, rough from use. I didn't know what Graham did in his spare time — I did not *want* to know, the less I knew the better, so far as I was concerned — but it wasn't hard to imagine him chopping logs or stacking firewood or repelling down cliffs. He was the outdoorsy type. He probably took his girlfriends camping. Real camping, as in sleep-on-a-bed-of-rock, build-your-own-fire, wipe-your-ass-with-wet-leaves camping. Not *my* version of camping, which only happened in a luxurious platformed yurt with WiFi access, a nearby hot spring, and a full menu of spa treatments. (Better known as *glamping*. Flo and I had spent a weekend doing exactly that at a retreat in the Berkshire Mountains last spring and it was, no-holds-barred, the most blissful weekend of my life.)

Graham's hands didn't look like he glamped. Graham's hands looked like... I forced myself to stop looking at Graham's hands before I started picturing them doing other insane things unrelated to the great outdoors. My eyes shifted to the denim-clad thigh he had pressed up against my display case. I stared at it for a long beat before I managed to force my eyes upward.

He was watching me, his eyes alert, and, it must be said, their startling green shade was even more of a sucker-punch from this proximity.

"Um," I said, rattled by the fact that he was standing on my side of the counter, with only the box at our feet to separate us. "You can't be over here."

He said not a word.

"Seriously. Staff only."

Still nothing.

"You're smudging up my counter," I said, trying a new tactic.

His eyes flickered down to his hand, splayed across my glass, for a brief second before returning to mine. Otherwise, there was no movement.

"It's already totally smudgy from that guy. I'm going to be Windexing until I'm ninety."

A low sound of exasperation rattled in his chest as he pushed off my counter, straightened to full height, and crossed his arms over his chest. "We need to talk."

I blinked. "Pardon?"

"Talk. You. Me." He glanced over his shoulder at the front section of the shop, where several customers were still milling around the shelves, pretending to read book descriptions while, in actuality, straining to eavesdrop on every word of our conversation. "Not here."

"We don't have anything to talk about."

"Wrong."

"Look, if you want a thank you so bad, I'll say it! If that's what it takes to make you leave."

"Come to think of it, you might want to hold off on the gratitude. Doubt you'll be thanking me after you learn why I'm here, Glinda."

"*Gwendolyn.*"

"Sure."

"What does that mean, I won't be thanking you?" I asked, belatedly processing his odd statement.

"Told you already, we'll talk about this somewhere private."

"You know what? Forget it. I've changed my mind. I don't care why you're here. I don't want to know."

"May not want to, but you need to all the same."

"I'm not listening to this anymore," I announced, bending to grab the box of amethyst, then whipping around and walking the length of the display case, toward the back of the shop. Madame Zelda's space was dark, her curtain pulled wide with a braided gold rope, seeing as the fortune teller had not yet arrived for the day. (This was not inherently strange — she made her own hours, came and went as she pleased — but later, when I looked back, would be the first clue that something was amiss in the small empire over which I ruled with, if not an iron fist, then at least an impeccably accessorized one.)

Two doors were embedded in the mossy green walls on either side of Zelda's space — one led to a small bathroom for customers, the other to our storage room. I headed for the latter, tilting the box of crystals against my chest as I fumbled one-handed for the knob.

"Goodbye, Graves," I called, just before I stepped inside, letting the door swing shut behind me.

Except, it didn't swing shut. A large hand shot out and caught hold of it before it could click into the latch. I whipped around to see Graham hot on my heels, a mere pace behind me. How he moved such a hulking frame in total silence across my creaky, historical hardwood, I could not begin to fathom. Especially not when he shoved the door wide and followed me inside.

He followed me inside!

"What are you doing?" I half-screeched.

"Talking to you somewhere private," he said, like it should be obvious.

Hellfire!

I backpedaled away from him, feeling my pulse spike as he stalked me deeper into the storeroom. As he did this, his eyes never left my face. In the dark, they seemed to glitter with emotion — what sort of emotion, I didn't know. I didn't *want* to know.

Unfortunately for me...

I was pretty certain I was about to find out.

CHAPTER THREE

If he's such a crafty devil, why doesn't he own a hot glue gun?
- Gwen Goode, attempting at-home DIY

The thing you have to understand about Graham and me is... it wasn't always this way between us. I didn't always hate him. In fact, there was a time when the things I felt for him were something more akin to the sensation you get when you haven't eaten all day and you see the waiter coming toward your table with your entree held aloft.

Pure, unadulterated, mouthwatering *hunger*.

So how, you ask, did we get here? To the land of verbal sparring and icy smalltalk and mocking nicknames? Well, it's kind of a long story. And to properly tell it, I have to take you back. Way back. As in, *fourteen years back,* to the summer I turned ten.

It was school break and, as usual, I was staying in Salem with

Aunt Colette — a much-needed hiatus from the existence Mom and I were eking out in a colorless town just off the New Jersey turnpike, where the closest thing to ethnic food for twenty miles in any direction was an understaffed Taco Bell.

Thankfully, Aunt Colette's house in Salem was nothing like our trailer. And Aunt Colette was nothing like Mom. She didn't ignore me or stare at me with ill-concealed resentment just for having the audacity to exist. In fact, Aunt Colette actually seemed to enjoy having me around — taking me to restaurants, cooking me dinners, letting me shadow her at The Gallows during business hours. I spent more rainy days curled up in the stacks flipping through occult texts than I could count.

Sunny days, however, were a different story.

When the skies were clear and the temperatures were soaring toward triple digits, I'd ride my bike across town to Winter Island, the small peninsula that jutted out into the Atlantic on the east side of town, as fast as my feet could work the pedals. By the time I got there, I'd be a sweaty mess — panting for air, windswept auburn curls blown out to *there* around my head with odd indentations at the crown courtesy of my sparkly pink helmet, my bathing suit in a serious wedgie from the narrow bike seat.

At ten, this did not particularly faze me. I was still trapped in that lovely un-self-conscious state of late childhood, just before puberty hits and saddles you with several excruciating teenage years of body dysmorphia, hormonal acne, PMS, and boy troubles. But even if I'd been old enough to realize my hair was out to *there* and my over-exerted face was a beet-red hue that seriously clashed with my messy locks, I probably wouldn't have cared. Because my attentions were fixed, with absolute focus, on the boy lazing in the lifeguard tower.

I'd told Aunt Colette I wanted to expand my growing seashell collection. The truth is, I didn't give two dingbats about seashells. Not since my first visit to the beach, anyway. Because as soon as I clapped eyes on that earthbound angel wearing a bright red bathing suit with white lettering, my bike rides to the beach had a far different motivation driving them.

He was, quite simply, the most beautiful boy my ten-year-old eyes had ever beheld. Several years older than me, at least fifteen or sixteen, with a head of dark, lush, slightly wavy hair that was just a shade too long, curling around his ears, nearly brushing his broad, sun-bronzed shoulders. His eyes were concealed behind a pair of shades when he was on duty, but even through his dark lenses I could tell they were always scanning the sand, watching the water for trouble. His chest was bare, displaying a rippled wall of abdominal muscle that tapered in the shape of the letter "V" at his chiseled hipbones. (That v-cut frame would go on to become the subject of much female interest by the time summer slipped away.)

But at the very beginning, he was all mine. My little secret. In early June, the weather wasn't quite warm enough to draw in the crowds, camping season wasn't yet in full-swing, leaving most of the sites at the water's edge empty, and I was often the only beachgoer on weekday afternoons. I'd scan for seashells, looking for sand dollars, determined to find a perfect one without any chips or cracks, and bring it home to Mom in September. Maybe, if I brought a gift, she'd actually be excited to see me for once.

I walked near the shallows, where the waves kissed the shore, eyes downcast, searching for that elusive specimen. Such was my determination, I didn't notice the urchin hidden in a clump of seaweed until it was too late. I stepped down on it with bare feet and the spines shot straight through my sole, piercing my skin like a dozen razor-sharp needles.

I yowled at the top of my lungs, falling to the sand and clutching my foot as tears leaked from my eyes in an unstoppable torrent. It hurt, *hellfire*, it hurt more than anything I'd ever experienced in my whole, entire life, including the time Mom's idiot boyfriend slammed my fingers in the car door and the other time Mom's *other* idiot boyfriend dropped a frying pan on my toe. And as I sat there in the sand, sobbing myself ragged, trying to work up the courage to pull those spines out of my foot or, at the very least, hop my way back to my bicycle and figure out how to pedal home one-footed... that's when I first heard it.

That voice.

His voice.

"Hey! Are you all right?"

I craned my neck back, blinking against the bright sunshine, and his face swam into focus. The sob caught in my throat as air halted in my lungs. Distantly, I felt the throbbing pain in my foot, the burning agony of the spines still embedded in my flesh, but I swear in that moment, I didn't even process it. That face, up close, without shades to obscure it, had commandeered every one of my senses.

And what a face it was.

Dark brows, furrowed together as he examined me. Straight nose, high cheekbones, and a firm, square jaw. His eyes locked on mine and I saw they were a startling shade of green, almost jade, and feathered by dark, thick lashes. They slid away far too soon for my liking and locked on the foot I was still clutching tight, my knee bent inward at an unnatural angle as I pulled it toward my chest.

"Shit," he clipped, exhaling sharply. "You're not all right."

I shook my head. Tears were still streaming from my eyes and my nose was beginning to run. "I st-st-stepped," I hiccuped. "On an ur-ur-"

"Sea urchin. Nasty little buggers."

Before I could say anything else, he dropped down in the sand before me, his knees hitting the beach mere inches away. His eyes slid back to mine for a moment as he took hold of my knobby-kneed leg and gently twisted it to get a better look. I tried very hard to hold still, but I was shaking. From the pain, yes, but also from the sheer emotional overload my body was experiencing as this beautiful, fallen-angel of a boy in his bright red bathing suit held my foot up to his face, examining the bottom with acute concentration.

"It's not so bad," he told me in a steady tone that instantly made me feel calmer. "Most of the spines didn't lodge. There are a few in there still, but they're shallow. Tweezers should do the trick. We'll have you back on your feet in no time."

I sniffled indelicately. I would've done it delicately, but there was too much snot leaking out my nose to be delicate. "Okay."

He looked at me, his face serious. "It must hurt."

My bottom lip was quivering, as was my voice when I whimpered, "Not too bad."

"Uh huh," was all he said, like he didn't believe me in the slightest — I blamed the snot, it was very hard to be credible with that much snot leaking from one's nose — and I noticed one of those dark brows arched upward as he lowered my foot back to the sand. For a moment, I thought he was going to leave me there to my own devices, but instead he did something that astonished me. He leaned forward, hooked his muscular arms around me — one behind my back, the other looped under my knobby knees — and rose to his feet with me cradled against his chest. Then, he looked down at me, stared straight into my tear-glazed eyes, and said something I'd never forget.

"I got you, Firecracker."

And he did.

He had me.

He brought me to the lifeguard tower — not to the top seat but to a smaller bench at ground level around the back side, setting me down like I weighed no more than a feather. I worked to regulate my breathing and get my tears under control as he retrieved his first aid box from somewhere out of sight. I'd managed to rein in the worst of the snot by the time he returned to me.

Once I was settled, he flipped open his kit, knelt in the sand, and took my foot in his large, steady grip. It looked very small and pale in his hands. I watched him, wary at what was to come, but he didn't hesitate as he wielded the stainless steel tweezers, not even for a second, moving with a self-assurance that belied his years.

I flinched each time he yanked one of the six — yes, *six* — spines from the soft arch of my foot, but managed not to make a single sound of protest. Not a sob. Not a wail. Not even a wince.

Despite this, he could tell I was suffering. I knew he could tell because, each time he pulled out a spine, he'd purse his lips and blow a soft stream of air onto the small wound it left behind, which was oddly soothing and somehow made me forget all about the sting of pain.

In what felt like a blink of the eye, he'd extracted them all with ease, like it was something he'd done a thousand times. Then, with a tenderness I'd never before been on the receiving end of from a single living soul — surely not a cool-as-heck, teenage boy, and absolutely not a cool-as-heck Lifeguard God such as himself — he applied a bit of gooey, translucent antibiotic ointment to the shallow punctures using a flat wooden applicator and wrapped up my foot with a long strip of gauzy, white bandage. He did this in silence, completely focused on his task.

"That should do it," he muttered, taping off the gauze. His eyes flashed up to mine and, once again, I noticed how sharply, starkly green they were. Mine were green, too, but they were a pale tea hue. Not like his. I didn't know the name of his particular color — somewhere between emerald and evergreen on the color scale — but it was, I decided instantly, my new favorite.

"You here alone?" he asked.

I nodded. It was not unusual for me to be out on my own. Aunt Colette was a free-wheeling, former hippie chick turned moderately-successful occult shop owner. As such, she did not only let me wander on my own, she openly encouraged it.

Can't taste the world through a sheet of glass, honey. Get on out in it. Try every flavor it has to offer.

"Someone drop you off?"

I shook my head.

His lips twitched. "You fly here on a broomstick or something?"

I stared at him, neither nodding or shaking, not knowing how to respond when a cool-as-heck Lifeguard God with gorgeous green eyes and thick, dark lashes was teasing me. Like we were *friends* or something. Like this was *normal* when the truth was, I'd never talked to a boy in my *life*, except the stupid ones in my homeroom class back in New Jersey. And they didn't *look* like the LG or *sound* like the LG.

Not even a little bit.

Not even *at all.*

"Firecracker? You still with me?"

"Um..." I swallowed. Hard. Then, I pointed at the metal rack by the parking lot, where my sparkly pink bike was sitting, helmet hooked over the handlebars, towel and flip-flops bundled in the front basket. "I rode my bike."

His lip-twitch disappeared, flattening out all traces of a smile. "Can't ride home on that foot. Got someone you can call?"

I stilled, eyes widening. I didn't want to bother Aunt Colette at the shop. Mom hated when I bothered her at the diner, and she let me know just how much she hated it by screaming at me, top volume, if I dared. Even when I got locked out of the trailer we were living in last December on one of the coldest days of the year because her loser boyfriend-of-the-minute forgot to pick me up from school like he promised he would.

Mom had been beyond pissed when I called from the neighbors' place. Not at her loser boyfriend for wandering off goddess only knew where. At *me*. Since she was working the graveyard shift and wouldn't be home until morning, she'd told me to crash on Jane and Stu's saggy sofa. Which I did, not for the first or the last time. At least, until we uprooted again a few months later and moved to a new trailer in a new town with a new 24-hour diner and, of course, a new boyfriend for Mom. New neighbors, too — unfriendly ones, who made it clear their sofa was not an available crash-pad for stranded kids.

When Mom got home the morning after the lockout incident, still in her apron, looking dead on her feet and mad as a hornet, I got an earful for bothering her at work, getting her in trouble with her manager. Even though I couldn't see how it was possibly my fault, seeing as I was only nine, I didn't say a peep. Mouthing off to Mom when she was in one of her moods was a good way to wind up with a belted bottom.

Aunt Colette was Mom's older sister, but she wasn't like Mom. She was generous and relaxed and funny. She laughed all the time. She never yelled. But they did share blood. So, whatever anger Mom had burning inside her... I figured Aunt Colette might have it, too. Maybe I just hadn't seen it yet. Maybe I just hadn't done anything to bring it out of her yet.

I really, really, didn't want to bring it out of her. Because if I ruined what I had going here in Salem, it would be devastating. The only thing that made leaving at the end of each summer tolerable was knowing in nine short months, I'd be back. And I needed that light at the end of the tunnel. I needed it like air in my lungs. It was the only thing that kept me from fading away completely in the dark.

I did not want to risk the air in my lungs, my light in the

dark, by calling Aunt Colette, tearing her away from work — especially since this time, it actually was my fault. But, seeing as I was stuck, and in a fair amount of pain, and there was a beautiful boy sitting six inches away staring at me, waiting on my answer... I figured I didn't have much of a choice.

I didn't share the reasons for my hesitation with the Lifeguard God. I merely took a deep, steadying breath, nodded, and held out my hand, palm up. He didn't say anything either, just passed me his cellphone and watched in silence as I punched in the numbers I'd memorized at Aunt Colette's insistence.

"You've reached The Gallows, this is your executioner speaking," her warm, familiar voice trilled over the line after one short ring.

"Hi," I murmured softly, hyper-aware of the LG's gaze on my face. "It's me. Gwen."

"Gwendolyn, darling! Is everything all right?"

I nodded even though she couldn't see me and screwed my eyes shut. Bracing for the worst. The words came out in a breathy rush of air. "I'm really sorry to bother you. Really, *really* sorry, I know you're at work and you're busy and I wouldn't call unless I had no other choice, I swear I wouldn't, it's just—"

"Gwendolyn." Aunt Colette's voice had lost none of its warmth, but now sounded far more serious. "Darling, what's wrong? What happened? Are you all right?"

"I'm fine. It was my fault. It was stupid." I scowled in frustration at my own carelessness. "I stepped on an urchin."

"Oh, no! Are you okay? Do you need a doctor? How bad is it?"

"The..." My eyes sliced open and cut straight to the LG. He was watching me carefully and something in his eyes made my breath catch again. "The lifeguard helped me. He bandaged it and put on the goopy stuff."

At this statement, his lips turned up at one side in a half-smile.

"Are you at the beach by Winter Island?" Aunt Colette asked in my ear. "I'll come get you."

"It doesn't hurt so much anymore," I lied, still staring into the boy's eyes. I couldn't look away. They were holding me hostage. "I can probably pedal with one foot..."

My words dried up as the boy shook his head, a flat rejection. He started reaching for the phone, no doubt prepared to expose my fibs to Aunt Colette, but before his fingers made contact I heard her voice again.

"I'll be there in five."

"But the shop—"

"I'm already on my way. Sit tight, Gwendolyn. I'll see you soon."

I heard the sound of the brass door bells as the shop door opened, and then she clicked off.

I blew out a relieved breath. She wasn't mad. Thank goodness she wasn't mad. I handed the phone back to the LG and he took it, sliding it into the pocket of his bathing suit.

"She coming?"

I nodded.

"Good." He was still staring at me. "Hey, Firecracker?"

My brows went up.

"You okay?" he asked, and for some inexplicable reason, I got the sense he wasn't asking about my foot.

"I'm fine," I told him, because I was. Or, I would be.

"Uh huh," he muttered, glancing away from me. His dark brows were furrowed in concentration and his eyes were fixed on the crashing waves. He didn't say anything else and neither did I. We just sat in silence until, precisely six minutes later, Aunt Colette's car rolled into the parking lot. It was hard to miss her arrival, seeing as she drove an exact replica of the infamous Thelma and Louise cliff-diving convertible — a turquoise blue 1966 Ford Thunderbird she kept in pristine condition.

The Lifeguard God wheeled my bike from the rack at the edge of the parking lot and stowed it in the trunk while Aunt Colette made a fuss over me, cooing and brushing at my tear-stained face, hauling most my weight up against the long length of her side and helping me hobble into the passenger seat. When I was settled, I heard her chatting to the LG by the trunk but, by this point, I was in the throes of deep mortification and couldn't bring myself to listen to their conversation.

The most beautiful boy I'd ever seen in my life had held me in his arms and carried me against his chest and blown on my foot and been my real, actual superhero, and that knowledge was as thrilling as it was humiliating. My small body simply could not contain all the emotions whirling around inside it. I was going to fly apart into a million pieces if we stayed here much longer, in plain view of those intense green eyes that seemed to see everything, all at once, every little detail and all the big ones, too.

Aunt Colette slid behind the wheel and strapped in. I listened to the click of her seatbelt, then turned to grab my own when she told me to buckle up. Swiveling in my seat, I saw the beautiful boy in all his glory standing there beside the passenger door, looking down at me. I tilted my face up to meet his eyes one last time and managed to overcome my mortification long enough to utter two words.

"Thank you."

He nodded. "See you around, Firecracker."

And he did.

Because not one week later, when my foot was fully healed and I was again allowed to take my bike out on sunny days, I rode straight back to that beach on Winter Island. I was practically giddy with anticipation to see the LG — my hero, my savior, extractor-of-urchin-spines and applier-of-goopy-stuff, the most beautiful boy to ever grace the beaches of Massachusetts, of New

England, of the whole freaking universe, so far as I was concerned.

But when I stowed my bike in the (surprisingly full) rack and walked down onto the beach, everything was different. The once-empty stretch of sand was peppered with towels and chairs. And on those towels and chairs... were girls.

Dozens of girls.

Dozens of gorgeous, older girls who filled out their bathing suit tops in a way I wouldn't for years and years to come. And they were not shy about showing off these attributes to the Lifeguard God.

My Lifeguard God!

But it was clear he wasn't just mine anymore. My secret was out. In the space of a week, he'd gone from the subject of one awkward preteen girl's hero-worship to the star of every girl in Salem's sexual fantasies.

I couldn't compete. I was ten. I was flat as a pancake. Flatter, actually. I couldn't get him to so much as look my direction, with all that perky flesh on display. Not to mention, he was five years older than me — an age difference that might not matter down the line, but most definitely did at that time. The five years separating ten from fifteen might as well have been five million lightyears.

I knew this.

I persisted anyway.

Day after day, I sat on my stupid polka-dotted towel in my stupid polka-dotted one-piece suit, crossed my spindly arms over my pancake-flat chest, watching my LG flirt with girls his own age — girls who had boobs and hips and midnight curfews — and positively *seething*. And then, as July slipped into August and he still hadn't looked my way, not even once, I finished seething and started the sad business of accepting reality.

This was something I was used to doing. Reality, more often

than not, sucked. In my experience, if you were lucky, you'd get three months of good for every nine months of bad, like my Salem summer arrangement. That was the way things worked in the world of Gwen.

So, I got up from my towel, plunked on my sparkly pink helmet, pedaled my way home to Aunt Colette's, and started going to a different beach on the other side of town to look for my shells. One where there were no lifeguards on duty and no sea urchins to step on.

Over time, I resigned myself to the fact that I wasn't going to ever look into those green eyes again, or hear that deep voice calling me *Firecracker* — which, for no particular reason at all, had become my favorite word in the entire English language.

I WAS WRONG, of course.

I did hear that voice again, but not for three whole summers. The wait was worth it, though, because, along with the voice, I finally got the name to accompany it. His name. And it was a good one.

Graham Graves.

It rolled off the tongue. It looked good in print, which I discovered when I wrote it in my journal about a hundred and twenty five times in a row. Better than that, his initials were G.G., just like mine, which was more irrefutable evidence from the universe that we were simply meant to be.

Graham Graves and Gwendolyn Goode.

I thought his was a perfect name for a Lifeguard God, who by then was no longer a mere beachside attraction but a full-on heartthrob. He was the talk of the town, which was how I learned his name in the first place. Everyone talked about the Graves family, seeing as they owned half the city and had done so since the 1600s, but they especially talked about Graham. He was the subject of relentless gossip — mostly about whatever new girl he was currently stringing along, whose heart he'd most recently left pulverized, and which lucky fool would be next.

At eighteen, he was a hometown hero. Salem's golden boy. Not only a high school sensation — Prom King, Class President, quarterback of the football team — but poised to be a college one, too. He was Harvard-bound, a legacy, but rumor said he had the grades to back up his family's longstanding tradition of enrollment. He was no longer Lifeguard God. He was just...

A god.

Period.

Girls swooned at his feet when he looked their way, grown men shook his hand when they saw him on the street. His picture was on the front of the local newspaper every other day during football season, it seemed, and I occasionally (okay, slightly more than occasionally) cut out these clippings and added them to my ever-expanding G.G. shrine, which I kept in a shoebox under my bed.

Three years before, I'd adored Graham Graves.

Now, *everyone* adored Graham Graves.

He was golden.

And me? I was five years behind and a whole universe away, awkward in a way only thirteen-year-old girls can be awkward. Not yet quite settled in my body, unsure of how to walk or talk or carry myself or style my hair. Still experimenting with makeup — and, for the most part, failing miserably in such experimentations. (Hello, turquoise eyeshadow.)

Needless to say, when I ran into Graham and a gaggle of his friends at a local pizza shop one July afternoon — a considerable number of whom were girls, including one specifically stunning blonde who was hanging on him like she'd fall out of the booth if he removed his hand from her waist — I kept my eyes downcast and pretended not to see him.

He wouldn't remember me anyway.

At least, I didn't think he would. For, though the sea-urchin afternoon was burned into my memory in indelible ink, fueling the raging torch I still carried for him from innocent childhood crush into ardent adolescent obsession, I was not naive enough to think it was a monumental moment in *his* life. In fact, I doubted he'd ever given me another thought after Aunt Colette's Thunderbird rolled away that day.

So, I hovered in the corner, waiting by the takeout counter, half-hidden from view by a display stand full of mini bags of chips, waiting for the checkout guy to call my order. Aunt Colette had sent me out to pick up our dinner at Flying Saucer Pizza, which was conveniently located a block away from The Gallows and just so happened to serve the best veggie pie in town. We were going to eat at the shop while she took inventory, then walk home together when it got dark.

"Got a takeout order here," the guy behind the counter boomed. "Gwendolyn?"

My head jerked up at the sound of my name. My eyes went not to the counter as I planned but, for some unfathomable reason, lifted right to the table in the corner where Graham Graves was sitting with his posse. Straight into a set of unwavering green eyes.

Eyes that pinned me to the spot in an instant.

My heart tripped over itself inside my chest as our gazes locked and I felt color bleed into my cheeks, a fierce blush stealing across my skin as the seconds slipped by. He was looking right at me. He was so stunningly handsome it stole my breath. And I...

I was...

Me.

Quite suddenly, I didn't want him looking at me. I didn't want those green eyes, the ones I'd spent so many nights wishing and hoping and dreaming would find mine again, to see how awkward and acne-ridden and flat-chested (yes, *still* — I was a late bloomer in that department, I couldn't even fill out a B-cup bra until my senior year of high school) I was, standing there in my cut-off shorts and faded black t-shirt, the one that said THE GALLOWS in spooky font that matched the sign outside my aunt's shop, with the letter "O" in the shape of a noose.

"Gwendolyn!" the takeout guy called again.

I ripped my eyes from Graham's and turned, flustered, toward the counter. Unfortunately, in my haste to get away from those piercing eyes, I wasn't looking where I was going and barreled straight into the display stand. It went over with a thud that made everyone in the joint jolt three inches in their seats. Bags of chips flew in all directions, scattering across the floor. Heads turned. Strangers winced their sympathy.

None moved to assist me.

I fell to my knees, scrambling to pick up the chips. My face, already red, burned with such heat I thought I might burst into flames. I'd collected nearly all the bags and was half-crawling to the fallen metal rack when, suddenly, a hand reached down and righted it with a powerful yank. Arms full of chips, I tilted my head up to look at whoever had helped me, expecting the guy behind the counter.

To my surprise, it was Graham. He was looking down at me, lips tugged up in a half smile, gaze curious. I tore my eyes from his and got shakily to my feet, shoving the mini bags of chips into the stand without a word. They were disorganized, definitely not back in the exact spots they'd flown from, but I was too embarrassed to do anything about it at that moment. It was all I could do to keep my jellied legs beneath me as I propelled my body toward the takeout counter and slapped down a twenty dollar bill.

"Keep the change," I murmured, hands curling around the cardboard pizza box.

The guy behind the counter gave a low grunt of thanks, blessedly not commenting on my graceless collision with his chip display. I turned on my heel, pizza box held out in front of me like a shield, and began to march toward the exit. My feet faltered when I saw Graham.

He wasn't back at his table with his friends. He'd just finished sorting the chips into their proper places, lining them up by brand so the logos were all facing front, and was now standing directly in my path, between me and the exit, with his arms folded over the broad planes of his chest. His t-shirt was faded red from many washes, and it said WITCHES on the front — the mascot of the Salem High football team. I tried not to notice how good it looked on him, against his tan skin and well-defined forearms. I tried not to notice anything about him, but that was difficult, seeing as he was... well...

Graham.

His eyes held a teasing light that made me nervous. Was he going to humiliate me in front of everyone? I'd already humiliated myself enough, I didn't need any help in that regard. He leaned in a few inches and I swear, all the air in the pizza shop seemed to compress inward. My heart was slamming away at my ribs like a jackhammer. It was all I could do to keep breathing.

"At least you didn't require first aid this time," he whispered lowly so only I could hear, obliterating any hope I'd had that he'd forgotten me entirely since our first meeting. "Progress, Firecracker. Progress."

More embarrassed than I'd ever been in my life, I scurried around him as fast as my feet could carry me and was out the door before he could say another word. But not before I heard the sound of a high-pitched, whiny, female voice drawl, "What was her deal? Little *freak*."

I'd never heard Graham's laugh, so I couldn't be sure whether or not he joined in with the rest of his friends as they all had a good chuckle at my expense. I told myself it didn't matter what they thought about me as I ducked into The Gallows with the pizza box, calling out to Aunt Colette as I moved through the maze of cluttered shelves. It did matter, of course, but there wasn't much I could do about it.

Aunt Colette could likely tell there was something on my mind, but she didn't push me to share. She distracted me instead. By the second slice, she had me laughing at crazy stories about her tenure with an Aboriginal shaman in the Australian outback, and an unfortunate incident with a kangaroo that had tears of utter hilarity leaking from both our eyes.

As we walked home that night, cutting across Salem Common toward Aunt Colette's stately, three-story colonial on Washington Square, I reminded myself that Graham was eighteen. He'd be off to college in the fall and even if he came back to visit his family on breaks, since I was only ever in Salem for the summers, there was a good chance our paths wouldn't cross again. I'd probably never see perfect Graham Graves again in my life.

I WAS WRONG ABOUT THAT, too.

I would see him again, but not for a very long time. Not for almost a decade. And that time — two years ago almost to the day, in fact — would change my perception of him forever. It would, in a single stroke, flip the coin of my affections from idolized infatuation to irreversible detestation so completely, and so quickly, the shift nearly gave me whiplash. I would walk away from the encounter finally, *finally*, cured of my stale childhood crush and delivered, without mercy, into a state of sheer, unadulterated loathing the likes of which I'd never felt before in my twenty-plus years on the planet.

It didn't help matters that I'd only recently moved back to town. That I'd endured some big losses that instigated said move, and was still finding my footing in their aftermath. That my grief was so thick, it seemed to coat my skin, to fill up my lungs until just breathing was a chore, until dragging my body out of bed each morning felt like a Herculean task. Even now, two years on, there were days the dulling film of mourning still followed me around like my own personal raincloud. Yes, they were rarer — a blip in my otherwise sunny existence — but not gone for good.

That night, though, the night Florence convinced me to come out for a drink, I was still in the thick of it. Still consumed by it. Still letting it eat me alive, body and soul.

It'll be fun, Flo assured me on the phone. *And you need some fun, Gwennie. I'll introduce you to Desmond, my new guy! He's pretty great. So are his friends. A few of them recently moved back to town, just like you.*

If I'd known who she intended to introduce me to, I would've stayed at home with my demons. But I was trying to be a good sport, a good friend. So I did my best to scrape together an autumn-chic outfit, fluffed my limp auburn curls into something resembling style, and walked the ten minutes from Aunt Colette's colonial on the Common into the heart of downtown.

The bar Flo picked wasn't far from The Gallows, and I found it easily enough. The wood shingle over the door was shaped like a cauldron and read *WITCHES BREW TAVERN* in old-fashioned gold lettering. When I stepped through the front doors into the cozy space, I liked it instantly. It had a neighborhood pub feel. A homey atmosphere, despite its fairly large size. There was a band playing cover songs on a small stage in the corner, a stately, circular bar made of hammered copper at the center, and a shoulder-to-shoulder crowd waiting for drinks.

I weaved a path through the mass of strangers, looking for Florence's dark glossy hair, and eventually spotted her at a table near the stage. She was standing with a small group of people, a mix of girls and guys around my age, with her side tucked tight against a lanky, bookish blond guy I assumed must be Desmond, her new boyfriend.

She didn't spot me as I walked up. Her eyes were fixed on the man standing across from her. His back — which I couldn't help noticing was particularly broad and muscular, even beneath the cool-as-heck vintage leather jacket he was sporting — was to me and he was speaking.

As soon as I heard his voice, I stopped in my tracks.

I knew that voice.

It had been years, but I knew that voice.

"—better not be your idea of another blind date, Flo, so help me god. I know she's your friend and she's new to town, so I'll be nice tonight. But don't expect a repeat performance."

"You should be so lucky," Flo said, narrowing her eyes at him. "She's beautiful and she's smart — not something you can say for many of your exes."

"Uh huh."

"Why are you such a jackass, Graham? Would it kill you to be kind? She needs kind, right now. She's going through a hard time."

I stiffened, hating her sympathetic words. Hating that I couldn't even deny them. I *was* going through a hard time. The hardest one I'd ever had, to be honest, and that was really saying something after a childhood like mine.

"She just inherited an occult shop here in town. She's in the process of renovating it," Flo continued, only to be interrupted by Graham.

"An occult shop? Are you fucking kidding me? Jesus Christ, she doesn't need kindness — she needs her head examined."

I was already stiff but, at this, my spine went ramrod.

"Shut up, Graham!" Flo glared at him, elbowing her boyfriend in hopes he would wade in. Desmond shrugged helplessly and took a sip of his beer instead.

"Don't look at me like I kicked your puppy, Flo. You know how I feel about that supernatural shit." Graham scoffed, the sound brimming with condescension. "I mean, really... just what this town needs. Another freak of nature."

Aunt Colette's face flashed behind my eyes and my hands curled into fists at my sides. Aunt Colette, who loved her store more than anything. Aunt Colette, who'd left that store to me when *she* left me, four months prior, a loss so unexpected, it damn near crippled me.

She was not a freak of nature.

She was my home.

The only home I'd ever known.

And now she was gone.

Graham wasn't finished. "You really think I'm going to waste my time with some chick cracked enough not only to buy into that crap, but to make it her life's work? I would sooner slam my dick in a doorway than shove it into some sage-waving, crystal-obsessed crazy girl who'll spend hours analyzing my star chart, then lay a curse on me when I break up with her."

"That's not—"

"Dick in a doorway, Flo. *Dick in a doorway.*"

"But—"

"No buts. If I have to listen to one more wannabe-Wiccan in this town tell me I have Scorpio energy, whatever the fuck that means..." He took a long pull from his beer bottle, swallowed harshly, then muttered, "Gotta be fucking kidding me."

"Gwennie," Flo whispered suddenly, going pale.

"Gwennie?" Graham repeated, voice changing from condescension to confusion.

"Gwendolyn! Wait, honey!" Flo was off her stool, pushing past her boyfriend, then shoving by Graham — sending him a rather scary glare in the process. "Gwen! Please!"

But I was already turning to leave. I had to get out of there, before I lost my cool. I wasn't ready for this. I needed more time. The grief was still too fresh, too close to the surface. I couldn't tamp it down. Couldn't get it in check. It was safer for everyone if I stayed home alone with my wine bottle and my bathtub, until I was once again able to function in society without having a breakdown.

Unfortunately, I only made it two steps before Flo caught up to me, latching onto my arm and whipping me around to face her. In the dim light of the bar, her expression was soft, gentle with sympathy, and I knew that *she* knew I'd heard every word.

"Gwen," she murmured. "He's a jackass. Don't let him bother you."

"He doesn't," I said, but even I could hear the hurt in my tone. "I don't care what he thinks."

"Then why are you leaving?"

"This was a mistake." I shook my head rapidly. "I'm not ready yet."

"It's been months, honey." Her eyes were still soft with compassion. "You can't just sit all alone in that big drafty house—"

"I'm sorry, I can't be here," I cut her off, breaking eye contact because if I kept looking into her soft, sweet, melted chocolate irises I was going to lose it completely. Regrettably, this meant my gaze locked on something else.

And that something was Graham.

He was standing several feet behind Florence, and his eyes were on me. Not just on me, but burning into me. I could feel the weight of them on my skin as they moved over my face and I wanted to look away, I *told* myself to look away, but I couldn't seem to make my eyes cooperate. I was staring straight back at him, hating him in part for what he'd said but mostly because if he'd been handsome as a teen, he was off-the-charts as a grown man. He was... *hot*, pure and simple.

People always say "clothes make the man" but in his case it was simply not true. He made those simple clothes spectacular. His jeans fit like they were created just for him. His shirt beneath the leather jacket was sculpted perfectly against every contour of his chest. He towered several inches past six feet, almost a head above me, even in my low-heeled boots.

Whatever traces of boyish youth his square jaw and angled cheeks held last time I saw him was gone completely, now. At twenty-seven, he was every inch a man and I hated, *hated*, that my body was responding to him as a woman. Just looking at him, I could feel something stirring in my bloodstream. A visceral reaction that gripped me from the inside out. It was intense. It was instinctive.

It was most unwelcome.

Because I could forgive him for talking about me, judging me without ever having met me. But I could not forgive him deriding Aunt Colette. Diminishing her shop, her life's work, into something idiotic and insane. I could not let it roll off. I could not take it as a harmless, off-the-cuff comment.

Not then, with her loss so fresh.

Maybe not ever.

But definitely, *definitely*, not then.

"Gwen?" Florence asked, calling my attention back to her. "Are you all right?"

With effort, I tore my gaze away from Graham's scorching one. And, as I did, I vowed it was the last time I'd ever waste my attention on him. From that moment on, he would cease to exist for me. Whoever he'd been as a young man — my good luck charm, my personal god on earth — was gone. This guy, standing before me, was an asshole, alpha-male jackass with heartbreak written all over his infuriatingly symmetrical face. And I'd already had enough heartbreak to last a lifetime.

"Of course I'm all right," I told Flo. "I'm always all right."

I smiled at her to assuage her worry. It didn't work — her brows remained furrowed, her teeth continued to chew her bottom lip.

"Honey..."

I squeezed her arm quickly. "We'll try again. Sometime soon."

"Promise?"

"Promise."

I could feel her worried eyes on my back all the way to the exit. Worse, I could feel another set of eyes — green, intense, biting into me like wolf's teeth — watching until I disappeared out the front door, into the chilly September night. I felt them on me the whole walk back to Aunt Colette's dark, empty house. I felt them even after I'd showered, scrubbed my skin raw, and climbed beneath the covers in the same bedroom I'd stayed in as a kid, back when I spent my summers in Salem.

I hadn't yet been able to bring myself to enter Aunt Colette's private chambers, let alone disturb her things. It would be another three months before I found the courage to do so. And three more after that before I'd force myself to call Flo so we could "try" again. But I made sure, when we did, that a certain towering, dark-haired jerk would not be in attendance.

That was a year and a half ago.

I'd seen Graham since, of course. Occasionally. In passing.

Once the shop renovations were complete and The Gallows reopened for business, I was a constant presence downtown. And, as a Graves, as the golden boy who'd grown into the golden man of the golden family... so was he. Salem was a city, but most days it felt more like a small town. Our community was close-knit. Everyone knew everyone, especially if you ran a local shop, like I did, and were friendly, like I was. (To *almost* everyone.)

When our paths did cross — meaning, when I was caught off guard and unable to avoid him by ducking into an alley or hiding behind a tree or engaging a baffled stranger in conversation on the sidewalk until he passed by — I was sweet. I forced a smile. I played my part.

Gwen Goode. The good time girl. She of the sunny disposition. She of the quick smile and easy laugh. She who never let her dark side show.

Except where Graham Graves was concerned.

No matter how many times I'd seen him since that night in the bar, my anger had not waned and my feelings had not changed. There was a part of me that had iced over as a result of his harsh words and it simply....

Would.

Not.

Thaw.

No matter how many times I tried to let it go. No matter how often Flo trained her melted-chocolate eyes on me, begging for me to please, for her sake, make nice with her boyfriend's best friend, so we could all go out for drinks without conversation growing strained or caustic looks being exchanged.

I couldn't do it.

Not even for Flo, who I'd adored since she adopted me as her best friend the summer I turned twelve, who'd written me letter after letter during our school year separations, who stayed in touch all through college with bi-monthly, marathon phone calls. Not even for Flo, who I still adored to this day, even more so now that we finally lived in the same zip code and could keep in touch simply by walking to each other's houses or meeting up for a glass of wine, rather than penning postcards and dialing long-distance numbers.

There wasn't much I would not do for Flo.

And yet...

Since I couldn't be my normally sweet self to Graham, I avoided him like the plague. On the rare instances we were forced to interact — say, if Flo and Desmond were having a party at their townhouse and we were both required to be in attendance — I did my best to smile and be civil while in his immediate proximity. It wasn't a very convincing charade. I was no actress. (I was a *freak of nature*, according to certain sources, but I was no actress.)

I knew I should let it go. I knew I'd let his words fester too long inside of me. But that was far easier said than done. And no matter how many times I resolved to turn over a new leaf, to make nice with the Spawn of Satan himself, as soon as I saw that smug half-smile tug up his lips on one side... as soon as those sharp green eyes hit mine...

I morphed into a total frigid bitch.

Ice Queen.

And as soon as he saw that ice, he returned in kind. He gave it right back to me, an arctic-level chill that would singlehandedly reverse global warming if directed at the polar caps.

Captain Cold.

We were at an impasse. One that became harder and harder to undo the longer we let it linger. Now, it had been going on so long, we were buried under such a thick sheet of frost, I doubted we'd ever be able to thaw it. Not even if we tried. Not even for the sake of Florence and Desmond.

It was easier, for the both of us, to simply avoid each other and do our best to be pleasant when said avoidance was absolutely unavoidable. Which did not explain why he was standing in front of me now.

Here.

In the dimly lit storeroom my shop, a place he had no business being. Not just standing, no less. Standing with his booted feet planted wide, his muscled arms crossed over his broad chest, and his green eyes fixed, with startling intensity, on my face.

I couldn't help but notice those eyes held not one trace of the ice I usually saw in their depths. They weren't cold. They were the exact *opposite* of cold. In fact, they were so damn heated, they set fire to every one of my senses as I backed slowly away from him, trying not to balk under the scorching gaze that tracked my every move.

I dragged an unsteady breath into my lungs.

What... the actual... hell... *was going on?*

CHAPTER FOUR

I thought "ghosting" meant he was a real freak in the sheets.
- Gwen Goode, wondering why her last date never called

The heavy door clicked closed behind Graham, enclosing us together in the dark storeroom. I forced myself to stop retreating like a coward, planting my feet on the tile floor. I hoped my face didn't reveal my deep unease at being alone with him. My grip was so tight on the box of amethyst, I was pretty sure I'd lost circulation.

"What the hell do you think you're doing?!" I hissed, my voice thrumming with outrage.

"I told you, we need to talk."

"We don't need to talk. We don't need to do anything."

He ignored this. His eyes flickered beyond me for a brief moment. "Anyone else back here?"

"No, but—"

"Good."

My mouth was gaping like a fish out of water so, with considerable effort, I clicked it closed. Graham's eyes scanned the L-shaped space, taking in the stock shelves — these were metal, utilitarian, nothing at all like the expensive, ornate, wood-carved ones in the shop — piled high with books and boxes of merchandise. Against the opposite wall next to some filing cabinets sat a small, organized desk — also metal, also utilitarian — where I often spent my nights pouring over the ledger books. In the far corner, beneath the only window in the elongated room, which looked out to the cobbled alley behind the building, was a mini-fridge, an industrial sink, and an old emerald sofa that had been there for as long as I could remember. I used to crash on it as a kid whenever I stayed late at the shop to help Aunt Colette with inventory, often falling asleep there while she sat at the desk trying to sort out what she called the 'Sisyphean horseshit' that came along with running a business. (Also known as paper-work.) The canvas slipcover was a bit frayed at the seams with age, but the cushions were so broken in they felt like a cloud when you sank down into them. I'd never get rid of that sofa, not in a million years. To this day, it was one of the only places I ever managed to get some decent shut-eye.

Graham appeared to examine and catalogue all these details in a nanosecond before his sharp gaze returned to mine. He took a step toward me and, despite my desire to hold my ground, I backpedaled with the box still clutched in my arms.

"You can't be in here," I informed him, retreating farther.

"I'm in here," he returned, following me.

I took three more steps, moving blindly backward through the shelves. I tried to tear my eyes away from Graham, but I couldn't seem to accomplish it. The look on his face as he advanced on me was not one you turned your back on. Not if you were smart.

"You scared to be alone with me, Glinda?" his voice was soft and, somehow, that was even scarier than the look on his face.

"For the last time, my name is Gwendolyn," I snapped to cover my unease.

"Not an answer."

"No," I clipped. "I am not scared of you."

"Uh huh. Is that why you bolt like a spooked horse every time I get close to you?"

"Maybe you just have that effect on women."

His lips twitched. "Not historically, no."

Arrogant!

My grip on the box tightened so much, the sides began to concave inward. Before I could destroy its structural integrity, I shoved it onto an empty shelf on my left, next to a bulk package of funky taper candles with whorls and spirals carved into the wax. They looked like they belonged on a ceremonial altar of blood, burning against the night to summon a demon. In other words, they were the absolute shit.

"Look," I said, turning back to Graham. "You—you—"

I stuttered into silence when I realized I'd repeated my mistake back in the shop. He'd used my momentary distraction to close the distance between us again, coming to a stop less than a foot away from me. I actually had to crane my neck to meet his eyes.

"Um." I swallowed. "What are you doing?"

"Watching you resist the urge to bolt."

I was, in an irritating turn of events, doing precisely that. But since I wasn't keen on sharing that with him, I locked my knees and held my ground. We were toe-to-toe, heavy black motorcycle boots to blush satin Manolo Blahniks. The room was dim, but a few weak shafts of late-morning sunshine were streaming through the window behind me, illuminating the angles of Graham's face. He was so handsome, standing there amidst the dust motes and sun beams, it actually took my breath away. I covered my breathlessness by adopting a bitchy tone.

"Sorry to disappoint, but I don't bolt in six hundred dollar stilettos."

His eyes flickered down to my feet for the briefest instant. "Didn't seem to stop you at the Fourth of July BBQ."

"Those were wedges," I said, again bitchily.

"Do I look like a man who cares about the intricacies of footwear?"

"A wedge is a platform, while a stiletto—"

"Glinda, fair warning, the only time I spare a thought to what a woman has on her feet is when she's got her legs wrapped around me, wearing nothing but those heels as I fuck her into next week."

My mouth fell open.

He did *not* just say that!

Did he just say that!?

"Pardon?" I squeaked.

Without bothering to respond, he stepped around me and walked deeper into the storage room, following the shelving units all the way to the back until he'd reached the sofa and mini-fridge area. "Do you have video surveillance back here?"

"Video surveillance?" I echoed, stupefied by the abrupt shift in topic. I was still recovering from his *fair warning* and caught in the throes of conversational whiplash.

"CCTV."

I shook my head, then realized he couldn't see me and murmured, "No. I thought about putting in a few cameras in the shop but..." I shrugged. "I'm not really into the whole video surveillance thing. I barely have time to catch up on my Netflix shows."

Graham grunted lowly. It was a grunt of grim acknowledgement, not surprise. I stared at his back as his head swung from the small window to the heavy black metal emergency exit door.

"Is this door alarmed?"

"Mildly perturbed, last I checked, but it's been having a tough time lately. Feeling neglected, since everyone uses the front entrance with the pretty brass bells..." I trailed off when he shot me an unamused look over his shoulder. "No, it's not alarmed."

"Why not?"

"Does it matter?" I blinked at him. "Why are you asking me about all this?"

"Just answer the question."

"It's not alarmed because it doesn't need an alarm, Graham Crackers. And I do mean *crackers* in the British sense of the word," I declared, planting my hands on my hips.

He ignored my declaration. "Anyone could just walk in off the street."

"No," I said, growing less patient by the second. "It locks automatically when it closes, so no one can enter from the alley. You have to prop it open with a brick when you haul the trash to the dumpsters, otherwise you get locked out and have to walk all the way around to the front entrance."

"Uh huh. And how often does that happen?"

"How often do I throw out our trash? Or how often do I accidentally get locked out while throwing out our trash?"

"Both."

I stared at him for a beat, still not understanding why I was subject to this line of questioning, from Graham of all people, but also reading the steely determination in his gaze and realizing perhaps the fastest way to get rid of him was simply entertaining his delusion, speedily answering his questions, and then sending him on his way. So, heaving a sigh, I told him what he wanted to know.

"The first, regularly. The second, less regularly after one particularly unpleasant experience involving a family of raccoons who'd taken up residence in our recycling bins and made their intentions to stay very apparent. Let me tell you, you do not want to find yourself locked out with four feisty trash-pandas hot on your heels."

He stared at me for a moment with a look of what could only be described as bewildered amusement. I couldn't tell if he wanted to throw his head back and laugh or have me pink-slipped on a 72-hour hold at the nearest psych ward.

"How many times a day do you go in and out of this door," he clarified. "On average."

"Assuming there are no trash-panda incidents?"

He gave a tight nod.

I scrunched my nose up in thought. "It varies. At least twice, sometimes three times. Hetti always empties it at six when we close, plus once before her lunch break. Sometimes, if we're really slammed in the morning, I'll empty it before things start to overflow. Old espresso beans start to stink up the place after a few hours."

"Then no one has been out this door yet today?"

"No, I don't think so." I shrugged. "It's still early."

Graham did not acknowledge this. Instead, he reached into his back pocket, pulled out a slim smartphone, tapped the screen a few times, and lifted it to his ear. "It's Graves." He paused. "Confirmed there's no CCTV in the shop. Alley door is one-way access, no one has been in or out yet today." His eyes slid to mine. "I'm going to bring her through now. You guys ready? Right. See you in a second." He hung up, slid the phone back into his pocket, and walked toward me.

"You ready?"

"Ready?" I shook my head rapidly, quick jerks of confusion. "Ready for what? You haven't told me anything! I have no idea what's going on here. You show up out of nowhere asking me all these bizarre questions—"

"Glinda."

"And now you're asking me if I'm ready, but you haven't given me the slightest indication of what is going on—"

"Glinda."

"—and I really think, if something is going on at my place of business, which it clearly is or I'm guessing you wouldn't be here in the first place, I should have the proper details to deal with it before—"

"Gwendolyn."

"*What?*" I exploded, so revved up I didn't even realize he'd used my actual name.

"There's a crime scene in your alley. Need you to look at it."

"A crime scene?"

His voice, unlike mine, was not squeaky with panic. It was the same as always — deep, level, highly controlled. "How are you with blood?"

"Blood?"

"You a fainter?"

"No, but—"

"You got a weak stomach?"

I blinked. "A weak stomach?"

"Yeah."

"I don't think so."

"You going to hurl if you see something... unpleasant?"

My eyes held his as my stomach clenched. "Whatever is in my alley is unpleasant?"

"Not many pleasant crime scenes, in my experience."

"Right." I swallowed. "Right."

"Glinda," he said, calling my eyes back to his face. I was so caught up in my own thoughts, I didn't even correct him. "I can't take you back there if you're going to fall apart on me."

I sucked in a sharp breath and considered this. Despite my immediate reaction to the rather scary news that there was crime scene in the alleyway behind my shop, despite the fact that this morning was going even more off the rails than it was before... I knew I'd rather see for myself what was going on than hear about it secondhand. And I knew, no matter what I was about to face, I'd seen worse. I'd lived worse.

I would not fall apart.

I was Gwendolyn Goode. I kept my shit together, no matter what happened. I was steady. I was strong. I was forged by a childhood of hellfire and brimstone. I wasn't going to crumble. Not then, not now.

"I won't fall apart on you," I told Graham firmly.

"Good."

Before I could protest, he reached forward, snatched my hand in his, and tugged me toward the emergency exit. I stumbled after him in my heels, unsuccessfully trying to extract my fingers from his iron-clad grip with every step. Then, the metal door swung open with a screech of rusty hinges and we stepped out into the leaf-strewn alley, harsh morning sunshine nearly blinding after the dimness of the storage room, and I found myself grateful for the strong, male hand wrapped so firmly around mine. Because, when the sunspots cleared from my eyes and the alley swam into focus... when I saw the cobblestones stained with blood and the utter carnage at my feet... I very nearly went back on my promise not to fall apart.

I sat on the stoop just outside the emergency exit, taking slow breaths in through my nose and out through my mouth. The door was propped open with a brick and I was leaned back against it, my feet planted on the cobblestones. I was so focused on my breathing, I didn't even care that I was likely ruining my favorite pair of wide-legged linen trousers, the high-waisted ones accented with six smooth pearlescent buttons. My eyes were fixed purposefully on the brick wall that divided my alley from a pay-by-hour parking lot. I was careful not to let them drift down and left, to the horrific site currently being taped off by uniformed police officers.

Graham was standing with them, speaking in hushed tones, but I was careful not to look at him either. I could feel his gaze on me, though, even across the distance. Studying me. Likely weighing whether or not I was about to fall into a fit of hysterics.

I was not.

I was holding it together.

(Barely.)

I didn't get squeamish around blood. Lord knew I'd seen enough of it spilled in my life, growing up the daughter of a certified loose cannon whose taste in men ranged from patently unpleasant to downright deranged. I'd witnessed violence first hand, up close and personal. But that didn't mean the sight of my alleyway hadn't sent a shockwave through my system.

When I'd stepped out with Graham twenty minutes earlier, it was all I could to do to keep my legs from giving way beneath me. He'd felt it, since his hand was still gripping mine, and he'd squeezed so tightly, I thought my bones were going to snap.

"You good?" he'd asked.

I hadn't answered. My eyes were fixed on the massacred animal in my alleyway, trying to make sense of something so horrific, so out of place in my generally drama-free existence, it nearly brought me to my knees.

I'd seen blood.

I'd seen death.

I'd never seen *anything* like this.

It was a donkey. Or, the remains of one. Whoever had killed the chestnut-brown beast had been beyond thorough in their execution. Its limbs were severed, as was its head, leaving the once-beautiful animal in six distinct pieces. Four legs, the torso, and the head. The cuts were not torn, not ragged at the edges. They looked as though they'd been made with a sharp blade, nearly surgical in precision.

The remains had been carefully arranged in a chillingly macabre circle, with the torso at the center, the legs fanning out in a ring at the bottom, the head at the top. The blood I'd seen was not spilled out from the violence of the massacre, but rather traced, with clear intention, in the shape of an encircled star around the carcass.

A pentagram.

Even more disturbing — and the donkey was pretty damn disturbing, so that was really saying something — was the accompanying message written across the back wall of my building. The dark brownish red of the dried blood formed one large, lopsided word across the pale beige siding.

RESURGEMUS

I'd read just enough Latin in old occult texts to know what that meant. And, let's just say, it did not give me a happy-go-lucky feeling inside.

WE SHALL RISE AGAIN

Somehow, I didn't think they were talking about bread dough.

"You need a paper bag to breathe into?"

I flinched at the sudden intrusion into my thoughts. My gaze sailed upward to Graham. I hadn't seen him leave the huddle of policemen, but there he was, two feet away, his hyper-alert eyes fixed on my face.

"I'm fine," I said, pushing shakily to my feet. "Or, I will be when you explain this to me."

"Which part?"

"The whole part." I gestured vaguely toward the donkey. My voice was barely a whisper. "Who would do this?"

"That's what we're tying to figure out."

"We?"

"Salem PD, and the boys on my task force."

My brows arched. "Your... boys?"

He nodded.

"On your... task force?"

He nodded again.

"I don't understand what you're doing here, Graham."

Now his brows were arching, too. "There's a dead donkey in your alleyway."

"I know why the police are here. Why are *you* here?"

"I'm a consultant."

"A consultant," I repeated slowly.

"At Gravewatch."

"Gravewatch..."

"Why are you repeating everything I say?"

I threw up my hands. "Because I'm hoping if I do, it will start to make sense."

"This shouldn't be confusing for you. You know I'm a special consultant for the police. You know what I do for a living. I overheard Flo tell you at Desmond's birthday last year."

I blinked, somewhat stunned he remembered such a minute interaction, but barreled past it to more important matters. "She told me you were a fixer."

"I am a fixer," he agreed instantly.

"I'm beginning to think our definitions of that word are not in alignment."

He waited for me to continue.

"See, I was under the impression you fixed things like... say... cabinets. Old furniture. The occasional leaky pipe."

A muscle leapt in his cheek. He was staring at me like I was a few watts short of a working bulb. "Let me get this straight. For the past two years, you've thought I was a handyman?"

"What's wrong with being a handyman?"

"Nothing, assuming that's what you are." His eyes narrowed and something flashed in their depths, something I didn't know him well enough to decipher. "Gwendolyn, I'm not a handyman."

"Oh," I said stupidly. "Then, when you say *fixer* you mean..."

"The police call me in to fix things they can't."

"What sorts of things?"

His eyes cut to the dead donkey for a brief instant before returning to mine. "Complex problems often require complex solutions. Solutions outside the parameters of law and order." He paused. "You wear a badge, you operate in a world of black and white. Good and bad. That works with about ninety-nine percent of cases. But for that occasional one percent... you need someone who operates in the gray."

"And... you're gray?"

"I'm gray," he concurred.

I was floored by this news. Almost, but not quite, as stunned as I'd been to step into my alleyway and find a donkey massacred in front of my dumpsters. In hindsight, I should've seen this coming. Not the donkey part, the handyman part. I mean... truth be told, had I thought it strange when Flo told me that Graham — Harvard-educated, uber-smart, golden boy Graham — was working as a glorified Mr. Fix-It?

Admittedly, yes.

Had I allowed myself to dwell on that information?

Absolutely not.

As with essentially everything that concerned Graham Graves, I did my utmost to expunge that factoid from my memory banks as soon as it entered. My own, personal 'the less I know about him the better' policy had, until this very moment, been working for me just fine.

Operative phrase being: *until this very moment.*

"A handyman," he muttered, running a hand through his thick, dark hair. "Christ."

"I can't fathom why you're so annoyed."

"Really? You can't?" His eyes narrowed on mine. "You wouldn't be annoyed if someone you've interacted with regularly for the past several years, someone who moves in your social circles and shares custody of your best friends, was walking around with an entirely skewed perception of who you are?"

Okay, he had a point. That would probably grind my gears. Not that I was going to admit that to him. "You make this sound like it's my fault! I can't help it that Flo didn't explain it better."

"Oh, please. You didn't even let her get a full sentence out before you changed the subject."

"That's not true."

"It is true."

"You can't possibly remember the exact conversation! It was ages ago!"

"I can, actually. You were standing in the kitchen wearing some ridiculous dress with no back — dropped all the way down to your ass, even though it was barely five degrees outside. Flo was telling you about Desmond's new teaching position at the university. Naturally conversation shifted to other professions, mine included."

My mouth was hanging open. I didn't know what to say so I blurted, "That dress is not ridiculous. It's designer!"

"Designed to give every man in the great state of Massachusetts a case of blue balls, maybe," he muttered.

"*Pardon?!*"

"Point is, even if I didn't remember the exact details of that night, I'd still know what happened."

"Oh? You're psychic, now?"

"I don't need psychic powers to predict your behavior. Same thing happens every time talk shifts to me or my life while you're in attendance." He eyed me. "You bolt."

"I do not!" (I totally did.)

"You do everything in your power to avoid me. That includes hearing about me or learning anything about me. Every time conversation turns my way, you make an excuse to leave."

"You're paranoid," I declared.

"I pay attention."

"To me?"

His eyes flared with unnamed emotion. "Don't flatter yourself, sweetheart. I pay attention to everything. I'm observant. Comes with the territory."

"As a fixer," I guessed.

"As a consultant for local and federal law enforcement and a licensed private investigator with Master's Degrees in Forensics and Criminal Justice." He leaned in. "Yeah. You could say I'm pretty fucking observant."

Degrees.

He said degrees.

Plural.

At this juncture, I wisely clamped my lips together and stopped talking. Thankfully, I was saved from further making an ass of myself by the arrival of a police officer in plain clothes. There was a gold badge clipped to his belt beside a holstered gun, glinting in the sun. His brown leather shoes were well-worn, his khaki pants had a few wrinkles. But his button-down shirt was crisp and white, and his shoulders filled it out in such a way that, should you find yourself pulled over for speeding, you wouldn't much mind the citation. He was seriously handsome. Great bone structure, killer facial hair. His full head of dark hair was streaked liberally with silver, his blue eyes were warm and steady as they met mine. Despite the silver streaks, I'd place him no older than his early thirties, give or take a few years.

"Miss Goode," he said, stopping beside Graham and extending his hand. "I'm Detective Caden Hightower, Salem PD."

"Gwendolyn is just fine," I told him, sliding my palm against his.

"Gwendolyn it is, then." Eyes crinkling in a smile, he gave a firm shake, then dropped my hand. "Quite a mess you've got here. Been on the force a while, never seen anything like it. Even in this town. And that's saying something."

"Not my typical Thursday morning either," I said weakly. I couldn't stop staring at him. He was a total fox. A *silver* fox. I think my mouth was watering. This was, admittedly, not proper crime scene decorum but I couldn't seem to help myself. His eyes were so deep blue, you could drown in them.

"You holding up okay?" he asked gently.

Cute *and* considerate! I was still salivating, but managed to nod. "I'll be fine."

"Graves here give you the run down?"

"I was starting to before you interrupted," Graham growled. He sounded even more peeved than usual. My eyes moved to him and I felt them get wide when I saw he was scowling at the — still crinkly-eyed and smiling — Detective Hightower.

"Well, don't let me hold you back. Carry on, Graves. After all, this is your show. You were the one who thought she needed to see this shit up close and personal."

"If you've got a problem with the way I do things, Hightower, we'll have a word when this is finished. Privately."

The men stared at each other, saying nothing more, but I swear they were engaged some kind of in-depth silent communication. It lasted for almost a full minute before they finally broke away. Hightower looked down at his shoes, blowing out a long breath.

Graves turned to me. "I understand this isn't exactly pleasant to look at. But I felt it was important you see what we're dealing with here as things progress."

"Of course," I agreed, hoping to smooth the sudden tension between the two men. "I do understand it's a crime scene. I won't interfere with your work and I'll talk to Hetti — that's my barista. We don't use the alley much except to throw away trash, but we can make alternate arrangements until you've finished." I looked at the handsome detective. "I should've said before, you and your officers are welcome in the shop any time — we have a bathroom you're free to use and an espresso machine. Hetti makes a killer pumpkin-spice latte. It'll knock your regulation-issue socks right off. On the house, of course."

Detective Hightower laughed. "That's mighty kind of you, Gwendolyn."

"You want a latte or you want to solve a crime?" Graham barked.

"Not sure why we can't do both," Detective Hightower replied jovially. His eyes cut to me, dazzlingly blue. "I'm a multitasker."

I grinned at him. I couldn't help it. But the grin slipped right off my lips when Graham sidled closer, cutting off my view and glaring down at me like I was the bane of his existence.

"Glinda, can you cut out the cutesy shit for a second and focus? I don't have all day."

"Sure thing," I said with false sweetness. "I'll cease my cutesy shit immediately."

Officer Hightower snorted.

Graham's glower intensified. "Have you ever seen anything like this before?"

"Have I ever seen a ritualistic animal sacrifice in the alley outside my place of business before?" I asked. "Hmmm. Let me think.... Yeah, that would be a big, fat *no*."

"Why do you say ritualistic?"

"What?"

"Ritualistic animal sacrifice. That's a specific description."

"That's what this is."

"Why do you say that?"

My eyes bugged out at him. "Are you joking?"

"Do I look like I'm joking?"

He didn't. His expression was stony.

"It's not like they chopped up Eeyore here for the thrill of it," I pointed out with a soft grimace. "Whoever did this not only killed him but placed his parts in some kind of... pattern." I didn't want to look, I really didn't, but I forced my eyes back to the scene. "It's not some meaningless slaughter. There's meaning to every part of this."

Officer Hightower sighed. "Witchy shit?"

"Witchy shit," I concurred.

"So you have seen this before," Graham said.

"In books, sure. Academic texts on the occult, historical volumes... stuff like that. Never in real life. Never with my own eyes."

"Is that your version of light reading before bed? Animal sacrifices?"

"I own an occult shop, Graves. My aunt owned it for thirty years before I inherited it. I've read my fair share of..."

"Witchy shit," Detective Hightower supplied succinctly.

I winked at him. "Exactly."

"But you don't practice," Graham said flatly.

I shot him a look. "No, I don't *practice*. I'm not a witch. This

75

may be a revolutionary concept for you, but you can have interests in a field, read for hours and hours about it, even build a career around it, without it defining who you are." My voice dropped to a mutter. "Jeeze, I also read historical romance novels, that doesn't mean I dress in whalebone corsets and reject all knowledge of antibiotics and refuse to be in the presence of a marriageable man without a chaperone."

The detective laughed again, louder this time.

"Glinda."

My eyes snapped to Graham's face. He wasn't laughing, but some of the severity had bled out of his stern expression. "I wouldn't normally ask, but since you do know a fair bit about this..."

"You want me to look at it."

He nodded.

I winced. I was hoping I could get away with leaving the alley without spending another single second staring at the ghastly scene, but I'd talked myself straight into a corner. "I'm not an expert."

"We know that. We'll have another set of eyes on it before the day is out. Still, anything you could tell us... little details we might miss..."

Taking a bracing breath, I stepped closer to the donkey parts and squatted down. It was gruesome as all hell but, now that I'd had a bit of time to adjust, I wasn't freaking out as much.

"It's a pentagram," I murmured after a moment. "See? The blood is smeared in the shape of a star inside the circle. But there are other markings I don't understand. These symbols..." I pointed to the odd shapes within the five star-point sectors. "I don't recognize them at all."

"What else?" Graham prompted.

"The..." I swallowed hard, staring at the severed head. The donkey's glossy eyes were lifeless, unseeing. Its tongue was lolling from between gaping teeth. I fought a shudder. "The parts are placed strategically. The head is upside down, which may have some significance. Again, I don't know what, but they put it like that for a reason. I don't have a compass on me but based on where the sun is right now..." I glanced briefly at the pale blue September sky. "I'd guess the legs are positioned pointing north, south, east, and west."

I craned my neck back to look at Graham and Officer Hightower. They were looking down at me with identical expressions of interest mingled with suspicion.

"Damn," I murmured. "I totally just made myself a suspect, didn't I?"

CHAPTER FIVE

*Why they decided to call it 'emotional baggage' instead
of 'griefcase' is simply beyond me.
  - Gwen Goode, loathing the English language*

I laid my cheek down on the cool, granite countertop and spun
the stem of my wineglass, watching the fading rays of sunset
that streamed through my kitchen windows refracting in the
deep pour of Bordeaux. Night was finally falling, bringing an end
to an excruciatingly long day. A day that started with verbal
harassment, continued with ritualistic animal sacrifice, and
eventually landed me in an interrogation room, sitting across
from two dizzyingly attractive men of the law who were
convinced I had something — if not everything — to do with the
blood-soaked scene in my alley.

After this delightful experience, I was delivered back to The
Gallows by Detective Hightower just in time to close up shop in

the company of one disgruntled barista, shooing out several college kids who'd been studying at a corner table for eight-plus hours, during which period they'd collectively spent under ten dollars on bottomless coffee refills.

Needless to say, I was drained.

I hadn't even changed or taken off my heels when I'd gotten home five minutes before. I'd walked straight to the kitchen, uncorked a bottle of wine, and filled my glass to the brim. Only after I'd sucked down several fortifying sips did I realize drinking on an empty stomach might not be the best idea and forced my tired bones to yank open the fridge in search of sustenance. I hadn't eaten anything since breakfast and, no matter how killer Hetti's lattes, pumpkin-spice alone was not enough to hold me over.

The microwave dinged just as my phone began to buzz against the slate gray granite. I retrieved my dinner — a reheated plate of Chinese takeout from the night before — as I answered the incoming call, toggling the speakerphone function so I could talk while wielding chopsticks.

"Hey, Flo."

"What the hell, Gwennie?" Florence's worried voice blasted at me, accusation apparent in every word. "Desmond just got home and told me what happened today at your store!"

I took a scorching bite of shrimp lo mein, scalding my tongue in my haste. *Ouch.* Steam billowed from between my lips as I asked, "How does Des know?"

"Graham told him! They usually have man-night, the last Thursday of every month."

My nose scrunched. "Man-night?"

"Poker, cigars, sports talk, whatever the heck else men do when unsupervised. I don't know, I don't ask questions. I'm just happy for an occasional evening alone where I can watch my trashy shows and do a mud-mask facial and drink a full bottle of sauvignon blanc without anyone around to say *boo* about it." She sighed heavily. "But I'm not getting my solo sav-blanc night tonight, Gwennie. You know why?"

I did know why, but I still gamely asked, "Why, Flo?"

"Because Graham cancelled man-night, on account of a new case he's working. A case that, according to him, involves you."

"And men say *we're* the gossips," I grumbled around a bite of egg roll. "They spill more tea than the Sons of Liberty did in Boston Harbor."

"That may be so, but it doesn't change the fact that you should've been the one spilling, missy! Why did I have to hear about this from Desmond?"

"I just walked in the door! There was no time to call you. My heels aren't even off, for Gaia's sake."

"I can hear you chewing. If you're chewing, you had time to call me."

I set down my chopsticks and took a large sip of Bordeaux. It paired surprisingly well with the leftover Chinese food. "Look, I'm sorry I didn't dial you immediately. It was a very long day. I'm tired. I needed a minute to myself to decompress before reliving it a second time for my best friend's benefit."

"I get that," Flo conceded immediately, her voice softening. "I'm sorry, honey. I'm just worried about you. When Des told me what happened... I freaked just hearing about it. I'm guessing you must be way more freaked, seeing as you're the one who actually lived it."

"I'm okay," I breezed. "Don't worry about me."

But the thing was, I wasn't okay. She probably *should* be worried about me. Or, if not worried, at least mildly concerned. Because after I'd given Graham and Detective Hightower my little crime-scene spiel, they'd decided to bring me in for a quote 'informal chat' unquote. Seeing as this chat took place in an interrogation room at the local precinct, it didn't feel all that informal to me. It felt about as informal as a black tie wedding with a four-string quartet and five-course dinner service, if you wanted my honest-to-goddess opinion on the matter. Then again, I'd never been interrogated by not one but two supremely hot detectives before, so my opinion wasn't worth all that much.

Once the men decided they needed to bring me in, a minor power struggle ensued. Detective Hightower wanted me to ride with him to the station; Graham was insistent he take me. With neither willing to concede, this left them glaring at one another in the alley for an uncomfortably long stretch of time, during which I stood between them, shifting my weight from foot to foot, trying to breathe through all the testosterone in the air.

I'm not sure how much time passed — enough for the uniformed police officers to finish blocking off the alley with thick, yellow and black tape, enough for the forensics technician to finish snapping her pictures of the slain donkey and head back to her own vehicle. She shot me a sympathetic look before she shoved her Nikon into her bag and scurried away from the Graves-Hightower showdown.

"Um," I'd interjected eventually. Two sets of eyes snapped to me with such intensity, I had to lock my knees to keep them from buckling. "I can just walk, it's not that far."

Both blue and green stares narrowed in a seriously scary way at this suggestion.

"Or not," I muttered.

"She's coming with me, Graves," Hightower said bluntly, turning his attention back to Graham.

"She's not."

"This is my investigation."

"Stopped being your investigation the minute my phone rang this morning and you know it."

"I don't need you or your boys on this."

"Clearly you do, Detective." Graham's tone was biting.

"You're so out of your depth here, you don't even realize you're drowning."

"The Mayor may think you shit gold bricks, the Chief may believe we need you, but I sure as fuck don't. You're here to consult, not to commandeer my entire case. That includes what happens with my witnesses and my sources."

"If thinking you're in charge helps you sleep at night, by all means..." Graham smirked. "Keep up the delusion."

My eyes moved back and forth between the two men as their words volleyed without relent. Neither seemed willing to back down and, if this continued to escalate, I had no doubt they'd soon be trading physical blows along with verbal ones.

With self-preservation in mind, I backed slowly toward the emergency exit door. This plan backfired. The instant I moved, both men's gazes snapped to me once more.

"I'll just... tell my barista I'm leaving..." I gulped. "And grab my jacket before we go..."

I didn't wait for a response, merely turned on a heel and darted across the alley, onto the stoop and into the storage room. I headed straight through, pausing only to unhook my camel brown cashmere jacket from the rack by my desk. As I crossed through the center of the shop, I noted that Madame Zelda still wasn't in attendance, her curtain pulled wide, the round table she used for readings clear of tarot cards or whatever other tools she used to confer with the spirits.

Truth be told, I didn't venture into her domain if it could be helped. Madame Zelda gave me the heebie-jeebies, but I kept her around because she brought in a good chunk of business. Desperate housewives seeking insight into failing marriages, giggling brides-to-be with gift certificates from their friends. Young, old. Tall, short. All ages, all sexes, all in need of spiritual guidance from a woman, it must be said, I would not trust to read my horoscope aloud from the local newspaper, let alone divine my fates from the heavens above.

Alas...

The morning rush was long gone and most of the tables at the front were empty. A handful of college students had parked themselves at the espresso bar. A couple of tourists browsed the bookshelves, flipping through a volume on ancient soothsayers. We stocked a *lot* of books, covering a vast swathe of bizarre topics, everything from modern moon phases to dark druidism to herbal healing arts to mystical energies. Reiki. Wicca. Voodoo. Paganism. Some were recent additions, hand-selected by me, but others had been hanging around collecting spores since I started helping out behind the counter as a kid. If they printed it, we stocked it, from *Alchemy For Dummies* to *Zombies: Mythos of the Modern Brain-Eater* and whatever weirdness fell in between. We even boasted a handful of honest-to-goddess grimoires predating the infamous Salem Witch Trials of the 1600s. (Those, we kept safe under glass.)

Hetti was wiping down the espresso machine, a bored look on her face. This wasn't unusual. Hetti's typical expression was one of practiced indifference. It coordinated sublimely with her black-on-black outfits and chunky, silver-studded jewelry.

I'm not sure how my own expression appeared in that moment. Probably shellshocked and pale from all that had transpired, but I hadn't glanced in a mirror. Whatever the case, as I approached, Hetti's heavily-lined eyes moved to me and widened. I thought I saw a flash of concern behind her mask of indifference.

"You okay, boss?"

I took her gently by the elbow and steered her to the far end of the espresso bar, away from the chit-chatting college students. I kept my voice low, speaking in a hushed tone as I gave her a brief explanation of what was going on.

"Huh," she murmured when I trailed off, taking the news in stride. "No wonder your aura looks like that."

"Like what?"

"Seasick. Sort of greenish gray. Like you're about to toss your cookies."

"My cookies, I assure you, are fine."

She merely shrugged. "So, you're going to the police station?"

"Apparently they have more questions and want to take my official statement or something." I sighed. "I don't know why they can't do that here, without interrupting my work day, but they didn't really seem up for a discussion about it."

"Wow, cops acting like alpha assholes?" She rolled her eyes. "I'm *shocked!*"

"Will you be okay here on your own?"

She stared at me like I had three heads. "Will I be okay refilling coffee mugs for the handful of customers we're likely to get this afternoon and ringing in the sale of maybe one, but probably zero, books before we close? Yeah, I think I'll manage."

"It's almost October. Things tend to get crazier with Halloween on the horizon."

"I'll manage," she repeated firmly.

"Right." I tried out a weak smile. "I should be back in an hour or so. I can't imagine this will take longer than that. If it gets too busy, just close up early and head home."

"It's a Thursday. It won't be busy. And even if it is, I can handle it."

"But—"

"Don't you have two alpha-male assholes waiting for you?" she asked. "Get a move on, boss. I've got this covered."

I swallowed hard and nodded. "Thanks, Hetti. You're a lifesaver."

Her eyes skittered over my shoulder, fixing on something behind me. For a moment, I thought she was examining my aura again. I realized this wasn't the case when she murmured, "Speak of the devil..."

I turned to find Graham standing on the other side of the espresso bar, arms crossed over his broad chest, boots planted firmly on the hardwood floor, eyes on me. Evidently, he'd won the battle of wills.

"Let's go, Glinda."

Hetti snorted at the nickname, but otherwise did not comment. I shot her a final look of gratitude, shrugged into my cashmere coat, and made my way to Graham. He watched me approach without moving a muscle but as soon as I stepped around the counter, his hand shot out and enveloped mine. For the second time that morning, he turned and tugged me along behind him, not seeming to care that my heeled feet were struggling to keep pace with his long-legged strides or that I was perfectly capable of walking without a leash.

"Hey!" I screeched softly, but my protest fell on deaf ears. "Slow down, would you?"

In a blink, with a clatter of bells, we were through the front door and on the sidewalk outside The Gallows. My shop was located on a pedestrian-only outdoor mall smack in the center of downtown, surrounded by dozens of other stores and restaurants. The only traffic we ever saw on the brick-laid street was of the foot variety. I was therefore surprised — but not entirely shocked — to see Graham's black Ford Bronco parked a dozen feet from my front door, directly behind two Salem PD cruisers. Whatever pull he had with the powers-that-be apparently extended to special parking privileges.

He marched me straight to the passenger side, yanked it open, and shoved me bodily inside, lifting me straight off my feet in the process since the Bronco was so high off the ground. My heels had barely cleared the frame when he slammed the door shut. I glowered at him through the glass windshield as he rounded the hood, opened his own door, and folded himself behind the wheel.

"You don't have to man-handle me," I hissed. "I'm not a criminal resisting arrest."

"Seatbelt," was all he said as he turned over the ignition.

I dutifully clicked it into place, then curled my hands tightly around my YSL clutch to keep from smacking him. His domineering attitude was grating on my last nerve.

He drove slowly, avoiding the stream of pedestrians as we rolled down the brick mall toward the main road. Rubberneckers shot us strange looks as we passed by, curious about our presence or, more likely, the police presence outside my shop. Nothing quite like a scandal to draw in a crowd. I had a feeling Hetti would be slammed with more customers than she could singlehandedly caffeinate by the time I got back.

"How long is this going to take?" I asked after a few minutes of silence.

"As long as it takes."

"I can't leave my barista alone all day."

"I think the dead carcass in your alleyway takes precedence over coffee, Glinda."

"*Gwen. Do. Lyn.*"

He stopped at a red light, wrist slung over the wheel, and leaned back against his leather seat. His jaw was tight, the line of it seemingly sharper than normal, and his attention was fixed on the intersection. Realizing I was staring, I forced my eyes away from his profile and studied the Bronco's black-on-black interior instead. I'd never ridden in it before, despite the fact that Graham had offered me a ride home from Des and Flo's townhouse on more than one occasion in the past. He'd owned it for a few months, but it still had that new car smell and looked like it had rolled off the lot mere days before. It was so immaculately clean, you could've done surgery on his center console — no dust on the windshield, no litter on the floor mats, no old coffee in the cup holders. A sterile environment, devoid of any traces of life.

I wondered suddenly what his home looked like. If he lived in a house or an apartment, if his decor style was as sparse as his car interior. Did he have a bachelor pad — all black and chrome with masculine red accents scattered about and a tacky LED fireplace operated by remote? Did he have a roommate? A pet? A houseplant?

I'd never allowed myself to wonder before. As with all things Graham, as soon as my brain began to wander down that path, I slammed a firm mental gate closed, then promptly diverted my thoughts elsewhere. I preferred it that way; preferred to keep his details unknown, his presence in my life intangible, as if knowing as little as possible about him would somehow counterbalance the years I'd spent fixated on him, back when I was a gawky teen girl with an out-of-control crush.

Unfortunately, my typical mental blockade wasn't so effective now that I was in his car, a foot away from him, the memory of his hand on mine still tingling across my palm like I'd stuck a fork in an electrical socket. His scent pressed in on me from all sides, a heady mix of crisp, woodsy soap and sheer male pheromones that invaded my senses.

Get it together, Gwen.

Curiosity clawed at me as we rode across town toward the police station, consuming my mind with so many questions it was hard to think straight, let alone make casual conversation. Luckily, Graham didn't seem interested in conversing, either. He was equally lost in thought as he drove, his grip relaxed but his brow furrowed.

The eight minute drive felt more like an eon. He'd barely come to a stop in the lot when I flung open my door and hopped out, the landing jarring my stilettos. Detective Hightower was waiting for us near the entrance to the brick building, just under a flag pole, holding two styrofoam coffee cups.

"It's not a pumpkin-spice latte, but..." He shrugged and extended one of the cups toward me. "Figured you might need a jolt, Gwendolyn."

"And me?" Graham asked, coming to a stop at my side.

"You can get your own coffee, Graves."

I smiled as I accepted my cup. "Thanks, Detective Hightower."

"Call me Caden. Or Cade, if you'd like."

"Cade," I echoed, testing it out. I liked the way it sounded coming out of my mouth. I liked the way his blue eyes flared when I said it even better.

"Can we get this over with?" Graham asked bluntly. "She's not here to socialize."

Detective Hightower — Cade — took a slow sip of his coffee, then turned and pulled open the glass door that led into the lobby of the station. I walked inside, eyes sweeping the space. It looked like every other police station I'd ever stepped foot in. A bit smaller than I'd expected, with low ceilings, fluorescent lighting, and a gray concrete floor. A long blue and gray reception desk sat opposite the doors, topped by a plexiglass barrier almost to the ceiling. A secretary was seated behind it, her neck cricked to cradle a phone handset to her ear as her fingers clacked rapidly across her keyboard. Her eyes shifted from her screen only long enough to see we were accompanied by Detective Hightower, then she went right back to whatever she was doing.

"This way," Cade said, corralling me down a hallway with one hand on the small of my back. I could hear Graham stomping along behind us, his heavy motorcycle boots thudding with violence against the concrete. We passed several doors — a glass-walled holding cell that was not currently holding anyone, a conference room, a dingy kitchenette, a space with lockers and workout equipment that smelled vaguely like old socks — before we were ushered into a cluttered, closet-like office with a stained carpet, a very small window, and a dead houseplant withering on the sill.

Cade grabbed a thick manila folder off the top of a teetering stack of paperwork, then turned to where we were lingering just inside the door. There was nowhere for us to sit — his desk took up the majority of the tiny room, his file cabinets took up the rest. He seemed to realize this only when he turned around and nearly bumped noses with Graham. From his unfamiliarity with his own office, I immediately got the sense that Detective Hightower did not spend much time behind his desk.

"We'll do this in the interview room," he said, jerking his chin toward the hall. "Just across the way."

The interview room was, in actuality, an interrogation room. It looked exactly like I'd imagined it would — stainless table at the center with a built-in bar for shackles, metal chairs bolted to the ground on either side, a camera in the upper right corner, and a mirror on the wall that I knew from every cop show I'd ever seen must be two-way. I took a seat, feeling a rush of nerves as the detective settled in across from me. Graham remained on his feet, leaning against the wall a few paces away. I hadn't done anything wrong, but sitting there beneath the heavy gazes of two — as Hetti would say — bossy alpha males was enough to make me squirm against the cold metal of my seat. I took a sip of my coffee, thinking it would steady me, and instantly regretted it.

"Told you," Cade said, laughing at the screwed-up look on my face. "Not a pumpkin-spice latte from your fancy machine."

I unscrewed my expression and forced myself to swallow. "It's not that bad."

"It's a criminal offense to lie to a detective, Gwendolyn."

"Right," I said weakly. "Well, in that case, that's got to be the worst cup of coffee I've ever had. And I grew up on sticks of instant I stole from the local diner."

"Gwendolyn..." Cade's voice was strangled with laughter. "I feel the need to point out, it's probably not wise to admit any past criminal offenses to a detective either."

"Right," I repeated, even more weakly. I contemplated taking another sip of coffee so my mouth had something to do besides self-implicate, but I still hadn't recovered from my first sip. "I was just kidding. So, how 'bout that slaughtered donkey?"

Graham shook his head and pressed his eyes closed.

Cade laughed full-out, but sobered quickly as he fingered file folder he'd brought from his office. "Okay, Gwendolyn. You may be wondering why we dragged you all the way down here. You may also be wondering why someone like Graves—" His eyes flickered briefly to Graham where he leaned against the wall. "— is involved in all this, when it's not exactly standard operating procedure to bring in a consultant at such an early stage in an investigation."

I shrugged. "No one's ever killed a donkey in my alley before. I don't really have any idea about procedure, standard or otherwise."

"Right." His lips twitched. "There's no question this morning's scene was outside the norm. But it's not actually the first scene like that we've found."

My eyes widened. I looked at Graham and he gave a shallow nod, confirming the detective's statement.

"I want you to take a look at these..." Cade flipped open the folder and began to lay out a series of photographs on the table in front of me. Four, in total. What I saw on the glossy photo paper was enough to make all the air in my lungs seize. A series of massacred animals, all hacked methodically into parts, all arranged inside bloody pentagrams of various sizes.

"This was the first," Cade said, tapping the first photograph in the row. "Or, at least the first one found. There may've been others before that we simply never discovered."

I stared down at the photograph. It depicted a cat — what used to be a cat. Mainly, I saw a few clumps of fur and the remnants of a tail lying at the center of a circle of blood, smeared on what looked like an asphalt sidewalk. It lacked the the precise, ceremonial reverence paid to the donkey I'd seen this morning. Only the pentagram was similar — though smaller and with far fewer symbols smeared against the concrete around it.

"Some locals found it at that dog park near the river, up by Bridge Street," Cade told me. "We figure, given the state of things, the canines found it before their owners did."

That explained why there was so little of the cat left.

"This one was next." Cade pushed the second photograph toward me. "Rooster. Down by Palmer Cove. There's a community garden there, folks from the neighborhood mostly use it to grow vegetables and flowers. They came across this in early May — luckily, before too much wildlife got at it. It's much better preserved."

He was right. The rooster looked totally undisturbed, its positioning precise within the pentagram. Its head had been lopped off at the neck. The wings were clipped and spread to their full span. Two scaly legs, cleanly severed. The proud plume of its tail fanned prominently, a riot of blue-black feathers arching across the hard-packed earth.

I swallowed hard, steeling myself for what was to come as the photo was swapped out for a third.

"Goat." Cade pushed it toward me. "A hiker came across it walking on the trails up around Gallows Hill."

"When?" I asked, eyes on the picture.

"Late June."

The goat was similarly slaughtered, its pieces artfully arranged by someone who put great thought into their actions. I clenched my hands together beneath the metal table, trying not to show how horrified I was. Not only by what I was seeing, but by the idea that there was someone out there in my community hurting innocent creatures — and, evidently, taking such pride in showing off their unhinged behavior.

I was reaching my limit for looking at murdered animals. I liked animals. I especially liked goats. Flo and I once did a yoga class with baby goats — they scampered all over us as we performed downward dog and child's pose, clattering around on their tiny hooves, their little kid bleats making us giggle. One even fell asleep in my arms afterward. Flo had to drag me to the car and check my purse twice to make sure I wasn't trying to smuggle it off the farm.

I tried not to look too closely at the severed parts. Instead, I studied the pagan hieroglyphs smeared on the lush, early-summer grass, and wondered what they meant. They were as much a mystery to me as those that decorated the cobblestones in my alley this morning. One looked like an inverted letter "Y" with a slash through its base. Another was like a yin-yang only more jagged, its lines sharper and somehow crueler in nature. A third appeared to be a set of imbalanced scales.

My examinations were cut short when the photograph was swapped for the fourth and final.

"Found this one last month. Beginning of August, some high school kids were tossing a football down on Bertram Field. Came across this behind the bleachers."

I glanced at it for only a few seconds, but the image seared itself into my brain in such a way, I knew I'd never forget it. The pot-bellied pig, hacked apart. Its head upside-down, snout pointing toward its torso. Legs spread out in a circle, forming the pentagram points. Curly tail and fuzzy ears artfully arranged, like finishing touches. Vivid scarlet blood clashing horribly against pale pink, peach-fuzzed skin.

"I'm sorry, I—" My words broke off as my stomach roiled. I pressed my eyes closed and sucked in a gulp of air. "I don't want to look anymore."

"That's fine, Gwendolyn."

In the wake of Cade's quiet assurance, I heard the sound of the photographs sliding against the stainless tabletop, hands shuffling them back into the folder. When the room fell silent, I risked cracking my eyelids open a sliver. The photographs were gone. The two men were staring at me. Cade looked solemn, but there was concern in his lively blue eyes. Graham was, as ever, inscrutable, his green gaze unflinching as it scanned my face.

"Sorry," I murmured.

"Don't be. Your reaction is normal." Cade tapped a finger against the closed folder. "This shit is not."

"It's just so violent. So... bloody."

"It isn't just the violence of it." Graham pushed away from the wall and approached. Planting his hands on the table, he ducked down slightly to catch my eyes. "Plenty of people do violent shit. Disturbing shit, even. But this... This is different. This is exhibitionist. Whoever is doing this takes great pride in his or her actions. They derive purpose from them. They may even feel they need to do this, compelled by some greater force."

"Like the devil?" I whispered, wide-eyed.

Graham just stared at me.

"Like mental illness," Cade offered gently.

"Oh. Right. Obviously." I swallowed. "So, my alleyway..."

"The donkey this morning makes five. Five animal sacrifices, scattered all across town." Cade sighed. "No known commonalities in their locations, so far as we can tell. It seems totally random. And, like I said earlier, there could be others we simply never discovered. We didn't even put it together that this may be some sort of pattern until we found the goat."

"What about the symbols? Surely they can tell you something about the reason for the sacrifices."

"We've had a parade of experts in to look over them. Historians, professors, even a self-proclaimed High Priestess from a coven of practicing Wiccans." Cade shook his head. "No one can make much sense of it. The pentagrams aren't following any traditional lore."

I bit my lower lip as I thought that over. My knowledge of the occult was not exhaustive by any means, but I hadn't been lying earlier when I'd told them I'd read my fair share of books on the subject.

"Spit it out," Graham ordered, bossy as ever.

My eyes snapped up to his. "Pardon?"

"Whatever you're thinking right now. Just say it."

"It's not really unusual that even experts in the field can't make sense of this. Many pagan circles create their own codes and rules and sigils. When a coven forms, they often hand-write their own grimoire." Seeing Cade's raised eyebrows, I clarified. "A spell book, that is. They'd probably refer to it as their Book of Shadows. A sacred tome detailing all their practices, rites, and rituals."

"Then if we find this book..." Cade trailed off.

"You find their book, you'll know what those symbols mean. You'll know why they're doing this."

"And where exactly would they keep something like that?"

I considered this for a moment. "Somewhere safe, where it won't be disturbed or stumbled upon by anyone outside their circle, but close enough for them to gather frequently at it. Probably on an altar."

"An altar?"

"A shrine of sorts, created to honor whatever deity they worship." I shrugged. "I have no clue, if I'm being honest. This is all speculation. There are as many sects of neopaganism as there are colors in the rainbow. You have to understand, it's not an organized religion like Christianity. There's no registry of practitioners. No official churches or meeting points." I glanced at the closed folder. "Those sacrifices could be carried out by a group of two or twenty or two hundred. There's no way of knowing."

"Probably not a lone wolf, though. It's surprisingly difficult to sever—" Cade's mouth clicked shut when he saw my blanched expression. "Never mind."

I lifted my hands from my lap and laid them atop the table. "I don't mean to sound ungrateful but... much as I appreciate the show and tell, I can't help wondering why you're telling me all this."

The men traded a glance. It was Graham who spoke, his voice rough. "Because whoever is doing this is escalating. Cat, rooster, goat, pig, donkey. Each bigger than the last. The symbols get more ornate, more elaborate, each time."

"Meaning?"

"Not much livestock out there bigger than a donkey, Glinda," he said pointedly. "We're thinking the next victim might not be from the barnyard."

My pulse spiked as a bolt of unadulterated anxiety shot through my system. "You think they're going to... to murder someone?"

The men traded another loaded glance. I got the sense there was something more to this, something they weren't telling me, but I didn't pry. I was still struggling to digest the news that the next pentagram they found might be far, far worse than anything I'd seen in those photographs.

"They've never left a message before today," Cade pointed out.

"*Resurgemus*," I murmured, seeing the bloody warning in my mind. "*We shall rise again.* Jeeze. Totally creepy. You'd better catch them before they decide to hack up one of the locals in their quest to *rise*, whatever that means."

They traded another glance and, again, I got the sense I was missing something. Something vitally important.

"What?" I asked. My heart was beginning to race. "What is it?"

"Christ," Graham muttered, looking grim. "Just tell her, Hightower."

"Tell me what?"

"Gwendolyn..." Cade blew out a breath. "The other locations have all been pretty remote. Public spaces. Parks, fields, gardens. But this morning was... different. We can't help wondering if there's a reason that donkey was left in *your* alley. Why that message was left on *your* wall."

"You think I'm somehow involved?" I asked, stunned. "I swear—"

"No, Gwen." Cade reached across the table and took my hand. I stiffened — and so, I couldn't help but notice, did Graham. "We think you might be their target."

CHAPTER SIX

Skeletons? In my closet?
Not with all these shoes.
- Gwen Goode, lamenting her lack of storage

I told Florence everything — in part because that's what best friends do, but mostly because I knew she'd eventually drag the information out of me, whether I wanted to share or not.

"So, after they told you that you're potentially a target in a string of ritualistic killings... How was the rest of your day?"

I laughed. "Busy."

"Tell me that's because you ended up having a threesome with the sexy detective and Graham."

"Hardly."

"Just Graham, then? One on one? A long overdue roll in the hay?"

"Give it up, Flo. It's never going to happen and you know it."

97

She growled unhappily through the phone. Flo, by the way, knew all about my childhood obsession with Graham. She'd heard it all — the sea urchin save, the lofty LG status, the hometown hero-worship phase. And, of course, she'd had a front row seat to our shaky introduction when I moved back to town, along with our past few months of strained interactions at various get-togethers. Despite this, she held out — severely delusional — hope that one day, I would develop a case of selective amnesia so immense, I'd drag Graham into bed with me to work out our myriad differences using a far more tactile approach.

Like I said... *delusional.*

"I simply don't understand how Des can call someone like him his best friend," I declared, not for the first time. Desmond, Flo's boyfriend, was one of the most genuine, gentlemanly guys I'd ever met. A professor at the local university, he taught courses on New England history and folklore, read copiously, tipped generously, and — most importantly — treated my oldest gal-pal like the earth-bound goddess she was. "They're nothing alike."

"Graham's not half bad, once you get to know him. He grows on you."

I snorted. "You know what else grows on you? Fungus. Bacteria. Mold. Leprosy."

"Come on, Gwennie. You've never even given him a chance! You've been so busy hating him, you've overlooked all his good qualities. It's almost like you try not to see his good side on purpose."

"I find it hard to believe he *has* a good side."

"Maybe you need to look harder, then. Or maybe you need your eyes checked. Seriously. Have you seen the man? He's like a cross between a badass action hero and an All-American heart-throb, with some deliciously domineering undercurrents that, you can just tell, make him a great lay."

She was not wrong — though I had no plans to admit as much. "Being attractive on the outside doesn't mean much if the insides don't match."

"They do, though, that's what I'm saying! Desmond told me Graham is the smartest person he's ever met. Do you know how difficult it is for a man who works in *academia* to admit there are intelligent people outside that strange, insular scholastic sphere? I mean, Graham hasn't even been published in a peer reviewed journal! Can you imagine the *horror*?" She giggled. "Plus, he's hugely successful. His consultant company, Gravewatch, makes bucketloads of money. He takes on cases for law enforcement agencies all up and down the east coast. He even works with the Feds sometimes. He's the real deal."

"About that..." I took a large sip of wine in preparation for her reaction. "Turns out... I may have misunderstood when you told me what he did for a living..." I quickly filled Flo in on the unfortunate *fixer* mishap. It took her a long, long while to stop laughing. So long, I had time to finish my final few mouthfuls of lo mein, rinse the plate, and load it into the dishwasher.

"Oh my god," she gasped, breathless. "That is very possibly the funniest thing I've ever heard."

"I'm glad someone is amused by the mess that is my life."

"Gwen, even you have to admit, that's hilarious. You thought he was a handyman. A *handyman*. Graham Motherfucking Graves! Badass extraordinaire! Crème de la crème of private investigators! Hold on, Desmond just walked in, I have to tell him about this..."

As she recounted the misunderstanding to her boyfriend — which resulted in both of them breaking down in yet another fit of hysterics — I finally kicked off my blush pink stilettos. The tile floor beneath my feet was icy, but it felt strangely good against my aching soles. I could practically see my breath, the kitchen was so cold. I fought off a shiver as I sipped my wine.

Like any self-respecting New Englander, I had stubbornly refused to switch on the heat, determined to make it to September's end before I caved to the plummeting fall temperatures. But soon no amount of cashmere sweaters or wool socks would be enough to keep me warm. While my house was gorgeous and historical, it was also drafty and poorly insulated. My heating bill each winter was astronomical.

It still caught me off guard sometimes — that it was mine. *My* house. *My* heating bill. For so long, it had been Aunt Colette's. A place of refuge for the summer months when I was a kid, then later a fun place to visit during breaks between my semesters at UMass Amherst, where I'd gotten a rather superfluous degree in interior design. Granted, the degree likely would not have been so superfluous if I'd actually gone into my field of choice.

I never got that chance.

Not for lack of trying, though. Shortly after graduation two and a half years ago, I had a job lined up in New York City. My dream career — or, so I thought at the time — at a fancy design firm where I'd be making six figures, plus hefty stock options and a signing bonus. It was more money than I'd ever dreamed of making right out of the gate. A far cry from the girl who grew up in a string of trailer parks, living off food stamps, intimately familiar with the act of going to bed hungry. It had taken years of studying, a hard-earned academic scholarship, seven letters of recommendation from my professors, and dozens of interviews... but I had finally done it.

I had gotten out.

I had left behind that life of switched-off utilities and repossessed cars and empty refrigerator shelves and eviction notices. No more particle-board furniture, no more houses on wheels. No more yelling or hiding or trying my hardest to disappear. Diploma in hand, I was poised on the cusp of a brand new sort of life at the center of the most vibrant city in the world, where I would live in a chic modern high rise full of stylish, solid wood housewares. I would dress to impress. I would sip black coffee while I power-walked down sidewalks and hailed taxi-cabs with a sharp, practiced whistle, just like the lovable workaholic stars of the cheesy romantic comedies I loved to watch.

But then, my phone rang.

There was a nurse on the other end. She told me she worked at Salem Hospital. I still remember her exact words — the words that changed the entire trajectory of my existence, picked me up off my chosen path and hurled me, without recourse, down an entirely unexpected one.

Your Aunt Colette has had a stroke, the nurse told me, her words punctuated by machines beeping in the background. *You need to come. Come quickly. You're her next-of-kin. You have power-of-attorney. You'll have to make some tough decisions...*

Just like that, nothing else mattered. Not the stock options, not the fancy apartment, not the rom-com montage. I emailed my prospective employers an apology for wasting their time, hopped on the first northbound bus, and hightailed it back here as quick as I could. And here I stayed, living in Aunt Colette's house and visiting her every day at the assisted care facility once she was transferred out of the ICU. There was no one else to visit her. She'd never married, never had kids. Her only other relative was my mother — her younger sister — and neither of us was holding our breath for her to show up and help.

After the stroke, Aunt Colette lost her ability to speak. Thankfully, we'd never really needed words. We got each other from day one. *Same wavelength*, that's what she always used to say. At her bedside, I'd sit and tell her stories from my crazy college days and read her the newspaper — she always liked the local crime blotter, as people called to report some objectively odd things in Salem — and try to help her drink syrup-thickened water like the rehab therapists had shown me, even though it was difficult for her to get anything down without choking.

I didn't resent Aunt Colette for derailing my post-grad plans. I owed her more than I could ever repay. She had been there for me as a kid, letting me spend every summer with her in Salem. Yanking me out of my dysfunctional childhood — which mostly meant yanking me away from my dysfunctional mother — long enough to show me a different sort of life, filled with art and music and books. A life empty of yelling and crying and Mom's parade of asshole boyfriends, each somehow worse than the last.

Those twelve weeks I spent with Aunt Colette each year were the only bright spots in the dark recesses of my childhood memory banks. They were also the only time I ever felt safe. Secure. The only time I knew I could go to bed without fear of being shaken awake in the middle of the night by Mom whispering that we had to leave, *right now*, that the car was already running in the driveway and I had two minutes to pack a bag before we left it all in our rearview. For the millionth time.

God damn it, Gwen! Quiet! You'll wake him and then we'll really be screwed...

When Aunt Colette needed me, I was there for her without question — just like she'd been there for me when I was at my most vulnerable, returning the favor the only way I knew how. Three months later, she was gone. She left everything to me. Her house — the gorgeous, three-story colonial in Washington Square, overlooking Salem Common, that had been in the family since the 1600s. Her classic car — the 1966 turquoise Thunderbird, à la Thelma and Louise. And her occult shop — The Gallows, a slice of prime commercial real estate smack in the center of the tourist district that, according to Aunt Colette, used to be a whorehouse, back in the day. (She always did love places — and people — with a tawdry history. Said it gave them character.)

Freshly turned twenty-two, I could've sold it all for a pretty penny, hopped on that bus straight back to NYC, and resumed the life I'd never meant to hit pause on. Hell, I could've booked myself a one-way ticket to Europe and spent several years as a wanderlusting expat, roaming until I got sick of fresh croissants and historic castles and seductive foreign men. (If such a thing was even possible.)

Instead, I stayed.

Frankly, it felt wrong to sell Aunt Colette's house. I couldn't picture boxing up her eclectic mix of belongings, couldn't envision selling her colorful wardrobe or listing her quirky furniture pieces on Craigslist to make a quick buck. It seemed like a betrayal of her memory to even contemplate such a course of action. And just the thought of The Gallows — which she'd built from the ground up and run for nearly forty years — shuttering put a similar pit in my stomach. I flat-out refused to stand by and watch it become a Starbucks or a Chipotle or some other soulless commercial chain. I might not have believed in the supernatural, but I was certain of one thing: Aunt Colette would haunt me from the other side if I ever let that happen.

Of course, it wasn't an easy adjustment. It took six months for her house to start feeling like *my* house. Another six after that before I worked up the nerve to clear out her closets and unpack my suitcases into them. Eventually, I stopped hesitating before grabbing her — *my* — car keys from the hook by the door. I stopped tiptoeing around like a guest in my own space. I stopped acting like this was just another summer-long stint and started setting down some roots for the first time in as long as I could remember.

I still occasionally caught myself marveling over the fact that this was my life. Certainly, it looked nothing like the one I had planned for myself. And yet... I wouldn't change a thing. (At least, not up until this morning, when I stepped into my back alley.)

I carried my wine with me upstairs, half-listening to the muffled sounds of Desmond and Florence giggling through the phone speaker. By the time she remembered I was on the other line, I was in my bedroom, changing into my favorite set of silk pajamas.

"Gwennie? You still there?"

"I'm here."

"Sorry. Des thought the whole handyman thing was a hoot. He just called Graham to ask if he'll come over and refinish our kitchen cabinets. I thought the phone speaker was going to blow out, Graham bellowed so loud."

"Great. Now he'll be even more of a jerk when I see him next."

"Which is when, exactly?"

"I don't know." Hopping on one foot, I tugged a pair of thick alpaca socks. Who needed central heating, anyway? "Hopefully *never*."

"But the case—"

"Detective Hightower said, as of now, they have no concrete suspects or evidence to warrant an arrest. It's creepy, but... animal sacrifice isn't the same as human homicide. I'm supposed to 'keep my senses honed to anything strange' — as if we don't live in a town where strange is the norm." I shoved my arms into a heavy wool sweater. "Yesterday, a man dressed as the terrifying clown from Stephen King's *It* asked if he could use our bathroom. Not only did he scare off my only paying customers, there was white grease paint all over the faucets by the time he was done in there. And let me tell you, Pennywise didn't spend a single penny in return for my hospitality."

"You need one of those signs that says 'Bathrooms For Paying Customers Only.'"

I shook my head. "I can't do that. Aunt Colette always said signs like that were for soulless chains and corporate America. *People don't walk through those doors looking to contribute to capitalism, Gwendolyn. They come looking for a respite from it.*"

"Right, but when Aunt Colette ran the place, it was about one bill cycle away from total bankruptcy."

A low laugh bubbled up my throat. "She was a kind soul. Not a particularly business savvy one."

"You've made other changes. You added a freaking espresso machine, for god's sake. And look how that turned out! The Gallows is a hipster hotspot."

This was true. When Aunt Colette ran things, it had been strictly an occult store. One big maze of shelves stuffed with musty, dusty old tomes and a shadowy stockroom of curiously-labeled vials. After I inherited it, I rearranged the shelves to open up the flow, added seating and coffee to lure in the co-ed crowd, upgraded the decor for our more aesthetically-inclined customers. I tried my damndest not to erase the original character of the place, but instead to unveil its full potential. And, let's be honest, to get our ledgers out of the red and into the black.

Aunt Colette was many things, but a businesswoman she most definitely was *not*. I liked to think she'd be proud that in just two years under my management, we'd not only begun to break even, but were actually turning a steady profit — especially now that Halloween was only six weeks away. More tourists flooded into the city every day, eager to explore Salem's unique magic, their pockets full of money happily spent on crystals and incense and charms and books. My little city was one of the only places I knew of where the end of summer didn't put an end to tourist season. In Witch City, the inverse happened — as autumn crept on, the air cooled but business heated up.

"Speaking of my hipster hotspot, I should probably get to bed."

Florence's eye roll was almost audible. "It's barely dark out, you old granny."

"I know. But tomorrow's Friday — it'll be a zoo at the store. Tourists are running rampant through the city. A whole ghost tour came in twenty minutes before closing and cleaned out all my candles. I'll have to stay late to restock and order more inventory."

"*Boo!*" Flo groaned. "Make Hetti do it instead. That's why you pay her, isn't it? To lighten your load?"

"Hetti's expertise ends at latte foam art. Besides, she already covered for me most of today while I was at the police station. By the time I got back to the shop to relieve her, she looked pale and annoyed."

"She's a goth. She always looks like that."

"Okay, well, she looked even more pale and annoyed than usual."

"What about Madame Zelda?"

"You think I would trust that old charlatan with my ledgers?" I shook my head sadly. "You must be as deluded as she is. Besides, she's in the wind."

There was a distinct pause. "She's gone incorporeal?"

"Not incorporeal. Incommunicado. She missed three appointments today. No call, no show."

"That's unlike her."

It was indeed. The woman was weird, but she was not stupid. She never missed an opportunity to line her pockets with any money she could convince vulnerable marks to fork over in exchange for missives from the Great Beyond.

"I'm sure she was just overcome by the spirits again," I said wryly. "I'll track her down tomorrow. Another line item on my list of joyful Friday activities."

"If you need an actual joyful Friday activity, that cover band we like is playing a set at The Witches Brew tomorrow night."

"The guys who go full on eye-rolling Exorcist mode while head-banging to *Zombie* by the Cranberries?"

"Yep."

Damn. She was right. I totally loved those guys. I'd hate to miss their set. "If inventory doesn't take too long... and I'm not dead on my feet... and assuming no other livestock is ritualistically slaughtered on my doorstep... I'll try to swing by afterward."

She whooped with glee through the line. "Excellent! They go on at eight, but I'll get there a bit early to grab our favorite table."

"No promises, Flo. I mean it, there's a good chance I won't—"

"See you tomorrow!" she chirped, clicking off before I could protest any more.

I stared at the dark screen of my phone for a long moment before I shook my head and sighed. There was no fighting with Florence. She was a gravitational force, refusing to be denied. After draining the last sip of my wine, I brushed my teeth in the master bathroom, washed my face, slathered on moisturizer, and climbed into bed.

It must be said, I freaking *loved* my bed. It was large and it was old, crafted of wickedly cool antique wood. It took forever to dust and polish all the intricate carvings on the headboard and posts, but I didn't mind. As soon as I'd clapped eyes on it last summer at a flea market, I knew it was meant to be mine. I'd haggled it down to half the original price, then bribed Desmond and Florence with dinner in exchange for their help lugging the disassembled pieces into their hatchback, then out of their hatchback, then through my historic — read: *narrow* — entryway and up my classic — read: *curved* — staircase to the second floor. Reassembling it took an entire day.

It was worth it.

Now, the master bedroom was finally complete, a result of months of pouring through architectural digest magazines and combing through what felt like a full palette of paint samples. Flo thought I'd lost my goddamned mind, but she didn't understand my fixation. In twenty-four years of life, this was the first bedroom I'd ever called my own, not counting college dormitories — which I didn't — and I'd been determined to make it utterly perfect in every regard, from the curtains to the color scheme.

I'd settled on a soothing array of cream tones, covered the walls in chunky gold-framed French art prints, and repurposed one of Aunt Colette's handwoven rugs from the downstairs living room to anchor the bed arrangement. The result was a space that radiated calm, that encouraged restful nights and peaceful mornings.

Something I'd certainly never had growing up.

The rest of the house was still, to put it generously, in transition. The vast majority of the rooms — and there were many of them, too many for any single person to know what to do with on her own — sat empty. I'd long since cleared out all of Aunt Colette's more eclectic belongings — the orange floral sofa, for instance, was straight out of the disco era, perfect for a hippie chick's abode but not exactly my style — and boxed some salvageable pieces away in the basement. The rest, I'd donated to a local charity, knowing that's what my ever-generous aunt would have wanted. However, after the big clear out, I hadn't found the time to redecorate in my own taste. Besides the master bedroom, attached bathroom, and kitchen, the rest of the house sat essentially vacant. A blank canvas, waiting to be painted and filled with furniture.

As soon as I had a spare minute, I told myself I'd pick a room at random and start. I'd always wanted a home office. No, not an office — a library. Full of built-in bookcases that soared to the ceilings, with a ladder that rolled the length of the room and a sunny picture window where I could curl up to read. If I had my library, maybe I'd finally feel settled enough to decorate the rest of this place. Maybe it would finally begin to feel like a proper home.

A permanent one.

Snuggling deeper beneath my thick ivory duvet, I switched off the lamp on my bedside table and switched on my e-reader. I made it approximately three pages into a book about a Regency-era debutante forced to marry a black-hearted pirate on the high seas before, like the timid Lady Scarlett beneath Captain Tristan's smoldering gaze, I too succumbed to the needs of my body, and fell into a deep, dreamless sleep.

CHAPTER SEVEN

I confess, I am full of sin.
- Gwen Goode, after eating approximately two deviled eggs

I stepped out into the sunny, late September morning and locked the front door behind me.

"Hiya, Mrs. Proctor!" I called, catching sight of my next door neighbor across the wrought-iron fence that divided our front yards as soon as I turned around on my narrow stoop.

I'd decorated for the season with pumpkins and gourds of various sizes and shades, two hay bales, and a pair of cornstalks lashed to the bannisters. A smiling scarecrow with button-eyes and straw filling stood guard beside my mailbox. It may've seemed a bit overboard, but my autumnal decor was tame when compared to the surrounding houses. Every season, my block looked like something out of *Better Homes and Gardens*. In the summer, buntings and American flags galore. In the winter, dazzling Christmas displays of white lights. Only white allowed, to keep the color scheme consistent. (One year, someone had the audacity to put up one of those tacky inflatable Santas... I think they were tar-and-feathered by the historical society.)

People were proud of their homes, proud of their long legacies. This whole stretch of town was historic — the little gold plaque beside my door proudly proclaimed "EST. 1672" — and since we directly abutted the Common, a nonstop parade of photographers and visitors and history buffs and Instagrammers wandered down our block. As such, my neighbors were a bit intense when it came to the aesthetics of our street. Mrs. Proctor — and her prize-winning gardens — was no exception.

"Good morning, Gwendolyn." The melodic reply drifted to me from the petite woman pruning her giant sunflowers. Her white hair was barely visible between the thick stalks. "How are you today?"

"Can't complain." I moved down the steps, onto my front walk. "Your sunflowers are looking great."

"Stop by and see me in a few days, I'll give you some of the seeds to plant next year." She paused pointedly. "They're easy to grow. Not much maintenance, even for a beginner gardener like yourself."

I eyed my own flower beds with a grimace. All my mums were dead as doornails. I wasn't a beginner gardener, I was a plant serial-killer. My thumb wasn't green, it was black. "Uh... thanks, Mrs. Proctor. That's sweet."

"You know, if you'd put half as much effort into your yard maintenance as you do your daily outfit selection, you'd have a thriving garden."

Okay, that was somewhat less sweet. In fact, it was borderline rude.

I glanced down at myself, taking in my attire. I was wearing my favorite wool skirt — knee-length with a front slit that stopped an inch short of scandalous. I'd layered it with my killer French-silk semi-sheer tights, the ones with seams down the back, and a pair of low heeled boots that elevated me from my usual 5'4" to 5'7". My top was gorgeous — single-sleeved with an asymmetrical neckline, it left one arm and shoulder completely bare and was constructed of the butteriest ivory cashmere on earth. I'd stacked six chunky silver bangles around my bare wrist, looped slim hoops through my ears, smoothed my metric ton of auburn waves back into a sleek twist, and spritzed perfume as a finishing touch.

Not too shabby, if I did say so myself.

Judging by her thinly-veiled disapproval, Mrs. Proctor evidently thought I was some self-obsessed shopaholic. I didn't really care. My wardrobe was the one thing I didn't ever feel guilty splurging on. After growing up in hand-me-downs and Goodwill castoffs, I had a special sort of appreciation for well-made, fashionable clothing. A good outfit was as vital as a suit of armor in the battle that was life. I hadn't forgotten the sidelong glances I used to get — from snickering kids in the classroom, from well-meaning strangers in checkout lines, from coaches and teachers and principals and peers' parents. Like I was some-thing to be mocked, manipulated, or worse — pitied.

Those glances didn't happen when you walked into a room looking polished and poised. People treated you like a player, not a pawn to move around the board at their own frivolous whims. These days, I rarely went anywhere without my outfit armor in place.

"I'll, uh, keep that in mind," I forced myself to say, pulling open my wrought-iron gate and stepping out onto the sidewalk. "Enjoy the weather."

"Have a lovely day, dear."

I made my way across the Common — the 8-acre public park

that separated me from the downtown district — in record time, cutting down one of the many criss-crossed paths by the bandstand. Only two sets of tourists stopped me to ask for directions to the Witch Museum. (A slow day!)

I dodged around a cluster of people snapping photos with their heads in the stocks, speed-walked past a man drawing caricature portraits, and cut straight through the middle of a walking-tour gathered outside the Hawthorne Hotel, which was reputedly haunted by several poltergeists. By the time I reached The Gallows, I'd worked up both a sweat and an appetite.

Hetti, already inside and setting up for the day, said nothing as I walked in. She did, however, slide a pumpkin-cheesecake muffin from Broomsticks Bakery across the counter at me as I walked past the espresso bar.

"Someone's angling for a raise," I murmured.

"Bad morning?" she asked, arching one silver-studded brow.

I took a bite of the muffin. It was divine. "It's improving rapidly," I told her, chewing as I made my way deeper into the shop, making mental notes of depleted stock on the shelves as I went. Both the candles and the crystals were running low again. We'd also had a run on sage and an unanticipated demand for vials of Sacred Gaia Tears — better known as tap water blessed by the goddess of my kitchen faucet beneath the light of a flickering candle. (Fall scented — authenticity was paramount.)

I heard the chime of the door bells behind me, announcing the arrival of our first customers as I made my way toward the back. Our resident psychic was still not in attendance. Her thick velvet curtains were drawn wide, the space beyond dark and vacant. I pulled out my phone as I stepped into storage room, scrolling one-handed until I reached the bottom of my contact list. But Zelda's phone didn't even ring — the call went straight to her voicemail box, which a robotic voice informed me was currently full.

Hmm.

The morning slipped by in a rush. I did inventory in the back until we were inundated with a flood of shoppers. Hetti manned the espresso bar at the front, glaring at everyone who dared place an order, while I manned the mystical curiosities section, ringing in sales at the antique brass cash register that had been around for longer than I'd been alive. We sold a considerable amount of books and baubles. We wouldn't be forming an IPO anytime soon, but it was enough to keep the lights on for another few months.

Hell, if it kept up like this, I might actually be able to hire on a part-timer to give Hetti an occasional day off. Not that she seemed to want any. In the six months she'd been working for me, she'd never once been late, never once called out sick, never once asked for a vacation. Ornery goth she may act, but the girl was dependable as a Girl Scout when push came to shove.

There wasn't a lull in the action until well into the afternoon, by which point I was hungry, Hetti was borderline homicidal, and the trash bin was overflowing with discarded coffee cups.

"I'll go grab lunch from Gulu-Gulu Cafe," I called to Hetti as I passed by the espresso bar. "You want your usual?"

She nodded without looking up from the milk fridge beneath the counter where she was crouched, restocking her supplies. Grabbing my clutch from below the cash register, I headed for the front door, lugging the overflowing trash with me as I went. It weighed a metric ton, filled to bursting. Throwing out the garbage was never my favorite task, but it was even less convenient today. With our dumpster still roped off with police tape, I'd be forced to carry it a block down to the alley behind the neighboring shops.

A pair of arriving Salem State kids held the door open for me as I struggled through it. I recognized both of them. Xander and Gus, two rail-thin, sun-deprived film students who never bought anything, but occasionally brought me donuts in exchange for permission to film their amateur B-roll in the shop after business hours. Apparently, The Gallows had the right ambiance for gothic noir. I didn't even like donuts, but they were good kids, and I didn't have the heart to charge them actual money.

"Hi Gwen."

"Hey guys," I said, hauling the bag across the threshold. It seemed to be getting heavier with each passing moment. "How's it hanging?"

They both cracked grins at my subpar gallows humor. "Do you need help with that?"

"No, no, I've got it. Get on inside, Hetti is just dying for company. You know what a people person she is. Make sure to ask her lots of questions about her day, her feelings, her every given thought."

They both laughed, knowing I was full of it, and disappeared inside. I continued to lug the overfilled trash bag down the brick sidewalk, dodging clusters of people buying cups of hot cider from a street vendor, skirting a crowd gathered to listen to a busking guitarist who went by Freddy Krooner and dressed exactly like the terrifying Wes Craven character of a similar name.

"*I put a spell on you,*" he crooned into the microphone, gripping the stand with knived fingers. "*Because you're mineeeee....*"

Freddy's voice faded as I stepped off the brick mall into the narrow alleyway that snaked behind Broomsticks Bakery. I was gasping for air by that point. Half-dragging the bag, I prayed it would not split open as I hefted it upward.

Thankfully, I managed to deposit it into the dumpster without incident, stumbling back a step as it sailed from my hands and landed in the bottom with a dull thud. Less thankfully, my heeled sole slid into a puddle of something slimy in the process. I glanced down to see what I'd stepped in, praying it would not be blood from another animal sacrifice. I was relieved to see it was merely a rotten banana peel, brown and molding.

Fixated as I was on wiping my shoe clean against the edge of the dumpster, I did not hear my attacker approach. Not until he was standing directly behind me. The slight scuff of a tan construction boot finally made me glance up, and I found myself staring directly at a wall of flannel — beneath which lay an impressively broad chest, across which two equally impressive muscular arms were currently crossed.

Eek!

So much for keeping my senses honed to danger.

"Gwendolyn Goode?"

"Um," I squeaked, trying not to cower beneath the seriously angry stare the flannel-clad lumberjack was aiming at me. "That depends. What do you want with her?"

"Just answer the question."

"You first," I retorted.

"No," he growled. "You."

"You!"

"*You*— Fuck, this is ridiculous!" The man's light blue eyes flared with exasperation. "What are you, in kindergarten? Just answer the damn question!"

"Sorry, I'm not at my most accommodating when I'm being accosted in alleyways!"

"Whoa, whoa, whoa. Who said anything about accosting? I'm not accosting." His hands — which were each approximately the size of a honey-baked ham — lifted in a placating gesture that did very little to assuage my worries. "I just wanna ask you a couple questions, that's all."

"Okay," I agreed, heart hammering. "Ask them when we're not alone, next to a dumpster where you can conveniently dispose of my body."

The lumberjack's eyes widened. "Jesus, lady, it's broad daylight."

"And?"

"You think I'm gonna off you in broad daylight? You're crazy!"

"Yes. That's right. I *am* crazy." I dropped my voice down an octave, hoping it had a menacing effect. "You don't want to mess with a crazy woman. There's no telling what she'll do when backed into a corner."

Menacing did not translate as well as I'd hoped. Lumberjack man was now staring at me like I had a few screws loose. That was fine. I wasn't trying to win a congeniality contest, I was trying to get back to civilization without ending up featured on a true crime podcast where two bored thirty-something housewives took it upon themselves to uncover the truth of my gruesome disappearance.

Gulping in some much-needed air, I took a few steps around him, but he blocked my path with his gargantuan form.

"Move out of my way," I hissed through clenched teeth.

"Look, I just wanna talk to you," he insisted, stepping nearer, forcing me to backpedal toward the dumpster. "I'm not gonna do nothing—"

"Don't come any closer!"

He froze mid-step. His ham-sized hands did the placating gesture again. "Okay, okay. Fuck, you're paranoid."

"Better paranoid than dead." I planted my hands on my hips and immediately regretted it. They probably smelled like trash and, thus, so too would my pretty wool skirt. "You have point two seconds before I start screaming bloody murder, so I suggest you talk fast."

He scowled. At least, I think he did. It was difficult to tell beneath his bushy, red beard. "Your psychic. Zelda. You seen her?"

I blinked, momentarily stunned. This was not where I had foreseen this conversation heading. "You're looking for Madame Zelda?"

He nodded, reddening slightly.

"*You're* a true believer?" I asked, my nose wrinkling. I couldn't help my skepticism. Even considering the psychic's varied clientele, he was an anomaly. Thirty-something men who looked like they were half Viking, half Unabomber didn't often seek out spiritual guidance from women in caftans.

He continued to redden, far more than slightly. I couldn't tell if it was anger or embarrassment. "It's a standing appointment set up, twice a month, at my mother's place," he rumbled. "She was supposed to come two nights ago. She never showed up."

I knew Zelda did house calls in addition to her readings at the shop. But as far as I was concerned, what she did on her own time was her business. I didn't interfere with her extracurriculars any more than she weighed in on mine.

"She hasn't been around for a few days." I threw out my hands in a 'what can you do' gesture. "I'm sure she'll turn back up soon. Just call to reschedule your appointment."

"Her voicemail is full."

"Right." I swallowed. "I'm sympathetic. I am. But I don't know what I can do to help you."

"She's your employee."

"Not exactly. She's more of a freelancer." I shrugged. "I let her use my space, she brings in a steady stream of clientele. Mutually beneficial relationship. Symbiotic. Sort of like a clownfish and a sea anemone."

He stared at me blankly.

I figured he wasn't well versed in clownfish coexistence, so I launched into an explanation. "See, the anemone provides a home for the clownfish, and in return the clownfish scares away—"

"I don't give a fuck."

"Fine! Jeeze." I held up my hands defensively at his blunt interjection. "Sue me for trying to spread a little knowledge."

"The only knowledge I'm interested in concerns where I can find Zelda."

"Right. Zelda." I shrugged yet again. "Like I said, she's not technically my employee. I don't pay her. I don't make her schedule or oversee her appointments. I don't keep tabs on when she comes and goes."

"You have her home address?"

My brows shot up. "If I did, I'd hardly give it to you."

"It wouldn't violate any privacy laws or nothin'. You just said she's not your employee."

"She may not be my employee, but she is an… associate. Whereas *you* are a stranger."

His face clouded over with a mix of anger and frustration when he realized I was not about to budge on this front. His hands, which were currently folded across his barrel chest, fisted tightly. "It's important that I see her as soon as possible. Today. *Now.*"

"Well, buddy, as I said, I have no idea where Zelda is. And I'm certainly not about to give up her personal information to a vaguely threatening dude who cornered me in an alleyway."

His eyes flared with undeniable rage. He took a lumbering step toward me. "Look, lady—"

I wasn't about to wait around to see what he intended to do next. I pointed at my bare wrist, as though there was a watch adorning it, and cut him off mid-sentence. "Would you look at the time? Your point-two seconds are over. I'll be going, now."

This time, when I darted around him, he let me go. But his voice called after me as I reached the end of the alley. "You see Zelda, you tell her Mickey is lookin' for her. You tell her he's not going away — not until he gets back what she took. You tell her she can run, but she can't hide. Not for long."

I picked up my pace, as if to outrun his threatening words. But they followed me all the way back to the main drag, sending a chill down my spine despite the sun-drenched afternoon.

BY THE TIME I left the shop for the night, darkness had fallen. Hetti was long gone — as soon as she shut off the espresso machine and wiped the tabletops, she disappeared out the door in a blur of black fishnets and magenta hair, lugging a bursting trash bag along with her. Hopefully, her alleyway experience would be less dramatic than mine.

Alone in the storeroom, I'd spent the next two hours hunched over my desk balancing the books, paying bills, processing payroll, and placing next month's inventory orders. The lead-up to Halloween was always our busiest time, the city increasingly overrun as the spirit of the season descended in full. Last year, Salem saw nearly a million visitors in October alone. By the end of the month, my shelves had practically been bare and I'd turned away plenty of paying customers with money to burn. I was doing my best not to repeat my mistakes this time around, unwilling to foolishly squander the income opportunity the next six weeks presented — even if it meant placing an order with so many zeros on the end of the total, my eyes bugged out of my head.

Anxiety furled through me, churning from the pit of my stomach up the path of my esophagus. The hard truth was, I might be making a massive miscalculation. I didn't have an MBA or any formal business training; I only had my gut to follow. I hoped like hell it wouldn't lead me astray. So far, the decisions

I'd made for the shop had been solid enough. And I didn't need a fancy degree to know that old adage was true.

No risk, no reward.

Business was a series of calculated wagers you hoped would pay off but could never quite be certain wouldn't come back to bite you in the ass. With a soft click, I shut my laptop, shoved it into my bag, and walked through the shop, flipping the lights off as I went. I locked up, listening to the reassuring thunk of the deadbolt sliding home. The wooden sign above my head groaned lightly in the wind, a forlorn soundtrack accompanying the steady clap of my heeled boots against the brick street as I walked down the pedestrian mall.

The night was lively, the fall Friday evening full of couples strolling hand in hand and young college kids equipped with fake IDs, eager to con their way into dark dive bars. I took a shortcut down a quieter side street, cutting across town toward The Witches Brew Tavern. Florence was already there — I knew this because she'd been texting me for the past twenty minutes on five minute intervals, telling me to get my nose out of my ledger books and into the real world. My phone buzzed again in the depths of my bag and I fished it out without breaking stride.

Around the corner, I texted her, peering down at the screen. *Be there in two.*

Great! she replied. *We're in the back.*

We?

Flo, rather suspiciously, did not answer.

With a sigh, I rounded the corner — and nearly leapt out of my skin as something bolted from the shadows no more than five feet in front of me. My heart sailed up into my throat. My phone clattered to the street, skittering dangerously close to a sewer grate. It was only when a feline screech split the night that I realized it was not Mickey the lumberjack nor a terrifying monster but a black cat, crossing my path. (If I'd been less distracted, I might have remembered that old superstition about black cats and crossed paths and the bad luck that would surely ensue as a result. But, as things stood, I was in a rush and paid little mind to old wives tales)

Cursing my own jumpiness, I bent to retrieve my phone from the gutter. I heard something rustle the fallen leaves behind me and turned, expecting to see the cat again.

Instead, I was met with a trio of cloaked figures.

My eyes widened and my mouth gaped, but there wasn't even time to scream. A pale hand emerged from the swathes of black fabric. Something was cupped in the outstretched palm — a pile of greenish silver dust that glittered even in the low light of the alleyway. The strange sight momentarily stunned me into stillness. Like a fool, I stood there, paralyzed in place as the middle figure in the trio bobbed forward, bent toward the aloft hand... and *blew.*

The dust exploded into a cloud that hit me directly in the face. There was no defending against it, no scrambling out of range. It shot up my nose and down my airway, filling my lungs with a searing sort of heat.

My nostrils stung. My throat burned. The phone in my hand fell back to the alley as my fingers went numb. My strength gave out in one abrupt instant. So did my knees — I felt them hit the asphalt. My last thought was not of my attackers or what they were going to do to me, but about the irreparable tears I'd no doubt just ripped in my favorite pair of fancy French silk stockings.

Then, everything went dark.

CHAPTER EIGHT

I'm more of a dog person.
- Gwen Goode, forced to hold a newborn

When my eyes opened, I found myself bound to a wooden chair in what appeared to be a basement. My head was pounding, my mouth parched. I had no earthly idea where I was or how I had gotten there.

Actually, that wasn't strictly true. Though the *where* remained a mystery, the *how* was immediately apparent; all evidence pointed to the cloaked trio huddled in the corner across the room from me, backlit by an alter of various chunky taper candles burning brightly. Melted wax from many previous lightings had hardened in dry rivulets that pooled on the edge of the table and hung toward the stone floor like stalagmites. (Or was it *stalactites*? I could never keep them straight. Geological formations weren't my forte.)

From the looks of it, my kidnappers had not yet realized I was awake. Their attention was fixed on one another, not on me. I aimed to keep it that way, moving only the tiniest amount as I tested my wrists against the thick rope that looped around each arm of the wooden chair in which I was propped. They were tied firmly and, besides, I still felt weak as a newborn kitten from whatever powder I'd inhaled back in the alley. For now, all I could do was observe though slitted eyelids and eavesdrop as if my life depended on it.

Because... it might.

Hellfire and brimstone.

"She'll wake soon," one of the figures was saying in a hushed — and decidedly feminine — voice muffled by her voluminous cloak. I thought there was something rather familiar about said voice, but I couldn't be certain. I strained my ears to catch the rest of her words. "...wish you hadn't gotten me involved. It's far too risky."

"You know full well, we had no other choice!" Another of the trio said. Also female. "This is a last resort. Should we fail..."

"We will not fail," the third woman interjected. "Because we cannot. The survival of the coven depends on it. On *her*."

Hold on a second...

Coven?!

Did she say *coven*?

As in coven of... *witches*?

Great. Just freaking great. I'd been kidnapped by the cast of Hocus Pocus. Probably the same practitioners who'd left that horrifying sacrifice in my alleyway yesterday. This, I thought, did not bode well for my survival. A series of images flashed through my head — five glossy photographs on a metal interrogation desk. Cat, rooster, goat, pig, donkey. Would I be the subject of the next crime scene snapshot Detective Hightower added to his case file?

I hoped not. I didn't want to die. Not at all, not ever, but especially not chopped into pieces with a pentagram of my own blood traced around me by a cabal of psychotic pagans.

At some point, as I processed this alarming development, the witchy trio had ceased their discussion and turned to look at me. I belatedly squeezed my eyes shut and feigned unconsciousness, but it was no use. I wasn't a good actress in the best of times and these, admittedly, were not those.

"She's awake."

"Yes, Agatha, we can see that."

"Don't say my name, you dingbat!"

"I'm sorry!"

"Don't be sorry, be smart!"

"Give me a break! I'm not a criminal mastermind."

"And yet, you manage to cheat at canasta every time we play."

"That's a blatant lie! I don't need to cheat to beat you."

"You couldn't beat me if I was a bowl of egg whites!"

"Your new nickname will be meringue after Sunday's meeting. Just you wait!"

"Bring it on!"

"Oh, I'll bring it." There was a contemplative pause. "I'll also bring my cheesecake."

"With the raspberry preserve?"

"Yes. Are you making those lemon scones again?"

Truth be told, I was struggling to keep up the unconscious charade. Whatever I'd expected (i.e.: torture, interrogation, threats, intimidation) it was *not* a conversation about card games and baked confections. Perhaps my captors realized they'd strayed from their intended course, because — with a rustle of fabric and a low huff of air, as though someone had caught a swift elbow to the midsection — they fell markedly silent.

I took a deep inhale, trying not to fidget as the seconds ticked on. And on. And *on*. Finally, when I thought I'd go mad from the strain, one of the voices broke the crushing silence.

"We know you're not asleep anymore, Gwendolyn," she murmured. "You might as well open your eyes."

Hellfire.

With a sigh, I peeled open my heavy lids and glared at the cloaked figures. They'd moved a bit nearer, now standing only a handful of feet away, but I still could not make out their features. In unison, they began to close the remaining distance between us.

"Wait!" I yelled, startling them to a sudden halt. I swallowed hard and lowered my tone to a reasonable volume, desperately trying to keep my voice steady. "If you kill me, you'll never get away with it! Livestock is one thing. I'm a *person*! People will notice I go missing." I gulped in a breath of air. "In fact, I'm sure they've already noticed. A friend was waiting for me when you grabbed me in that alley. She'll call the police if I don't show up."

At least, I hoped she would. Flo had a tendency to get lost in the music as soon as the band went on. It might be well into the first set before she realized I'd never made an appearance.

The cloaked figures looked at each other.

"*Kill* you?" one asked, sounding bewildered. "Why on earth would we kill you, Gwendolyn?"

"Why did you kill all those innocent animals?" I retorted immediately, heart thudding hard against my ribcage. "Why did you leave that donkey butchered in my alley?"

The trio traded another glance.

"It *was* you guys, wasn't it?" I asked. "Don't tell me there's more than one crazed coven of witches running amok in this town."

"We do not associate with the Heretics," the central cloak decreed, her voice conveying a deep sense of disgust at the mere implication. "We cast them out. Banished them, many years ago. But they have returned."

I blinked. "Heretics?"

"Yes. A dark sect of witches, who once shared this territory with our coven. It is they who conduct blood sacrifices. It is they who pervert the teachings of the sacred goddess with their twisted practitioning. Not us."

My brows were so high on my forehead, they'd probably disappeared beneath my hairline. "Then... if you aren't the ones who left the donkey in my alley... what do you want from me?" I asked, trying to sound entirely unrattled, though I was anything but. Shake me to the beat and call me a maraca, baby, because...

I.

Was.

Rattled.

The central figure — the one they'd called Agatha — emitted a long sigh from beneath her hood. "We don't want anything from you, child. Merely to talk."

"To *warn*," her companion corrected.

My eyebrows shot up. "Warn about what?"

"You are in grave danger."

"Yeah, see, the police already told me that yesterday. Plus, I mean, I sort of put that together on my own, what with the series of disembodied, decapitated farm animals and the creepy message left in blood. So, this whole kidnapping was really not necessary..."

"Do not be glib!" Agatha snapped. "This is not a joking matter."

"I wasn't joking—"

She cut me off. "Don't you understand? As soon as they learned of your existence, you became a target. Before you moved back to town, they thought the bloodline was dead. Extinguished. They thought there was no chance to undo the binding curse we laid upon them so many years ago. But you have changed all of that."

My eyes were bugging out of my head as I stared from one of the cloaked figures to the other, waiting for them to yell, "gotcha!" and start laughing. Waiting for the hidden cameras to appear, for Flo and Des to step out of the shadows and declare it all a practical joke at my expense. But the seconds ticked by and nothing happened.

"You have given them hope they once thought lost, to reclaim that which we took," Agatha continued. "And they will not rest until they have eradicated the Goode lineage from the face of this earth. You will not be safe until they are cast from these lands once more."

This was beginning to feel more and more like some sort of fever dream. Perhaps I'd slipped and hit my head in that alley. Perhaps I'd had a bad reaction to that silvery fairy dust I inhaled. Perhaps I was hallucinating. That would make more sense than anything she was saying.

"Look, I respect that you're trying to warn me about some seriously witchy impending doom, but... I think you've got the wrong girl. All this talk of bloodlines and curses and casting out Heretics?" I shook my head back and forth rapidly. "Not my cup of tea. I'm a coffee girl. I don't even drink tea! And if I did, it certainly wouldn't be to divine my future in the leaves at the bottom of the mug. I'm not a true believer. I'm not anything, really. Just an ordinary girl leading an ordinary life."

Silence descended, thick as fog, cold as ice. The trio seemed decidedly unhappy with this revelation. The vibes in the basement — which, admittedly, were already rather creepy but in a cool, gothic sort of way — became *genuinely* creepy, sending a shiver of unease down my spine. The candles on the altar behind them began to flicker as if a draft of wind suddenly swept through the room. Which was pretty odd, since there were no windows anywhere I could see.

"I told you this was a waste of time," one of the trio — the one who had spoken the least and stayed farthest away, half-hidden by her companions — muttered. She kept her voice hushed, but again I was struck by the thought that there was something distinctly familiar about it. "She's never shown even the slightest flicker of inheritance."

"And yet," Agatha hissed. "She is the one."

"How can you be certain?"

"There is no one else!" She sighed. "And even if we are wrong, the Heretics believe she is the one. The key. They will not stop until she is dead."

I did not like the sound of that.

Like, *at all*.

"Um," I interrupted softly. "Look, if you know who these Heretics are, why not just report them to the police?"

Agatha snorted. "Do you know nothing? No ordinary task force can handle this. No jail cell can properly contain a practitioner of dark magic. Gaia above, she really is a simpleton."

"Intuitive as a turnip," the second witch added.

"Hey!" I snapped defensively.

"I told you," the quiet one murmured. "Waste of time. It seems the gift has skipped a generation."

Inside my sluggish brain, something finally clicked. In shock, I jolted against my rope bonds as my eyes flew to the face concealed behind the third cloak. Because I'd finally recognized the voice that was whispering from beneath its rim.

"*Mrs. Proctor?*" I half-shouted, incredulity dripping from each syllable. Of all the people I'd suspected of kidnapping me, my elderly neighbor with a penchant for gardening was not at the top of the list. In fact, she wasn't even *on* the list. "Oh my god, Mrs. Proctor, is it really you?"

Silence fell once more. The trio traded glances.

Agatha sighed again. "Eliza, I think—"

"Hush, you old coot!" Mrs. Elizabeth Proctor — *Eliza* — exclaimed.

"Me, an old coot? You're the one who can't properly disguise her voice. Don't blame me for her recognizing you."

"You didn't have to confirm her suspicions!"

"She may not be a true believer, but she's not entirely unobservant, Eliza."

"Oh, put a sock in it, Sally," Eliza barked at the third witch. "Agatha's right! You are a dingbat!"

"I'm not the one who got us recognized!"

My gaze moved from one woman to the other as they traded jabs, unsure whether to be amused or concerned by the rapidly fraying situation. Fixing my eyes on my neighbor's cloaked form, I adopted a breezy tone. "I know it's you, Mrs. Proctor. You might as well drop the theatrics."

A hushed oath slipped from her mouth. Reaching up, she pushed back her cloak to reveal a face I knew quite well. One I saw just about every morning across the wrought-iron fence that divided our yards. Her owlish features were enhanced by the round glasses she wore perched on the bridge of a tiny, upturned nose. Her white hair was, as always, perfectly coiffed, never a strand out of place. I'd bet she slept with it in rollers. Not even my Dyson Airwrap provided such gravity-defying volume.

"Gwendolyn," Mrs. Proctor greeted me — rather belatedly. "I'd hoped to do this without needing to bring our personal lives into it."

"Maybe you should have thought of that before you dragged me into a basement. Call me crazy, but *abduction* seems pretty damn personal."

I peered at the other two women. Agatha and Sally had also pushed back their cloaks to reveal their faces. They both looked like they were approaching eighty, with wrinkled cheeks and warm eyes. It would be easier to envision them baking cookies for their grandchildren than holding me captive in a basement.

And yet... here we were.

"How did the three of you get me here, anyway?" I asked.

"Just because we're old doesn't mean we're fragile," Agatha retorted, eyes narrowing on mine. "Even if you do weigh more than a hay bale."

Rude!

I scowled. "I do not."

She merely pursed her lips and shrugged.

"Can we focus, ladies?" Eliza clapped her hands three times to call everyone's attention. Now that she'd revealed herself, it seemed she was stepping into her natural role as leader of the deranged trio. Her eyes locked on me, steely through the shining lenses of her spectacles. "Gwendolyn. We are aware that you are not a true believer. We are aware that, unlike Colette, you do not possess the gifts of the goddess. Still, we are honor bound to protect the bloodlines of all coven members. Even those who have passed beyond the mortal veil. Do you understand?"

"Not remotely," I admitted. "What does Aunt Colette have to do with this?"

The trio looked at one another, their expressions torn between incredulity and amusement.

"What?" I asked impatiently. "Just tell me, already."

"Before she passed," Sally said slowly, as though I was the most imbecilic creature to ever cross her path. "Colette was a member of our coven."

"Not only a member," Agatha added. "She was our leader."

"High Priestess," Eliza murmured, "Of the Bay Colony Coven for over fifty years. Her loss is one from which we will never recover."

I shook my head, attempting to rattle my thoughts into order by sheer force. "Are you telling me... Aunt Colette was... a *witch*?"

They all bleated out soft laughs.

"Of course, child." Agatha rolled her eyes heavenward. "Did you really not know?"

I hadn't.

Not really, anyway. Sure, I'd heard the talk around town about Aunt Colette when I came to visit as a kid. *The Goode Witch,* they'd whisper. *She's an odd one...* And, sure, I knew she dabbled in all things occult. She was a true believer, and proud of it. But she never gave me the slightest indication, as she poured over old grimoires at The Gallows and taught me about Gaia, that she was the High Priestess of a practicing coven. Never in my wildest dreams did I imagine her casting spells (*Hexes? Curses? Enchantments?* I wasn't up on the correct terminology) or dancing naked in the light of the full moon with her spirit-sisters.

I'd foolishly assumed her interest in witchcraft was purely academic. A hobby — much like my fascination with ancient architecture, or my penchant for clicking my way down a never-ending black hole of Wikipedia pages in a futile attempt to learn all I could about any given random topic, like the Kennedy curse or the history of marshmallow fluff or the evolution of deep sea creatures.

"Look at her face," Sally said, not unkindly. "We've shocked the poor girl. She's white as your backside in January, Agatha."

"You leave my backside out of this, Sally."

"I might be able to, if it wasn't so large. Can you still fit through the front door without turning sideways?"

"At least my knockers aren't down to my waist! Tell me, Sally, do you have to special order your bras from the local quarry? I'd think they're the only ones capable of handling boulders that size."

"You bitter cow! Take it back!"

"You started it!"

I swallowed down a laugh, trying not to let my amusement show as my eyes bolted back and forth between Sally and Agatha. A deep, martyred groan from Eliza drew my gaze. Her lips were pursed, her eyes narrowed behind her owlish lenses.

"You two! That's enough," she chastised her accomplices. "Focus. You can fight later."

They instantly fell silent, but continued to exchange sneers and vulgar hand gestures behind Eliza's back, like little girls on the school yard. It was a struggle to keep my expression serious as I stared at my neighbor, who was regarding me solemnly.

"Gwendolyn. You really must heed our warning. You have no idea the danger you will be in if you don't."

"What do you expect me to to?"

"Leave," she said simply. "Leave Salem and never return."

My mouth gaped open like a fish on dry land, making soundless gulps for air. "But..." I shook my head. "I can't just leave."

"You can and you will if you know what's good for you." Her expression was resolute, no trace of sympathy or softness to be seen. "Put your house on the market. Find someone to run the business in your stead. Or better yet, sell it off. There are plenty of eager buyers, and we are not entirely without resources. We could find someone in a matter of days."

Okay. Now, I was getting annoyed. Actually, it was more than annoyed. I was getting downright *angry*.

"I am not selling Aunt Colette's house," I growled through gritted teeth. "And I'm not passing off the shop to some random stranger. You say you cared for my aunt... how do you think she would feel to hear you encouraging me to liquidate all her assets and erase her legacy?"

"*You* are her legacy, Gwendolyn," Eliza insisted. "Not a shop. Not a house."

In the space of a heartbeat, my eyes started stinging with unshed tears. An overwhelming wave of longing swept over me, through me, hitting me square in the heart. I wished Aunt Colette were here with a fierceness that stole my breath. If she were here, none of this would be happening. If she were here...

I blinked the gathering tears back and grasped onto my simmering anger instead. If I stayed angry, perhaps I wouldn't fall apart.

"Forget it," I snapped. "I'm not going anywhere." *(Literally.* Those bonds at my wrists were inescapable.)

"Don't you understand?" Eliza took a half-step closer to me. "You are Colette's only living descendant. You were like a daughter to her. She cherished you with her whole being. She would want you safe. She would want you protected. That's why we are here. That's why we must intervene. If you won't leave of your own free will... if you won't heed our warnings..." She paused, glancing at the other women. As if they'd been waiting for this cue, Sally and Agatha stepped forward so the three of them were standing shoulder to shoulder in a unified line before me. "Then, you give us little choice," Eliza finished softly.

"What?" I looked from Sally to Agatha to Eliza, my gaze beseeching. "What does that mean?"

"The Heretics cannot regain their foothold here, child," Sally whispered, round cheeks flushing. Several mousy brown tendrils had escaped her chignon and frizzed around her temples. "We cannot allow them to break the binding curse we cast so many years ago."

"You cannot be serious!" I wanted to laugh. I wanted to cry. I wanted to scream. (I went with the third option.) "THIS IS RIDICULOUS! THERE'S NO SUCH THING AS CURSES! OR SPELLS! OR WITCHES!" I yanked at my bindings. "*LET!*" Yank. "*ME!*" Another yank. "*GO!*"

The ropes didn't even loosen.

"The cost of their malevolence is far too high for any of us to pay," Agatha said, as though I'd never spoken. (Shouted.) "It's your blood they need to break the curse. Should they succeed in unlocking their powers... it would be the end for us all. Best to keep you out of their hands." She nodded with conviction. "Best to keep you here."

"*WHAT*?!"

"Only temporarily, of course. Until we can make other arrangements. More permanent ones, somewhere out of town."

"WHAT DO YOU MEAN BY *OUT OF TOWN*?"

"This measure may seem extreme to you now, Gwendolyn," Eliza said in an eerily calm voice. "But in time, I hope you will see the wisdom in it. The necessity behind it." She paused. "In time, I hope you will forgive us."

"FORGIVE YOU?" I was really starting to panic as the reality of my situation settled around my shoulders. With effort, I managed to lower my tone a fraction, so I was only half-hollering. "Forgive you for what? You're not really planning to keep me here, are you? Please, tell me you're joking!"

The trio exchanged another lingering glance amongst themselves, then turned away in a whirl of black fabric. In unison, they slipped their hoods back up over their heads and began to move toward the far side of the basement.

"*HEY*!" I yelled after them as they began to walk away from me, again struggling furiously against the binds on my wrists. "Wait! Where do you think you're going?"

They gave no response. They didn't even pause. And then, in the space between two blinks, they seemed to disappear into thin air, fading into the dense shadows beyond the altar's pool of light, leaving me utterly alone.

There must be some sort of passage out of here. A storm cellar door, perhaps. A secret tunnel.

Unless... they really could do magic.

"You can't just leave me down here!" I called to the empty void, my voice cracking with rising panic.

But they had.

Those horrid, unhinged....

Witches!

As full quiet descended in the wake of their departure, I took stock of my situation.

Okay. No point in panicking, Gwen. It's really not so bad. You're unharmed, for the most part. Sure, you've been witch-roofied, tied up, and held hostage by three paranoid, paranormal octogenarians who think your blood is the key to unlocking an ancient curse they laid upon a rival sect of dark pagans...

A half-laugh, half-cry bubbled up my throat, a byproduct of sheer hysteria at the ridiculous nature of this whole scenario. All laughter dissipated as the quiet of the empty basement echoed back at me. On the stone altar, the candles were burning low. I wondered how much longer the wicks would last before spluttering into darkness. The basement was already unpleasant; I had no desire to still be here when it was plunged into pitch black.

With fresh urgency, I tugged at my bindings until my skin was raw and my bones were smarting. But I was bound fast, unable to gain even a millimeter of slack in the heavy, braided rope. I was officially stuck until they came back for me. Goddess only knew how long that would take. They weren't exactly spry spring chickens. I could be here forever. I might actually perish down here without any food or water. Assuming I didn't lose my mind from sheer boredom before dying of thirst. They could've at least left me some reading material to pass the time. Or a nightlight to keep the ghosts at bay!

The left side of the space held nothing but a few empty, half-rotted storage crates. On the right, a rickety set of wooden stairs were bolted to the stone wall. They looked like they'd been built by the original settlers of Salem back in the 1600s. Not very promising, as escape routes went. A lump of fabric bundled on the bottom step caught my frantic eyes — my camel coat and patent leather tote bag, I realized with a rush of foolish hope.

Was my phone still inside my bag?

There was a good chance they'd ditched it back in the gutter of that alleyway outside The Witches Brew. But on the off chance it was still inside... I had to get to it. Somehow. I had to try, at least.

Rocking back and forth in my chair, I hoped I might scoot it across the floor or maybe tip it over and splinter the wood arms, setting myself free in the manner of a badass secret agent heroine of a spy movie. Unfortunately, since I was not a badass secret agent and this was reality, I soon realized the chair was made of oak so heavy, it might as well be the Iron Throne, forged of a thousand melted swords. No amount of squirming lifted the legs off the ground. My struggles only succeeded in stealing my breath, sapping my strength, and breaking my spirit.

Hellfire and brimstone.

Hope fading, I craned my neck to examine the cobwebbed wood planks high overhead. The utter lack of sound left me with little confidence that anyone was up there; that anyone would hear my screams for help. That didn't stop me from trying, though.

I screamed and screamed and screamed until my throat was hoarse and my lungs were aching, until the word 'help' had lost all meaning, morphing into mangled, guttural muddle of letters that barely made it past my lips.

After that, I screamed some more.

CHAPTER NINE

He's a walking red flag. Thankfully, red is my favorite color.
- Gwen Goode, justifying a recent crush

Glass shattered somewhere overhead.

I jolted awake at the muffled sound. In an instant, I sat upright in my chair, spine ramrod straight. I'd slumped over as I slept, worn out by what felt like hours of screaming and struggling in vain.

Maybe not entirely *in vain...*

Someone was here.

Someone had come.

I stilled, straining my ears to listen as footsteps echoed down through the floorboards overhead. It was difficult to hear over the sudden roar of my pulse between my ears. I felt a ticklish sprinkle of dust falling against my face. I couldn't see it; I couldn't see anything. The candles had burned out several hours ago. It was dark as a crypt in the basement and cold as ice. I shivered, regretting my choice of a fashionable skirt and tights instead of, say, a set of thermal footy-pajamas to ward off the chill.

The footsteps stopped their thudding. My heart skipped a beat as the door at the top of the half-rotted staircase creaked open on rusty hinges. For a second, nothing happened. Whoever was up there seemed to be listening for signs of life. Or signs of impending danger. But then, a narrow shaft of light spliced the pervasive dark — the beam of a flashlight, shining down into the basement, pooling on the dense earthen floor. It fixed for a long beat on my tan leather bucket bag, sitting with my coat on the bottom step.

I opened my mouth to call out for help, but clamped my lips together before a single syllable escaped. For all I knew, whoever was up there was in cahoots with the Bay Colony Coven biddies who'd left me in this rather uncomfortable position. Or worse! What if it was a Heretic? What if it was just your standard, run-of-the-mill serial killer?

A foot thunked down on the topmost step, then paused before continuing, as if testing whether or not it would splinter. I didn't dare draw a single breath as the boots began to pound their way downward. The wood groaned precariously in protest. I kept my eyes on the bobbing beam of the flashlight as it reached ground level, wincing against the sudden flare as it swept sharply across the space and snared me in its glaringly bright crosshairs.

"Agh!" I yelled, slamming my eyelids shut. My retinas were searing. "Watch it!"

There was a terse beat of silence, and then a low voice growled, "*Watch it?* Really? I come here to rescue you, and that's all you have to say to me?"

My eyes sprang back open. "*Graham?*"

He grunted in response to my low, incredulous inquiry. I blinked rapidly, adjusting to the brightness, and he came slowly into focus. He was dressed in all black from his boots to his jeans to his leather jacket to his stormy expression. His hands were crossed at the wrists — one gripped a flashlight, the other had a finger poised on the trigger of a sleek black handgun.

"Jeeze! Don't shoot!" I yelped.

The gun lowered slightly. "Anyone else down here?"

"No, they've been gone for hours." My voice was small. "It's only me."

With a short nod, he tucked the gun into the back waistband of his jeans. In two short strides he was there in front of me, crouched by my battered knees, which were bloodied from my fall in the alley — and, if I had to guess, from being dragged unceremoniously across rough pavement by three little old ladies. The tights were torn, the skin scraped away. Pain throbbed through me, a constant undercurrent.

"What are you doing here?" I whispered, half-convinced I was imagining Graham's presence.

He didn't answer. It almost seemed like he hadn't heard me speak. He was staring at the dried blood on my knees, his eyes far seeing. With aching slowness, he reached out and skimmed a fingertip across my right kneecap, his touch light as a feather on the wound. I sucked in a sharp breath at the contact. Hearing it, he pulled away instantly. His eyes finally lifted to lock on mine, the raw emotion in their depths burning bright even in the darkness.

"Who did this?" His voice was a low rasp of rage. "*Who hurt you?*"

"Um," I squeaked, a little afraid of him in that moment. Much as I was annoyed at Eliza, Sally, and Agatha for their over-protective antics, their hearts had been in the right places. (For the most part.) I certainly wasn't about to set Graham loose on them. Not when he looked fully capable of committing triple homicide. "I'm not hurt. A little freaked out, sure, but I'm fine. Really."

His eyes narrowed. "*Fine?*"

"Fine," I echoed, nodding. Because I was. Mostly. I mean, sure, I had to pee pretty desperately. Yes, I was so hungry I'd contemplated chewing through my rope bindings — not for escape, but sustenance. And, okay, I could admit to being a teeny, tiny bit scared that I was going to die down here, alone in the dark, forgotten by the world, never to be heard from again. But I wasn't about to admit any of that to Graham, of all people.

"Gwendolyn."

I blinked at his use of my real name. It was jarring, after months of *Wizard of Oz* mockery. Not entirely unpleasant, though, even if he was saying it in a rather intimidating, scolding manner. I wished suddenly that I knew him well enough to read his facial expressions, because the one he was giving me...

Wowza.

It was a doozy.

"Um." I swallowed hard. "Yeah?"

"You've been missing for six hours. You're tied to a chair. Your wrists are rubbed raw. Your knees are shredded. You look pale and shaken, not at all like your usual smartass self. So forgive me if I call bullshit on your claims to be *fine*."

"I'm not a smartass," I grumbled, somewhat affronted. "I'm a sweetheart. Everyone says so."

"I must be the exception, then."

Rude!

"Are you going to proceed with this rescue mission or did you come here to insult me?"

His brows furrowed in a scowl as he tucked the flashlight in the crook of his neck, freeing his hands to undo my binds. As he worked at the knots, he began to interrogate me. "Let's start at the beginning. Who attacked you in that alley?"

My head tilted in surprise. "How do you know about the alley?"

"When you didn't show up to the bar, I went looking for you."

He'd been at The Witches Brew.

Damn Flo and her meddling!

"Didn't take me long to find your phone at the scene," he continued. "Along with clear signs of a struggle."

"Signs? What sort of signs?"

"The leaves were crushed and scattered, as though someone had been dragged off through them. Found one of your bracelets in the gutter. Scuff marks from your boots on the curb. Smears of blood from your knees..."

"Wow. You're like a regular Magnum PI. A modern Sherlock Holmes. Watch out, Maltese Falcon, he's coming for you!"

He ignored me, laser-focused on his task. He'd already freed my left side and moved on to my right. I lifted my arm and rolled the wrist, wincing a bit as feeling rushed back with a fierce tingle. The skin was rubbed raw where the ropes had chafed during my struggles. I had a feeling it would hurt like a bitch when my adrenaline wore off.

"Almost done," Graham murmured, yanking at the remaining binding with strong, impatient fingers. "There we go."

Free at last.

I flexed my fingers, grimacing in discomfort. "Thank you."

His eyes were on mine again. He hadn't moved away — he was still crouched by my legs, staring into my face with an unfathomable expression. "You about ready to get out of here?"

"I was ready six hours ago."

His lips tugged up at one side in a fleeting half-smile. I barely had time to process it — or to smother the swarm of nervous butterflies in my stomach the sight of it inspired — before he reached out, grabbed my hand, and tugged me to my feet. "Come on. Let's get out of here before they come back."

I didn't have the heart to tell him that the likelihood of three octogenarians returning to wreak more havoc in the middle of the night was slim to none. I'd bet my ass that Sally, Agatha, and Eliza were home in bed, curlers in their hair, hearing aids powered off, fast asleep until the morrow.

Graham led me toward the rickety stairs, pausing only to grab my leather bag and wool coat from the floor. He managed to tuck them both beneath one arm like a football without ever dropping my hand or the flashlight. Impressive coordination skills. It was taking all my concentration not to trip over my own feet as I followed him up the dark steps.

"Where are we?" I whispered to his broad shoulders.

"Abandoned house on the west side of the river, by Furlong Park."

"That's... random."

He grunted noncommittally.

"How did you find me here?"

"Tracked your laptop." His hand tightened briefly on mine. "Damn lucky they didn't think to ditch it when they grabbed you."

I blinked, stunned by his casual announcement. When I managed to summon words, they came out in a voice choked with disbelief. "You... you... *you tracked my laptop?*"

We'd reached the top of the stairs. Graham led me quickly through the first floor of the house, which was totally empty except for some litter and a dirty bare mattress leaning up against one graffiti-covered wall.

I jerked my hand against his grip, but he held fast. "Graham!"

He grunted again.

"Is that even legal? Tracking my laptop?"

"Seriously, Glinda? I didn't look at the Chris Hemsworth nudes saved on your desktop, if that's what you're worried about."

Oh, goodie, we were back to nicknames. I rolled my eyes. "I don't have any porn saved on my desktop, Graham Crackers. And even if I did... *Thor*? He doesn't do it for me. Captain America, on the other hand..."

This, he did not deign to answer.

"All I'm saying is," I babbled on, for reasons unknown. Looking back, I think I might have been in shock. "It's not about you looking through my computer. I have nothing to hide." *For the most part.* "I'm just pointing out, it's sort of an invasion of privacy—"

"You'd have preferred I left you to rot down there? Good to know. I'll remember that for next time." He sounded seriously peeved. His pace increased along with his annoyance, until he was dragging me through the dusty, abandoned house at such a clip, I nearly lost my footing on a loose floorboard.

"Would you slow down?" I scowled at his back, avoiding a particularly thick cobweb. "I'm in heels, here."

He sighed, but his pace slowed. Marginally. We reached the entryway. My eyes widened when I saw the window panel in the front door had been smashed out — presumably by Graham when he broke in earlier.

"Careful," he muttered, kicking some of the glass shards out of my path before he yanked open the door. He pulled me onto the front stoop, then down a set of uneven steps. Tufts of grass were shooting up between the bricks of the walkway. The hedges lining the chainlink fence were so overgrown, they practically formed a thicket around the gate.

It was pitch black out, the full moon hidden behind a thick blanket of clouds. The street appeared deserted, every house on the block dark and quiet. A few were boarded up, like the one we'd just exited, with faded foreclosure signs planted in their overgrown lawns, but most were patently ordinary. It looked like any other neighborhood in any other average American town. Not at all what I'd expected as the site of my kidnapping. Then again, nothing about my kidnapping had gone as expected.

We walked half a block, turned a corner, and stopped beside a familiar vehicle. Graham's black Ford Bronco. He jerked open the passenger door, snagged me around the waist, and planted my ass inside before I could even think about struggling.

"You don't need to manhandle me, I'm—"

The door slammed shut before I could finish.

I settled back against the smooth leather of the seat, trying not to let annoyance get the best of me. He had saved me, after all. If anything, I should be grateful. But my heart was racing with other emotions — a mix of pure adrenaline, simmering anger, and residual fear from the past six hours. I pressed a hand against my chest as though I might somehow calm my thudding pulse. It was still twice its normal speed when Graham folded his tall frame into the driver's seat beside me. He had a cellphone pressed to his ear. His words were low and clipped as he spoke into it.

"I've got her." He paused, listening for a beat. Whoever was on the other line said something that made his brows furrow inward. "Because you didn't need to know, that's why." Another pause. "You're cracked if you think I was about to put her at risk by announcing my presence with a light show courtesy of Salem PD at the scene. I made a judgment call. Deal with it."

My brows shot up in curiosity. I opened my mouth to ask who he was talking to, but was startled into silence before I had a chance as Graham reached suddenly into into my space to open the glove compartment. I shrank back against the leather seat, eyes locked on him as he retrieved the sleek, black handgun from the back waistband of his jeans and stashed it away. I heard the distant click of the compartment closing, but all my attention was fixed with laser-like focus on the back of his head. The fall of his lush hair, inches from my nose. I had the strangest urge to run my fingers through it.

Get it together, Gwen.

His warmth was there and then gone, so quickly I might've imagined it — except for the undeniable tingling on my thigh, where his forearm had pressed against it for the briefest of moments. I don't think I took a proper breath until the gun was shut out of sight and he was back on his side of the cab.

"I haven't gotten the details yet." His eyes flickered over to me, zeroing in on the hand at my heart. I hadn't realized it was still pressed there, and instantly pulled it down to my lap. "Because I was a bit busy untying her from a fucking chair in a fucking basement, that's why."

Who is it? I mouthed at him.

He glanced away, ignoring me as he listened for a moment. "Oh, fuck off. I'm not doing anything half-cocked. I never do. And if I chose this to be the first, I certainly wouldn't admit it to law enforcement." He paused, voice lowering to an ominous growl. "You don't get to lecture me on calm. You didn't see her down there."

My breath caught.

"I'm going to hunt these fuckers down and make them regret they ever touched a hair on her fucking head," he continued lowly. "And when I do, they'd better pray I'm in a more forgiving mood."

Um.

I shivered at the undiluted rage in his vow. His fury was in check — but only barely. It burned just below the surface, like a volcano on the brink of an eruption. Graham was silent for a moment, listening to, what I gathered from his expression, was an unwanted attempt at placation from the other caller.

"No. Not until she gets some sleep." He paused again. "Tough shit, Hightower. Tomorrow or never."

Hightower?

Caden!

Without saying goodbye, Graham disconnected, tossed his phone into the console tray by his gear shift, and jammed his thumb into the ignition button. The engine roared to life.

"Seatbelt," he ordered, not looking at me as he reached for his own. Hearing his tone — which was simmering with wrath — I didn't think it wise to argue. For once, I simply did as I was told. And as we peeled away from the curb and began to career down the street at twice the legal limit, I was glad for the safety measures. Graham's hands were tight on the steering wheel, the knuckles white with tension. His jaw was clenched, his brows furrowed in a dark expression that mirrored his brooding mood. He said nothing, and I didn't dare shatter the silence. Despite his claims about my so-called smartassery, I was not completely immune to his intimidating demeanor.

I glanced out my window. We'd crossed the bridge and were headed back toward the center of town. I watched until unfamiliar streets became recognizable once more, the seedy outskirts swapped for the well-lit suburban downtown I called home. It wasn't until we sped past the turn-off that would lead to my neighborhood that I risked a glance back at Graham's severe profile.

His scowl had deepened in the ten minutes of silence. A muscle ticked rhythmically in his cheek, like a bomb set to detonate. Swallowing down my anxiety, I cleared my throat with a light cough.

"You missed the turn."

The muscle in his jaw leapt again. "No, I didn't."

"But that's the fastest way to my house—"

"We aren't going to your house."

My mouth dropped open. "What?"

"Did you get hit over the head?"

"No."

"You experiencing hearing damage or something?"

"I heard you," I snapped, instantly annoyed at him — which, oddly, made my world feel more normal than it had in hours. "If you aren't taking me home, where are you taking me?"

"My place."

"Your— But— You— I—"

"You having a seizure? Should I pull over?"

"I don't want to go to your place!" I finally managed to get out, the words choked with rising panic.

"Tough."

"Graham!"

"Snap at me all you want. Won't change our destination."

"Graham." I strove for a calm tone. "Please. I've had a long day. I want to go home. I want a glass of wine the size of my head. Actually, wine isn't going to cut it — make that a glass of whiskey the size of my head. I want to take a long, hot shower. I want to climb into my bed and forget all this ever happened. Cant you understand that?"

He nodded. "Sure."

"So, you'll take me home?" I asked, brightening.

"Nope."

Hellfire!

"Why?"

"Nothing you just listed that you can't do at my place."

"But—"

"I have a bottle of Macallan. I have a damn nice shower. And I have a big fucking comfy bed."

I so did *not* want to think about Graham's big fucking comfy bed. In fact, such thoughts were in direct violation of my *avoid-any-*

information-about-Graham-at-all-costs policy. Such thoughts were a gateway drug to even more dangerous contemplations. Like, for instance... what Graham would look like totally naked, on top of me, in said big fucking comfy bed. What Graham would look like in... *me*.

The sudden ring of an incoming call filled the cab, jolting me out of my illicit thoughts. I flinched violently in my seat — *jumpy, party of one* — as Graham's phone connected automatically to the Bronco's bluetooth speakers. The center console display declared "DESMOND BOURNE CALLING" in persistent letters. Glad for the distraction, I watched as he punched a button on the steering wheel, silencing the shrill ring.

"Des," Graham said by way of greeting.

"It's Florence!" Flo sounded half hysterical, her voice slurred with tears. "Please tell me you found her!"

He shot me a brief glance. "She's here. She can tell you herself."

"Flo?" I whispered thickly, leaning forward in my seat until my face was close to the center console, as though that might somehow bring me closer to my best friend.

"GWENNIE! Oh my god, what happened? Where were you? Are you okay?"

"I'm fine."

Graham scoffed under his breath.

"You promise?" Flo sounded no less calm. "I was so worried, you have no idea. When you didn't show up... I should've realized right away! But you know how I get when there's a live band, I was caught up in the set. They were doing that cover of Howlin' For You by The Black Keys, with the electric guitar solo..."

I nodded, fully understanding. "That's a killer cover."

Graham scoffed again.

"Totally." Flo sniffled audibly. "Anyway, thank goodness

Graham realized something was wrong and went to look for you, or it might've been too late..."

My eyes flickered over to the man in the driver's seat. His eyes were fixed on the road, but I knew he was listening. That muscle in his jaw was ticking again.

"God, I don't even want to think what might've happened to you!" Flo's voice cracked. "I'm a terrible friend."

"You aren't."

"Where are you now?"

"In Graham's Bronco."

"Tell him to drive you over here!"

"Sounds good," I agreed instantly, thrilled by the idea.

"Absolutely not," Graham said at the same time, his tone bossy as ever.

I scowled at him. "Would you be reasonable?"

"Not in my wheelhouse, babe."

The endearment hit me like a punch to the stomach. I reeled back in my seat, too startled to speak. Graham just smirked at me, his lips half-tugged up at one side in a way that made my mouth go completely dry.

"Hello?" Flo said through the speakers. "Anyone there?"

Tearing my gaze away, I refocused on the call. "I've asked Graham — repeatedly — to take me home, but he's being completely uncompromising—"

"You wouldn't know compromise if it bit you in the ass," Graham muttered lowly.

"What was that?" Flo asked.

"Nothing," I snapped. "Apparently, I'm not permitted to go home. Or to your place."

"What?" Flo cried, outraged on my behalf. "Why?"

"He's insisting I spend the night at *his* place."

Silence blasted over the line before Flo sucked in a sharp,

audible breath. When she spoke again, her tone had heartened significantly. "Good. That's good."

Good?

Good?!

"Flo!"

"Don't *Flo* me!" she fired back. "Graham will keep you safe."

"But you know—" I broke off into silence, feeling my cheeks heat. I'd never been more aware of Graham listening to my every word than I was in that instant. "You know I can't— You know I don't—"

Don't sleep in anyone's bed but my own, I finished inside my head, unable to voice the embarrassing confession aloud. I could feel Graham looking at me, could feel his curiosity thickening the air between us, but I kept my eyes on the center console.

"Oh, Gwennie..." Flo sighed in sympathy. She knew all about my insomnia issues. She also knew I'd never spent the night with anyone. Not a date, not a boyfriend, not a slumber party. I didn't crash on friend's couches after late-night benders, didn't doze off during movies or boring conversations, never climbed into someone else's bed — at least, not with the intention to go to sleep. I couldn't get my eyes to close with someone lying next to me, couldn't get my body to relax enough to drift into dreamland if I wasn't completely on my own.

Solo.

Safe.

"Flo," I said a little desperately.

"I know, honey. And I sympathize, I do... but at the same time, I don't want you to be on your own after what you've been through tonight."

"I said I'm fine!"

"Yeah, but I know you well enough to know when you're *not* fine," she said gently. "Even if you insist otherwise."

My scowl deepened.

"One night won't kill you," she assured me. "Rules are meant to be broken. Or, at least, bent a bit."

"But—"

"Seems like you're in good hands. I'll let you go. We'll check in tomorrow."

"Flo!"

"Sleep well!"

"*FLO!*"

The speakers chimed as the call disconnected. I collapsed back against the leather seat and sank my teeth into my bottom lip, trying to quiet my jagged breaths. Anger and frustration were pooling in my gut, bubbling up my throat with the urge to scream and cry like a kid having a tantrum. I balled my hands into fists in my lap and swallowed down the gathering emotion, determined not to let Graham see me shaken.

He swung the Bronco sharply to the left, down a narrow side street that looped onto Pickering Wharf. We pulled up outside a brick building a stone's throw from Salem Harbor. Graham hit a button on his visor, triggering an automatic door, and drove into a triple-bay garage. The other two spots were occupied by a sleek motorcycle and a not-so-sleek SUV with windows tinted so dark, it was impossible to see inside. Like the Bronco, both vehicles were black.

I guessed Graham had a favorite color.

The door shut behind us with a smooth clunk, enclosing us in the garage. Graham jabbed the ignition button and the engine rumbled into silence, leaving us in startling quiet. My eyes drifted — with considerable reluctance — over to the man in the driver's seat. He'd already removed his seatbelt and sat there silently, half-turned to face me with one arm slung over the gap between our seats. His hand was planted on my leather headrest, mere inches from my face.

I sucked in a sharp breath, trying not to squirm as his fingers pressed into the leather — five small indentations. He wasn't even touching me, he was touching my freaking *seat*, yet for some unfathomable reason, that touch felt more erotic than anything I'd experienced in my entire romantic history. A shot of pure, undeniable arousal shot through me like a bolt of lightning.

"Please," I half-whispered, not above begging if it meant getting away from him — and the unwelcome feelings he was stirring inside me. "Just take me home."

"No."

"I don't understand why you're so insistent on me staying here."

"Beginning to realize there's a lot about me you don't understand."

My eyes narrowed. He was so damn arrogant. And rude. And... alarmingly attractive.

Hellfire.

It wasn't fair. It made no sense at all. I couldn't stand this man. I loathed him to my core and always would. Right? So... why was I sitting in his passenger seat, torn equally between the impulse to wrap my hands around his throat and strangle the life out of him, and the urge to wind my arms around his neck and press my mouth against his?

No, Gwen.

Bad, Gwen.

Squeezing my thighs together, I shifted on the leather seat and tried my damndest to ignore the insane magnetic pull between us. I blamed sleep deprivation. And post traumatic stress. That was the only reasonable explanation for the feelings fluttering around inside my chest — not to mention several other, slightly *lower* places on my anatomy that I felt disinclined to acknowledge at this point in time.

"Besides," Graham murmured, leaning forward into my

space so his face was only a few inches from mine. I could've pulled back, but I seemed to be paralyzed. All the air in the cab compressed inward, squeezing the oxygen from my lungs. My eyes were fixed on his lips as they continued, "My place has one thing yours definitely doesn't."

"Um," I breathed, trying not to think about his big fucking comfy bed. "A state of the art security system?"

He shook his head.

"Attack dogs?"

Another shake.

"A moat full of flesh-eating piranhas?"

Shaking his head one last time, his mouth tugged up in a familiar half-smile and his eyes flared with warmth. Slowly, he leaned another inch into my space. I fought the urge to squirm in my seat, clenching my thighs together so hard, I was pretty sure I stopped circulation to my toes.

"Then what does it have?" I asked, afraid of the answer. His face was alarmingly close to my own. I could smell his body wash, could see the tiny flecks of darker green in his irises, could hear every breath that pumped in and out the broad column of his throat. Alarm bells began to sound in my head.

PROXIMITY ALERT!

PULL BACK!

REVERSE COURSE!

But those alarms stuttered into silence as Graham's smug, smirking mouth gave me an answer.

"Me, Gwendolyn. It has me."

CHAPTER TEN

A special place in Hell? For me? That's actually so thoughtful.
- Gwen Goode, flattered by an enemy

I shadowed Graham from the Bronco across the garage bays, through a fortified steel door that he unlocked with a passcode of six numbers, up a dim stairwell, and into his home. It was dark inside, the only light coming from the wall of glass directly opposite us, which opened out onto a harbor-facing terrace. The water beyond was a spill of ink, white boats bobbing like ghosts on the surface, hulls catching the moonlight as they drifted on their mooring lines.

"Lights," Graham commanded as the heavy door swung shut at my back. Overhead, a wrought iron track of exposed-filament bulbs instantly flared on, illuminating the space. Any expectations I'd had about his home (namely: a consummate bachelor pad dripping with modern touches, garish leather accents, and a complete absence of artwork — an aesthetic I collectively liked to call *frat-boy-chic*) instantly vanished. It took effort to keep my mouth from dropping open in shock as my eyes swung around the roomy loft.

His decor didn't feel like any particular style I could put a name to. Not modern or transitional or bohemian or eclectic. It simply felt like... him.

Like Graham.

Highly attractive, blatantly affluent, and yet, not ostentatious. Everything from the smell — something deliciously musky, spice and sage edged with smoke — to the colors he'd chosen for his furnishings — deep, camel brown leather and warm, varnished woods — to the custom built-in bookshelves behind his heavy oak desk screamed *Property of Graham Graves* in undeniable, bold letters.

It was all one massive open space, with a textured partition wall to separate the sleeping alcove from the kitchen and dining area. Thick wood beams spanned the vaulted ceilings, along with exposed ducts painted matte black. Brick dominated the walls, lending warmth and character, a pleasing contrast to the thick hardwood floors beneath our feet where oriental rugs of supremely high quality were scattered here and there to create a natural flow. The light fixtures were heavy and industrial in a way that seemed hand-crafted; the furnishings were a mix of old and new, antique and classic, simple enough in style but clearly selected with great care. Huge abstract art prints dominated the walls, tying everything together into a pleasing, richly rustic visual palette.

Nothing about the loft was overtly masculine, but at the same time it was abundantly clear a man lived here. There was no clutter. No throw pillows, no tchotchkes, no knickknacks. Not even a candle on the impressive mantle over his fireplace. There was also not a speck of dust anywhere to be seen, not a dirty dish left out on the butcher-block countertop, nor an item out of place on his imposing, harbor-facing desk.

A furl of appreciation stirred in my stomach as I took it all in. I was a sucker for a good sense of interior design, and Graham's place appealed to me on an almost visceral level. I wondered if he'd decorated it himself or hired a professional. I hoped it was the latter, because the possibility that he had such good taste — taste that was, in fact, rather similar to my own — was a dangerously appealing quality.

"Gwendolyn."

My eyes jerked away from the loft to the man himself. While I'd stopped in my tracks to gawk, he'd moved deeper inside, depositing my coat and bag on the kitchen countertop along the way. He now stood in the seating area arranged around the mammoth fireplace, watching me with an unreadable expression on his face.

"Come here," he said, his voice softer than I'd ever heard it.

My feet jolted into motion before I made the conscious decision to acquiesce, as though he'd yanked on some invisible tether that connected us. My knees felt a bit weak as the distance between us shrank from feet to inches. I locked them tight when I rocked to a stop before him, head tilting back to hold his gaze.

For a long beat, nothing happened. We merely stared at one another, not speaking or touching, taking each other's measure in the gathering silence. The tension between us mounted, the tether going taut as a bowstring.

Graham was the one to break the spell. Jaw locking, he looked away from me, shrugged out of his leather jacket, tossed it down on the arm of the sofa and then settled on the cushion beside it. When a few seconds passed and I failed to join him, he sighed and muttered a terse, "Sit."

I stood my ground. "Bathroom?"

"Past the kitchen. There's a door in the alcove to the left."

He'd barely finished speaking when I scurried away, desperate for a little breathing room. Being in his space was confusing my head. I barely knew which way was up. I needed a bit of distance, that was all. Some space to get my thoughts in order. And as soon as I saw an opportunity, I fully planned on doing what I did best when it concerned Graham Graves.

Bolting.

I closed myself in the bathroom, relieved for a moment of solitude. All the emotions I'd spent the past few hours suppressing were starting to claw their way to the surface. I knew it was only a matter of time before they overwhelmed me. And I wanted — no, I *needed* — to be alone when that happened. Being vulnerable in front of other people wasn't a weakness I allowed myself. Not if I had any other choice in the matter.

Graham's bathroom was, like the rest of his space, surgically clean and surprisingly colorful. Dark teal walls, heated ceramic tile floors, a lively Picasso print over the freestanding pedestal tub framed in the same metallic copper as the sink and tub fixtures. There were curtained windows that overlooked the terrace. A gorgeous walk-in shower with floor-to-ceiling glass doors took up almost half the space. But the thing that caught my attention was the woman in the mirror.

I stifled a shriek at my reflection. I looked ghastly — pale and shaky, my expression drained of its usual color. My smattering of freckles stood out like bullet holes on the bridge of my nose. My mascara was smeared beneath my eyes in a way only Hetti would've approved of. My pretty ivory, single-sleeved top was wrinkled and streaked with goddess knows what, as was the skin of my bare arm. And I was missing one of my chunky silver bracelets.

Did Graham have it, or was it still sitting in that alley gutter?

My hair was the worst of all — an unsalvageable mess of

waves and frizz. I didn't even attempt to tame it. But, after taking the world's longest pee, I did wipe away my ruined eye makeup with a tissue and pinch a bit of color back into my cheeks. I wished rather desperately that I'd paused to grab my purse before bolting to the bathroom. I'd been in such a hurry to escape Graham...

Ugh.

I eyed the closed door, dreading the moment I had to walk back through it. That thin panel of wood was all that separated me from an interrogation about the events of this evening. I wasn't sure I was ready for that. More, I wasn't sure I was ready to be back in Graham's presence. The more time we spent together, the harder it was becoming to keep him in the safe, little box I'd shoved him into two years ago. My attempts at hating his guts were severely hindered by constant proximity to his muscular body and intoxicating smell and perfect taste in interior design and domineering-yet-devastatingly-appealing propensity for dishing out orders...

Get a hold of yourself, Gwen.

Conscious I'd been in the bathroom for a very long time, I steeled my shoulders, took a deep breath, and walked back into the loft. Graham was sitting on the sofa, forearms planted on his knees, eyes on the fireplace. He'd lit it in my absence; several wood logs were already engulfed in flame in the grate, emitting loud pops and crackles as they caught. He didn't turn to look at me, but his back tensed beneath the fabric of his black t-shirt as my footfalls sounded against the floors, bringing me to his side.

Saying nothing, I dropped down onto the opposite cushion, as far away from him as I could get — and nearly groaned as I sank into the soft, buttery leather. Now that my adrenaline had officially worn off, exhaustion was catching up with me. I fought off a yawn as I knit my hands together in my lap, resisting the urge to get too comfortable.

"So," I said, shattering the silence.

"So," Graham echoed, straightening in his seat, turning toward me.

My heart stuttered stupidly in my chest. I made a point of glancing around the loft, avoiding his eyes. Avoiding his proximity. Avoiding the tension that was, once again, charging the air between us. "So... this is your place."

"Mmm."

"It's nice," I offered.

"I'm aware."

My lips pursed. "You know, arrogance isn't an attractive trait."

"Who says I'm trying to attract you?"

"Do you always have to have the last word?"

"Why does it bother you so much when I do?"

"As I said before... *arrogance*. It's not exactly a likable quality."

"I'm an arrogant prick because I agreed that my place is nice?"

I gritted my teeth. "That's not what I'm saying—"

"What are you saying? That I shouldn't agree with an accurate assessment? That I should play coy, for the sake of propriety?" He shook his head. "Not how I operate. I like nice things. I spend a fuck of a lot of money acquiring them, surrounding myself with them, and caring for them. I have no qualms about admitting that."

I sighed. "Do you always have to be so... blunt?"

"Blunt, honest... What's the difference? I call it like I see it. Always." He shrugged. "You may live your life running away from anything that threatens your perfect world order, but I'll choose authenticity over artificial bullshit any day."

Instantly, I was enraged, all sense of exhaustion fleeing in a heartbeat. "Where the hell do you get off saying something like that to me? I do not run away from things! My world is not perfect! *Obviously*. Or have you not been paying attention at all these past few days?"

He sighed. "Gwen—"

"In case it slipped your mind, I was just kidnapped! And tied to a chair in a grimy basement! I could've died! Then, I was rescued by a *total jerk*—" I glared at him, my volume scaling up at least two decibels along with my anger. "—who, for some reason known only to him, will not let me go home! Which, I will point out, is where I want to be! Because it's the middle of the night! I'm exhausted! My wrists hurt! I'm starving! There's dirt under my fingernails! My knees are all crusty with blood and... *It. Is. Gross!*"

"Gwen, you need to calm down—"

"Not to mention," I barreled right over him. "My favorite tights are ripped to shreds — and they were *expensive*! Seriously, more money than anyone has any right to charge for a freaking pair of stockings! Frankly, I should've known better than to buy them in the first place, but the salesgirl was very convincing when she said they were practically indestructible! Some new composite weave that even terrorist bullets couldn't tear through during a shoot out—"

"Gwendolyn." Graham sidled closer to me, eyes narrowing. "I mean it—"

"But you know what? She *lied*. I wasn't even in a shoot out but they're completely in tatters! She lied and I *fell for it* and now they're ruined, and tomorrow I should go back to that store and show her the rips because, truly, it's not good business to *lie* to your customers, especially in the event that they get *kidna*—"

Graham — who had evidently grown tired of my semi-hysterical tirade — closed the remaining distance between us in one swift lunge. His hands planted in the leather around my head, his face angled down, and his lips pressed firmly against mine. He swallowed the second half of the word *kidnapped* with a fast, furious kiss.

My brain short circuited.

As quickly as it began, the kiss ended. In fact, I wasn't even sure it counted as a kiss, seeing as I was too thunderstruck to participate in it. He pulled back, looping his arm over the back rest of the sofa, looking completely calm and not at all like he'd just put a stop to my sleep-deprived tantrum by quite literally kissing me silent.

"You just kissed me," I said dumbly, when I was once again able to speak.

"Seemed like the quickest way to shut you up."

I stared at him, bug-eyed. Surely, I'd just hallucinated that. My brain was manufacturing delusions. I was shaking, my whole body trembling head to toe. "You can't just kiss me."

"Too late."

"Graham! What the— Where are you going?"

"Stay."

Like I was a dog!

He was already up off the couch, crossing the loft to the kitchen area. I kept my wide eyes on the fireplace, trying desperately to get myself under control. I needed to get the hell out of there. ASAP. But, strangely, my limbs seemed incapable of movement no matter how many times I ordered myself to get to my feet and walk over to the door. I simply sat there, listening to the sounds of a cabinet opening, a bottle unstoppering, footsteps approaching.

When Graham reappeared, there were two lowball glasses of amber liquor in his hands. He passed one to me in silence. I accepted it, not knowing what else to do. My hands were shaking so much, the whiskey sloshed a bit as I brought it to my mouth and took a large sip. Truth be told, it was more of a gulp. It burned all the way down my throat, a hot rush of fire that exploded in my empty stomach. I immediately sipped again, knowing it would steady me once the after-burn subsided.

"Better?" Graham asked after a while.

I nodded.

"You calm?"

I nodded again, still not looking at him.

"You going to freak out?"

I shook my head.

"Good. I'd hate to have to kiss you again."

My eyes flashed over to him, brows furrowed in a glare. "Oh, in your wildest dreams!"

His eyes were glittering with amusement and something else. Something... decidedly heated. It set off another rush of fire in my stomach, one that had nothing to do with the contents of my glass.

"Finish your drink," he murmured. "Then, you're going to tell me everything that happened, every detail you can remember about the people who took you."

Hellfire.

My mind raced as I contemplated how much to tell him about my unlikely kidnappers. I hadn't forgotten what he'd said on the phone to Detective Hightower.

I'm going to hunt these fuckers down and make them regret they ever touched a hair on her fucking head. And when I do, they'd better pray I'm in a more forgiving mood.

Would he truly track down three grandmothers and exact vengeance for their — admittedly misguided — attempt at protecting me? I didn't think so. Then again, I didn't have him kissing me on my BINGO card for the evening, either. If there was even the slightest chance he planned to go after Aunt Colette's friends... I wasn't going to be the one who enabled it. Better to talk to them on my own, try to reason with them in the light of day. Preferably somewhere with plenty of witnesses, so they couldn't repeat that whole witchy-roofie-powder maneuver.

I took slow sips of my whiskey, making small appreciative hums in the back of my throat with each swallow. A languorous glow began to spread through me, warming me from the inside out, chasing away the residual chill from the dank basement. I fought off a face-splitting yawn. The urge to curl up into a ball in the corner of Graham's ultra-comfy couch was growing stronger by the minute.

"Gwendolyn."

I looked over at the man sitting beside me. His whiskey was barely touched. The glass looked fragile in his large hand, the amber inside it catching the firelight as he slowly swirled it around, his strong wrist making absentminded rotations. He watched the small vortex spinning for a moment before his eyes lifted to pierce mine. They were the same shade of green as the painting on the wall behind him.

"Tell me what happened tonight," he said softly. But it was a deceptive softness. There was steel beneath it. This was no request; it was a command. I'd been lulled into a false sense of security by his quiet reprieve, I realized. I'd fallen so easily into the trap he laid for me, relaxed by the whiskey he provided, soothed by the soft leather and low lighting and crackling fire.

Damn, he was good.

"Gwendolyn," he prompted a second time.

I tightened my grip on the glass in my hand. It was almost empty. "I don't know what you want me to tell you, Graham."

"The truth, for starters."

"There's not much to say. It all happened so fast, and I was unconscious for most of it."

"Just start at the beginning."

"Okay." I blew out a sharp breath. "I was walking to meet Flo at The Witches Brew—"

"Leaving from where? Work?"

I nodded.

"So, you left The Gallows. What time was this?"

"Maybe around eight? Eight-fifteen? I stayed late, doing inventory."

"Alone?"

I nodded again. "My barista left at six, when we closed. After I locked up, I cut straight across town."

"Was anyone following you?"

"Not that I was aware of. But I can't really say for sure. There were a zillion people out. You know how it is on Friday nights. The sidewalks were mobbed with ghost tours and tourists and couples and costumed street performers..."

"Mmm."

"So..." I heaved a sigh. "I took a shortcut."

Graham made an unhappy noise. It was almost a growl.

I glanced at him. "What?"

"Your shortcut. You mean a dimly lit alley with no security cameras."

"I'll have you know, I've taken that shortcut a hundred times."

"And on your hundred-and-first, you got fucking kidnapped," he pointed out, jaw tightening. "Reckless behavior doesn't get any less reckless just because you've done it before and walked away unscathed. If you continually put yourself at risk, your luck will eventually run out."

"Please, spare me the lecture. I can handle myself."

"Is that what you were doing in that basement? Handling yourself?"

Fury and frustration flashed through me. I spoke without thinking. "If you saw what I'd seen growing up, if you took a walk through the places I spent my formative years, you'd know I've been in far more dangerous places than little old Salem. That basement was a freaking palace compared to some of the shit-holes I called home, trust me."

Graham tensed. It was small, almost imperceptible, but I saw it nonetheless. I clamped my lips shut, wishing I could snatch my words back, but it was too late.

Get a hold of yourself, Gwen.

Curiosity sparked in Graham's eyes as they moved over my face but, thankfully, he didn't push me to elaborate. He said nothing. Asked nothing. Merely took a small sip of his whiskey and gestured for me to continue.

"As I was saying... I took the shortcut," I told him, summoning my most measured tone through sheer force of will. "I was looking down at my phone, answering a text from Florence—"

Graham made another unhappy noise. "Distracted. Perfect target."

I pointedly ignored him and finished, "That's when they grabbed me."

There was a long silence. I got the sense he was waiting for me to continue. When I didn't, he slammed down his glass on the coffee table. I flinched at the sudden impact. I flinched a second time as he exploded, "*And?*"

"And what?"

"That's it? That's all you're going to say?"

I shrugged, trying to maintain composure. "What else do you expect me to say?"

"I was hoping for a bit more in the way of detail. A physical description, maybe. Were they male, female, tall, short, fat, thin... What kind of car did they drive? Make, model, plate number, color... You must have seen something useful."

"Well, I didn't," I lied. "Or, if I did, I don't remember. There's just a blank space in my memory between walking through that alley and waking up in that basement, tied to a chair. I was there a long time. Hours. And then... you were there."

Graham did not look satisfied by this explanation. Not remotely. If I'd expected him to take my word on blind faith, I should've known better. For the next few minutes, he proceeded to pepper me with questions, rapid-fire. Almost like he knew I was lying and was attempting to trip me up.

How many were there? More than one? More than three? Yes, it matters. What did their voices sound like? Did they speak with any accent? Southern? Boston? English? It's hard to believe they didn't say anything at all. Uh huh. Did they smell like anything in particular? Gasoline or cigarettes or pot or incense or perfume or bad BO? Everyone smells like something. Think back. Then think harder, damn it. Come on.

"I don't know," I told him over and over, a persistent refrain. "I don't remember."

By the time he ran out of questions, Graham's cheek muscle was ticking like a bomb again as he stared at me, jaw clenching and unclenching. I resisted the urge to wilt against the couch cushions, drained by his interrogation. I liked to think I was a decent enough liar — goddess knew I'd had the need for it, growing up with a mother like mine — but those green eyes seemed to cut straight through my bullshit. Straight through *me*, down to my soul. It took all my resolve to keep from squirming in my seat as he eyed me with an unreadable expression. It might've been disappointment. It might've been something far more intimidating — something I was afraid to put a name to, to be perfectly frank.

Moving with deliberate slowness, he pushed to his feet and walked the length of the couch until he was towering over me. The breath caught in my throat and my lungs convulsed as he leaned down, planting his hands on the leather cushion of the back rest to either side of my head. Just as he had right before he kissed me. Only this time, his lips stopped short of mine — so close, I could feel his breath fanning my lips.

I was statue-still. Unblinking. Unbreathing.

"Gwendolyn."

"Y-yes?" I stammered.

"Are you lying to me?"

"Why would I lie?" I was unable to look away from his eyes. They were so close to mine. Closer than they'd ever been. My palms were sweaty as I knit them tightly together in my lap, digging my fingernails into the thin flesh above each knuckle. My heart was experiencing such palpitations, I was pretty certain I was going to go into cardiac arrest any second.

"That's a good question. One I intend to find out the answer to — with or without your cooperation." Graham's eyes, just for a second, flashed down to my mouth. His voice was thick. Almost a rasp. "Go get in my shower. There are cobwebs in your hair."

Sliding sideways, I shot off the couch like a bullet from a gun. I didn't dare look back.

WATER BEAT DIRECTLY DOWN on me from the giant rainfall shower-head, the temperature one click away from scalding. I'd been in the shower for what felt like a full hour, telling myself I'd leave once the tap started to run cold. But my fingers were pruny and it was still hotter than a geyser. Graham must have a fantastic water heater.

A fist rapped against the door — three hard knocks that made me jump. My eyes cut across the steam-filled room in terror. He wasn't about to burst in here, was he?

"I'm naked!" I screeched, scrambling to cover the bits of my flesh I wasn't altogether eager for Graham to see.

"That an invitation?"

"Only if you have a death wish!"

His low chuckle was muffled by the door. "Relax. I was just checking to see if you were still alive in there. Glad to know I won't have to deal with your waterlogged corpse. It's been a long enough night already."

I scowled at him, even though he couldn't see it. "I'll be out soon."

There was a long pause. "There are towels in the cabinet beside the tub. Spare toothbrushes in the drawer under the sink. Use whatever you want. I'll leave some clothes for you to sleep in by the door."

Swallowing against the sudden lump in my throat, I croaked out a thank you and turned to press my face against the tile wall. *Hellfire.* That was actually kind of... thoughtful. I much preferred it when he was rude. It was easier to deal with him.

I pressed my face harder, wishing I could hide out in the shower for the rest of the night. Or possibly for the rest of my life. But I'd already shampooed, deep conditioned, and scrubbed my body head to toe twice, using a liberal helping of Graham's expensive body wash. Any more exfoliation, I'd look like a piece of sandpaper when I finally rejoined the world of the living.

With reluctance, I reached out and shut off the valve, stopping the steady flow of water. I found the towels right where he said they would be and dried myself off, my limbs moving at a pace that would impress a sloth as I dabbed water droplets from my skin, then wrapped it around me in a tight sarong. In the drawer beneath the sink — which, like the rest of the loft, was freakishly organized — I found a spare toothbrush still wrapped in plastic and a hairbrush. I made unapologetic use of both.

The mirror was fogged over. I wiped a small window away, so I could see my face. My skin was pink with heat and softened by the steam. My auburn hair was a shade darker than usual, still damp from the shower. There were deep bags beneath my eyes. Still, I looked significantly better than I had the last time I caught my reflection.

Cracking open the door a sliver to peer out, I found the kitchen beyond encased in darkness. Only the light from the dying fire in the grate illuminated the loft, warm flickers of red and yellow that danced across the heavy beamed ceilings and textured brick walls. Graham was nowhere in sight, but my eyes fell on the stack of clothing he'd left for me on the threshold of the bathroom. I snatched it and slipped back inside to get dressed.

The t-shirt fell well past my thighs, more dress than top. The sweatpants were laughably large on me. I rolled them several times at the hips, but they still pooled at the ankles, inches of excess fabric dragging on the floor with each step.

Oh well.

I wasn't walking in Paris Fashion Week. And it was either this or my own grimy outfit — which I had no intentions of ever letting touch my flesh again. The bloody, torn tights were already wadded into a ball in his trash bin.

Before I could talk myself out of it, I shut the lights and slipped out the door. My footsteps were silent as I made my way through the kitchen. I set my bundle of dirty clothing on the countertop where Graham had left my other belongings, and bent to set my boots to the floor. Rising back to full height, I nearly screamed when I saw a mammoth shadowy figure standing less than a foot to my left.

"Hellfire! You scared the bejeezus out of me!"

Graham's grin was a flash of white in the darkness. "Sorry," he said, sounding not the least bit remorseful.

"It's bad manners to sneak up on people."

"Occupational hazard. I'm used to moving in silence."

My head tilted as I eyed him, vision slowly adjusting to the darkness. He'd changed into sweatpants that matched the pair I was wearing — dark grey, hanging low on his hips. He was shirtless, his broad chest on full display, his abdominal muscles defined in eight distinct indentations, the v-cut lines somehow even sharper than they'd been during his teenage Lifeguard God tenure.

Christ.

I sucked in a breath and forced my eyes not to wander south of his chin. "Can you put on a shirt?"

"Babe, the pants were a concession. I usually sleep naked."

My eyes bugged out. "If you're trying to entice me to sleep here, it's not working."

"If I was trying to entice you, you'd know it."

"From the nauseated sensation?"

His head tilted down, stopping dangerously close to mine. "You can talk as much shit as you want, smartass. You're still sleeping here, with or without my enticement."

"What are you going to do if I try to leave? Tie me to a chair in your basement?"

"Effective method, if unoriginal. But I was thinking of tying you to something else. My bed would work nicely."

"Do you often have to resort to threats to get women into your bed?"

"Usually, I have more trouble getting them out of it."

"*Arrogant!*"

As if he hadn't heard me at all, he dropped suddenly into a crouch before me. I stared down at the top of his head, baffled, as he began to push the fabric of my pants up my left leg.

"What are you doing?" I squeaked as his large hands found my battered kneecap. His strong fingers were unbelievably gentle as they probed the torn skin. "Graham—"

"Shh," he muttered, reaching into his pocket. A small tube of antiseptic ointment materialized, along with two bandages. "I'm busy."

I blinked. Hard.

Ripping the paper packaging open with his teeth, he made quick work of bandaging my knees, one after another. It took all my concentration to remain completely still as his fingertip smoothed a dollop of the ointment onto my cuts, as his hands affixed the adhesive edges, pressing them firmly against my skin.

Memories flashed through my mind unbidden, a kaleidoscope of watercolor images. A little girl on a beach with a foot full of urchin spines. A gorgeous lifeguard with a first aid kit, telling her everything would be all right.

I got you, Firecracker.

"There," he said when he was finished, unrolling my pant legs again. "Good as new."

I tried to speak, tried to form a *thank you*, but the words kept getting lodged in my throat. Graham didn't seem to mind, though. He was standing again, even closer than before, staring down at me.

"Time for bed," he announced.

"Bed?"

"Bed. Sleep. You. Now."

"I'm not tired."

"I don't care."

My eyes narrowed. "Why do you have to immediately follow up every nice thing you do with something so annoying?"

"You haven't seen how nice I can be, yet, babe. Not by a long shot."

The blatant suggestion in his tone frazzled my brainwaves. "That's— you're— I'm not—"

"Gwendolyn," he cut off my inarticulate splutters. "I'm going to brush my teeth."

"Congrats."

Ignoring my flippant remark, he took a step closer. I automatically moved backward, exhaling sharply when the countertop bit into my spine. *Damn it all to hell.* I had nowhere to run.

"That should take me about two minutes," he continued, planting his hands on the butcher block, bracketing me inside his arms. His bare chest was so close, I could almost feel the heat of it. "Three, tops."

"I guess gum health isn't a top priority, huh?"

"And when I get back," he said, as if I hadn't spoken. "You'd better be in my bed."

I jerked my chin up, indignant. Unfortunately, this brought my face within a hairsbreadth of his. My heart, already pounding like a drum, tripped over itself inside my chest. Even though I knew no good could come of it, I couldn't stop myself from asking, "And if I'm not?"

He grinned again — and, let me tell you, up close that grin was nearly enough to knock me flat on my ass — as if I'd said exactly what he wanted to hear. As if I'd thrown down some sort of challenge. One he couldn't wait to partake in.

Without another word, he pushed off the counter and walked away. I remained immobilized, unable to breathe or blink, let alone make my legs function. Before I heard the bathroom door click shut, he called out one last time.

"Timer starts now."

Hellfire.

CHAPTER ELEVEN

Dating a man for less than a month is not a relationship. It's a free trial.
- Gwen Goode, unsubscribing

Two minutes felt like two years as I lay in the dark, waiting for him to return. His king-sized bed was ridiculously comfortable, the duvet a brushed beige linen, the mattress itself a perfect balance of firm and feather-soft. Despite this, I couldn't relax. I stared up at the ceiling, heart racing like I'd just run a marathon. The small clock on the bedside table read 3:46AM in glowing white numbers. Now that the fire had completely burned down to embers, it was the only source of light besides the shafts of moonlight that slanted in through the skylight directly overhead.

My pulse spiked when I heard the soft click of the bathroom door, followed by the steady patter of bare feet crossing the loft. Through the kitchen. Around his office area. Past the sofa.

Wait.

Past the sofa?

As in... he isn't planing to *sleep* on said sofa?

The footsteps kept coming and, seconds later, a shadowy form rounded the partition and entered the sleeping alcove. Graham walked directly to the other side of the bed, pulled back the duvet, and slid in beside me without a flicker of hesitation.

I jerked the covers up to my chin. "What are you doing?"

"Playing soccer."

I rolled my eyes. "Hilarious. I mean what are you doing *here*? In this bed?"

"It's my bed."

"Aren't you planning to be a gentleman and crash on the couch?"

"Nope." He shifted against his pillows, glancing over at me with one hand propped behind his head. "I've never been much of a gentleman."

"At least you're self-aware."

"Finally, she compliments me."

"That wasn't a compliment. It was an insult."

"No walking it back now. You've admitted I have at least one admirable trait." I could hear the smile in his voice. "Now, shut the hell up and close your eyes. It's four in the morning and my alarm is set to go off at six-thirty."

"Makes sense," I muttered. "The antichrist *would* wake at such an ungodly hour."

He chuckled lowly but said nothing else. Clearly, he was done talking. I listened to him shifting around on his side of the bed — which, thankfully, was so spacious, there was no chance of limbs tangling awkwardly in the night — as he found a comfortable sleeping position. After a few minutes, his breathing began to level out as he drifted off.

I continued to stare up at the skylight, unable to sleep despite the deep exhaustion crashing through my system in relentless waves. The moon was clearly visible, a luminous orb peeking through the sparse clouds. It was still almost full and seemed abnormally close to earth, twice its normal size.

"Fun fact," a drowsy voice said from the other side of the bed. "When your eyes are open, you aren't sleeping."

"Really?" I gasped. "I had no idea."

"Go to sleep, Gwen. I mean it."

I rolled onto my side to properly glare at him. "I know you love giving orders, but I'm so sorry to disappoint you—"

"Doubt that."

"—you can't physically order me to fall asleep. It's impossible. Unless you're some sort of hypnotist."

Growling in frustration, he also rolled onto his side so he was facing me, punching his pillow into a more comfortable shape before his face settled on top of it. "I can tell you're exhausted. After your shower, you looked about ready to collapse. Why can't you sleep?"

"I just can't."

He was silent for a long beat. His throat cleared and his voice softened before he spoke again. "You're safe here, you know. You're... safe with me."

I nodded, unable to think of a coherent response. And, if I was being honest, somewhat afraid of what might come out if I risked opening my mouth.

"No one is going to come after you."

"I know that."

His eyes narrowed a shade. "Then why can't you sleep?"

"I don't..." A blush heated my cheeks and I merely shook my head. "I can't..."

"Is this about what you told Flo, back in the car? You said you can't... *what*?"

Goddess, he didn't miss a trick. I could tell he wasn't about to let this go until I gave him an answer. Running a hand through my still-wet hair, I heaved a heavy sigh. "I don't sleep with people."

He made a strangled sound of disbelief. "You're not a..."

"No, I'm not a virgin." I rolled my eyes. "I screw people, Graham. I just don't sleep with them."

I think I'd shocked him silent. He was quiet for a very long time. When he finally did speak again, all he asked was, "Why?"

My chest felt like there was an anvil resting on it, slowly compressing all the air out of my lungs. I never talked about this — about my past. But for some reason — maybe it was the dark, maybe it was the sleep-deprivation, maybe it was because there was some deranged part of me that still went weak in the knees whenever this infuriating man came within a half-mile radius — the words started to spill out. Words I'd never told anyone. Not even Flo. Not even Aunt Colette.

"I didn't grow up like you. Silver spoon, perfect family, all that. I didn't even grow up like Desmond or Florence, comfortably middle class, not rich but not poor. My mother was — still is, I suppose, though I haven't seen her in almost a decade — a pretty big mess. She could barely take care of herself, let alone me. Though, honestly, she didn't ever express much interest in taking care of me. Or in me, period." I took a shaky breath. "We bounced around from town to town, from trailer park to trailer park. Never the same place for long. Mostly because Mom moved through boyfriends even faster than she moved through employment opportunities. Which was to say, *warp-speed*. I learned pretty quickly how to take care of myself during the day. Got myself to school, figured out how to use the microwave. But at night, if she wasn't working she'd be home... and that was somehow worse than being by myself all the time. Because she never came alone."

Graham listened without interruption, so still he was like a shadow. If I didn't look at him, I could almost convince myself he wasn't there at all. Or that he'd fallen asleep, and I was just speaking to the darkness.

"She partied a lot. Drugs and booze and other stuff, with whatever dickhead she happened to be dating at the time. I saw a lot of things no little kid is supposed to see — especially when their mother is the one doing them. And I never had any way to escape it. It was a trailer. So, I never had..."

"A room of your own," Graham finished softly.

"A room?" I laughed without humor. "Try a door. Try a lock. Try a bed." My voice lowered, barely audible. "My so-called *bed* was the convertible dining room table where she snorted lines of coke and rolled joints. I can't count the number of times I fell asleep curled up in a ball on the cushions, and woke up to some random skeezeball, drunk off his ass, staring at me."

Graham's body went solid as he tensed. The air seemed to charge, like a live current had started spitting raw power into the room. "Did anyone... did they ever..."

"No. No, I suppose I was lucky in that regard. When they got too interested, Mom would drag them off into the back bedroom and shut the door."

Some of the tension ebbed.

"But even then, with that door shut... I could never sleep. It wasn't until I came to Salem... until I started spending summers with Aunt Colette... that I finally got a good night's sleep."

Graham blew out a long breath. "How old were you? When you started coming here?"

"Eight."

"Been a long time since then."

I nodded at the ceiling, saying nothing. He was right. It had been a long time. But some scars don't fade. Some wounds alter you on a molecular level, rearrange your body-chemistry in such a way that there's no undoing the damage.

"You've never shared a bed with anyone?" he asked after a while, a dubious edge to his voice. "Even in college?"

"I requested a single every semester."

"And... relationships?"

I felt a bit squirmy, but persevered. "If nighttime cuddling is a dealbreaker for a guy... Well, I guess he's not my guy."

Graham was silent. I could almost hear the wheels turning in his head as he mulled over everything I'd told him. Honestly, I was in a bit of shock that I'd spilled the beans so thoroughly. I half-expected to feel panic clawing at my throat, desperation to snatch back every word that had come out of my mouth and shove them back inside, deep down where they would never again see the light of day.

To my surprise, all I felt was... calm. At ease. Like I'd set down a heavy load I hadn't even realized I was carrying. It was odd and more than a little unsettling to know that Graham Graves was capable of pulling the truth from me when no one else ever managed. For my own sanity, I decided not to examine that fact too closely.

"Besides," I said, forcing a lighter tone. "I've also been known to sleepwalk."

"Seriously?"

"*Occasionally*," I stressed, defensive.

"I thought that was something people only did in books and movies."

"If only."

Now, why hadn't I just told him that from the start? It was a much simpler explanation than my traumatic backstory.

Way to overshare, psycho...

"So, you're a sleepwalking insomniac with trust issues?"

"*Occasional* sleepwalker," I amended. "But yeah, I guess that's generally accurate."

"I'm sorry."

I jolted at the unexpected apology. "Why? It's not your fault."

"Just because it's not my fault doesn't mean I don't wish I could fix it for you."

That quiet statement, for whatever reason, made my eyes sting with tears. I blinked them rapidly away. What the hell was the matter with me? My emotions were like a rollercoaster tonight. I blamed the lack of sleep. And the lack of dinner. I'd planned to eat at the pub with Florence. My mid-afternoon snack — a greek yogurt and granola from the work fridge — had digested hours ago.

"You want me to go sleep in the bathtub?" Graham offered, fighting off a yawn.

I snorted at the image of his long limbs trying to fit horizontal in his pedestal tub. "That won't be necessary."

"You sure?"

"Don't start being nice to me now, Graham. You'll kill your street cred."

"God knows we can't have that," he muttered dryly, then added, "I'm fading here."

"So, sleep. I'll be fine."

He grunted and rolled over. When he spoke again, his voice was somewhat muffled by his pillow. "I'll take you home as soon as it's light out. You can get some rest once you're home in your own bed."

"But the store—"

"Don't worry about the store."

"But it's a Saturday—"

"We'll talk about it tomorrow."

"I can't just—"

"*Tomorrow.*"

He sounded so weary, I found myself unable to fight with him any longer. We fell silent and, after a few moments, I wondered if he'd drifted off. But his voice came again, thick with sleep.

"My Kindle's in the nightstand. Passcode is 2929."

"Thanks," I whispered, oddly touched. "Goodnight, Graham."

"Night."

If I couldn't sleep, I might as well read. I found his e-reader right where he said I would and, with the brightness setting turned down low, scrolled his library for something to keep me occupied until morning. He had an eclectic mix of nonfiction, memoirs, thrillers, and mysteries. Some bestsellers, some I'd never heard of before. No steamy pirate romances... but that wasn't exactly surprising.

Nothing jumped out at me until I reached nearly the end of his library. I was stunned to see one of my favorite books — a very un-Graham-like book, at that, since the pages practically dripped with paranormal prose — sitting there in his collection.

The Night Circus by Erin Morgenstern.

Grinning in the dark, I clicked it open and allowed my eyes to devour the first page, falling instantly back into a story of two rival magicians who spiral deeper and deeper into forbidden love...

I STARED bleary-eyed at the toaster, waiting for it to pop. I'd read until the letters began to swim on the illuminated screen, the night slipping away chapter by chapter, listening to the steady metronome of Graham's breathing beside me. As the sky began to lighten in slow degrees, dawn peeking over the horizon with pale pink fingers, I'd slipped out of bed and sought out the only thing that would hold my deep exhaustion at bay.

Coffee.

I took a long sip, humming in satisfaction as the warm liquid pooled in my rumbling stomach. I was ravenous. So much so, I'd decided to pilfer through Graham's cupboards without waiting for permission. Not exactly proper guest etiquette, but I figured he could spare a few pieces of sourdough in penance for making me stay here against my will.

The only thing I'd dared take from his impeccably organized refrigerator was a dollop of milk for my coffee. The inside was too intimidating to touch — orderly reusable containers full of fresh ingredients, drawers jam-packed with organic produce, doors full of unusual condiments like lemongrass paste and miso seasoning and homemade aioli. All of which told me that he cooked — and cooked well, I might add.

Goddess, the man grew more annoying by the minute.

The toaster popped with a low chime. I buttered each piece, fingers practically shaking with hunger. Before I could take a bite, a hand reached over my shoulder and snatched my breakfast right out of my grasp. I heard a crunch and whirled around to see Graham's strong white teeth chomping away at my sourdough.

"I was planning on eating that," I said grumpily, glaring at him. He grinned around the toast in his mouth, unapologetic. His eyes were still half-lidded with sleep. His hair was tousled, the dark locks falling over his forehead in a sexy, mussed sort of way that made my heart pulse faster.

"*Was* being the operative word, babe," he murmured, moving closer. His arms landed on the butcher block, caging me in with his body. I tried very hard not to look down, knowing the sight of his bare chest and chiseled abs were more than I could handle while in the throes of sleep deprivation.

Graham exchanged my stolen toast for my coffee, bringing to mug to his lips for a long sip without a beat of hesitation.

"That's my coffee."

"Not big on sharing, are you?" He grinned again. "Let me guess... you're an only child."

"I don't see what that has to do with anything."

"Trust me, you grow up with two twin hellion kid brothers, you learn about sharing. Quickly."

"I didn't know you had brothers."

"How would you? You didn't ask. You never ask anything about me. It's like you're actively trying not to get to know me."

"That's not true."

"Until a few days ago, you thought I was a handyman."

Color flooded into my cheeks. "I didn't know one tiny, little thing. That was an isolated incident."

"Then name five other things you know about me."

I stared up at him, wishing he wasn't standing so close. It was making my empty stomach somersault. "Can you back off?"

"Why? Am I making you nervous?"

"No," I lied. "But your morning breath leaves something to be desired."

He chuckled and took another sip of my coffee. "You're grouchy in the morning."

"I am not grouchy! I just enjoy my personal space."

"Name five things you know about me and I'll give you all the space you want."

I glared at him. "You're the most arrogant man alive. That's one."

"I don't know if that's a fact so much as your opinion on the matter, but I'll let it slide. Next."

"You went to Harvard to study Criminology and Forensics."

"Next."

"You have two younger brothers," I said smugly. "*Twins*."

"I just told you that twenty seconds ago."

"So?"

"So, that doesn't count."

"It totally counts. You didn't stipulate any rules regarding how long I've had to know these personal factoids."

"Fine," he conceded, eyes flashing with amusement. "You're up to three. Let's hear another."

Hellfire, he was attractive when he was being playful. It was hard to hold onto my train of thought. I dug my teeth into my bottom lip to ground myself in reality. Unfortunately, this only caught Graham's attention; his gaze dropped to my mouth and stayed there, fixated.

"Stop that," I muttered, fighting against the fierce flush that was threatening to turn my cheeks the same color as my hair.

"Stop what?"

"Looking at my mouth."

His eyes flickered back to mine. They were incredibly green. "Why? I like your mouth."

"*Excuse me?*"

"It's a great mouth, babe. I like looking at it. Especially when it's firing insults at me."

I blinked, stunned momentarily silent.

"Think I'd like doing other things to it, too," he murmured, before I had a chance to formulate my thoughts.

"Wha— That— You—" I was spluttering. "You can't say things like that!"

"Just did." His hand, the one planted on the butcher block beside my hip, shifted. Before I could blink, his finger was tracing the outline of my bottom lip, soft as a whisper. "Every time you talk, I find myself distracted. Watching your mouth move. Wondering if your lips are as soft as they look... what they'd feel like on my skin."

I was no longer breathing.

His thumb pressed harder against the supple pillow of my lip, forcing it into a pout. He stared, hard, for another few seconds before he finally pulled back and looked at me. "They are, for the record."

"What?"

He leaned down, until his mouth was only a millimeter from mine. When he whispered, I felt his exhale against my lips — tiny, torturous puffs of air that set my nerve endings aflame. "Just as soft as they look."

Gaia, help me.

My head was spinning with exhaustion and exhilaration at his nearness. I couldn't think straight when he was so close. I couldn't even breathe when he was staring at me like that. "Um..."

"Tick tock, Gwen. Two more to go."

"I can't think straight with you looking at me like that!" I blurted stupidly.

The heat in his eyes flared hotter. Rather than backing off, he shifted even closer, bringing his entire body flush with mine. I sucked in a sharp breath as the firm plane of his chest pressed against me, the hard lines of his thigh muscles lining up with my own through the fabric of our matching sweatpants. I locked my knees to keep them from buckling.

"Why?" he whispered, bowing his head down to the crook of my neck. I felt his hot breath on the sensitive skin of my earlobe and fought off a shiver. "Am I distracting you?"

"No," I lied, breathless. "Not at all."

His low chuckle sent a pulse of attraction shooting straight downward from my stomach to places best left unnamed. "You all out of factoids already?"

Steeling myself, I lifted my hands to his chest and pushed him back, so I could breathe again. His muscles were like steel under my fingertips, but he conceded a few scant inches.

"You're from one of the oldest families in Salem. One of your great-great-great grandfathers was the judge who condemned all the witches to death." I paused, staring into his eyes. "I guess despotic malice is in your blood, huh?"

He tensed for a second — a barely noticeable ripple in his otherwise nonchalant demeanor. But I was close enough to see that I'd thrown him off his game, even if only for an instant, with the mere mention of his ancestry.

Interesting.

"That's four," he growled. All the playfulness had bled right out of his voice and I felt a bolt of unease shoot through me. Graham Graves definitely did not enjoy discussing his familial legacy. "What else have you got, Gwen?"

Eager to have this interlude over and done with — and, admittedly, rather caught up in the thrill of besting him — I didn't think about the implications of what I was about to say before blurting, "You spent summers working as a lifeguard at the beach on Winter Island when you were a teenager, before you left for college."

His head titled to one side, eyes narrowing to slits as he stared down at me. There was an undeniable question in his stare. Belatedly, I realized my mistake. I'd revealed something I had no logical reason to know about him.

Yes, I knew you back then.

Yes, I adored you from afar.

No, you don't remember me.

At least, I didn't think he did.

Since he barreled back into my orbit two years ago, he'd never given the slightest indication he had any memory of the awkward, accident-prone redhead who once stared at him with unguarded longing. His little Firecracker, with the foolish crush on an older boy so out of her league, it was like a tee-ball player trying out for the MLB. As far as I knew, he'd forgotten me entirely... and I was in no rush for him to remember. It was best for everyone if the torch I carried for him stayed buried six feet beneath the earth. Where it belonged.

The longer he stared at me with that curious look in his eyes, the more my anxiety mounted.

"That's five," I declared, suddenly desperate for a change of subject. "I win. Now, back off."

Lips twitching as if he found me highly amusing, he finally backed off, leaning against the kitchen island with his arms crossed over his chest. His eyes never shifted away from mine as I hurriedly glanced down at my toast and took a large bite. It was now ice cold.

Perfect.

"Did you sleep at all?" he asked after a moment.

I shook my head, still chewing the cold toast. I forced myself to swallow, then discarded the rest with a grimace.

"You look like crap."

My eyes rolled skyward. "Gee, thanks."

"I mean you look tired."

"That's a symptom of not sleeping for two nights."

"Two?" He paused. "Did you not sleep the night before last, either?"

"You mean the night after I learned I was the target of crazed pagans and shown a series of disturbing photographs depicting ritualistic animal slaughter? *That* night?"

"Ah. Right. Fair enough."

I shot him a pointed look. "And how did *you* sleep?"

"Soundly."

"Mmm. I could tell from your thunderous snoring."

He scoffed. "I don't snore."

"Oh, you do. It was reminiscent of a freight train. Or a wood-chopper." I suppressed a smile at my blatant fabrications. "What? Your exes didn't tell you? Maybe they didn't want to hurt your feelings. That last one — Mara, was it? — seemed to think you farted moonbeams and sneezed watercolors. What ever happened to her, anyway? Too nice for you?"

There was a marked pause. "You seem rather fixated on my past love life. Been keeping tabs on who I date?"

"I couldn't care less who you date."

Okay, so, this wasn't strictly true. I had a tendency to take notice whenever Graham had a new girl in his life. Which, seeing as he was Graham, and he looked the way he looked, happened pretty regularly. He wasn't a serial dater or anything, but over the past year and a half, he'd brought a handful of different girls around as his plus-one to barbecues and boat trips on Desmond's speedboat. Always gorgeous, always charming, always looking at him like he'd personally hung the sun in the sky just for them to get a tan.

But they never stuck around for very long. It was rare to see them at more than one consecutive social engagement. Having seen his perfectly ordered loft, I wondered if he was too much of a control freak to let anyone invade his space for very long before cutting them off.

"Uh huh," he said, bringing me back to the present. I could hear the smug smile in his voice, but I purposefully didn't look at him, fixated on my lukewarm coffee instead. "And what about you?"

"Me?" I squeaked. "What about me?"

"You haven't dated anyone in... what? Six months? Why is that? Sworn off men?"

"Who I date — or don't date — is frankly none of your business." I took a deep breath, working up the nerve to meet his stare agin. It was amused, crinkles feathering the skin around his eyes. "Do you have my phone?"

"Why? Want to check your Tinder matches?"

I rolled my eyes. "I need to check in with my barista, tell her I'm going to be late to open the store today."

He walked across the room to the couch, where he'd left his leather jacket the night before, and pulled my smartphone from the pocket. He frowned down at the screen as he returned to me, his bare feet moving soundlessly across the hardwood floors. In the pale pink light of sunrise, he looked like some sort of fallen angel — all dark, chiseled angles and dangerously attractive edges. Lucifer incarnate, the devil made flesh. I swallowed the lump in my throat as he passed me my phone.

The screen said 6:49AM. The battery bar said 8%. The notifications said 24 MISSED CALLS.

"All from Florence," Graham noted.

"I'll call her back. She's probably worried."

"She knows you're with me."

"Exactly. She's not worried about the kidnapping; she's worried I caved to my baser instincts and smothered you in your sleep."

Graham's chuckle was drowned out by the sudden vibration of the phone in my hand. I peered down at it, not at all surprised to see FLORENCE LAMBERT flashing across the screen in bold letters.

"Hi, Flo," I said as I lifted it to my ear.

"Hi! Let us in!"

"What?"

"We're outside! Des and me. We brought breakfast."

I glanced at Graham. He was leaning back against the kitchen island, watching me with that inscrutable expression he so often wore, arms crossed over his broad, bare chest. His brows lifted in question.

"Florence and Desmond are at your front door," I told him, shrugging lightly.

If he was shocked by this information, he didn't show it. He merely pushed off the counter, muttering, "I'll buzz them in."

"He'll buzz you in," I reiterated to Flo, watching the rippling muscles in Graham's back as he moved across the loft to the front door, where a sleek intercom panel was embedded in the wall. He walked with the lithe, athletic grace of a former athlete; like all the best quarterbacks, he was deceptively light on his feet for such a big man.

I'd bet he was a fantastic dancer. My mind flashed with the insane vision of him in a groom's tux, steering me across the dance floor in an elegant waltz, my white gown floating around me in a cloud of tulle. I shook my head to banish it.

"Great!" Flo chirped in my ear, bringing me crashing back to reality. "See you in a sec!"

She disconnected before I could say anything. I used the brief moment of solitude to haul in a series of deep breaths, trying to calm my racing heart and clear my expression of all emotion, calling upon the years of customer service training to summon the cool, composed mask I used whenever shit hit the fan. Then, I went about the business of pouring three additional mugs of coffee. One for Florence... milk and two sugars. Another for Desmond... black with one sugar. And a third for Graham...

Only, I didn't know how he took his coffee.

I thought of him casually sipping from my mug, like we'd shared beverages a thousand times before on mornings just like this one, and felt a strange, unfamiliar sensation take hold of my heart, like a fist squeezing until pain began to radiate. The man was right about one thing; I had gone out of my way to avoid getting to know him. But I was beginning to realize that endeavor was entirely one-sided. Because while I might've spent the past few years ignoring his existence, it was abundantly clear that Graham had been paying attention.

Close attention.

To *me*.

This realization set off a spiral of contradictory feelings that made it difficult to draw a full breath into my lungs. Panic, surely. Annoyance, most definitely. And last but not least, something I was barely able to admit, even to myself...

Exhilaration.

Being around Graham these past few hours was a shot of pure epinephrine, a chemical dose of adrenaline that skyrocketed all my senses off the chart. When he was near me, I felt alive in a way I'd never felt before.

It wasn't just that he'd saved me or that he was so damned mouthwateringly gorgeous to look at, especially when his shirt was off and his lips were within kissing distance. (Okay, so, it was partly that.) But it was *also* that ravaged look on his face when he found me in that basement. It was the grip of his hand on mine as he led me down the sidewalk. It was the half-smile his lips tugged into whenever I cracked a dumb joke. It was his strong fingers, so achingly careful as they tended to my injured knees. It was his sleep-roughened voice, telling me his Kindle password. It was his attentive silence as he absorbed every single word of my story last night, without interrupting or ordering me to shut up and go to sleep or seeming at all bored by the things I was telling him.

This was a new Graham. One I'd never let myself know; one he'd never shown me. He'd never acted quite like this before — so openly considerate, so forthright. And so blatantly, outrageously flirty.

I assured myself it was no more than some new, nefarious battle tactic in our never-ending war of attrition, designed to throw me off my game. I needed to get my head screwed on straight. I wasn't some innocent wallflower. I shouldn't be so enthralled by his every innuendo and heated look. I shouldn't be so turned on by him when I knew, better than anyone, that he was just playing a game with me. Toying with me for his own amusement, like a cat with a mouse between its paws.

Men like Graham lived for the challenge of a new conquest. I had no intentions of being the next girl in the long line of starstruck exes he sent packing once he tired of their charms. Surely, I was stronger than this. Stronger than whatever inexplicable animal attraction had gripped me the first time I laid eyes on the man, all those years ago, long before he was even a man — just a boy in a lifeguard tower, who looked into my eyes and stole my heart without even trying. Even as a kid, he'd captivated me like no one else. Infatuated me like no one else.

It was just that, though. *Infatuation.* There was no substance behind it. That boy was long gone; the man in his place was a brute who'd only break my heart if I gave him the chance. He was high-handed and bossy and unlikable. The sooner I got away from him, the better.

I had no doubt once I was back in my own space, with several blocks of distance between us, this bizarre feeling that had seized my heart would fade, and we would go right back to hating each other.

All would be right in the world.

At least, I hoped it would.

CHAPTER TWELVE

I bring a lot to the table. (Mainly charcuterie.)
— Gwen Goode, attending a dinner party

"Oh my god, *Gwennie!*"

Florence rushed into the loft through the garage stairwell door and raced for my side in a blur of dark glossy hair and faded denim. She threw her arms around me, the impact rocking my whole frame back against the countertop. "I'm so relieved you're okay! I've been freaking out!"

I hugged her back, closing my eyes for a moment as her warmth sank into my bones.

"Really?" I asked, chuckling. "That's odd, I couldn't tell from the twenty-four missed calls."

She pulled back to smack me lightly on the arm. Her chocolate brown eyes were glossed over with tears. "Don't joke. I've been a basket case. Ask Des if you don't believe me."

"It's true," her boyfriend agreed, setting down a large white bag that said *Bagel World* on the counter. "You have no idea how much effort it took to convince her to wait until daylight to come here."

"Sue me for being worried about my best friend!"

Desmond ignored his girlfriend's indignant pouting as he stepped closer, looped his lanky arms around the both of us, and squeezed tightly. I felt his lips brush the top of my hair in a brief, brotherly kiss. "Glad you're okay, Gwen. For a few hours there, I was worried I'd have to put Flo in a padded cell."

"Oh, as if you wouldn't need a matching straight jacket," she snapped. "You were just as crazy worried as I was!"

My eyes began to prickle. All I could manage to croak out was an emotion-clogged, "You guys..."

Both of them simultaneously tightened their arms around me, so I was fully ensconced in love from all sides. We stayed like that for a long while, until I was afraid I might actually lose the battle against my gathering tears. Blinking hard, I forced myself to squirm out of their hold and cleared my throat.

"Okay, okay, that's enough. You're suffocating me."

Drifting away, Flo reached into the bag and pulled out four breakfast sandwiches wrapped in paper. They smelled delicious. Way better than cold sourdough. The memory of Graham chomping playfully into my toast earlier flashed through my head. I resisted the urge to look toward the bedroom alcove, where he'd disappeared. I could hear the low murmur of his voice as he spoke into the phone, but couldn't make out any of the words.

Focus, Gwen.

I topped off my own coffee from the pot after directing Flo and Des toward their mugs, trying not to trip on the long legs of my sweatpants as I moved around the kitchen. Desmond plunked his tall frame down on one of the kitchen island stools.

His gaze was gentle behind the translucent bookish frames he wore as Florence passed one of the wrapped sandwiches into his ink-stained hands. Professor's hands. She shot him an equally warm glance before hopping up on the stool beside him, bumping her shoulder against his as a smile played at her lips.

Seeing the wordless exchange of affection made my heart turn over. I didn't think it would be long before Desmond popped the question — assuming Florence didn't beat him to the punch. They were so head-over-heels for each other, it would've been nauseating if it weren't so danged cute.

"I got your favorite," she informed me around a bite of her onion bagel with cream cheese and lox. Her words were almost unintelligible. "Scrambled, extra cheddar, no bacon, on a toasted asiago."

My mouth was already watering, but I resisted the urge to sink my teeth into my own sandwich. "You're a goddess. I just need to call Hetti before I eat."

"Why?" Des asked around a huge mouthful of his own.

"To tell her we're going to have to open a bit late. I'm running on zero sleep and I can't exactly wear this to work." I gestured down at the getup I'd borrowed from Graham. "There's no way I'm going to make it to the store by nine to open."

Flo wrinkled her nose. "Can't you just stay closed for the day?"

"On a Saturday, less than six weeks from Halloween?" I shook my head. "No way. This will be one of the most profitable days of the year. I can't afford to lose that business."

"Then let me help."

"What?"

"Let me run the shop for you."

I eyed my best friend dubiously. "Flo..."

"Don't look at me like that! It's not like I haven't helped out before."

This was true. Florence was an elementary school teacher and, as such, had her summers off. On more than one occasion in the past, she'd kept me company at The Gallows on rainy days, clearing tables and washing used coffee mugs. Still, there was a major difference between helping out on a slow August afternoon and running the show solo during a high-season weekend.

"I appreciate the offer, Flo, but it's too much to ask you to do that," I said as gently as possible. "It'll be a madhouse this afternoon."

"I run a classroom of unruly second graders five days a week in an underfunded public school. I'm pretty sure I can handle entitled hipsters and wide-eyed tourists for a single day."

"But—"

"But nothing." She grinned at her boyfriend. "Besides, Des will help me. Isn't that right, sweetheart? You can grade papers in the back office and help out if it gets really crazy."

Desmond just nodded his head indulgently and continued eating his breakfast.

"Besides, it's not like I have to make fancy latte art or anything," Flo pointed out. "Hetti will be there for that."

"Hetti can be kind of moody," I warned.

Flo scoffed. "I've met the girl a hundred times. No amount of eyeliner will intimidate me."

"Okay, but the cash register drawer sticks. You have to press on the left side—"

"I'm sure we'll figure it out."

I tensed, torn between gratitude and guilt. The bottom line was, I needed their help. And I knew they were offering it without any strings, because they truly wanted to support me. Because they loved me. But knowing that *theoretically* didn't make it any easier to accept it *actually*.

Maybe it was just me — maybe it was a byproduct of growing up without a penny to my name — but I hesitated to

196

take a handout from anyone. Even my best friends. Experience had taught me better. When you've got nothing, you learn early on that nothing is really free. There's always payback involved.

This isn't charity, Gwen, I scolded myself. *They just want to help. Let them.*

I forced my shoulders to un-tense and blew out a breath I didn't realize I'd been holding. "Okay. I just need to get an couple hours of shut-eye, take a shower, and locate some real clothes."

"There's no rush." She paused, looking at my makeup-free face and wild hair. "Seriously. Take your time. Eat a breakfast sandwich. More importantly, brush your hair."

My cheeks heated. It had not escaped my notice that my hair was out to *there* after letting it air dry all night. A wild riot of dark red curls cascaded around my shoulders, less like my usual look — a blatant emulation of Jessica Chastain's sleek loose waves — and more like Merida from *Brave.* "Are you sure you don't mind doing this on your day off?"

They both shook their heads in tandem.

"Well... thank you. You're saving my ass."

"Yeah, yeah," she murmured, licking cream cheese off her upper lip. "Make sure to remember us in your memoirs."

"I'll be in by noon," I promised. "No later. I just need to get home—"

"I'll take you," Graham cut in, walking toward us. He was yanking on a brown thermal henley. He'd changed into dark wash jeans at some point during my conversation with Flo and Des. There were faded brown boots on his feet, a wickedly cool scuffed leather pair I instantly wanted in my size.

"I just spoke with one of my guys in the field," he continued, eyes on mine. "He's done a preliminary sweep of your property and the surrounding streets, made sure no one is watching your house. My tech guy is at base reviewing traffic camera footage from the past few hours, double checking for anything suspect.

When we get there, I'll do a quick walkthrough to make sure no one is inside."

I stared at him for a moment. "You have *guys* on this? *Plural?*"

"Why is that surprising?"

"I didn't realize my kidnapping warranted such manpower. Don't they have more important things to be doing? Catching criminals, taking compromising photos, planting corporate espionage wiretaps, beating the truth out of sources, that sort of thing?"

His lips twitched. "Where'd you get your concept of private investigations? A cartoon?"

"Old episodes of Moonlighting, mostly," I admitted quietly.

Amusement flared in his eyes and his lip-twitch tugged up into a full-fledged grin. "Much as I appreciate the concern, all my cases are currently covered. Though, it'd help matters if you could avoid being kidnapped again. We're stretched thin with three of my guys out of state after skips."

"Skips?"

"Bond skips. People who are FTA in court." He closed the final bit of distance between us, eyes still dancing with humor. "FYI, Gwendolyn, that's *failure to appear*, not Future Teachers of America."

"I knew that," I grumbled, even though I hadn't.

Graham stopped next to me at the kitchen island, standing so close I had to fight the urge to skitter sideways. His arm brushed mine as he unwrapped his breakfast sandwich — everything bagel, double bacon, double fried eggs, with a crispy hash brown layer at the center — and took a large bite. The low sound of satisfaction that came from his throat as he swallowed made my stomach clench, but I tried my best to ignore him.

This attempt was unsuccessful, seeing as the second he'd swallowed, he leaned down and took a bite of *my* sandwich before I could jerk it out of range.

"Hey!" I squawked. "Would you *stop* doing that?!"

Graham's mouth was fighting a playful grin as he chewed. "Sorry, babe. For some reason, breakfast just tastes better when it's yours."

I scowled at him and purposefully sidestepped out of range. Taking a large bite of my — *my, not his!* — breakfast, I looked up and found Flo and Des watching Graham and me with what could only be described as befuddled fascination.

"What?" I snapped.

"Nothing!" they said in unison, glancing down at the countertop. They couldn't quite hide their matching smiles.

I rolled my eyes and looked at Graham. He'd already put a significant dent in his breakfast sandwich. As if he felt my gaze, he glanced my way, that playful smile still tugging at his mouth, and I quickly turned my attention back to my own breakfast.

"So, Graham," Desmond said, cutting through the mounting tension. "You working any other cases lately? Besides figuring out this mess Gwen is caught up in, I mean."

"I actually have to meet with a new client at nine."

"Anything interesting?"

"Potential case of fraud. Someone's been scamming his mother out of her life savings, draining what would otherwise be his inheritance. He wants me to look into it..."

As Graham and Desmond began to chat about his new case, my gaze met Flo's across the island. Her eyes bugged out at me, flickering from me to Graham and back again in a pointed way that, in best-friend-code, clearly meant: *What the fuck is going on between the two of you?*

I pinned her with my best stare, the one that said: *Nothing is going on, mind your own business!*

She volleyed back with a slow, intentional blink. *We're going to talk about this later.*

I rolled my eyes back in the sockets. *There's nothing to talk about.*

"Right," she said aloud. "Sure. Whatever you say."

Both men stopped their chatter to look at her in confusion.

"Talking to yourself again, sweetheart?" Desmond asked lightly, his forehead creased with concern. "Maybe we should reconsider institutionalization after all..."

I smothered my laugh behind my sandwich.

Nerves fluttered in the pit of my stomach as I shoved my key into the lock and listened to the low thunk of the deadbolt sliding open. I was hyper-aware of Graham standing approximately six inches behind me on the top step of my shallow front stoop, waiting for me to open the door. He was insistent on walking through the whole house, making sure there were no would-be kidnappers lurking in the broom closet or beneath my bed frame.

I could've told him the truth — that my kidnappers were far more likely to be in Mrs. Proctor's stately Victorian next door, playing canasta in the parlor and showing off pictures of their grandbabies — but that was a can of worms I thought it best to leave unopened at the moment.

"You know..." I hesitated with one hand on the shiny gold knob. "You really don't have to come inside. I'm sure it's perfectly safe—"

"Open the door, Gwendolyn."

I sighed and did as he said, trying to remain poised as I led him inside. After seeing his loft, which was more thoughtfully curated than some exhibits at the nearby Peabody Essex Museum, the empty walls and unfinished rooms of my own place seemed even more desolate than usual.

"You need a security system."

I sighed again. He was so danged bossy. "I'll think about it."

"How many other people have copies of that key?"

"Just me." I narrowed my eyes. "Oh, and I of course mailed one to each member of BTS, just in case they ever need a place to crash if they come to town."

With a low grunt of what could've been amusement or annoyance — it was hard to tell with him — Graham turned on his heel and walked away. He clearly wasn't holding his breath for me to give him the grand tour. Then again, he didn't seem to need one. He walked right through the foyer to the double-wide archway that led into my kitchen, as if he already knew his way around. Which was impossible, seeing as he'd never once been here. With the exception of Florence a handful of times over the past few years, *no one* had been here.

It was bizarre to have another person in my space. Especially when that person was Graham. His green eyes swept around, taking in the furnishings — or, lack thereof. I trailed in his wake, fighting the urge to wring my hands together as his critical gaze moved over every nook and cranny, catalogued every infinitesimal detail.

"Haven't you lived here for two years?" he asked, moving beyond the kitchen into the vacant dining room that adjoined it. I'd always thought it would look fantastic with a giant farmhouse table, big enough to serve a basketball team... or a bucketload of kids. A thick, jute rug. Maybe a wrought-iron chandelier, the kind with chunky taper candles and heavy black suspension chain. Unfortunately, right now, like most of the first floor, all it housed were a few cobwebs and dust bunnies.

"Um. Yeah."

He turned to look at me. "Where's all your stuff?"

"What stuff?"

"You're telling me you've been living like this? In this giant ass house? For two whole years?"

"For your information, there's absolutely nothing wrong with the way I live."

"Didn't you study interior design?"

My tone grew defensive. "What does that have to do with anything?"

"I just figure most interior designers would relish the chance to decorate a blank canvas like this." His eyes narrowed fractionally. "But I guess it makes sense. Plumbers always have the leakiest pipes. Mechanics always need a new muffler. Shrinks are always in need of the most therapy."

"I'm too sleep deprived to listen to this," I announced, ripping my gaze from his and stomping into the next room. Though, truth be told, it was rather hard to stomp, given that I was barefoot, half-tripping over the too-long sweatpants with every step. "Besides, I thought you were here to look for intruders, not psychoanalyze me."

In grudging silence, he shadowed me through the rest of the rooms on the first floor. At each threshold, he made a low grunt, as if the sight of yet another vacant room was confirming some deeply-rooted suspicion. I grew more and more annoyed by these small sounds of self-affirmation as we moved up the grand staircase to the second floor, the steps creaking beneath our feet as we climbed.

"I am planning on decorating. Eventually." I clenched my hands into fists as we peered into the sun-drenched room I'd always envisioned as my library-slash-home-office. All it needed was a coat of paint... and custom built-in bookshelves with rolling ladders... a plush nook for reading by the picture window... a few thousand dollars worth of furnishings... plus a few hundred books... oh, and a rug... and...

"Uh huh," Graham murmured doubtfully.

"I am! I just haven't had the time. I've been a bit busy running a small business."

"Uh huh."

"Stop with the *uh huh*'s and say whatever you're clearly so desperate to say."

His head swung around and he pinned me with that intense stare. "Fine. You and Flo have time to go sit in vats of mud with cucumber slices on your eyelids four, maybe five times a year. I'm pretty sure you have the time to decorate."

Rude!

(Though, it must be said, accurate.)

My chin jerked higher. "You don't know anything about me or how I spend my free time."

"Not for lack of trying."

"What?"

He ignored my frazzled exclamation. His eyes narrowed a shade, as though if he looked at me hard enough he might see through my bullshit. "I think you're scared to decorate this place."

I laughed; I couldn't help myself. It was ridiculous! *He* was ridiculous. "Excuse me?"

"You heard me. I think you're scared — scared to put down roots, scared to settle in. Scared to call something permanent. Scared to let anyone know you, besides maybe Florence, and that's only because she met you long before you threw up those sky-high walls you keep around yourself for protection."

His words clawed their way into my brain, tearing at me from the inside out. I told myself he was wrong about me, that he spoke lies, but deep down I knew better. Much as I might like to pretend this place was my home, there was a part of me that would always be that girl in the trailer, looking for escape routes, ready to pack up her whole life at a moment's notice and move on.

"You don't know what you're talking about," I lied, heart thudding twice its normal speed. My hands clenched into fists at my sides to keep myself from flying apart in a million directions. "You're way off base."

"Am I?"

"Lightyears."

He took a step closer, forcing me to tilt my head back to maintain eye contact. "Then name one person besides Florence you've allowed to know you since you moved back to town. The real you, not the sunny facade you let everyone else see. Not the bullshit customer service smile. Not the designer outfits. Not the poised, perfectly coordinated shopkeeper. *You.*"

"Desmond," I said immediately.

"Doesn't count. He and Flo are a package deal. You only let him close because he's fused to her side eighty-six percent of the time." He paused. "As for everyone else? You keep them at arm's length."

My heart was jackhammering my ribs. "That's not true. I'm a nice person. Plenty of people know me. Not only know me, they like me!"

At least, they seemed to. I had a growing base of loyal customers. I was a good neighbor. (Admittedly, my exterior fall facade could use some work, but I never threw loud parties or left my trash cans on the street after pickup.) I was a goddamned national treasure, damn it! Or, if not a national treasure, at least... a well-liked local trinket. He was making me sound like some antisocial old hag who lived in the swamps, unable to mingle with the ordinary townsfolk.

"People do like you, Gwen," Graham murmured. "They'd even love you, if you let them. But you don't."

"And just *what*," I said, ice dripping from my every word, "Is that supposed to mean?"

He ran a hand through his hair, looking suddenly frustrated.

"Every guy you've brought around these past few years has stared at you with the same half-whipped, puppy dog expression, wondering how the hell he's going to get through. How he's going to make you let down your guard long enough to love you. And every one of them has failed."

"That's not true!"

"It is. I've seen it happen, over and over, again and again. You may let them have your body, but you never let them in your head. Under your skin." He took a stride closer and, before I could stop him, pressed his big hand flat against the left side of my chest. Directly over my heart. "You never let them in here."

I froze.

Too scared to move.

Too scared to breathe.

Too scared to speak.

"You push them away, keep them at a careful distance, until they have no choice but to walk out."

I flinched back, and he dropped his hand. "So, I suppose it's *my* fault I've been cheated on? It's my fault I've been ghosted? It's my fault I've been screwed over and dicked around?"

"Don't put fucking words in my mouth," Graham growled, eyes flashing. "I'm glad you never let those assholes in. They didn't deserve you. But even if they had, I doubt it would've changed a goddamn thing. Not when you're determined to be alone."

"News flash: I've been alone my whole damn life!" I half-bellowed, my self-control finally cracking. "I'm perfectly fine all alone!"

"You love that word, don't you? *Fine.* No matter whether you've been kidnapped or injured or hurt or scared, you're always just *fine*," he bellowed back. "Christ, Gwen! Don't you understand? You deserve so much more than *fine*! You deserve—"

He broke off abruptly, locking down his jaw to contain the rest of his words. His eyes were burning into mine, a stare so intense I could feel it in the marrow of my bones.

"This," I hissed, furious, "Is none of your business."

He leaned forward, equally furious. "I'm *making* it my business."

My mouth fell open in shock at his audacity. This was a fatal mistake — primarily because it meant my lips were already parted when he closed the final bit of distance between us, grabbed me by the shoulders, and slammed his mouth down on mine in an angry, breath-snatching kiss.

Holy.

Hell.

The first time he'd kissed me, back at his loft, it was strictly to shut me up. To stop me from spiraling. This kiss was different. It wasn't calculated. It wasn't planned. It was hard, fast, furious. Not like he wanted to do it; like he had no choice in the matter. Like his desire got the better of him, snapping his iron-clad control until he couldn't help himself.

I tasted simmering anger on his tongue as it tangled with mine, felt his ill-concealed frustration in every satin-steel brush of his lips as his head slanted sideways to deepen the kiss. His fingertips tightened on my upper arms, dragging me up against his body. His hold was so tight, it nearly hurt. But in that moment, I was beyond processing pain. I was beyond processing anything except his mouth on mine as passion spiked to a fever pitch, a reaction as uncontrollable as it was unexpected.

I wish I could say I held onto my convictions. That I resisted temptation, stood strong in the face of unparalleled passion. But...

Goddess help me, I kissed him back.

I arched up onto the balls of my feet, pressing more firmly against his strong frame, giving him better access to my mouth.

My tongue stroked against his, eliciting a low growl of pleasure from deep in his throat, and I felt a shiver of pure pleasure move down my spine. If I'd been capable of rational thought, I would've been screaming at myself for letting this happen with him.

Alas...

My brain was a blank of static, hijacked by several other, decidedly more primal organs in my body.

My hands hit his chest then slid around to his back, and he loosed another low sound of desire in response to my touch. I swallowed down a moan of my own as his teeth grazed my bottom lip, then sucked it into his mouth.

Hellfire, that felt good.

I can't say how long it lasted. Less than a minute, maybe. But what a minute it was. There was nothing gentle about the way we explored one another. Nothing sweet or tender. This was a full-frontal attack. An assault of the senses, a battle for dominance. I wasn't sure how, or if, a winner would ever be declared in such a battle — frankly, I was feeling like a winner regardless, seeing as it was the hottest kiss I'd ever experienced in my life.

At least... until Graham finally broke away to gasp for much-needed breath. Between ragged inhales, he muttered something against my lips. Something that made my blood run cold, evaporating any passion I'd felt in a single heartbeat.

"That was a fuck of a lot better than *fine* and you know it."

My body locked. Sanity came crashing back in an instant. What the hell was I thinking, kissing him? Was I a total idiot? I'd played right into his hands! This was all a game to him. His way of proving a point. His way of besting me.

The professional fixer, fixing a situation by any means necessary.

The realization was enough to make me forget all about the drugging desire I'd felt only seconds before. In its place, rage came crashing in like a flood. On its heels, resentment. Bringing up the rear, a burning sort of humiliation I refused to examine too closely.

I jerked back, out of Graham's arms, and backpedaled a stride away. I tried to form words, but they were lodged in my throat, along with a thick tangle of emotions I could barely breathe around.

"You..." I broke off, too worked up to be articulate. "You..."

His dark brows quirked up. "If a kiss steals the power of speech, can't wait to see what an orgasm does."

Of all the arrogant, egotistical things to say in that moment...

Rage boiled my blood.

I saw red.

Before I could stop myself, my hand cocked back and I slapped him clear across the face. I'm not sure who was more shocked by the strike, him or me. We both froze as the red handprint bloomed on his right cheek, a vivid imprint of my anger.

"Oh my god," I whispered, shocked by my own actions.

"What the fuck!" he exclaimed, brows furrowing. He lifted a hand to rub his reddened skin. "What was that for?"

I shook my head, unable to speak. Mortification consumed me. I'd never struck anyone in my life. I'd been on the receiving end of too many slaps from my mother to ever lift my own hand against anyone else. A thick tangle of emotion settled in my throat, blocking my airway. I was ashamed at myself for acting on my baser instincts, and more than a little angry at him for driving me to that newfound low. If I'd needed any more irrefutable proof that I was better off staying far, far away from Graham Graves...

Here it was, in bold red.

"Gwen—" he started, stepping closer.

"Don't!" I snapped. "Just... don't. Okay?"

"No, not okay. We need to— Gwen!"

He called out after me but I'd already turned away from him, exiting the room and storming down the hall to my bedroom.

"Damn it," he cursed lowly, following after me. "Would you wait a second—"

"Nope!"

"Gwen—"

"No! Don't you say my name. Don't even *think* my name!" I yelled, shoving open my door so violently, it rattled on its hinges. "Thanks *so* much for the security check. I've never felt more secure in my life!"

A growl of frustration sounded at my blatant sarcasm.

"I should've known you'd take the opportunity to belittle me," I continued, storming deeper into the room. "You just can't resist, can you? Any chance you get to take me down a peg, you simply have to take it!"

"That's not what I was trying to do—"

"Right."

"Fuck! If you'd just listen to me—"

Reaching my bed, I whirled around in time to see him enter the bedroom. His eyes swept around the beautifully finished space, taking in the stunning carved headboard, the fresh flowers on my vintage dresser, the carefully selected artwork, the lush accents scattered thoughtfully around on every available surface. His gaze lingered for a long beat on my bed. For some reason, I didn't think he was memorizing the throw pillow arrangement or the duvet pattern. The look on his face was raw, the fading outline of my handprint still visible on his cheek. I had to avert my eyes, too ashamed to look at him when my mark still stained his skin. I hated myself for losing control — not just with the slap, but the kiss that proceeded it.

"Don't you get it? I don't want to listen to you, Graham." I was breathing hard, my words a tangle of fury and frustration and fear. Yes, fear. Because there was a part of me that knew, as

209

angry as I was at him for saying it... he was right. Right about my walls. Right about *me*. "I want you to leave."

"No."

"*No?*"

"Not until you listen to what I have to say."

"I think I've heard enough."

"And I think," he said, walking toward me with slow steps. "You're just proving my point. Repeating your pattern."

"How's that?"

"Pushing away anyone who tries to get close. Anyone who tries to really know you." His eyes flickered briefly to the room behind me. "You don't like me in here. Your inner sanctum. Your safe space. The only place you can really rest. Why is that?"

"Maybe I just don't like you."

"Or maybe you like me so much, it makes you avoid me like the plague."

I shot him an incredulous look. "Do you even hear yourself? You're delusional. Truly. If anyone here needs psycho-analysis, it's you. Get a consult. Tell them you've got a raging case of undiagnosed narcissistic personality disorder and a propensity for arrogance the likes of which no one has ever seen!"

"Is it arrogance if I'm right?"

"Can you please just leave already?" I shot him a death-glare. "You've done your security sweep. Unless you want to check for feral dust bunnies in the basement, I'd say I'm safe enough."

He stared at me, stone-faced. Unmoving.

"Go! I mean it," I snapped. "I need to get to the store."

"The store can wait."

Ugh!

I curled my hands into fists. "That's not your decision to make. You're not my boss or my boyfriend. Hell, you're not even my friend. Now, *please*, get out of here. Or I'll call Detective Caden Hightower and have you removed."

The words hit him like a bucket of ice water. My mouth snapped closed with a click as I watched him flinch, like I'd struck him again. I swallowed down the guilt that flared through me and tried not to fidget under the weight of his intense glare. He stood there for a long beat, arms crossed over his chest, taking long drags of air through his nose — as if he was striving to calm himself. The muscle in his cheek was ticking rhythmically as his jaw clenched and unclenched. I'd never seen him so worked up.

It took a few moments but, eventually, he regained control — the fury bled out of his eyes and they returned to their typical icy indifference. His expression smoothed, all traces of frustration disappearing between one breath and the next. His fists unclenched. His jaw unlocked. His arms fell to his sides.

Without another word, he turned on his cool-as-shit leather boots and stalked out my door. I listened to him thud down the stairs and waited for the crash of the front door. Only it didn't come. In the silence, I heard a heavy sigh, followed immediately by a shout that made me jump about three feet off the ground.

"*Lock the damn door!*"

And then, with a slam, he was gone.

THREE AND A HALF HOURS LATER, I dragged my half-dead carcass through the front door of The Gallows. The bell chimed merrily overhead. I glared at it, resentful. My head was pounding from lack of sleep — and, quite possibly, from the altercation with Graham. Fury still sizzled through my veins, hot as lava.

"Nice of you to show up, boss," Hetti called from behind the espresso machine. "It's like the tenth circle of Hell in here."

"There are only nine."

"According to who? *Dante*?" She snorted. "What the fuck did he know about anything?"

Near her elbow, at least six paper to-go cups were lined up, awaiting their caffeinated confections. A line of customers four people deep crowded the counter, impatient to place their own orders. Every table in the front section was at capacity. Even the espresso bar was jammed, a cluster of giggling preteen girls taking selfies with their frappuccinos occupying the space usually populated by students with laptops.

My eyes scanned deeper into the shop, past the busy shelves where people perused our eclectic book selection, around the display of colorful incense sticks, over the ever-popular essential oils table, down the short flight of steps into the mystical curiosities section, where Flo was manning the secondary cash register. She was busy chatting with a customer as she loaded a set of creepy, corn-husk poppet dolls into a bag with black tissue paper. When I managed to catch her eye, she shot me a reassuring wink and a wave to let me know she had things under control.

"Sorry I'm late," I told Hetti, rushing around the back side of the counter.

"Are you wearing jeans?"

The alarmed note in my barista's voice made me glance down at my outfit. I'd been far too tired to conjure my typical outfit-armor today. I was in an ancient pair of faded Levis I'd owned since my teenage years and a light blue babydoll t-shirt that proclaimed I'M WITH SATAN in capital letters.

"Am I breaking the nonexistent dress code?" I asked, eyeing her own outfit. She was in fishnets, combat boots, a black pleated leather skirt, and a corset top that, if she'd had even a slightly more ample chest, would've made her look less like Wednesday Addams and more like Dita Von Tease.

"I've just never seen you so... casual."

"I haven't slept in two days. My bloodstream is currently 85% caffeine. No brainpower leftover for outfit coordination."

"Guess that explains your aura."

"Let me guess, it's black as death."

"No... more of a dark red, with lighter orange edges. But there are these little flecks of gold sparkling through..." Her eyes were half-focused, studying the air around my head. "Huh."

"*Huh*? What do you mean, *huh*?"

"You head-over-heels for someone, boss?"

My mouth dropped open. "What?"

"It's just... that particular mix of frustration, excitement, and terror usually signals a pretty intense crush."

Color flooded my cheeks. "No! I don't— That's not—"

"Hello? Excuse me!" a girl in line called impatiently. "Are you planning to take my order anytime soon?"

"Yep," I called, not looking away from Hetti. I crossed my arms over my chest and pinned her with my most serious *I'm the boss, I mean business* look. "Stop reading my aura. It's creeping me out."

"Or what?"

"Or you're fired."

She rolled her eyes, not at all worried about my empty threat. She knew I would never fire her in a million years. Certainly not today, with an endless line of customers in need of slightly over-priced beverages. "Whatever you say, boss."

"I mean it!"

"Sure you do."

Grumbling under my breath about ungrateful employees, I wadded my thin gray leather moto jacket into a ball, shoved it beneath the counter, and grabbed a spare apron from the hook on the wall. By the time I took up position at the register, the girl at the front of the line looked seriously peeved. I pasted on my sunniest customer service smile and grabbed my sharpie.

"Welcome to The Gallows. How's it hanging?" I grinned weakly at my own pun.

"I've been waiting, like, an eternity. I'm dying over here."

"Then you've come to the right place." My smile never wavered. "What can we get started for you..."

CHAPTER THIRTEEN

Putting the die in diet since three hours ago when I decided to eat healthier.
- Gwen Goode, resisting temptation

"Swing by again, sometime!"

I shut the door behind our final customer of the day and flipped the sign from OPEN to CLOSED. A massive gust of air rushed out of my lungs. I'd barely had time to take a breath all afternoon.

We'd never been so busy. I thought I'd been dead on my feet when I arrived. Now, I was thinking death might not be so bad. I needed to be horizontal ASAP — even if it was in a coffin.

"Jesus," Flo wheezed, collapsing down on the plush green velvet loveseat by the window display. "That was pure insanity. I kept waiting for a lull and it just... never... happened. Nonstop sales."

"You're a lifesaver," I said, falling down beside her and laying my head on her shoulder. "I owe you. Big time."

"True."

"What do you want? I'll give you anything. My firstborn child—"

"That seems more like a punishment than a reward."

"Okay. How 'bout I buy you dinner?"

"If by *dinner* you mean a nice bottle of wine, you have a deal."

"Done." My eyes slid closed. "If I fall asleep, just leave me here. In fact, if I die, just leave me here. My rotting corpse will add to the occult aesthetic. Eventually, I'll become a friendly poltergeist that haunts the shelves."

"Are we entirely certain you don't already have a ghost? Madame Zelda gives off strong spectral vibes."

"She's flesh and bone beneath that caftan, as far as I know." My eyes cracked open again as a thought occurred to me. "But it is odd she didn't come in again today. That's nearly a week she's been MIA. A dozen missed appointments, and that's not even counting all the walk-ins we've turned away."

"People were pissed when I told them they couldn't get a tarot reading."

"I know. She's missing out on a lot of money. And that woman loves money. I thought she was just off on an another ayahuasca trip — and I do mean *trip* in the psychedelic context — but now I'm starting to get really worried." I paused. "Plus, something kind of strange happened the other day..."

"Strange? In this town? I'm shocked."

"This wasn't *spooky* strange, though... It was just *strange* strange."

I proceeded to tell Flo about the altercation I'd had with the Irish giant by the dumpsters, describing his semi-menacing manner and clear desperation to get in contact with our resident psychic.

"Jesus Christ, Gwen!" Flo pushed me up off her shoulder so she could properly glare at me. "Why didn't you tell me this right when it happened?"

"Um. Hello? I was a little busy..." My eyes shot to Hetti, who was meticulously wiping down the gold espresso machine across the room. I dropped my voice to a whisper. "...getting *kidnapped* last night! Then, I was forced to stay at Graham's place. And we were slammed with customers until literally five minutes ago. When was I supposed to find spare time to tell you about some weird moment with a vaguely hostile lumberjack-looking dude named Mickey?"

"Fair enough. But did you at least tell Graham about weird dumpster dude?"

"Why would I tell him about it?"

"Oh, I don't know," she drawled, voice thick with sarcasm. "Maybe because he's running point on your case and trying his best to keep you safe?"

"First of all, it's not *my* case. It's a case about animal sacrifices that, coincidentally, involves the alley behind my shop. Secondly, he doesn't give a hoot about my safety. I just happen to be caught up in his crosshairs at the moment."

"Is that seriously what you think?"

"That's seriously what I know," I declared. Though, for some inexplicable reason, at that exact moment a memory of Graham's moonlit face in bed last night popped into my head unbidden.

You're safe here, you know.
You're safe with me.

I bit my lip hard enough to banish the deep timbre of his voice to the darkest recesses of my brain.

Flo merely shook her head, almost as if she was disappointed in me. "I don't know what it's going to take for you to remove the horse-blinders you seem to put on whenever he walks into a room—"

"I have a secret!" I cut her off, not wanting to go down the delusional *GG + GG = SOULMATES* road she was dragging me toward with all her might. "About last night."

She was instantly intrigued. Her brown eyes widened in expectation and her voice became breathless. "Well? What is it?"

I glanced again toward Hetti, knowing she was in earshot. The barista seemed thoroughly occupied with washing dirty coffee mugs in the industrial sink. Plus, even if she was eavesdropping, I figured she wouldn't bat an eye at the details of my unorthodox abduction.

"Is it about Graham?" Flo pestered. "Did something happen between you two?"

She was hopeless.

"No! Of course not!"

Okay, so, that wasn't strictly true.

I generally wasn't a fan of lying, especially not to Flo. But in this instance, I was willing to fib to my best friend if it meant keeping the memory of Graham's lips on mine locked away in the iron-clad vault at the back of my brain where I'd shoved it as soon as he walked out my door that morning. Self-preservation took precedence over full transparency.

Flo's hopeful expression crumbled into disappointment. "The way you two were flirting this morning, I thought maybe..."

"We were not flirting!"

She waggled her eyebrows. "He bit your bagel."

"It was a breakfast sandwich!"

"That is so not my point."

"What I have to tell you is way better. Trust me." Dropping my voice to a whisper, I launched into the story, telling her everything I'd kept from Graham about Agatha, Sally, and Eliza. About the Heretics and the blood curse. About Aunt Collette being the former High Priestess. As I spoke, Flo's eyes got wider and wider and wider, until she began to look like an anime character.

"Obviously I wouldn't be able to live with myself if I got Aunt Colette's friends in trouble with the police," I said to wrap up the saga, shrugging lightly. "And I seriously hesitate to sic Graham on them."

Flo nodded in agreement. "Sending three octogenarians to the can would be kind of cold. But at the same time, it wasn't great of them to kidnap you. Or tell you to split town. I mean, how could they think selling Colette's house was an option? And the shop?" She glanced around. "This place is an institution. You can't sell it. As her friends, they should know better than anyone how much this place meant to her."

"That's the thing. They *do* know. They still want me to leave. Which means..."

"They're seriously rattled about this whole Heretic situation," Flo finished.

"*Shh!* Not so loud. This is a secret, remember?" My eyes cut to Hetti again. Thankfully, she seemed completely absorbed in tying the overly-full trash bag closed, and didn't appear to be paying us even the smallest ounce of attention. "I need to find a way to talk to the coven again, try to get them to see reason in the light of day. I'm sure we can find a solution that doesn't involve me fleeing Salem forever. But..."

"You need backup."

"I need backup," I confirmed.

"I'm totally in. Just give me a time and place, you know I'm ride-or-die."

"Thanks, Flo."

"Of course." She grinned at me. "By the way, can I just say, I always knew Aunt Colette was cool-as-shit, but... High Priestess of the Bay Colony Coven?! How badass is that?"

"Totally."

"And you're her ancestor! That means her badass witchy magic passed on to you!"

"Now you sound like Eliza Proctor."

"She might not be on target about the whole dark-witches-out-for-blood thing, but she's definitely right about you inheriting a bucketload of Colette's special brand of magic. Maybe it doesn't work for spells or potions. But you have her charm and her warmth and that way of enchanting everyone you meet."

Out of nowhere, my throat felt thick. That was, hands down, the nicest thing anyone had ever said to me. Ever. "Flo..."

She reached out, took my hand, and squeezed hard enough to crunch my bones. "Don't cry. Or I'll cry. And I'm not wearing waterproof mascara today."

"Fine. No crying." I laughed softly. "I just miss her so much."

"Me too." Another hand squeeze. "All those rainy summer days we'd spend here in the shop... She had the best stories. She gave the best hugs. Always made me laugh my ass off or cheered me up when I was having a shitty week."

"It's a shame she's not here now. She'd know what to do."

"We could always have a seance, get her opinion on things."

"Absolutely not. Knowing the two of us, we'd accidentally conjure a chaos demon and set off an apocalyptic event."

Flo harrumphed. "If Madame Zelda ever comes back, maybe she can peer into her crystal ball and channel Colette from the Great Beyond."

I snorted. "I'm pretty sure the only channel Zelda knows how to tune into with any kind of success is the Home Shopping Channel."

"Is that where she buys those caftans?"

"Almost certainly."

Flo shook her head slowly, brows furrowed. "I for one still

think the seance is a fun idea. You never know, Zelda might surprise you. Even a broken clock is right twice a day."

"I'm not letting Zelda channel Aunt Colette." I rolled my eyes. "But I really should try to track her down. If the next few weeks are anything like today, we're going to need all hands on deck to deal with the customers."

"Do you have her home address?"

"Yeah, I think so. It's jotted down somewhere in my personnel files in the back office... Why? You think I should do a wellness check?"

"No, I think *we* should do a wellness check. No way in hell are you going to track down that old flimflammer alone."

An uncharacteristic bleat of laughter came from the direction of the front door, where Hetti was hauling the trash bag. By the time I glanced over, all traces of amusement were wiped from the barista's face. She stared at me and Flo on the sofa with her typical apathetic expression.

"I'm out of here, boss," she said. Her fingers, which were painted with chipped black polish, tightly gripped the plastic bag, which appeared full to bursting. "I'll toss this in the dumpster behind the bakery on my way home."

"Our alley should be cleaned up soon," I promised her. "I'll check in with Detective Hightower tomorrow, see if we're clear to use our dumpsters again."

Hetti nodded and turned for the door.

"Thanks for all your help today!" I called after her.

The only answer I got was the tinkle of bells as the door slammed closed. I took no offense. This was a standard exit for Hetti.

"That girl needs some serotonin," Flo muttered, pushing to her feet. She pulled me up after her, ignoring my groan of protest as my tired bones screamed for sleep. "Come on. Let's go get Desmond and get the hell out of here. Ten bucks says he fell asleep grading papers at your desk in the back. Twenty says there's ink all over his adorable geeky face."

"I'm smart enough not to take that bet."

As we moved through the shop, I took mental note of all the things that needed to be handled before we opened for business tomorrow morning. The book display tables were a mess. The bundles of hanging herbs were depleted. Half our crystals were cleared out. (*Surprise, surprise...* we still had plenty of citrine.) The glass apothecary cabinets needed reorganization. The relic cabinets needed dusting and (*ugh*) Windexing. The bathroom needed fresh toilet paper and a proper scrub...

"Stop it."

My brows shot up at Florence's abrupt statement. "Stop what?"

"Hyper-fixating on everything you need to handle."

I rolled my eyes. She knew me too well. "If I scratch some of it off my list tonight, there will be less to do before we open—"

"Gwen. No. You're dead on your feet. You're going to go home, get in your shower, and then sleep." She pushed open the back door to the storage room. "In the infamous words of Scarlett O'Hara: *tomorrow is another day.*"

Tomorrow came around far too fast.

I nearly punched my alarm clock across the room when it chirped violently at half past seven. I'd slept, deep and dreamless, for nearly twelve hours, but it barely made a dent in my bone-deep weariness.

Fighting a yawn, I brewed extra-strength coffee and decided to skip my typical Sunday morning jog. Pretty much every week, like clockwork, I took a long run around town before heading to work, since The Gallows opened at noon instead of nine on Sundays. But I simply wasn't up for it today.

It was the first of the month. Officially October. My favorite month of the year. As I sipped my coffee, I grabbed a familiar jar from my spice rack and wandered to the front door. Stepping out into the crisp early-morning air, I hopped from foot to foot to keep warm as I shook a healthy sprinkle of cinnamon across the front stoop, just as Aunt Colette taught me to do when I was a kid.

Cinnamon signals abundance, Gwendolyn. Place one teaspoon at your threshold on the first of each month. When it blows inside, it will bring good fortune into your home.

It wasn't that I truly believed a common kitchen herb could have a tangible impact on my finances. But the ritual was something we used to do together. Now that she was gone, I continued the tradition because it made me feel close to her.

"Good morning, Gwendolyn."

I whipped around, hot coffee sloshing over my fingers, cinnamon jar tumbling down the front steps and rolling to a stop in the garden beds. My heart was thumping double-speed.

"Mrs. Proctor," I greeted stiffly.

She stood by the wrought-iron fence that separated our front yards, dressed in her typical gardening get-up — worn canvas apron, dirt-streaked gloves, pruning shears. She looked every bit the harmless grandmother, her hair smoothed back in a sleek chignon, her clear blue eyes untroubled behind her round spectacles. Not at all like the cloaked coven member who'd left me in a dank basement two nights ago.

Hellfire.

I'd wanted to talk to her, but not like this. Not unprepared. Definitely not alone.

"I see Colette did teach you some of our ways," Eliza noted, staring at the sprinkled cinnamon by my feet.

"She also taught me that when someone shows you who they are..." I narrowed my eyes at her. "Believe them the first time."

"You're angry with me."

"That surprises you?" I descended down onto the bottom step, never taking my eyes off her. My spine was ramrod with tension. I was ready to react at a moment's notice if someone sprung out of the hedges and tried to grab me. "You kidnapped me! Who's to say you aren't about to try it again?"

"I admit, we acted rather rashly the other night. I apologize for my part in it." She shook her head and sighed. "Truth be told, it wasn't my plan to begin with. But Sally and Agatha can be... over-excitable."

"Look, lady, the only reason I didn't call the police was out of respect for my aunt. That courtesy will expire if you, or any other members of your coven, come after me again."

"You don't need to threaten me, Gwendolyn."

"It's not a threat. It's a fact."

"We have much to discuss." Her eyes drifted over my shoulder at the sound of a door swinging open. Two lively male voices spilled out into the morning. Dan and Rich, my other neighbors, who'd recently renovated the townhouse to the left of my colonial, must be headed to brunch.

"Our methods weren't perfect, but our intentions were good," Eliza continued, lowering her voice so it didn't carry beyond my yard. "Surely, you must see that."

"You think I'm in danger."

"You *are* in danger!" Her voice rose, despite her efforts to remain calm. "We are all in danger! The fact that you are too ignorant to see, even now, how much risk your existence poses is precisely why we took such drastic measures!"

"And if you had bothered to *talk* to me about it, before taking those measures," I countered, my own volume climbing. "You might see that I can be a pretty open-minded person! But I tend to lose some of my open-mindedness when I'm tied to a freaking ch—"

"Morning, ladies!" A male voice called. "Everything okay, here?"

Swallowing down the rest of my words, I turned toward the street. Dan and Rich were standing by my front gate, staring from me to Eliza and back again. They both looked uneasy, not at all like their usual jovial selves. I realized immediately how this scene probably looked to them — like I was out here badgering an old lady, or something.

Goddess, if they only knew the truth...

"All good, gentlemen," I said, trying to smooth over the tension. "You headed to brunch?"

Rich nodded, but his eyes remained on Eliza. "How about you, Mrs. Proctor? Are you all right?"

She fluttered a frail hand toward her chest. In an instant, her voice was all sugar, no steel. "Oh, yes, Richard. Just a small tiff about the garden beds with Miss Goode. I'm sure I'll be quite all right in a moment." She blinked at him, guileless, and smiled her best innocent-granny smile. "It's just... my blood pressure goes up when I get upset..."

Oh, she was good.

Dan was flat out glaring at me, now. "Gwendolyn, I think it's best you go inside."

"But—"

"Let us make you a cup of tea, Mrs. Proctor," Rich was saying, turning his back on me. Dan followed suit. "Our reservation isn't until nine-thirty. We have plenty of time."

"That's not necessary, boys."

"We insist."

I watched as they stepped into her front yard and began to usher her up the steps of her stately Victorian. My blood was already simmering with frustration. It began to boil when her words drifted back to me just before the front door closed.

"It's so nice to know *some* of my neighbors actually care about an old woman…"

Gah!

Snatching my cinnamon jar from the flower bed, I stomped back inside and slammed my own door. A cloud of cinnamon drifted in after me.

So much for good fortune.

So far, it hadn't brought me anything but trouble.

SUNDAY at the shop was only slightly less busy than Saturday. Thankfully, the nonstop crowd kept my mind occupied. I was too busy to think about Eliza Proctor, let alone any of the other chaos of late. Before I knew it, the crowds had thinned out and the clock was marching toward six. Hetti was already halfway through her end-of-shift cleanup, making sure the espresso bar was shipshape for Tuesday morning. We were closed on Mondays, thank the goddess. I needed a day off to decompress and get my life back in order.

Much as I enjoyed the crush of customers that came with our rising popularity — and, let's be honest, the financial cushion those customers provided — it was getting harder and harder to keep up with the demand. I'd have to put out a want-ad for part time help — and soon. I could use a backup barista. If Madame Zelda didn't come back soon, I'd be in the market for a new psychic as well.

"So, like…" My final — I hoped — customer of the day turned the piece of amethyst over in her hand, her eyes captivated by the multifaceted depths of the purple gemstone. "What does it do?"

"Amethyst is known to block negative vibrations. It provides calming, healing properties. It can also help with meditation, sleep problems, mental clarity..."

"Wow." She snapped her gum. "So I just, like, stick it under my pillow and it fixes my whole life?"

"You should really charge it first, but yeah. Essentially."

"Charge it? Like an iPhone?" She brought it close to her face. "Does it have a hidden plug?"

I suppressed a laugh. "No. But if you leave it out in the moonlight, ideally on a full moon, it will infuse with natural energy..."

Feeling the weight of a stare from the front of the shop, my eyes drifted over the customer's vacuous expression. A familiar tall, muscular body was leaning against the coffee counter, sipping from one of our to-go cups. When our gazes met, he lifted his cup in a cheers motion.

"Would you excuse me for a second?" I murmured, not waiting for an answer as I left the customer to mull over her crystal purchase alone. My eyes never shifted from the man as I walked up the two mahogany steps into the front section. His eyes scanned me up and down, taking in every detail of my outfit with blatant appreciation. I was glad I'd chosen a good one, today — I was wearing an ultra short witchy-chic Free People dress with long, lace-edged bell sleeves that I'd bought for a song at Modern Millie, a vintage store around the corner. My boots were pale suede, with elaborate stitching. (They'd cost far more than a song. Closer to a full discography.) In addition to looking cool-as-shit, they went up over my knees, thus concealing the not-so-chic bandaids I'd applied to my scratched kneecaps.

"Detective Hightower," I said, smiling up at his handsome face as I came to a stop before him. "You must've read my mind — I was going to call you later today."

"Planning to ask me out? I'm free Tuesday."

"Don't tease, Detective, a girl might get the wrong idea."

"Who says I'm teasing?" he asked, winking playfully.

"What brings you here?"

"Would you believe me if I said it was for the triple-shot cappuccino?"

His eyes twinkled with good humor. He looked great — even cuter than I'd remembered, with his thick silver-streaked hair and piercing blue eyes. Six-foot-three inches of pure muscle in dark khakis and a fitted button-down. No tie. His badge was clipped beside the gun holstered at his hip.

"Our cappuccinos are good, but I doubt they warrant a trip across town."

His grin widened. "True."

"What can I do for you? Please don't tell me there's another sacrifice in my alley."

"No, no. Nothing like that." He paused. "I wanted to see for myself that you were all right. Graves has been rather tight-lipped about everything that went down the other night."

"Oh..." My heart turned over, touched by his concern. "That's sweet. I'm right as rain."

"Relieved to hear it." His grin faded into a slight frown of disapproval. "You never came in to give a statement."

"I know..." I shrugged helplessly. "I didn't think it was neces-sary, I suppose."

"Graves says you don't remember much?"

I nodded, feeling nervous butterflies burst to life in my gut. It was one thing to fib to Graham about what had happened. It was quite another to lie to an officer of the law.

Cade's eyes narrowed a shade. They were alarmingly blue. Dizzyingly blue. "Can we maybe take a walk? I know you're wrapping up for the night, but there are a few things I need to discuss with you. In private."

"Um." I swallowed hard, trying to banish the butterflies back from whence they came. "We close in about fifteen minutes. Do you mind waiting until then?"

"Not at all."

"Thanks."

I finished up with my final customer, making idle smalltalk as I bundled her crystals and candles into black tissue paper and placed them inside one of our custom gift bags — black paper, silver ribbon handles, white font, trademark noose replacing the letter 'o' in the shop name. I was entirely too conscious of Detective Hightower's eyes on me as I worked.

Once the customer left, I locked the cash register, then bustled into the storeroom to grab my purse and flip off the lights. My typical end-of-night checklist sat on my desk, a reminder of the many tasks I still needed to tackle before we reopened on Tuesday. I didn't like to leave things unfinished, but with a handsome detective waiting on me, it couldn't be helped. I hurried to the espresso bar and said goodbye to Hetti.

"I'll come back to straighten up the shelves and tackle the bathroom later tonight," I assured her. "Don't forget to update next week's purchase order. It's on my desk. Lord knows we don't want to run out of oat milk again... the hipsters will revolt."

"You got it, boss," she said, not even looking up at me.

"Thanks, Hetti. I'll see you Tuesday, okay? Don't forget to lock up when you leave. And enjoy your day off!"

She merely grunted in acknowledgement, cranking up the stereo to blast the angry alternative music she'd switched on as soon as the door closed behind the final customer of the day. My acoustic indie playlist was not to her liking, a point she'd made clear on more than one occasion.

Detective Hightower followed me out onto the street, discarding his cappuccino cup in the bin on the way. His long legs easily matched my pace as we strolled down the brick-laid pedestrian walk.

"Your alleyway is clear for use again, by the way," he informed me. "The forensics guys are finished and the carcass—" He winced. "—is gone. Feel free to use your dumpsters."

"Oh, that's great."

"How are you holding up? I know the past few days have been... a lot."

I glanced over at him. "Checking up on me?"

"Occupational hazard." He shrugged unapologetically. "I hope you know I'm here if you ever need to talk about the case. Or anything, really. Night or day."

Was the sexy, silver fox cop hitting on me? I tripped over my own feet at the thought. Cade reached out instantly to steady me, his strong grip warm even through the fabric of my dress.

"Whoa there," he murmured. "You okay?"

"Historic cobblestones and high heels — not always a great mix. If I was a practical girl, I'd donate them all to Goodwill and buy some flats."

"Now that would be a shame."

Yep, the sexy, silver fox cop was *definitely* hitting on me. I sucked in a breath. "Hey, you're a hotshot detective — you have pull! Think you could make a few calls, get the city to lay some level sidewalks? Something designed for the modern gal-on-the-go instead of, say, a seventeenth-century Pilgrim?"

His blue eyes glittered with amusement. "I'll see what I can do."

"Thanks. As a tax-paying citizen, it's good to know my hard earned dollars are going to support my interests in a concrete manner."

We took a left down a side street, walking without any particular destination in mind. It was a glorious October evening, blustery and warm despite the sun's early descent. We passed by Witch Trials Memorial, where clusters of tourists were snapping photos, and meandered by The Burying Point, a historic cemetery smack dab at the center of town, where the judges who'd condemned the witches were buried in mossy tombs. Graham's great-great-great grandfather among them. There was a line of people waiting outside the Wax Museum, eager to see creepy life-sized models of historical figures — for what reason, I could not fathom.

"I have to admit, I'm still not used to all this," Cade confessed, eyeing the droves of witch-crazed customers.

"Have you lived here long?"

"'Bout a year."

"Where were you before?"

"Baltimore." He paused. "This beat is... different, to say the least. I went from baseball and crab cakes to..."

"Costumes and ghost tours?"

"Exactly."

I laughed as we stepped around a woman dressed like Morticia Addams. "*Different* is a good way to describe Salem."

"Are you a lifelong resident?"

"Me?" I shook my head. "No. I spent my summer breaks here as a kid, but I only officially moved here two years ago, when my aunt passed away."

"I'm sorry for your loss."

I smiled softly. "Thanks."

"The Gallows was hers before it passed to you, then?"

"Yep, Aunt Colette ran it for almost forty years. She loved that old place. Somehow keeping it running feels like keeping her with me, even though she's gone."

"That's a nice way of looking at it."

A bit farther down, on the corner, a barefoot man dressed in a red and white striped shirt, torn trousers, and a black tricorn hat bearing skull and crossbones was trying to recruit some of the people to abandon the Wax Museum line in favor of the nearby Pirate Museum. When he spotted me in the crowd, his face split into a wide grin and he waved enthusiastically.

"Ahoy, Gwen!"

"Hi, Peg-Leg Pete!" I waved back. "How's business tonight?"

"Arrrr, the doubloons aren't flowing fast as we'd like, lass. Those scalawags across the way have taken all our business." He shot a glare across the street, where a brand new rival pirate-themed museum — cheekily named the Real Pirates Museum — had recently opened its doors. Even from here, I could see there was a crowd gathered outside, awaiting admission.

I grimaced in sympathy. "Sorry, Pete."

"Bloody mutineers will scuttle our business before the season is out! If things don't pick up soon, we'll be sunk. Savvy?"

"You can't go out of business, Pete! The original Pirate Museum is an institution around here."

"I know, lassie. I know. A crying shame, I tell you. Son of a biscuit eater! It's enough to make a man walk the plank. Straight to Davy Jones Locker, the lot of us..."

"Does he ever break character?" Cade asked under his breath from beside me.

"Never once since I met him," I murmured back, not looking away from the forlorn pirate. "Have you tried passing out flyers, Pete?"

He glanced back at me and burnished a thick stack of black pamphlets advertising half-off admission. "Aye, aye, I've given one to every landlubber who's crossed me path this week." He cast a dark look at the people in line for the Wax Museum, who were steadfastly ignoring him. "Some can't even be bothered to look up from their cellphones, let alone return my friendly Yo-Ho-Ho's when they pass me on the street."

"You're welcome to leave some flyers at The Gallows. I'll make sure Hetti passes them out."

"Fair Henrietta! A wench like none other. Shiver me timbers, if she'd give an old sea dog like me a chance, I'd consider it the finest bounty of all."

I could barely suppress my giggle at the thought of Peg-Leg Pete asking Hetti out on a date. A pirate and a goth — what a match. "You probably shouldn't call her a wench when you ask her out."

Beside me, Cade coughed to cover a laugh.

"Aye, aye. A fine point, lass." The pirate gave a final wave. "Smooth sailing, Gwendolyn, until we meet again!"

"Bye, Pete."

We rounded the corner and fell back into step. I felt a brief flicker of trepidation as Cade led me across the street toward the harbor, knowing we were only a stone's throw from Graham's loft. The last thing I needed was to run into him right now.

He doesn't own this city, I reminded myself firmly. *He doesn't control where you go or don't go.*

On the docks, several boats were backing out of their slips, headed out for a Sunday night on the water. Pickering Wharf was busy as ever, the outdoor patios overflowing with people sipping cocktails and snacking on appetizer plates of fried seafood beneath heating lamps. My stomach rumbled, reminding me I hadn't yet eaten today. After a few moments of silence, I glanced over at Cade and found him studying me curiously.

"What?"

He shrugged. "Just trying to figure you out. You're a bit of an enigma, Gwendolyn Goode."

"Is that a compliment or an insult?"

"Just an observation."

"Honestly, there's not much to figure out. I'm pretty ordinary."

"We'll have to agree to disagree on that front." He stopped on the sidewalk and I automatically followed suit. The crowd parted around us, a steady stream of traffic moving down the wharf. "I was wondering…"

My heart leapt.

Was the sexy, silver fox cop about to ask me out?

Moreover… did I want the sexy, silver fox cop to ask me out?

I stared up into his eyes. So blue. So beautiful. "Yes?"

"Would you maybe want to—"

But whatever Cade was about to ask me never made it past his lips. Instead of his voice, I heard someone else's. A deep, familiar rasp that paralyzed me from the crown of my head to the soles of my feet.

"You conducting a case interview without me, Hightower?"

CHAPTER FOURTEEN

I thought "bread-crumbing" was a Hansel + Gretel reference.

- Gwen Goode, learning new lingo

Detective Hightower and I turned in unison to face Graham.

He looked irritatingly good. His dark hair curled around the collar of the thick-knit fisherman's sweater he wore. The white wool offset his bronzed skin. He could've passed for a J.Crew model — until you looked into his eyes. They were so sharp as they swept up the length of my body, they seemed to pierce every exposed slice of skin.

A shiver moved down my spine as our gazes tangled. The memory of the last time I'd seen him sizzled hot in the air between us. He didn't say a word to me; he didn't need to. His silence alone was enough to make my knees quake.

"I wouldn't dream of it, Graves," Caden drawled finally, shattering the thick tension. "She's all yours... when it comes to the case, at least."

Graham's jaw tightened in an alarming way as his eyes shifted to the detective's, blue and green clashing together like swords on a battlefield. Their poses were mirror images — feet planted, arms crossed over chests, expressions devoid of all warmth. My discomfort grew as the silence stretched on. Neither seemed particularly inclined to end it.

"Thought we had an understanding," Graham said eventually.

"Your jurisdiction covers the case," Cade returned. "Doesn't extend beyond that, as far as I'm aware."

"Then adjust your awareness."

My eyes volleyed back and forth between them as their sparring match grew more and more hostile.

"Here I thought you were a professional, Hightower."

"Nothing unprofessional happening in my eyes, Graves."

"Maybe you need to visit an optometrist."

"Never thought you were one to play by the rules. From what I've heard, you don't think they apply to you." Cade paused. "Makes me wonder if that's what your involvement here is actually about."

Graham's jaw clenched. A muscle leapt in his cheek as his gaze flashed to my face for the span of a single heartbeat before returning to the detective. "We have a string of macabre sacrifices, no suspects, no resolution in sight. She's been targeted. We still don't know why or what their next move will be. It's a damn mess. I don't need you complicating things further by crossing the line."

"Oh? You sure that's it?" Cade's smile was biting. "Or are you just pissed I found the balls to make my move first?"

Graham's jaw was so tight, I thought his teeth might crack. "Watch it, Hightower."

"Are you threatening a member of the force? Not smart, Graves. Even for someone with your connections."

"*Boys!*" I interjected before this could further deteriorate, stepping between them with my arms thrown wide. "Enough. Hellfire and brimstone, what are you, fourteen years old? I don't know what this pissing contest is about and, frankly, I don't really care. Whatever your problems are... I'm sure you're capable of working them out without this ridiculous show of machismo. Now, why don't we all take a deep breath and— *Hey!*"

My squawk of protest was summarily ignored as Graham — who, sometime during my speech, had reached out, grabbed me by my outstretched hand, and yanked me to his side — began dragging me down the sidewalk, leaving Cade in the dust.

"Let go!" I hissed.

"No."

"You're *embarrassing* me!" I tugged futilely against his grip. "People are looking at us!"

He stopped walking, but did not release my hand. When he glared down into my face, I sucked in a breath at his thunderous expression. He was breathing hard, his self-control poised on a knife's edge.

"We need to talk," he clipped tersely.

"So, talk."

"Alone." His gaze cut back to Cade, who was still standing several feet away, watching things unfold. "It's important."

"I don't care how important it is, I was in the middle of—"

"You can flirt with the dreamy detective later."

I glared up at him. "You're a real asshole sometimes, you know that?"

"You have five seconds to say goodbye, or I'm throwing you over my shoulder."

Gaia, save me.

That statement shouldn't have been so damn hot. Nonetheless, a furl of pure heat bloomed in my gut, instantly incinerating the nervous butterflies that had taken up residence there. Tearing my gaze from Graham's, I looked back at the detective somewhat helplessly.

Cade's eyes were on my hand. More specifically, on Graham's hand, which was still tightly enveloping it.

"Caden..."

"Go on, Gwendolyn." He lifted his gaze to mine, giving me a reassuring nod and a half-smile. "This seems important. We'll talk soon."

"I'm sorry," I called over my shoulder. I'd barely gotten the words out before Graham was moving again, tugging me along behind him heedless of the thick crowds on the sidewalk.

"That was seriously not cool," I informed his back.

He didn't bother to respond.

We sped down the wharf, passing a row of busy restaurants. The last time I'd been to his building, we entered through the garage on the back side, which faced the harbor. This time, Graham led me through the front doors, into a street-facing office that encompassed the first floor. The glass window read GRAVEWATCH in a clean, opaque, capitalized font. I barely had time to take in the sleekly decorated reception area before he marched me past a polished onyx desk where a stunning platinum blonde woman was sitting — and, I might add, openly gaping at us — through a thick set of double doors, down a long hallway lined with more closed doors, and finally into a private conference room with windows that looked out at the water.

It was a nice view, spanning the docks, the old sail loft, and *The Friendship*, a wooden 171-foot, triple-masted, old-timey schooner that called Salem its home port. Not that I could appreciate said view. All my focus was on the seething man who'd just dragged me into the room without even a hint of gentleness. His mood was tangible, aggression and frustration pouring off him.

The door swung shut behind us with an audible click. Graham was still holding my hand. I belatedly jerked it away and took a few steps toward the bank of windows, not stopping until the stately wood conference table was between us. For whatever reason, I felt safer that way.

"Okay, Graham," I forced myself to say, aiming for a light tone. "You've got me here. Are you going to tell me the big emergency or do I have to tickle it out of you?"

I was trying to lighten the mood. It didn't work. Serious as a heart attack, he planted both his hands on the conference room table and pinned me with that intense stare. "Madame Zelda."

I blinked, startled by the sudden change in topic. Whatever I'd expected him to say, it was not that. "What about her?"

"She's your psychic."

"Yes."

"She conducts business out of your shop."

"Yes," I repeated. "Look, what is this about—"

"When was the last time you saw her?"

"I don't know. About a week ago? She hasn't been in."

He processed this information for a moment. "You didn't report her missing?"

"She has a tendency to disappear. She's sort of flighty. It isn't entirely abnormal for her to fall off the face of the earth, then wander back in a few days later like nothing happened." I paused, narrowing my eyes at him. "Why? What does Zelda have to do with you?"

"I met with a new client yesterday morning. Mickey O'Banion."

Mickey!

The guy from the dumpsters. It had to be him. Statistically speaking, it was borderline impossible that there were two separate Mickeys running around Salem, looking for my psychic. I tried my best to hide my reaction to this realization, keeping my expression as blank as humanly possible.

"That name mean something to you?"

"No," I lied immediately. "Should it?"

"You've never heard of the O'Banions?"

I thought about this for half a second, then felt my eyes grow wide. "O'Banion as in... *those* O'Banions? The ones who own that seedy bar by the bridge?"

Graham nodded stiffly.

There weren't many places Aunt Colette told me were off limits when I was a kid. The Banshee was one of them. It wasn't until I reached adulthood and learned the bar was home base for the O'Banion family — who reputedly had ties, *deep* ties, to the Irish mafia scene, ties that hadn't really been cut, even when their notorious uncle Whitey went to prison and the Winter Hill gang was wiped off the streets of Boston — that I figured out why she was dead-set against me getting anywhere near it. In all my time in Salem, I'd never stepped so much as a toe inside The Banshee, and had no plans to change that policy anytime soon.

"Guessing you've heard the rumors about that family, seeing as you've gone white as a sheet," Graham said bluntly.

It was a good guess.

"Mickey O'Banion came to me yesterday," Graham continued. "Usually, they like to do their own dirty work. Handle things in house. But they've been hitting roadblocks in their own search and asked for my help. Apparently, someone has been stealing O'Banion heirlooms and selling them to the highest bidder. Someone with access to his ailing mother, who makes regular visits to the home, who has a history of criminal activity..." He paused. "Were you aware your psychic has a criminal record?"

"Um. No?"

"You didn't think it wise to run a CORI check on someone in your employ?"

Goddess, not this again.

"She's not *in my employ*. She just uses my space. It's a mutually beneficial relationship! Sort of like a sea anemone and a cl —" I stopped short at the dark look on his face, which told me in no uncertain terms that he was not interested in a marine biology lesson. Heaving a martyred sigh, I asked, "You really think Madame Zelda is conning old ladies out of their costume jewelry?"

Graham's jaw clenched. "An emerald the size of a golfball is no worthless bauble. Mickey estimates up to half a million dollars of priceless items are gone."

I paled. *"Half a million dollars?"*

"Madame Zelda — given name Jennifer H. Custer — was arrested twelve years ago for passing bad checks, and again six years ago for grand larceny. Served four years in Rhode Island before she moved here." He crossed both arms over his chest, his corded muscles apparent even through his thick sweater. "Which you would know if you'd done even the slightest bit of research about the people you surround yourself with. How can you be so careless with your safety?"

"I'm not careless with anything," I said, my own anger bubbling to the surface. "You have no right to judge the way I live my life or the way I run my business."

"Except when the way you run your business becomes *my* business." He exhaled sharply. "I've been hired to track down your psychic. O'Banion won't go to the police, for obvious reasons." Graham's brows furrowed darkly. "Mickey, hell, all four of the O'Banion brothers are batshit crazy. I don't want you anywhere near him."

Hmm.

Graham didn't seem to realize I'd already had the displeasure of meeting Mickey. The memory of our interaction by the dumpsters made my hands go clammy with hindsight anxiety.

"Do you know her address?" His gaze, already searching, became frighteningly sharp. "It's not on file with the city or in any of the government databases. Wherever she's staying, it's either under a fake name or not registered at all."

My mouth opened, then clicked shut as my mind whirled with contradictory thoughts. Part of me wanted to tell Graham the truth, come clean about everything that I knew and trust him to handle it. But a louder, more insistent part of me was adamant that Graham had his own interests at work. He was representing Mickey O'Banion, not Madame Zelda. Anything I told him would be used against her. And while she might not be my favorite person in the world... I wasn't about to throw her to the proverbial wolves. At least, not until I had definitive proof she deserved to be tossed there.

"Gwen, focus," Graham said tiredly. "This is important."

"Mickey O'Banion..." I lifted my gaze to meet his. "What's he going to do to her?"

"I don't know. He's paying me to find her. That's where my curiosity ends."

"But what if he's planning to hurt her? Make her swim with the fishes or something?"

His lips twitched. "Swim with the fishes?"

"Sue me, I'm not up on my mafia lingo."

Graham shook his head slowly back and forth, looking like he wasn't sure whether to laugh at me or throttle me. "All I can tell you is, your psychic fucked with the wrong people. The O'Banions are not big fans of getting ripped off. They're even less thrilled when it's their bed-bound, soon-to-be-in-hospice-care family matriarch getting ripped off." He paused, all traces of humor leaving his face. "What they *are* big fans of is retribution, in whatever form that comes. That does not bode well for Zelda."

My whole body locked, every muscle going solid as a rock. "And, knowing that, you're just going to hand her over to them?"

"Like I said, my job begins and ends with locating her. Anything else is the client's business."

"How can you think that way? Even if she screwed up... she's still a human being."

"She's a career criminal."

"What happened to innocent until proven guilty?"

"That's for the judicial system to sort out. You want black and white, call your precious detective. Me? I'm not bound by those parameters. I do my job, I get paid. That's it." His eyes glittered darkly as the muscle in his jawline clenched and unclenched. "Told you once before, babe. *Gray*. Remember?"

Oh, I remembered.

I stared at him, wondering if he was truly as callus as he wanted me to believe. I knew, deep down, there was a heart that beat inside his chest. I knew he cared about people. I'd even seen it in action, been on the receiving end of it. But in this moment, staring at him, I saw only the cold mask he was so fond of wearing to intimidate others into submission. And I knew, with sudden clarity, that I couldn't tell him the truth — not about Zelda's potential whereabouts, not about the incident with Mickey by the dumpsters, not about a damn thing.

I swallowed harshly. "Fine. Got it. Good luck tracking her down."

"Gwen—"

"Like I said, I have no idea where she is or what she's up to these days. If you find her, tell her to call me."

"Gwendolyn," he repeated more firmly, his tone totally no-nonsense. I got the sense he wasn't buying my bullshit. Not at all. "This woman is not your friend. She is not part of your inner circle."

"So?"

243

"*So,*" he stressed, his tone softening a smidgen. "I've seen a lot of cases like this, involving people like this. Rarely works out with a fairy tale ending, carriage ride into the sunset, if you catch my drift. The way I figure it, Zelda's made her bed. She's shit where she eats, she's shit where she sleeps, she's shit everywhere. And when that shit hits the fan — and it will hit the fan, that I guarantee — I don't want you getting splattered. I don't want you anywhere near this mess."

He's worried about you.

I banished the unwelcome intrusive thought with a ferocious mental shove to the dark recesses of my brain. "What do you expect me to do, Graham? Zelda's off the grid. I've been calling her for days. Her voicemail is full."

"She comes into the shop, you call me. Immediately."

"I don't have your number," I retorted — and instantly wanted to insert my foot into my own mouth. I did *not* want his number.

"You do," he informed me. "I programmed it into your phone the other day."

"You did?"

He nodded. "Gwen. Hear me when I say this: Mickey O'Banion is not a nice guy. He's got a violent streak. All the O'Banion boys do — his older brothers are so wild, they make Mickey look like a fucking monk. And right now, those boys are seriously pissed off that someone's been taking advantage of their senile mother. They're the type to swing first, ask questions later. No matter who gets in their way." He paused. "You are not going to get in their way. You hear me?"

"I hear you."

"You'll call me the moment Zelda comes into the shop," he reiterated.

"I said I hear you."

"You'll steer clear if Mickey O'Banion — if any of the O'Banions — tries to contact you."

"For the last time, *I hear you!* Jeeze. Lay off."

He eyed me severely, his gaze sharp as ever. "You really have no idea where Zelda might be?"

"I have no clue where she lives or where she goes when she's not telling fortunes in the back room," I told him truthfully. "Now, if that's all, I need to get back to The Gallows."

"It's six thirty. You're closed for the day."

My chin jerked up in surprise at his familiarity with my schedule. I suppose I shouldn't have been so shocked. He was a private detective, after all. Knowing things was sort of his whole business model.

"Right," I murmured. "We're closed to customers, but I still have a shedload of uncompleted items on my end-of-week cleaning checklist, including about six straight years worth of Windexing, so if you don't mind..."

Trying to breathe deeply, I avoided his gaze as I rounded the table and beelined for the exit, my boots rapping audibly against his polished marble flooring. I was nearly at the door when Graham cut me off at the pass, stepping into my path and blocking my escape with his large form. His large hands settled on my biceps, effective as shackles. His face tilted down to stare into mine, those piercing green eyes inescapable.

"You're not lying to me again, are you Gwendolyn?" he whispered, his words a velvet blade between two ribs.

"*Again?*" I bleated, heart pounding. "What do you mean *again?*"

He didn't answer right away. After a few long seconds, I realized he wasn't going to answer at all. He was just going to let me suffer, wondering which one of my fabrications he'd seen through.

Bending forward, his mouth brushed my ear. "You've got a

bad habit of underestimating my ability to see through your bullshit."

Hellfire!

"Or..." I whispered back. "Maybe you don't know me as well as you think you do."

This was the wrong thing to say. I knew it the moment the words left my mouth. I'd thrown down a challenge and, alpha male that he was, Graham couldn't resist the urge to best it. His fingers flexed against my arms, his eyes flared with unchecked intensity. A rough sound moved in his throat.

"More likely, I know you twice as well as you want me to. Which freaks you out, gives you the urge to bolt even more than normal." He moved closer, his hands leaving my biceps to circle around to my upper back, sliding featherlight across the fabric of my dress. His voice dropped to a low whisper. "But the thing is, I'm not letting you do that anymore."

"W-what?" I stuttered.

"This dance we've been dancing, these past few months? I'm done with it. I've waited for the ice to thaw on its own. I've waited for you to admit how you feel. I've waited for you to get over your trust issues and come to me. I'm not waiting anymore. I'm done with your boundaries and your bullshit excuses."

My mouth fell open in shock. I didn't know what to say, so I simply blurted, "My excuses are not bullshit!"

"They are, babe."

"If that's how you feel, why are you holding me here?"

I couldn't see his smile, but I felt it against the skin of my neck. And it felt *great*. So great, my knees nearly buckled.

"Because," he said lowly. "God help me, I happen to think your bullshit is pretty fucking cute most of the time. I like watching you panic when I manage to work my way under your defensive perimeters. I like watching you squirm when you realize you've forgotten to hold me at arm's length."

"That's not very nice," I pointed out.

"Never claimed to be nice." Graham's breath was hot on my neck, sending shivers down my spine. "You drive me fucking crazy, you know that? Half the time, I tell myself you're not worth the effort."

My spine snapped straight. "Well, excuse me—"

"But somehow," he cut me off, still whispering. "No matter how much you piss me off pretending to be indifferent to this..." His fingertips slid down my spine as his lips pressed against the hollow of my throat. I shuddered as I felt the barest flick of his tongue against my skin. "Fuck, Gwen, I still want more."

My lungs seized up, all air flow halting entirely. His fingertips put pressure on the small of my back, bringing my body into full contact with his. I gasped involuntarily as we collided. My hands fell to his hips, gripping the belt-loops of his jeans to keep myself upright.

"What—" I breathed, rattled. "Graham, what are you doing—"

His mouth skimmed the column of my throat. The tip of his nose dragged along my jawline. And then, in a blink, his lips were hovering a hairsbreadth above mine.

"*More,*" he whispered.

Then, his head slanted to the side and his mouth sank onto mine, a kiss nothing at all like our last — not designed to shut me up, not hard or fast or harsh, but sinfully slow and achingly thorough. He devoured my mouth, his lips moving over mine in a way that made me gasp and clutch at him for balance.

The second my lips parted, his tongue demanded entry, spearing inside like he was dying to taste me. I wish I could say I didn't kiss him back right away, that I put up even the smallest bit of a fight, but the truth was, I was just as needy for him. Just as ravenous. I arched against him when his hands slid into my hair to yank my head back for better access, moaning into his mouth when my breasts pushed up against the firm planes of his chest.

Goddess, that felt good.

My arms tightened around him, sliding around his back, anchoring my body to his. His muscles were like steel under my fingertips. I couldn't get close enough. It was electric, insatiable. I'd spent most of my life wondering what it would be like to finally, finally kiss Graham Graves. Envisioning the feel of his lips, picturing the heat of his skin. Imagining his taste, his touch, his scent. But my daydreams were no match for reality.

Reality was so, *so* much better.

Years worth of pent-up pining, months of verbal sparring, weeks of heated glances, days of sexual tension... all of it exploded between us in a dizzying instant that set off fireworks beneath my ribcage and between my legs. He pushed me back against the conference room table and, before I was aware of it happening, he'd dropped his hands to cup my ass and lifted me up onto it. My thighs spread to accommodate him and he moved in without hesitation, shoving my dress up nearly to my hips so we were flush together once more. He loosed a low growl as my thighs cradled his body, and I tried not to whimper at the feel of him — his length, hard as steel through the fabric of his jeans, rubbing torturously against me; the rough scratch of denim against the bare, sensitive skin of my upper legs.

Hellfire.

Our mouths were fused together, the already heated kiss turning molten as the passion mounted. My arms wound around his neck, my fingers threading through the overgrown locks of dark hair that brushed his nape. His hands were at my hips, each fingertip digging in with such force, I thought I might have bruises tomorrow. We were wild for one another. Neither of us showed any sign of stopping, even though a small voice in the back of my head suggested, rather impolitely, that we probably should.

But then, his tongue was in my mouth and he was grinding into me, his hips rolling in a way that made my mind blank completely. His mouth moved more fervently over mine, head slanting this way and that, deepening the kiss until I couldn't breathe. Couldn't think. Couldn't do anything but cling to him and kiss him back.

My legs lifted, looping around his waist as he pressed me farther onto the table. His hands were working their way beneath the hem of my dress, calluses dragging deliciously against against the thin lace of my underwear. I writhed impatiently as his fingertips toyed with the elastic waistband, wanting to feel those hands *inside* my underwear with a desperation I could hardly fathom, let alone find the words to express aloud. I kissed him harder, delving my hands deeper into his hair, hoping my desires were conveyed nonverbally. I needed him to touch me, *now*, right this moment, because if he didn't, I might explode into a million pieces, fractured apart by sheer lust.

"*Ahem.*"

We froze at the sudden clearing of a throat. Graham didn't move a muscle except to pull his mouth off mine, just enough for him to get a few words out.

"What is it?"

"You have an urgent call, Mr. Graves," a feminine voice said, sounding rather embarrassed.

That made two of us.

"Take a message, Brianne," he clipped at his receptionist. His fingers were still hooked in the lace of my panties, for Gaia's sake.

"But... it's Holden. He's in the field. And you said..."

"Fuck." Graham's forehead tipped forward to rest on mine.

He exhaled, his breath warm as wildfire on my still-wet lips. "Tell him I'll be there in two."

The door clicked closed.

For a moment, neither of us moved. I felt like someone had dumped a bucket of ice water over my head, leaving me numb and cold in the wake of fiery passion. I didn't know what to do in this situation besides what I always did when things with Graham got complicated.

Bolt.

"Let me go," I said flatly.

"Gwen—"

"This never happened." Pushing him back with all my might, I hopped off the table, grabbed my purse, and hurtled headlong toward the door.

"The fuck it didn't," he growled, prowling after me.

"Then we're going to *pretend* it never happened."

"The fuck we are!"

"Graham. Don't be stubborn." I ran my fingers through my hair, hoping like hell it wasn't all mussed from his roving hands. I pressed my lips together, knowing they were swollen from his fervent kisses. "We had a momentary lapse of judgment. I plead insanity."

He made a choked sound of disbelief. "You *are* insane if you think I'm just going to let you leave after we finally—"

"Don't you have an urgent call waiting for you?"

He cursed lowly.

I reached the door, but only managed to get it open a crack before his hand shot out and slammed it shut again. His words were a low, ominous rasp. "Where do you think you're going?"

"Home."

He fell silent, but I knew better than to mistake quiet for calmness. I felt the heat of his body hovering an inch behind mine, felt the rapid rhythm of his breathing against the nape of

250

my neck. Anger and frustration and pure sexual desire were rolling off him in visceral waves.

"You're fooling yourself if you think we're finished talking about this," he gritted out between clenched teeth. "Go on. Run home. Convince yourself this was a — what did you call it? *Lapse in judgment.* But Gwen?" He pressed into me and my knees nearly buckled when I felt the rigid length of him against my ass. "I'll be here when you're ready to lapse again."

CHAPTER FIFTEEN

They say you attract what you fear most... I am soooo scared of all-expense-paid vacations.
- Gwen Goode, dreaming of a white sand beach

I couldn't go home. I didn't want to be alone with my thoughts. And, hell, I was half-afraid of Graham showing up at my front door to finish what we'd started on his conference room table before his perfectly put-together receptionist saw fit to interrupt. I should've been thankful she did so but, instead, all I felt was burning resentment that I'd finally, *finally*, after several eons of waiting, been essentially flat on my back beneath Graham Graves, only to have the experience cut short. Seeing as I had no plans to ever in a million years repeat said experience, I would've liked to at least get an orgasm out of it.

But I digress.

I speed-walked the five blocks from Pickering Wharf to

Desmond and Florence's place, which sat just around the corner from The House of Seven Gables, a local landmark made famous — at least, in literary circles and high school English classrooms — by Nathaniel Hawthorne. At first, I admit, my brisk clip was simply to put some immediate distance between me and Graham. But as I passed by the dark harbor, skirting around clusters of tourists and handholding couples, I couldn't shake the uncomfortable sensation that someone was watching me from the shadows.

Following me.

I glanced around, half-expecting to see Mickey O'Banion and his horde of batshit brothers barreling my direction, or the witchy trio of Sally, Agatha, and Eliza blocking my path or, scariest of all, Graham Graves charging down the sidewalk after me with mouthwatering desire in his frosty green eyes. Yet, no matter where I looked, I recognized no one in the crowd.

Chalking my frazzled senses up to the tidal wave of arousal still crashing through my system, I dismissed the paranoia, picked up my pace, and carried on my way. By the time I reached the yellow townhouse, I was practically running.

Flo answered the door after a single knock.

"Hey! This is a surprise."

"I know, I'm sorry." I fidgeted under the soft glow of the front porch light. "I was in the area, and—"

She waved away my apologies. "Come in, come in. We're just about to sit down to dinner. Des made his famous mushroom risotto. I'll set another place for you."

"I made out with Graham," I blurted.

Florence froze for five endless seconds, her mouth a perfectly round '*O*' of surprise. Her wide eyes scanned my face, trying to discern if I was messing with her. I knew I was probably flushed with embarrassment and shock and — I wasn't too proud to admit — a bit of residual lust from the feeling of Graham's body against mine, his teeth nipping my bottom lip, his hands delving into my hair...

Focus, Gwen!

"Des, sweetheart?" Flo called down the hall toward his study, never looking away from me. "Eat without me, okay?"

She didn't wait for his response. Finally coming unstuck from her daze, she grabbed me by the hand, yanked me through the kitchen — pausing only to grab the uncorked bottle of Bordeaux off the table, which was fully set for dinner, along with the glasses sitting beside their empty plates — and led me out onto the small back patio they shared with their next door neighbors.

"Pour," she muttered, shoving the bottle at me.

This was not the reaction I'd been expecting. Frankly, I'd been expecting her to do cartwheels down Derby Street. Blast off a few fireworks. Maybe rent out one of those planes that wrote sky messages, proclaiming her pure joy at the news.

"Flo—"

"Shh! I'm processing."

"But—"

"*Pour.*"

I got to work filling our glasses while she flipped on the gas fire pit. It wasn't until we were settled in our chairs, thick flannel blankets draped over our laps, sipping our wine and watching the flames dance, that my best friend spoke again.

"Okay. I've processed." She narrowed her eyes at me over the rim of her glass. "So, you made out with Graham."

"Um." I took a large sip of my wine. "Yeah."

"When?"

"Just now. I came straight here."

"Where?"

"His office."

Her brows arched. "The Gravewatch office?"

I nodded. "On the conference room table."

"*Christ!*" She took a massive swallow. "How did this happen?"

"Honestly, I have no idea. We were butting heads, like we always do, and then, somehow... suddenly... we... *weren't,*" I finished weakly.

Her eyes narrowed to slits.

"He basically did it to win an argument," I hastened on, clutching my glass tighter. "He was asking me some questions, he sensed I was withholding information from him... but I wasn't budging. Since he couldn't rattle me with his words, I guess he tried a new tactic. That's all it was."

Her mouth pursed in barely-contained rage.

"Flo," I murmured hesitantly. "I'm not sure I understand your reaction right now. Haven't you been the staunchest advocate of this? Haven't you been desperately hoping for something to happen between Graham and me? Now, it finally does, and you seem... angry."

"Damn straight I'm angry!"

"Why?"

"Because I've been dreaming of this day for years — *years!* — and when it finally happens, it's all messed up! Just... totally wrong!"

"What do you mean *wrong?*"

"You aren't supposed to have an angry make out session with that man in the middle of a verbal sparring match and, five seconds after it happens, convince yourself it was a mistake! You're supposed to *look inside your heart and admit to yourself that you've been in love with him since you were ten!*"

"How do you know I think it was a mistake?"

"Please!" She rolled her eyes. "I took one look at you and could tell you were ready to book a one-way ticket to Timbuktu rather than face the facts. When it comes to Graham, your fight or flight instinct kicks in almost immediately. I can only imagine how fast you high-tailed it out of there. Tell me, did you break the sound barrier? I thought I heard a sonic boom over the harbor about fifteen minutes ago."

I took another sip of my wine.

Flo did the same.

"I haven't been in love with him since I was ten," I grumbled sulkily after a long silence.

"Who do you think you're talking to here? I know you. Sometimes, I think I know you better than you know yourself. And I love you, Gwennie. I don't want to see you get hurt." She shook her head, her expression torn between anxiety and anger. "As much as I've been rooting for you and Graham to finally pull your heads out of your asses and admit there are some very deep, very real feelings there... I can't help worrying you're going to end up in an even worse position if you let this become about manipulating each other in some part of the weird twisted battle of wills the two of you are always locked in. God! I've never met two more stubborn individuals in my life. Makes me want to smack your skulls together, knock some sense into you both."

I digested this for a while. "I know you think he and I are meant to be, but honestly... sometimes I can't stand him. He makes me so unbelievably mad. There's no one in the world who can get under my skin like he does."

"I'm well aware," she said wryly.

"With everyone else, I can keep it together. But for whatever reason, he's got this ability to slip behind my defenses and rattle me to my foundations." My fingers tightened on the delicate stem of my glass, twirling it absently so the firelight refracted in the deep red Bordeaux. "My childhood... I... I grew up... rough."

"I know, honey."

"I used to think it was lousy karma. That maybe I did something terrible in a former life to deserve the nightmare that was my mother." Flo's mouth opened to refute this, but I barreled on.

"I know better, now. It's not fate or predestination. It's purely luck of the draw which cradle you wake up in. Some people are born with Lady Luck on their side; born into happy homes with stable parents. And some of us... aren't."

Flo nodded in silent agreement.

"I knew from the start she wasn't on my side," I continued, clearing my throat lightly. "Lady Luck, that is. Looking around at other kids who never had to worry about the electric getting switched off or their mom going off on a three-day bender or some creepy drug dealer coming around in the middle of the night to collect his due..." I narrowed my eyes on my glass, afraid if I looked at Flo, my courage to share would falter. "But then, I came here. To Salem. To Aunt Colette. One random summer afternoon, I stepped on a sea urchin — which normally would've seemed like the *epitome* of bad luck. Only, that day, I looked up into the eyes of an honest-to-god hero in a red lifeguard suit. My personal savior, sent down to keep me safe from all the darkness that shrouded my life." I laughed but there was no joy in the sound. "I needed so desperately for something — someone — to believe in back then. For a long time, I was stupid enough to believe that someone was Graham."

I heard Flo suck in a sharp breath. "Gwen..."

"He was more than a childhood crush for me. He was... hope. Hope for a different sort of life, hope for a better sort of future. He made me believe my luck was finally changing. That the tide was finally was turning from bad to good. And I freaking *worshipped* him for it." I could hear the sadness in my own voice. "Though I guess it's true, what people always say — never meet your heroes. I should've known he wasn't my protector. He wasn't a god. He wasn't my good luck charm. He was just one more twisted thread in a string of rotten luck."

"Gwen, honey..."

"You know, as pathetic as it sounds, there was a part of me

that still clung to that old infatuation when I came back to town two years ago? I was so lost after Aunt Colette passed, after I had to toss all my post-grad plans down the garbage chute. My luck never felt worse than in those first dark days living here. But in the back of my mind... he was still there, like this shiny beacon of goodness and light, warding off the shadows that kept pushing in on me." My brittle laugh burst out again. "Then, the very first time I saw him again, he shattered every illusion I'd ever had that Lady Luck might finally be on my side."

"He didn't mean to hurt you that night, Gwen. It wasn't intentional, those things he said about you and your aunt..."

I shook my head sadly. "That's not the point."

"What is, then?"

"It's not just that he humiliated me in front of you and Desmond and a whole bar of witnesses. It's not even that now, with him working this case, he takes every chance he gets to push my buttons. It's that..." I steadied my shoulders, forcing out the words. "I can't even look at him without feeling unbelievably stupid. Unbelievably *angry*. Not at him — at myself, for wasting so many years believing he was something special, when he's not. He's just an ordinary guy I hung all my foolish hopes on, for no good reason. And that makes me feel..."

Weak. Like a scared little girl, living out a nightmare, unable to control her own environment or her emotional responses.

"Gwennie," Flo interjected gently. "You can't punish yourself for needing someone to pin your dreams on as a kid. That's not fair — not to Graham, and definitely not to yourself." Flo shook her head. "Have you ever considered the fact that, despite what you say, you still have him up on that godlike pedestal?"

I flinched, eyes flying to her. "I do not!"

"You do, though. You hold Graham Graves to a higher standard than anyone else in your life. You expect miracles from him.

You expect perfection. But he's not Superman. He's a human, like everyone else. He makes mistakes. He miscalculates."

"Oh, trust me, I know he makes mistakes."

"You should cut him a little slack."

"Cut him slack? *Cut him slack?!*"

"I just mean—"

"No," I declared, vehement. I was suddenly breathing so hard I was almost panting, emotions churning inside me in an unstoppable vortex. "You're right, Flo. He's not my Superman, here to save the day. He's my freaking *kryptonite*. He's an emotional crutch I leaned on for way too long. He's not a sign of shifting fortune. Not good luck. If anything, he's my freaking *bad luck charm*."

"Gwen? Honey?"

"What?!"

"Don't get mad at me, but... do you think it's remotely possible... you might be twisting things in your head to justify all the mixed emotions you're feeling toward Graham right now?"

"They aren't mixed. They're clear as day. Loathing. Hatred. Resentment. Wrath."

"Okay! Okay. If you say we hate him, we hate him. Solidarity, sister." She set down her wine glass on the side table and scooted her chair closer to mine, so she could look into my face. "I just think, *maybe*, there's a chance that... it's easier to hate him than to admit what you really feel."

"Aren't you supposed to be on my side, here?"

"I am on your side! But..."

My brows arched. "What?"

"Love and hate are two sides of the same coin, that's all I'm saying. The way you describe your feelings for him... the way he's able to rattle you like nobody else... that's not something to just throw away because it scares you."

"You act like I've never dated before. I've had relationships with plenty of men! Nice, well-adjusted men, who didn't drive me insane or push my buttons just for the fun of it, who didn't goad me into a reaction because it amuses them."

"Right. But — and don't kill me for saying this — you didn't love any of those men. When those relationships ended, you barely blinked. You weren't heartbroken. You weren't shattered. You weren't even upset."

I chewed my bottom lip. "So?"

"So, Graham is different. You know this. It's why you've been avoiding him for so long — even when he's made it pretty damn apparent he'd like you to *stop* avoiding him." She hesitated for a beat, as if deciding whether or not to say the next part aloud. "Graham can absolutely come across like an arrogant asshole, but... I think deep down he's just as scared of starting something with you."

"Graham Graves? *Scared*?" I snorted. "He's not scared of anything."

"Fine. Whatever." She threw up her hands, exasperated. "I'm just saying, be careful. Love — especially new love — is so delicate. So unbearably fragile. It can shatter if you don't handle it correctly. And those shatters can cut you. Deep."

"I don't want to *handle it*, delicately or otherwise. Don't you understand? I have no interest in falling in love, Flo! Not with him, not with anyone. I'm perfectly content with my life, just as it is. I don't need a partner. I have friends, I have the shop, I have my house. I live in a cute, quirky town with cute, quirky people. Everything is—"

Fine.

There was that word again. I caught myself before it slipped out, wishing I couldn't hear Graham's voice in my head.

Christ, Gwen! Don't you understand? You deserve so much more than fine!

I shook the memory off, returning my focus to my best

friend. "I know you don't understand. You have Desmond, he makes you happy. Seeing that makes me so happy for you. But the way I grew up, the way that I am... I just don't think that sort of a relationship is ever going to be in the cards for me. I'm not built for that longterm, lifelong, finish-each-other's-sentences, can't-eat-can't-sleep-without-you, star-crossed soulmates sort of thing. I'm used to holding everything together on my own. To counting only on myself. I don't know how to be any other way."

"It breaks my heart to hear you say that," Florence whispered, her voice thick with emotion. "Because, Gwen, you may not think you're built for a relationship like that, but I don't know anyone on this planet more deserving of one."

I didn't know what else to say, so I didn't say anything at all.

"What were you doing there in the first place?" she asked eventually, steering the conversation into safer waters. "At Graham's office?"

"He dragged me in there and ambushed me about Madame Zelda."

"Is he looking for a tarot reading?"

I quickly filled Florence in on everything I'd learned about the psychic's criminal enterprises, the O'Banion family, and Graham's involvement.

"Let me get this straight," she murmured. "The psycho dumpster dude from the other day is *Mickey O'Banion?* And he's hired Graham to track down Zelda, because he suspects she stole *half a million dollars* worth of jewelry from his *dying mother* during their private readings at the family home? A family which, by all accounts, is not just *any* family, but an offshoot of a *mafia* family full of hellions and hotheads, most of whom have already served time, all of whom are out for blood and clearly willing to serve more?"

"That pretty much sums it up."

"And when Graham finds her, he's going to hand her over to said psycho family?"

"Seems that way."

"Even if she's innocent?"

"Apparently, he doesn't care."

"Damn." Flo blew out a breath. "I guess that explains why she's been out of work."

"Yep. And I doubt she'll be back until this is all resolved. Which leaves me seriously in the lurch — right before Halloween, no less. I was counting on the foot traffic she brings in. The shop's profits will take a big hit without her." I ran a hand through my hair, frustration consuming me. "But even putting my own selfish needs aside, I can't throw her to the wolves. She may not be my favorite person in the world, but I'm not willing to see her hurt by a hothead like Mickey. If I find her before he does, maybe I can get her to return the jewelry."

"And if she won't?"

"Then I'll call Caden Hightower. He'll know how to handle things without anyone ending up dead."

"Plus, you'll have an excuse to see the sexy, silver fox detective again."

"That's not a priority, but I'm not totally opposed to it either."

Cracking a smile, Flo took another sip of wine. Her head tilted to the side as thoughts stirred in her eyes.

"What are you thinking?" I asked, recognizing her *I've got a plan* expression a mile away. "So help me, if you even suggest stepping foot inside The Banshee..."

"I don't have a death wish." She rolled her eyes. "But *you* have Zelda's address. No one else does. That's an advantage we shouldn't waste."

"Meaning..."

"*Meaning,* tomorrow we pay a visit to the Madame." Her eyes glittered with excitement, firelight dancing on her irises. "We just have to get to her before Graham does."

THE ENGINE RUMBLED like a freight train beneath me as I nudged the beefy muscle car down a narrow side street, disturbing an otherwise quiet Monday morning.

"Cut the lights!" Flo hissed from the passenger seat. She was staring down at the directions on her phone screen, practically shaking with anticipation as we crept closer to our destination.

"It's daylight," I noted drolly. "The headlights aren't on. And we aren't exactly incognito, headlights non-withstanding. We stick out like a sore thumb in this thing."

Aunt Colette's car — a 1966 Ford Thunderbird — was a turquoise behemoth that drew attention no matter the time or place. When we'd hatched out our scheme the night before, we'd originally planned to take Florence's far more discrete Ford Focus hatchback. Said plan went awry around dawn when she phoned me, frantic. Evidently, Desmond was giving a guest lecture at a college way out in Western Mass today — otherwise known as the sticks — which left us without a suitable getaway car.

Enter: *The Thunderbird.*

"You know, I think this car is perfect for this mission," Flo declared. "We're totally channeling Thelma and Louise energy right now."

"Weren't they in love?"

"A love that dare not speak its name." She waggled her brows at me suggestively. "Go through this stop sign, then take a left onto the dead end. It should be the last house on the right."

I followed her directions, slowing to a crawl as we approached. The dead-end street where Zelda lived was on the fringes of town in a working-class neighborhood called The Point. Once a notably sketchy area, it was slowly gentrifying as the university expanded and dilapidated tenements became prime student housing. Still, there were traces of its rougher past everywhere you looked. For every newly refinished home, there were two with sagging front porches, rusted chainlink fences, and broken down cars rotting in the driveway.

"It's that one." Flo pointed to the double decker with chipped navy shingles at the end of the row.

It took two tries, but I managed to park the Thunderbird (relatively) close to the curb. We scampered out, glancing up and down the abandoned street for signs of life. No one seemed to be around, but I couldn't shake the sensation that someone was watching us.

I'd had that feeling a lot lately. Frankly, it was getting old.

"Come on," I muttered, starting up the cracked concrete walkway to the two-family home. "Let's get this over with."

A pair of doors waited for us at the top of the steps, each with a labeled doorbell. If the names scrawled in messy sharpie were accurate, Apartment No. 1 was occupied by someone named *HALLOWAY*, Apartment No. 2 merely by a single letter.

Z.

"Gotta be that one," Florence said, reaching out and jamming her finger against the doorbell button without a moment's hesitation. We heard a resulting muffled ring from somewhere above, then total silence. No approaching footsteps, no answering bellows promising to be right down. After thirty seconds of waiting, Flo tried again, this time holding her finger against the bell for such a prolonged stretch, I finally reached out and smacked it away.

"Hey!" Flo protested.

"You really think she's going to come down if you annoy her to death?"

"Maybe."

"She's not coming." I expelled a deep sighed. "She's probably not even home. I sure as hell wouldn't stick around town if the O'Banions were after me."

Flo planted her hands on her hips and glared at the door. "Well, this was an anticlimactic secret mission. I can't believe I called out sick for this."

"Sorry to disappoint. It's still early, though. You could make it in for most of the day."

"Nah, that's okay. I'm supposed to be teaching fractions. I freaking *hate* fractions." She paused, brightening with a fresh idea. "Want to go get pancakes at Red's instead?"

"Um, obviously."

We walked slowly toward the Thunderbird, resigned to our thwarted plan but, ultimately, not too shaken up by it now that we'd pivoted to brunch. Ahead of me, Flo was chattering animatedly about the double order of hash brows she planned on eating.

I'm not sure what made me glance back at the house. There was no sudden sound, nothing at all to draw my attention. But I stopped in my tracks, looked over my shoulder, and, sure enough, when my eyes landed on the second-floor window, I saw a familiar face peering out at me. It was there and gone, quickly darting out of sight behind a thick velvet curtain. Too late, though. She'd seen me and I'd seen her.

"She's home."

"Huh?" Flo asked, stopping short. "Hey, wait for me!"

I was already racing back up the walk, bounding onto the porch, pushing my finger against the doorbell. My fist began to pound against the wood panel. "Zelda! Come on, I know you're in there! I saw you through the window!" I rang again, even more persistently. "I'm not leaving until you talk to me!"

Finally, I heard the clomp of footsteps on the stairs. I released the doorbell and the shrill peal tapered into silence. The door jerked open and there she stood.

Madame Zelda herself.

Her tall frame was swathed in a loose-fitting caftan — lime green with purple peacock feathers running down the sides. She was unusually bare-faced, no penciled on brows or bold purple lipstick, no heavy blush caked on the apples of her cheeks. It was the first time I'd seen her without her sky-high turban. Her mousy blonde hair sat limply atop her head, the length pulled back in a severe knot by her nape. Her cloudy blue eyes were fixed on me with undisguised displeasure.

"Gwendolyn. What an... *unexpected...* surprise."

"Aren't you a psychic?" Flo asked, nose wrinkling skeptically. "Didn't you know we were coming?"

Zelda's unhappy gaze shifted to her. "And you are?"

"Florence Lambert, Gwen's best friend. The Thelma to her Louise. The Rose to her Blanche. The Sookie to her Lorelai. The Waldorf to her Van der Woodsen."

The psychic looked back at me. "Is she speaking English?"

"I've been calling you for days, Zelda," I said, getting straight to the point. "Where have you been? What's going on? You've missed all your appointments. People are pissed."

"I needed a bit of me-time."

"*Me-time?*" I blinked. "Then your sudden disappearance doesn't have anything to do with Mickey O'Banion?"

She jolted in surprise then quickly covered it, adopting a disinterested expression. Her voice was the quintessence of casual as she asked, "How do you know Mickey?"

"For starters," I said, growing more irritated by the second, "He cornered me the other day while I was taking out the store's trash. He was trying to track you down and seemed seriously annoyed that you'd blown him off. He said to tell you he's not going away until he gets back what you took. He said..." I adopted a poor imitation of Mickey's gruff tones. *"You can run but you can't hide."*

Her sparse brows pulled inward in a scowl at this news. Stepping back, she swung the door wide open. "You'd better come inside for a moment, Gwendolyn." Her gaze darted over my shoulder to the street beyond. "Prying eyes everywhere."

Flo and I traded a glance before we followed the psychic's silk-shrouded form up the creaky staircase, into a rather rundown apartment. There was no decor scheme, so far as I could tell. Nothing matched. The furniture was eclectic in the extreme, but all of it looked shabby. (And, it must be noted, *smelled* shabby.) Thick, woven rugs blanked the floor in a colorful canvas. Chiffon scarves were draped over every lampshade, casting the entire apartment in muted rainbow hues. Most startling of all, on a tall, excrement-encrusted perch by the window, a brilliant blue macaw parrot with yellow neck feathers stared at us with beady, intelligent eyes. It cocked its head as we came closer, taking our measure, talons tightening on the wooden rungs.

"Mercury reenters retrograde," the parrot cawed in greeting, black tongue poking from its beak. *"The moon is square Venus!"*

Flo and I glanced at one another again.

"That's Hecate. My familiar. She is an accomplished oracle." Zelda gestured toward a threadbare fuchsia sofa as she settled into a green brocade armchair. "Do sit down."

We sat, the springs creaking beneath us in a rusty chorus.

"Can I get you anything? Wine? Brandy?"

"It's nine-thirty in the morning," Flo murmured.

Zelda merely stared at her and took a defiant sip of her mug. I was guessing its contents weren't tea. Her eyes slid to mine, their murky blue unsettling as always. "What is it you're seeking here, Gwendolyn?"

"I wanted to see if you were all right. It's unlike you to miss appointments, especially during the high season."

"*Death inverted,*" the parrot interjected. "*Purge the past, purge the past.*"

"Spiritual beings cannot be beholden to the whims of what you deem appropriate business hours. Time is but a construct." Zelda gestured vaguely in the air. "I must go where the energy calls most strongly."

"It calls you *here*?" Flo asked doubtfully, eyeing the parrot. A dollop of greenish brown poop plopped to the floor, landing atop a large pile of dried droppings that had accumulated on the rug over what must've been months. Maybe even years.

I guess that explained the smell.

"Zelda," I persevered. "This man who is looking for you — Mickey O'Banion. He claims you stole some of his mother's jewelry."

"What use would I have with jewelry?" She fluttered her unadorned fingers. "Material wealth means nothing to the truly enlightened, for you cannot carry it with you to the other side."

"Right... It's just... he seems pretty dang convinced that you stole half a million dollars worth of his mother's belongings and are planning to pawn them on the black market."

"*Blind the third eye,*" Hecate added. "*She sees! She sees!*"

Madame Zelda stared at me blankly, totally unruffled by my accusation. Eventually, she took another long sip of her... tea... and sighed. "And you believe him?"

"It's not about what I believe or don't believe. But the O'Banion family is not known for their friendliness, especially when they think someone has ripped them off. This Mickey guy..." I glanced briefly at Flo. "He's hired Gravewatch — one of the top private investigation agencies in the state — to track you down. It's only a matter of time before they find you here. Actually, if you ask me, it's sort of a miracle they haven't tracked you down yet. When they do, they're going to hand you over to

Mickey. And I get the feeling he's more a fan of *an eye for an eye* than *forgive and forget* when it comes to meting out justice."

"The O'Banions are no threat to me."

"But Zelda—"

"You have a good heart, Gwendolyn. I appreciate you coming all the way here over something so trivial. Your concern is noted but, I assure you, ultimately unnecessary. I have no knowledge of this missing jewelry." She paused a beat. "Even if I did, I surely wouldn't be foolish enough to keep it here at my apartment, in plain sight of anyone who strolls through my front door."

Flo and I traded another loaded glance. Her eyes were bugging out of her head in her patented *oh-my-god-this-bitch-is-loco* look. I wasn't sure how I'd expected this visit to go, though I figured Zelda might show a flicker of concern about her own wellbeing, if not mine.

"Just to make sure I understand this correctly... you don't know Mrs. O'Banion?" I asked, disbelief thick in my voice.

Zelda shrugged lightly. "I didn't say that."

"You do know her, then."

"We have had a longstanding arrangement, stretching back several years. Twice a month, I visit her home and give a private reading as she is elderly and unable to come to me. It pains me to know I'm being accused of wrongdoing after I've been so accommodating of her limitations."

Flo scoffed. "Right. I'm sure you make private house calls out of the goodness of your heart. Nothing at all to do with the whopping fees you can extort from a little old lady who's just addled enough to write you a blank check. "

"And why shouldn't I collect a profit for my services?" Zelda asked, sounding a bit miffed.

"I don't know," Flo murmured, then added in a low whisper. "Maybe because your services are bullshit?"

I shot my best friend a sharp glance, telling her to quit while she was ahead. Insulting Zelda wouldn't get us anywhere.

The psychic's smile turned sharp — she hadn't missed Flo's whisper. "Believe what you will about the validity of my readings. I give the O'Banion matriarch a few hours of simple companionship and spiritual consultation in exchange for compensation." She paused. "It's odd. You say her son claims she's senile?"

I nodded.

"She speaks to me quite clearly whenever we discuss her future. In fact, at our most recent visit, she was rather candid concerning her wishes to alter her last will and testament before she passes. She holds a significant fortune from her father. Not to mention, all the family properties are in her name — including that dirty hole-in-the-wall bar they hold so dear. Her boys have been battling over who will inherit it for years." Zelda's pause was rich with implication. "It makes you wonder what the true motives are behind these false accusations of thievery."

"You think Mickey is trying to frame you?" I asked, incredulous. "That he stole the jewelry himself, and is... what? Throwing his brothers off the scent?"

"*The hanged man sees true,*" Hecate cried, beak clicking. "*Too late to go back!*"

"I do not concern myself with what a weak figure such as Mickey O'Banion does or does not do." Zelda waved one hand dismissively. "He is naught but a nuisance; an unenlightened bug to be squashed if it flies too close to my face."

Flo and I traded another loaded glance.

"Now then..." Zelda pushed to her feet in a swirl of lime green fabric. "If the jewelry is what you came here for, I'm sorry to say you'll be leaving disappointed. I have a busy morning of meditation ahead, so if you don't mind...." She gestured toward

270

the front door with her teacup, making it clear she wanted us to walk through it and never return.

"Are you ever coming back to the shop?" I asked, rising off the sofa with a screech of springs. "Or should I start advertising for a replacement psychic?"

Zelda studied me for a beat. "Your choices are your own."

"And if Mickey O'Banion comes after Gwen again?" Flo half-growled. "What then, huh? Don't you feel at all guilty for dragging her into this?"

"As I stated before..." The psychic shrugged. "I have nothing else to say on this matter."

"Listen here, you crazy old bi—"

The rest of Flo's sentence cut off as Hecate began to screech, a piercing cry of alarm several decibels louder than any of her previous squawks, drawing all our attention to the window.

"*Enemy at the gates,*" the parrot cawed, flapping her bold blue wings in warning as her head cocked to the side. "*Ding dong! Ding dong! Ding dong!*"

A half-second later, the piercing toll of the doorbell filled the apartment. Someone was at Zelda's front door. Slamming down her teacup on the side-table, she whirled on me, murky blue eyes flashing with anger as her pointy acrylic nails sank into the flesh of my long-sleeved black turtleneck sweater.

"Ow!" I exclaimed.

"Who else did you bring here?" She shook me — *hard*. "Who, damn you?"

"No one!" I stepped back, trying to escape her grip, but she held fast. She was surprisingly strong. I guess those flowy caftans were hiding a fair bit of muscle. "I swear, Zelda, it's just the two of us—"

"Then you were followed," she said, spittle flying from her lips. "You've led them right to me!"

The doorbell came again, an insistent knell, this time accompanied by the pounding of a fist on the door. Zelda stared into my eyes, wrath written all over here face, and hissed a single word that made all the hair on the back of my neck stand on end.

"*Mickey*."

"Maybe it's not him," I reasoned hopefully. "Maybe it's someone who works for the census."

Flo snorted. "Right."

"Or," I went on blithely. "A delivery guy with a package! Order anything lately? Maybe some of that enzymatic stain and odor eliminator for your carpet?"

Zelda opened her mouth to respond, but before she had a chance, a man's violent roar ripped up the stairwell and through the front door of the apartment.

"*ZELDA*! OPEN UP, YOU FUCKING BITCH! DON'T MAKE ME KNOCK THIS DOOR DOWN!"

Hellfire.

CHAPTER SIXTEEN

People who give out apples instead of candy are the scariest monsters on Halloween.
- Gwen Goode, stocking up on snack-size chocolate bars

My eyes flew to Zelda's face.

"O'Banion," she whispered, paling slightly as her fears were confirmed. Her fingernails dug more sharply into my arm as her expression morphed from fear to rage. "You led him right to me, you idiot!"

"How was I supposed to know I was being followed?" I cried, struggling against the stinging grip. "Zelda, you're hurting me!"

"Good!" she snapped.

"Let go of Gwen, you old dingbat!" Flo yelled, jumping into the mix. She began to tug on Zelda's arm, trying to get her off me, but those acrylics were sharp as blades, digging into the cashmere with vengeance, refusing to release.

The doorbell rang again, punctuating another bellow from Mickey. "I'M NOT GOING AWAY, YOU THIEVING CUNT!"

We all flinched.

"Zelda, I'm sorry, but you're in real trouble," I whispered quickly, blinking back tears of pain. My arm was throbbing. "Let me call for help. I know a detective who works for Salem PD. He can—"

"*No!* No police." Her grip tightened and I swallowed down a whimper. She shook me, rattling me hard enough to give me whiplash. "I did my time! I'm not going back. Certainly not because of a pissant little fool like you."

"Excuse me?!" I glared at her, any sympathy I'd harbored evaporating instantly. "I came here to check up on you because I was worried—"

"You should've kept your nose out of my affairs!"

"*Ding dong!*" Hecate parroted, mimicking the ringing bell. "*Ding dong! Enemy at the gates! Enemy at the gates!*"

I tried to shrug Zelda off again, but she only tightened her hold. The wrath in her eyes was bordering on scary, now.

"You wanted me to leave," I reminded her. "Let me go!"

"You're not going anywhere," she hissed, getting right in my face. Her murky blue eyes were narrowed, her mouth pursed into a dozen deeply scored wrinkles from decades of smoking two packs a day. "You brought this mess to my doorstep. You're going to help me clean it up."

I didn't know what that meant, exactly, and I was not interested in finding out. I began to struggle in earnest, attempting to peel Zelda's bony fingers from my bicep. In response, she shook me again, even more violently this time. My brains were beginning to feel like scrambled eggs. Which, honestly, I blamed for the action I took next.

I didn't think; I just knew I wanted her off of me, right freaking *now*, and I reacted instinctively, lifting one low-heeled leather boot and aiming for her midsection. Unfortunately, beneath all that fabric, it was difficult to tell where her true form began. I managed only to graze her. (And piss her off further.)

The momentum of my kick sent us both lurching several uneven steps sideways. We rocked to a sudden halt, slamming up against the back of the sofa. A low pulse of pain shot through my hipbone. Ignoring it, I kicked at Zelda again. (And missed, again.) In retaliation, she reached out and grabbed me by the hair with her other hand, yanking the thick rope of my ponytail, jerking my head back. My scalp burned with pain and a muscle in my neck spasmed sharply as it twisted at an unnatural angle.

"*Ow!*" I yelled loudly.

Blinking away the dizzying pain, I leveled another blind kick at my psychic's midsection — and felt no small amount of satisfaction as this one connected. Zelda loosed a low *oof* of pain, then released my hair. Unfortunately, her vise-like grip on my arm remained, keeping me within arm's reach even as I tried to reel away.

"Let me go!" I cried, kicking at her again.

"LET ME IN!" Mickey bellowed distantly.

"*Let the chips fall!*" Hecate squawked, much less distantly. "*Fall as they may!*"

While Zelda and I grappled, both breathing hard as we clawed at each other with increasing violence, Florence (who had, until this point, been watching from the sidelines) picked up a heavy paperweight off the coffee table — a massive chunk of onyx, from the looks of it — and raced toward us.

"*Enough!*"

Both Zelda and I stopped grappling long enough to look over at Florence. She was standing less than a foot away, the stone held aloft in both hands, her pretty face contorted into a hellbent expression I'd never seen before. (And, over the course of our decade-long friendship, I'd seen most of Flo's looks.) She appeared fully prepared to bring the heavy onyx down on Zelda's head if she didn't release me, pronto.

"Listen to me, you old bag," Florence growled at the psychic. "*Let. My. Best. Friend. Go!*"

Hecate, sensing her master was in trouble, chose this moment to join the fray. The massive bird swooped down from her perch, sailing straight toward Florence with her razor-sharp, curled talons poised to do some serious damage.

"Flo!" I shouted. "Behind you!"

She dodged just in time, ducking for cover behind the green brocade chair. The onyx went tumbling across the floor. Hecate — and her talons — missed Flo's face by mere inches. Zelda's grip loosened as she turned to see what was happening and I used the opportunity to finally wrench myself free.

"LAST WARNING, ZELDA!" Mickey roared.

The pounding at the door downstairs grew louder. More violent. I wondered how much force it would take to knock it clean off its hinges. Probably not much, given the ramshackle state of this place, and the size of the man doing the pounding. Mickey O'Banion was built like a Mack truck.

The thought had scarcely occurred to me when I heard the unmistakeable sound of wood splintering.

We all froze for a heartbeat. (Even Hecate.)

Hellfire and brimstone.

Footsteps started pounding up the stairwell, coming at us full-clip.

Zelda regained her senses first. Reaching into the deep folds of her billowing caftan, she pulled out a tiny, purse-sized pistol. It looked like a toy in her hand, but I had no doubt its bullets would feel very real embedded in your flesh. My eyes were wide as dinner plates as she checked the chamber for a bullet and clicked off the safety.

"Um, Zelda—"

"Out the back," she snapped, gesturing toward the dingy dining area with the gun. She was still breathing hard from our catfight. "The window beside the stove. There's a fire escape. Use it."

"What about you—"

"*Go!* Before I change my mind!"

We went.

Flo and I raced into the narrow galley kitchen, which was painted a sallow mustard hue and piled high with dirty dishes on every surface. We stepped over a mountain of moldering takeout boxes and shoved the grime-coated window upward. The pane was practically fused shut from layers of old paint along with lack of use, but after a few seconds of brute force, it finally lurched open.

Florence exited first, slipping through the gap with admirable grace. I could hear Hecate behind us, swooping around the living room, shrieking at top volume — *"The devil doesn't bargain!"*— as I straddled the sill and shimmied my way out onto the rusty spiral staircase bolted to the back of the house. Flo was already halfway down. I stared at the top of her head, glossy brown hair flying behind her like a flag, as I began to follow her.

A splintering sound of another door being kicked in boomed from the open window, followed by the pulse-spiking report of a gun firing — once, twice, three times. Zelda's unhinged cackles of laughter chased me the rest of the way down the spiral staircase. Goddess above, she was enjoying the shoot-out. I'd always known the woman had a few screws loose; I'd failed to realize she was genuinely insane.

"For the record," Flo said when I reached the ground,

reaching out to grab my hand. "I was wrong about this secret mission being anticlimactic."

"Noted."

Fingers tightly intertwined, we took off across the overgrown lawn, our boots crunching on fallen leaves from several large maple trees. The property had a sizable yard that wrapped all the way around the margins of the house. We ran until we hit the street, never pausing long enough to catch our breath. By the time we reached the Thunderbird, both of us were winded. I could hear Flo panting behind me as I rounded the hood, headed for the driver's side.

I was so focused on getting the hell out of dodge, I didn't notice the dark SUV careening down the dead-end street until it slammed to a halt ahead of us, angled diagonally at the curb. The windows were tinted so darkly, I couldn't see who was inside — and I didn't feel the need to stick around and find out for myself.

"Now who the hell is that?" Flo yelled, staring at the SUV with eyes that were just as wide, if not wider, than mine.

"Don't know, don't care," I fired back, fumbling for my door handle, tearing it open. "Let's motor!"

I didn't need to tell Flo twice. She strapped herself into the passenger seat as I folded in behind the wheel. I was shaking head to toe, my bloodstream a rush of pure adrenaline as I shoved the key in the ignition and turned over the engine. It thundered to life with a throaty growl. My hand froze on the shifter when Flo's startled whisper filled the cab.

"Oh my god."

She was staring through the windshield, mouth gaping. My gaze followed suit, just in time to take in the sight of two dark-haired men alighting from the SUV. One sprinted directly into the house, too fast to get a real look at him. All I saw was a flash of black leather and a blur of motion. But the second man began to advance on us, closing the distance between the SUV and the

Thunderbird with long legged strides. It was not lost on me that there was a gun gripped casually in his hand.

"Go, go, go!" Flo shrieked, spotting the gun at the same time I did. "Give it some gas! Peel out! Before he shoots us!"

Regrettably, it wasn't really possible to *peel out* in the Thunderbird, seeing as it had the turning radius of a Panzer tank and we were parked on an extremely narrow dead-end street with an SUV angled inconveniently in our path. Thus, I had no choice but to execute not a three or even a four but an *eight*-point turn, my cheeks growing redder and redder in embarrassment as I shifted from forward to reverse again and again, slowly maneuvering the beast of a car away from the curb, back the way we came.

Throughout this rather humiliating process, the gun-toting guy stood by the curb, arms crossed over his chest, face an unreadable mask as he watched us execute our escape. His gun was, in a small stroke of fortune, now holstered. He appeared not to want to shoot us.

"Could you be *any* slower?" Flo cried as I reversed for what seemed the thousandth time.

"Probably," I snapped back, spinning the wheel and slamming the shifter violently into forward gear. "If I really tried."

Flo leaned forward in her seat, trying to get a better look at the guy on the curb. "He's just... staring at us."

"Yes, thanks, I can see that."

"What do you think he wants?"

I pawed the shifter again, gears crunching as I reversed a few inches. Almost there. "How the heck am I supposed to know, Flo? Would you just let me focus?"

"Oh, please! I'm not the one who can't make a simple u-turn!"

"You want to try driving this thing? It takes serious finesse."

She was silent for a long beat. "*Finesse* seems like a stretch."

"Keep it up and I'm leaving you here," I warned.

Ignoring this, she ducked lower in her seat, frowning through the window at the man. "You know, he looks sort of familiar."

I grunted noncommittally. So long as he wasn't shooting at us, I wasn't really interested in his identity.

"He's also kinda... *hot*," Flo added, staring harder out the window. "Do you think he's with Mickey? One of the other batshit O'Banion boys?"

"Doesn't matter," I muttered. "As far as I'm concerned, we were never here."

Finally, the nose of the Thunderbird cleared the curb. I jammed my foot down on the gas pedal and we vaulted down the street, leaving the scene of the crime — and the watchful gaze of the tall, dark-haired stranger — in our rearview. Yet even when I turned onto the main street and headed back toward Flo's townhouse, far beyond his sight, I could still feel the heavy weight of his stare on the back of my neck, making all the hair stand on end.

"Ouch!"

I winced as the metal tip of the hot-glue gun scorched my fingertips. Abandoning the mess of crafting supplies on the counter, I raced for the sink and shoved the burn under the tap. The cool water soothed the rapidly-reddening patch of skin on the pads of my fingers.

It was my own fault, frankly. I hadn't been paying attention to what I was doing. My mind kept wandering to the events of this morning instead of the task at hand. I'd been distracted all day, since I dropped Florence off hours earlier — with promises to never again speak of our misguided visit to Zelda's — and headed back home.

I'd gone for a run to clear my head, winding up at The Gallows when I was breathless and sweaty. Since we were closed-to-business, I used the rare customer-free opportunity to organize the messy bestseller section, restock our depleted candles, sort out the incense display, and (*sigh*) Windex until every display case shone like the day they'd rolled off the factory floor.

Once I was satisfied with my efforts, I'd locked up the now-pristine shop and headed back home. Irritatingly, my restless energy followed me, thoughts of Mickey and Zelda churning through my brain until I thought I'd go crazy. Three times, I picked up my phone to call Graham. And three times, I set my phone down, knowing he'd flip his lid if he ever found out what Florence and I were up to that morning.

I sought out any source of distraction I could find, weeding out my closet for old clothes in need of donation, cleaning my bathroom top to bottom, trying my hand at cooking an elaborate dinner — so elaborate, in fact, I ended up burning it and ordering takeout from Passage to India instead. But even their delectable chicken tikka masala wasn't successful in taking my mind off matters. Nor was my tried-and-true fallback of cracking open my Kindle and getting lost in a fictional world to ignore the chaos of the real one I was currently stuck in. I'd read the same page of my romance novel six times in a row before conceding that my mind was too preoccupied to pay attention — even to the roguish charms of the Pirate King.

Desperate times called for desperate measures. After dinner, I'd hauled my trusty DIY kit in from the garage and gotten to work. Five hours later, my kitchen looked like a '*dark academia aesthetic*' Pinterest board threw up all over it, and I'd successfully created the foundations of a new window display for the shop. It featured suspended picture frames I'd spray-painted black along with ghost-like mannequin forms draped in gauzy gowns that would blow in the haunted winds of All Hallow's Eve. (Okay, okay, so the haunted wind was actually a rotating floor fan I'd plug in beneath the display, but what the tourists didn't know wouldn't hurt them.)

I'd fashioned six nooses out of coarse rope to hang around the mannequins — a nod to the shop name as well as an homage to the original Salem women who lost their lives in the infamous Witch Trials. Now, I was hot-gluing dozens of old books onto a canvas sheet, creating a textured backdrop out of torn pages. As a finishing touch, I planned to scorch some of the edges with matches. Then again, seeing as I was already nursing a smarting burn, I should probably quit while I was ahead.

The sudden buzz of my cellphone startled me. I shut the sink tap and raced across the room before the call disconnected. I'd expected it to be Florence, calling for the fifth time (*"We got in a catfight! With a psychic!"* she'd gasped between giggles the last time she phoned. *"And a parrot!"*) but the name flashing across my screen made my stomach drop straight to the cold tile floor.

GRAHAM GRAVES CALLING

I sucked in a breath. Stock-still, I watched it ring three more times before he was directed to my voicemail. He didn't leave a message. I blew out a shaky breath of relief as the screen turned dark once more. But the relief was short-lived.

Why was he calling me? It was 10PM on a Monday night... not exactly a reasonable hour for idle chitchat. Had he somehow found out about my trip to Zelda's this morning? I prayed he hadn't, seeing as I'd lied straight to his face about not knowing the psychic's address... and considering he'd explicitly warned me to stay as far away from Mickey O'Banion as possible...

There's no way he knows, I assured myself, steeling my shoulders against the intrusive thoughts. *He's not the Eye of Sauron. He doesn't see everything you do, Gwen.*

Assurances aside, I couldn't stop myself from dimming the

lights in the kitchen to their lowest setting. Nor could I prevent peeking out the window by the breakfast nook to see if a familiar black Bronco was parked in front of my house. Thankfully, the street was dark and quiet, no signs of Graham or anyone else prowling about in the moonlight. My recent sensation of being watched had only gotten worse as the hours ticked on. I was actually looking forward to work in the morning. The chaos of customers would keep me far too occupied to worry about Graham or Zelda or rogue witch covens or the O'Banion boys.

Shaking off my lingering unease, I double checked my locks, cleaned up my crafting supplies, and made my way upstairs for the night. I wasn't tired. In fact, I was the opposite of tired, thoughts jumping around inside my skull like popcorn kernels. I went through the motions of my evening routine anyway, changing into my favorite set of silk pajamas, washing my face clean of makeup, brushing my teeth, and climbing into bed.

I lay in the darkness, staring up at my ceiling, and conjured up what I liked to call a mental vacation. It was a tactic I'd used a thousand sleepless nights before. I'd come up with it years ago, when I was just a kid, back in the days I'd felt too exposed to sleep, too nervous to shut my eyes for fear of what might find me in the dark. The idea was to trick my brain into a state of relaxation by pretending I was somewhere exotic, in places I'd seen only in magazines and glossy textbook pages in my History class textbooks.

I wasn't there, in that beige-on-beige trailer in a no-name town off the New Jersey Interstate. I wasn't in a makeshift bed that doubled as our dining room table. I was far away, somewhere full of color and light and sound. The Grand Canyon, maybe, or Mount Rushmore. A white sand beach on the panhandle coast of Florida or a winding mountain route through the snowy Rockies of Colorado.

I'd envision every detail I could think of, from the sky's shade of blue to the dirt's gritty crunch beneath my boots to the feel of the wind blowing through my hair. Then, I'd imagine myself there, weave myself into the illusion. Not *me*, per se, but an older, wiser version of myself, one who wasn't ruled by fear or held hostage by the whims of a wild mother. One who could sleep through the night with ease.

A Gwendolyn who trusted easily. A Gwendolyn who let people into her heart without anticipating the pain that would result when they inevitably broke it. A better, stronger, more capable Gwendolyn.

I was supposed to be her by now.

Unfortunately, that version of me seemed just as fictitious as my mental vacations.

When you're a kid, you think by the time you're an adult, you'll have it all figured out. Life, that is. As though you'll turn eighteen and, with the simple flip of a calendar page, be somehow better equipped to handle everything that the world throws at you.

Of course, when you actually turn eighteen, you realize pretty quickly that you're just as much of an idiot kid as you were at eight — albeit with slightly better sense of style and slightly worse taste in men. But surely, you tell yourself, you'll have it figured out by twenty-one. Old enough to legally drink. A whole year outside of your teenage wasteland.

And yet, twenty-one feels just as overwhelming as ever. Twenty-two is even worse. Twenty-three offers no further enlightenment. As you slowly begin the march toward twenty-five — halfway through the defining decade of your life — you begin to accept the truth. There is no age at which you'll ever have it figured out; no magic number where every missing piece falls abruptly into place. You will get older, there's no stopping that, but there's no guarantee you'll ever get wiser. If anything, you merely get better at pretending. Acting like you have all the answers, holding all the loose threads of your life together in one fist, so they resemble a rope strong enough to guide you along until your time on earth expires.

I wasn't that little girl anymore, lost and alone and so, so afraid of everything that went bump in the night. And yet, in many ways, I'd always be her. I carried her deep inside me, an inner shadow locked away within my soul. I shared her same worries, felt her same fears.

Never take anything you're not able to pay back.

Never let in anyone who might do real damage.

Never drop your guard, even if you think it's safe.

It's never safe.

Tonight, as I fell back into old insomniac patterns, painting myself into a rich mental image of the lush, tropical landscape of Hawaii, feeling the salt air kiss my cheeks, the hot sand between my toes, watching the sway of the palm trees and the crash of the waves, that inner shadow of mine felt perilously close to the surface. She was with me as my overtaxed mind eventually succumbed to the illusory relaxation I'd conjured, and she was with me as I tumbled over the edge of consciousness, into the obliterating dark.

CHAPTER SEVENTEEN

Relationships are basically algebra. Haven't you ever looked at your X and wondered Y?
- Gwen Goode, thinking back on old flames

The stairs creaked beneath the weight of someone's shoe.

I sat bolt upright in my bed, heart in my throat, instantly awake. It was still full dark outside my windows — I hadn't been asleep for long. I strained my ears for a long moment, half-convinced I'd imagined the sound that woke me, when it came again. The unmistakable creak of the old wood steps. This time, closer to the top.

Someone was coming up my stairs.

Mickey O'Banion's face, contorted with rage, flashed through my head. I was out of bed in a flash, moving in utter silence as I ducked down beneath my bed and grabbed the baseball bat I kept there for just such an occasion. Creeping behind my bedroom door, I pressed myself close to the wall and took up a batter's stance. My pulse was a steady thud, pounding like a battle drum. My grip was so tight on the bat, my knuckles turned white. I didn't dare breathe as the doorknob began to twist under the grip of the intruder.

The door cracked open slowly, and a dark figure stepped through. He took two soundless strides toward the bed — impressively stealth for such a large man. As soon as he cleared the door frame, I swung for his head. I swear I didn't make a sound, but he somehow sensed the blow coming. He managed to spin around and grab my bat just before I made contact, halting me mid-swing.

Hellfire.

Normally, this would've spelled disaster — he was definitely stronger than me, fully capable of wrenching my weapon away with one tug. But this wasn't the first time I'd had to defend myself in the middle of the night, and I wasn't going down that easily.

The first rule of survival?

Always, *always*, have a backup plan. Mine came in the form of a tube sock, which I'd layered over the bat — a trailer park trick I'd learned from my mother, who was well-practiced in the art of driving off unwanted male attention. When the intruder yanked at my bat, he came away with nothing but fabric in his grip.

"What the—"

Grinning in the dark at the intruder's confusion, I cocked back the now-bare bat and swung a second time. He dodged, swift on his feet, but I managed to clip him on the shoulder hard enough to elicit a low grunt of pain. I was preparing to swing again — this time, for his cranium — when he did something unexpected. He dropped low and lunged at me, planting his shoulder in my stomach and lifting me clear off my feet.

The bat clattered out of my grip as I went airborne. I tried to scream, but he'd knocked the wind from my lungs. I kicked violently at the air as he began to march me across the room, pounding the planes of his back with my fists. He didn't even seem to notice. His stride was unhurried as he carried me toward the bed.

"Let go of me, you bastard!" I screeched when I finally regained my breath. "I'll kill you if you touch me!"

He was silent as he flung me none-too-gently off his shoulder onto the mattress. I landed hard, bouncing several inches into the air, then felt myself flattened against the duvet as a heavy male body settled on top of me. Before I could even attempt to push him off, my arms were jerked up over my head, held within the iron-like grip of one massive hand against the pillows. I bucked and thrashed in pure, undiluted terror and tried, unsuccessfully, to headbutt him.

"Get off me!"

"No."

I stilled at the voice. My eyes, which had clouded over with a film of fear, finally cleared enough to take a proper look at my attacker. The face hovering inches above mine came into focus and I felt all my fright crystalize into cold, hard, untempered fury. Because *Graham Motherfucking Graves* was lying on top of me, pinning me to my bed with his not-inconsiderable weight, his green eyes narrowed to slits, his breathing labored.

"What the hell are you doing?" I cried, outraged.

"Showing you how easy it is for someone to get to you if they want to," he gritted out between clenched teeth, his rage a perfect match for mine. "I thought you needed a more effective demonstration, since me telling you with words didn't make much of an impact."

"*What?!*"

"It seems our earlier conversation didn't stick. You know, the one where I told you to stay away from the mess with

Zelda? Where I warned you Mickey O'Banion was a dangerous guy?"

Oh, shit.

I swallowed hard. "Um..."

"Did you listen to me? Of course not. You never fucking listen." He leaned in, so our faces were even closer. "What did you do? You marched your pert little ass straight into the middle of the chaos and took a seat at the table."

My voice was a half-screech. "So, you wanted to teach me a lesson by breaking into my house in the middle of the night?!"

"I didn't break in. I have a key."

"You have a key?" I blinked, stunned. "How the hell do you have a key to my house?"

"I made a copy."

"When?"

He merely stared at me, refusing to answer.

Rude!

I scowled up at him, still burning with anger. "I thought you were a rapist or an axe-murderer! You scared me half to death, you asshole!"

"Good," he clipped. "I want you scared. If you're scared, maybe you'll start taking your safety seriously." His nostrils flared on a sharp, furious exhale. "You put yourself at risk this morning. Not only that, you put Florence at risk. What were you planning to tell Desmond when his girlfriend came back from a playdate with you full of bullets?"

"We weren't hurt!"

"You were lucky. That's all. Lucky my men were keeping tabs on your location, lucky the fake psychic is such a crap shot, lucky O'Banion didn't see you when he made it into that apartment."

His men.

I guess that explained the tall, dark, handsome stranger who'd watched our every move, and the one who'd raced headlong toward the firefight. Graham probably got a full report about our hectic escape from the scene of the crime as soon as we were out of sight. Goddess, he really was like the Eye of Sauron. He knew everything.

"Is Zelda okay?" I asked tentatively.

"She emptied her full clip when O'Banion burst through her front door, shot him in the shoulder. Barely a flesh wound, but enough to buy her some time to slip away. Mickey was..."

"Pissed?"

"Pissed doesn't cover it."

"Then Zelda's okay?"

"Mentally? Nothing is *okay* about that old quack. Physically, I'm sure she's fine."

"Did she leave Hecate behind?"

He stared down at me blankly.

"Her familiar."

The blank stare continued.

I sighed. "The parrot."

"Not that I'm aware of. There was no sign of a bird in the apartment when we did a sweep. Even if there was, it's not your business."

"But—"

"*Since*," he cut me off sharply. "You're planning to give this mess a wide berth from now on, like you promised. Remember?"

"Yes, yes. Wide berth."

I got the sense he didn't believe me. Mainly because, as soon as I spoke, his grip tightened on my hands, which still locked over my head. His frame pressed me more deeply against the bed, his weight stealing my breath as his brows furrowed in a look of raw frustration. "Do I need to tattoo this message on your ass for you to comprehend it?"

"That won't be necessary," I informed him, my tone uppity.

"I have a strict *no-needles-near-my-flesh-unless-I'm-at-the-doctor* policy."

"Uh huh."

When he didn't shift off me, I forced my tone to be ever-so-slightly less uppity. "Look, Graham, you've made your point. I said I'd stay away from Zelda. Now, get off me."

"No."

"*No?*"

"No," he repeated, glaring at me.

Of all the insane intimidation tactics...

With a low grunt, I bucked against him, trying to escape. He merely dropped more of his weight onto me, pressed me harder into the mattress until my struggles were absorbed by the plush pillow-top. I stopped thrashing, realizing it was getting me precisely nowhere. This was around the same time I realized Graham's body had settled firmly against mine, bringing us flush together, my curves tight against his rock-hard chest.

Since I was wearing only my skimpy silk shorts and tank top, my bare legs brushed the denim of his jeans and I fought off a shiver that had nothing to do with the cold temperature of my bedroom.

"Graham..."

The grip on my hands tightened almost to the point of pain as his name tumbled from my lips. "What, Gwen?"

"I'm sorry."

His eyes narrowed. "For what?"

"For lying to you about not knowing where Zelda was. For getting involved when you told me not to." I chewed nervously on my bottom lip as I stared up into his furious face. "I just wanted to talk to her. In my defense, I didn't know the situation was going to devolve into a shootout."

"In my line of work, a shootout is never off the table," he

gritted out, still clearly pissed. "That's why I asked you to let me handle it."

"I was worried you were going to hand her over to Mickey O'Banion — who is so not a nice guy, by the way, he totally tried to bully me the other day — without even giving her a chance to explain herself! And she had some alternate theories about why the sons might be so interested in their mother's money..." I trailed off when I felt his entire body stiffen with sudden tension.

"*The other day*," he echoed harshly, stormy expression clouding over into a mask of pure rage. "What the fuck do you mean, *the other day?*"

"Um..."

"Gwen, so help me God—"

"He came by the shop a few days ago," I forced myself to say, pushing the words out in a rush before I lost my nerve. "He sort of, well, cornered me by the dumpsters and tried to get me to tell him where Zelda was. And, when I refused, he was... unhappy."

"Are you fucking kidding me?!" he thundered.

"No, I am not fucking kidding you."

"And you chose not tell me about this, *why?*"

"Maybe because you have a tendency to overreact? Such as, I don't know, just off the top of my head... breaking into my home in the middle of the night?" I glared up at him, my pulse roaring between my ears. "Besides, it happened well before I knew he'd hired you. There was no need to tell you."

"No need... *Christ.*"

"I don't know why you're so upset." I tried to shrug but it was impossible with my arms pinioned overhead. "It's not like I typically come crawling to you with my personal problems. We aren't... *close.*"

For a long moment, he glowered down at me in terse silence. I was pretty certain he was contemplating the most efficient ways to dispose of my corpse once he was through murdering me for being such a monumental pain in his ass. But, for whatever reason, he decided against homicide. I had a front-row seat to watch as he locked down his fury, banking the fiery rage burning in his eyes, relaxing his brows from their deep furrow. When he finally spoke, his voice had calmed — marginally.

"From now on," he said. "Something like that happens, anyone corners you, threatens you, intimidates you, anyone so much as blinks at you in a way you don't like... you tell me. Not three days after the fact. You tell me *immediately* when it happens. Got it?"

I nodded.

His eyes dropped to my mouth. I was still chewing nervously on my lip, but released it when I felt the heavy weight of his gaze.

"Gwendolyn."

"Y-yes?" I stammered.

"Something else you need to wrap your mind around."

"Um... what?"

"You and me." His eyes flickered back up to mine and I sucked in a breath at what I saw in their depths. "We're close."

"Wh—"

My startled question was cut off as his head slanted down and his mouth sank onto mine. All the anger and tension burning inside my bloodstream was gasoline; Graham's lips were the match. In an instant, we were aflame. I bowed up on the bed, pressing into him as his mouth claimed mine. A low growl of satisfaction rumbled deep in his throat as I met his kiss, matched it, and then kicked it up a notch, sliding my tongue between his lips and getting my own taste of him.

He still had my arms locked above my head and, though I'd never admit it in a million years, there was something deliciously erotic about being restrained. Unable to touch him. Captive and submissive beneath his hard, capable body.

His teeth tugged at my bottom lip, drawing a gasp from deep

within me. I felt the tip of his tongue slide over my jawline, to my ear, and then his teeth were there, too, a sharp graze that felt so good I practically convulsed against him. Our bodies rubbed together, my thighs pressing in against his hips, cradling him closer, pulling him into the very core of me, where delicious warmth was gathering.

My bones went liquid when I felt his rigid length pushing through the confines of his jeans, hard and ready, the thin silk of my pajama shorts doing little to cushion it. I was unbelievably turned on already, but I thought I might explode when he began to move against me in shallow thrusts, his hips rolling rhythmically, the fabric of our clothing rubbing with delicious friction against the most intimate part of me. An ache began to spread through me, growing more intense with each passing second. His lips moved at my neck, kissing, sucking, nibbling, as we ground against each other. I tried — *failed* — to yank my hands free from his grip, a mewl of frustration slipping from my mouth. I wanted, no, I *needed* him to let me go so I could touch him.

"Hellfire," I breathed, the word a half-moan as he kissed the fragile hinge of my jaw, his hips rolling harder against mine.

"That feels good?"

"Mmm."

"And this?" he asked, his hot mouth nipping at my ear, sending a shiver of pure lust down my spine. "How does this feel?"

"Amazing."

"And this?" His teeth clamped down on the sensitive lobe and he sucked lightly.

I nearly purred, it felt so good.

"Use your words, Gwen."

"Good," I gasped. "It feels so good."

"Then I guess you're lucky it was me who came after you tonight, huh? Because I promise you, your evening would be going differently if Mickey O'Banion was here in your bedroom, Gwen." His mouth left my ear, his hips stopped their rhythmic torture, his voice turned totally hollow. "He's got a temper, especially when it comes to women. That temper has landed him in jail twice already in his twenty-nine years — once for assault during an ugly bar fight at The Banshee, once for trying to rape his high school girlfriend after breaking into her bedroom while her parents slept on down the hall."

My blood turned to ice.

Graham wasn't done. "Do you think, if he was here now, he'd bother turning you on? Getting you primed to come? Pulling those little mewls of pleasure from your mouth? Or do you think he'd just take what he wanted from you, then leave you broken after he'd had his fill, like a sadistic little boy with a porcelain doll he knows he's too rough to play with but can't stop himself from squeezing till it shatters apart in his hands?"

My body locked, every muscle going tight with tension, and my half-lidded eyes sprang fully open. For a long stretch of time — it felt like years, but I knew it was only seconds — I could only stare up into Graham's face in utter shock, taking in the hard set of his mouth, the cruel bend to his brows. The switch from passion to pain was like a catapult inside me, a complete 180 degree u-turn that slingshotted me out of the grips of drugging desire and back into cold, hard reality.

He'd done this — kissed me, touched me, reduced me to a squirming, panting, pleading mess — just to teach me a lesson.

"Get off me," I bit out, my tone icy with wrath. "Now."

For once, he actually did as I requested. He rolled away, then rose off the bed and walked to the window. His back was to me as he stared out into the dark night, but his shoulders moved up and down as ragged breaths rocked through him. As if he was barely holding on to his temper. As if he was too full of rage to even look at me, let alone be near me.

Too.

Freaking.

Bad.

Frankly, I didn't care what he was feeling. The rage *I* was feeling in that moment was more than enough to override every warning sign that told me to run headlong in the opposite direction. I scrambled to my feet, tugging my silk shorts back into place with as much dignity as I could muster, then stormed in his direction. He turned just as I reached him, the indifferent mask I'd come to know so well firmly in place as he regarded me. He didn't even duck or dodge as I reached out, planted both hands against his granite-hard chest, and shoved him with all my might. Annoyingly, the impact barely made him rock back on his heels.

"Don't you ever do that again!" I snarled at the top of my voice. "Or I will make sure you regret the day you were born!"

"Do what?" he asked, infuriatingly calm in the face of my fury.

"You know exactly what! Don't you dare kiss me to... to.... to punish me or to prove a point!" I glared at him, burning with resentment and rage and more than a little embarrassment. "In fact, don't kiss me *at all*! Ever!"

"Funny, you didn't seem upset about me kissing you when your tongue was in my mouth and you were moaning under my hands. Let me guess — another lapse of sanity?"

"Precisely," I bit out, turning on my bare heel and storming toward the door so he couldn't see how flaming red my cheeks were. "I was half-asleep. I can't be held responsible for my actions."

"Uh huh. Where do you think you're going?"

"Away from you."

"We're not finished talking about this."

"There's nothing more to discuss!"

"How about us?"

I stumbled over my feet, nearly falling flat on my face. I grabbed the door to keep myself upright. "*Us?*"

"Us," he concurred. "You and me."

"There is no you and me," I told the door, too chickenshit to turn around and face him.

"Only because every time I try to change that, you run scared."

"Or maybe because I loathe you with every ounce of my being!"

"Tell that to your nipples, babe."

I glanced down at my silk tank and, sure enough, my nipples were standing at full attention. I was undeniably turned on, the buzz of arousal in my veins a distracting undercurrent to my wrath at the man standing behind me.

"Leave my nipples out of this," I seethed. Finally gathering the strength to turn, I pinned him with my iciest glare. "In fact, just *leave.*"

He didn't move a muscle. His tone was blunt. Matter-of-fact. As though we were discussing seasonal weather patterns. "Deny it all you want. You're attracted to me, Gwen."

"If by *attracted* you mean repulsed, annoyed, irritated—" I ignored the hammering of my pulse. "Shall I go on? The list is quite extensive."

"Oh, I'm sure it is. I'm sure you have a whole stockpile of little lies you tell yourself over and over about just how much you loathe me. I'm sure that's easier than the alternative, which would be admitting that whenever you see me, your stomach is in knots, your breathing is altered, your body is on fire. Hell, I'm sure you probably even convince yourself, at least some of the time, that your breaths are so short because of *annoyance*. But we both know your thighs are shaking with a different sort of frustration. The kind you're dying for me to satisfy." He paused, lips twisting in a dark smirk. "Sorry, was that too arrogant? I know how that irks you."

My heart was pounding double-time. Heat was flushing through my body in a great tide, centering in the pit of my stomach and drifting downward to the very core of my being. I did my best not to clench my thighs together, determined not to prove his point — even if it was true. I *was* attracted to him. But it would be a cold day in hell before I ever owned up to that fact. Especially when he'd used that attraction against me like weapon, to teach me a lesson.

I tossed my head haughtily. "For a private detective, you really are clueless."

"Am I?"

"Yes." I swallowed. "There's nothing remotely attractive about your overly-inflated sense of self. If you think otherwise, well, you've been fed a line of bullshit. Maybe the string of girls you've dated in the past were happy to blow hot air and stroke your—"

"Stroke my what?"

"Ego," I finished firmly. "But I have no intentions of adding to the pile."

"You know, that's the second time you've brought up my dating history."

"Point being?"

"I had no idea you kept such close tabs on my exes."

"It's like a car wreck," I said sweetly. "Hard to look away."

"Keep lying to yourself, babe. Just going to make it more satisfying when I finally get you to admit the truth."

"You want the truth? Fine. The truth is, you came here tonight to punish me because you were pissed off I disobeyed your orders. You wanted to scare me, and guess what? You succeeded. I was terrified when I thought you were an intruder. But that wasn't enough for you, was it?" I shook my head and backed away when he tried to step nearer. "No! Don't you dare come near me. I mean it."

He stopped walking. "Gwen—"

"Don't *Gwen* me. I may not be able to control my body's reaction to you, but I can sure as hell still make up my own mind. Sex isn't a weapon you get to wield against me. My body isn't a wind-up toy for you to play with when it strikes your fancy. You want to make a point? Do it some other way. Any other way. Or I swear, I will cut you out of my life with surgical precision and never look back."

He absorbed this in silence for a moment, his expression flashing between exasperation, anger, and something else — something I couldn't decipher. His voice cracked out like a whip, harsh enough to make my heart skip a beat. "You really think that's all this was? Me, trying to... what? Fuck you into submission?"

"Sure seems that way!"

"And yesterday? At my office? What was my nefarious plan there, huh? More mind tricks?"

"Knowing you, I wouldn't doubt it!"

He ran both hands through his hair, mussing it instantly. "Jesus Christ, Gwen. You'll twist anything to make it fit the evil version of me in your head, won't you? The truth could bite you in the ass and you'd deny it had teeth."

"Oh, goodie," I snapped, planting my hands on my hips. "More insults."

"I'm not insulting you. I'm trying to fucking *talk* to you—"

"I'm done talking."

"That's not how this works. You don't get to unilaterally decide when we're done. You want to monologue? Join a theater group. We're having what I like to call a *conversation*. And a conversation is between two people. You and me. We both get to decide when it's done. You don't get to order me out just because you don't like what you're hearing."

I glowered at him, unable to refute his points.

"Fine," I grumbled. "Then say what you need to say."

He glowered back at me in silence, jaw tightening in anger.

"What are you waiting for?" I asked. "A drum roll?"

He took three deep breaths — in through his nose, out through his mouth — and I knew it was taking all his patience to keep from roaring at me. His gaze cut to the bed, which was rumpled from our tussle, for a long moment. When it finally met mine again, I shivered under the chill in his eyes.

"Let's get something straight," he rasped lowly, advancing a step in my direction. It took all my strength not to cower back against the doorframe. "You've somehow convinced yourself that what's happening between us is me trying to manipulate you. But that's not what this is, and deep down you know it. If you'd stop trying to twist it into some Machiavellian scheme, maybe you'd see that I didn't kiss you as a punishment or a ploy or a power move. I kissed you because *I wanted to*. I kissed you because I haven't been able to stop thinking about getting my lips back on yours since the moment you left my office. I kissed you because..."

He pulled in a ragged breath. "For the past two years, it's been pure fucking torture being near you all the time, watching you date dickhead after dickhead — none of them making you happy, none of them even *seeing* you, the real you, or even bothering all that hard to try. Two fucking years of standing in the shadows. Every boat day, every backyard barbecue. Watching while they touched you like you belonged to them. Trying not to turn fucking feral because they got to taste something that always should've been *mine*."

I jolted in place, too startled to speak.

His?

I wasn't his. I wasn't anyone's. But my mouth refused to form the words. In fact, my brain wasn't relaying any sort of executive orders to my body.

The weight of Graham's stare pinned me in place more effectively than an anvil on my feet. His eyes scanned slowly up my frame, lingering on my bare thighs, on my panting chest, on my neck. When they finally reached my face, all the ice had melted out of them. Instead, they were burning with heat.

"Is that clear enough for you?" he snapped softly. "Or do I need to spell it out further?"

I shook my head, suddenly desperate for him to stop talking. It was too much to process all at once. My eyes began to sting with tears. I blinked rapidly to fight them back, appalled to be reduced to such an emotional state in front of him. Try as I might to hide it, he plainly saw that I was balanced on the razor's edge of a breakdown. His angry expression slipped. Softened into something far, far more treacherous.

"Gwendolyn—"

"Please," I choked out, my voice thick with impending tears. "Please, can you just go?"

"I don't want to leave you like this."

"I'm only like this because of you," I retorted, incapable of being reasonable in such a moment of weakness. He physically flinched, as though the words had dealt a direct blow to his heart. I wanted to snatch back my cruel words, to hit the rewind button back five minutes to before this conversation. But I couldn't.

"*Please*," I repeated.

He stared at me for another long moment. "You need space. I can see that. And I'm happy to give it to you — for now. But not forever, Gwen. Not even for long. I have no intentions of giving you enough time to twist this around in your head, change us into something we're not." He turned for the door, but paused before stepping out into the hallway. "I'm a patient man. I've been patient for years, waiting for you to drop your guard. I'll keep being patient as long as it takes you to feel safe enough to do that. But so help me God, if you don't stop trying to actively push me away just because you're scared... then I guess I wasted my energy, because you aren't the girl I've been waiting for all this time."

When he was gone, I collapsed onto my bed in a heap, curled into a protective ball, and did something I hadn't done since the day after Aunt Colette's funeral. I wept like a heartsick child, salt streaming out of my eyes in a great flood, ragged sobs racking my whole body. I wept until there were no more tears left inside me, until I was a dried out, emotionless husk. All the while, Graham's words haunted me, echoing over and over inside my skull.

You aren't the girl I've been waiting for all this time.

With swollen eyes and a hollow heart, I drifted off into a fitful sleep.

CHAPTER EIGHTEEN

Sure, I have a magic wand. It's in my nightstand.
- Gwen Goode, enjoying six unique vibration patterns

My sneakers pounded the pavement, matching the tempo of the music blasting into my ears as I neared the final mile of my favored running route. The song choice — 'Monsters' by All Time Low — matched my mood as well as the atmosphere. While October usually gifted Massachusetts with glorious autumn weather, that morning was overcast and gray, the air thick with mist that rolled off the Atlantic.

Each breath I hauled in felt damp inside my lungs, like swallowing a gulp of dry ice. My ponytail swung behind me in a thick rope as I increased my pace, the weight of it tugging at my temples with each stride. My throat was burning. So were my thighs. I'd pushed myself far faster than normal. Maybe I thought if I ran fast enough, I might somehow outrun my problems — and by problems, I meant Graham.

It had been six days since his unexpected appearance in my bedroom. Six days of silent reflection on a kiss that made me simultaneously the most turned on I'd ever been and the most furious I'd ever been. Six days of riding an emotional roller coaster, second guessing everything I thought and felt, playing it back over and over until it was burned in my brain, every second of it, from the rasp of his voice to the brush of his lips to the heat of his body pressing into mine.

I hadn't called him. He hadn't called me, either. Our paths never crossed, not even once — not on the street or at the shop or at The Witches Brew, when I met Florence and Desmond for a midweek drink. As the days passed without any contact whatsoever, I found myself bracing for him to pop back into my life as he always did — appearing out of nowhere to stick his perfect nose into my affairs. Yet, after a week of seeing neither hide nor hair of him, I was left to assume he was avoiding me.

Which was fine.

Totally fine.

I didn't care at all, not in the slightest. What that man did in his spare time was not my business. The fact that I'd grown so accustomed to his constant presence in my life was alarming in and of itself.

You know you can't afford to depend on anyone like that, I scolded myself, pacing the length of my bedroom in the wee hours of the night when sleep refused to come. *Especially not Graham Graves.*

It was not lost on me, however, that my dark mood did miraculously improve midweek when Desmond let it slip over our second round of drinks that Graham was out of town, consulting on a case for the Feds up in New Hampshire. I'm not sure what my expression looked like in that moment but, evidently, it had been enough to alarm my best friends, seeing as Flo slid her stool closer to mine and Des reached out to grab my hand across the table, squeezing as he assured me his best friend never took jobs that lasted more than a few weeks.

So... maybe he wasn't avoiding me. Maybe he was just out of town. Not that I cared.

At all.

The only thing that kept me from going completely off the rails was the fact that I quite simply did not have the time. Halloween season was in full swing and things at The Gallows were busier than ever, a nonstop parade of sales that kept me occupied from the second I stepped through the front doors at the start of each day to the instant I bolted it behind me each night. I went in early and stayed late nearly every day, the overtime necessary to restock our rapidly-emptying display cases and set the book tables to rights after tourists ripped them apart.

Setting up the new window display turned out to be a monumental endeavor, one that took two full nights to finish even with Flo's assistance. She, as ever, could be bribed into servitude with wine and copious amounts of gossip — about Madame Zelda's potential whereabouts, about whether things with the dastardly O'Banion clan had cooled down at all, about Hetti's new hair color, which was a vibrant violet shade... about everything except the one thing I probably need to gossip about the most.

Graham.

I didn't tell her about what had happened between us, mostly because I wasn't sure how to put it into words without spontaneously combusting. I did experience a good degree of guilt over this omission, especially since she sacrificed two nights in a row to help me make my window display absolutely perfect. In the end, our long hours of toil paid off. It looked fabulous — and I wasn't just saying that because I'd spent so damn long getting the nooses to hang right, or positioning the hidden floor fan to waft the witches' dresses in a seriously spooky-cool way.

There'd never been so many tourists stopping to take pictures of the storefront before. Half of them ended up wandering in, buying coffee or a book or a bauble before they went on their way. (Okay, so, most of them only bought coffee.) Hetti, to her credit, was never daunted by the constant influx of patrons, even when we had a line out the door and every seat in the cafe section was occupied. She was *so* getting an early Christmas bonus once Halloween was behind us.

Sales only ramped up as the week slipped into the weekend. Yesterday, Saturday, was not only our craziest day of the week for sales but also — joy of joys — delivery day from our biggest supplier. I'd stayed at the shop until nearly midnight unpacking new books, rearranging candles, hanging bundles of dried herbs from the ceiling rack, and fiddling with our new line of essential oils. By the time I got home, it was beyond late and I was beyond exhausted. Still, bone-tired or not, I hadn't slept well. I hadn't slept well all week. My chateau-chic bedroom, which once felt like my safe haven against the world, was now full of memories that attacked with a vengeance every time my eyes slipped closed, Graham's voice on constant replay in my head.

You didn't seem upset about me kissing you when your tongue was in my mouth and you were moaning under my hands.

They got to taste something that always should've been mine.

I've been patient for years, waiting for you to drop your guard.

He was haunting me. Even in sleep, even in dreams, he was there. Inescapable.

I'd awoken early this morning, slipped on my running shoes, and headed out on my typical four-mile loop, the same one I ran every Sunday. The route brought me from my neighborhood out to Salem Willows Park, which jutted into the Atlantic at the eastern tip of town. In the summer, the area was bursting with life and sound and color. But the attractions were closed for the season — the carousel quiet and still, the arcade abandoned, the food shops shuttered. The beach was deserted, a barren stretch of coarse sand and rotting seaweed. Even the harbor had begun to empty out as boats were hauled and stored for the winter in yards across town.

I felt like the only living soul in the world as I jogged back homeward, following a disjointed path that snaked along the waterfront. It was still quite early. Too early for commuters or tourists to be out and about on a sleepy Sunday, even in the heart of downtown. I had the streets to myself as I jogged up Charter Street and slipped through the black gate into the The Old Burying Point cemetery.

The graves here were old, dating back to the 1600s, and they looked every bit their age, coated with fuzzy green moss, slanting at odd angles, crumbling at the edges. A handful of larger tombs lined the perimeter, housing notable figures from Salem's past. Many of the names were illegible, their letters worn into nothingness by the elements, but others were still chiseled clearly in the stone, including one Jonah W. Graves, a prominent judge during the Witch Trials... and Graham's direct ancestor.

I rolled my eyes as I passed by it. There was a certain irony in the fact that I was purportedly descended from one of the witches his great-great-great-grandfather condemned to an untimely death.

Fitting, really, I thought, pausing to catch my breath beneath a huge, gnarled ash tree, its leaves a riot of red and orange and yellow. *Even our ancestors were sworn enemies. We never stood a chance.*

A cramp stitched through my ribs, making me fold nearly in half. Panting through the pain, I began to stretch — shaking out my tight muscles, flexing my shins against the trunk of the tree, lifting my arms high overhead until the tension ebbed out of my system. A psychoanalyst would probably have a field day with the fact that in the moments I felt most alive — lungs on fire, muscles spasming, heart pounding in my veins — I liked to surround myself with the dead. Macabre or not, there was something peaceful about graveyards.

The sun was beginning to break through the thick cloud cover as it rose higher in the sky. Once I'd finished stretching, I walked the winding gravel paths between the headstones that jutted from the grass like crooked teeth, toward the gate at the other end of the cemetery. I wasn't far from home — a ten minute stroll if I took my sweet time — but my mind was already outpacing my body, running through the checklist of things I needed to do before we opened at noon. Shower, pull together an outfit, blow dry my hair, eat breakfast...

I didn't see the body at first. Partly because I was distracted, partly because, well, the only dead people I associated with cemeteries were the skeletons buried six feet beneath my feet. I wasn't expecting to see an actual dead person. But there it was.

There *she* was.

As soon as I rounded the final curve in the path, I spotted her sprawled across the rectangular stone slab of a crypt at the very heart of the graveyard. I jolted to a sudden stop, staring across the fifteen or so feet between me and the body, my mind trying to rationalize what I was seeing.

It's just some sort of prank, right? An early Halloween trick, set up to scare the tourists?

Of course. It had to be. This was Salem, after all. Someone must have purchased a fake corpse and staged her here for maximum effect. Otherwise, it was a paid actor about to scare the bejeezus out of me. I was probably being recorded for a viral TikTok video at this exact moment. Any second now, she would sit up, yank the prop knife from her chest, and start chasing me around the graveyard like a zombie come alive.

My eyes narrowed on the dead — more like '*dead*' — woman. I had no plans to become fodder for the amusement of strangers on the internet. Hauling in a deep breath to steel myself, I stepped closer, taking in some of the details. Really, it looked quite real. I was impressed by the commitment to the scene. I couldn't see her face yet, but it was clear it was a woman. Her bare feet dangled over the edge of the crypt's stone slab top. She was dressed in a flowy white nightgown that covered her to her ankles, the old fashioned kind I'd only ever seen in historical period pieces on the BBC, with a high neckline and frilly lace around the wrists. The blood from the stab wound in her chest was a vibrant red, seeping through the snowy fabric, pooling around her body.

Wow, I thought, dazed. *That's a lot of fake blood.*

The tomb itself wasn't particularly tall — about chest height — and it looked quite old, the stone discolored and cracked, the lettering on the side faded completely. Moving off the gravel path, I stepped onto the grass, my white running shoes crunching on fallen leaves. I was close enough now to see the silver knife was covered in glyphs and occult symbols, with a rounded pentagram at the very base of the hilt. We had some similar pieces locked away in the very back cabinets at The Gallows. Collectors items, mostly. Antique relics with ties to ancient covens.

This particular knife looked very old... and very real. Alarmingly real. So real, I couldn't help leaning in closer to get a better look at it. I ignored the faint warning bells of alarm that had begun to chime inside my head as I came within a handful of feet of the body. I was so, so certain it was all just a prank, I'd nearly reached the 'dead' woman's side before I realized... she wasn't sitting up. She wasn't pulling the knife from her chest. She wasn't chasing me around the graveyard. No one in the distance was shouting, "Gotcha!" or laughing hysterically at their own antics. There were no hidden cameras capturing this moment on film.

Was it possible... that this... wasn't a prank at all? That... this woman... was actually... *dead*?

Not 'dead' in quotation marks.

Really dead.

Actually dead.

Dead dead.

No. Not just dead, I thought, staring at the knife that pierced her heart. *Murdered.*

Panic bolted through me like a lightning strike, locking up my muscles and stealing my breath. I knew, quite abruptly, that this was no harmless Halloween trick. I knew it in the marrow of my bones, beyond any shadow of a doubt. There was no special effects makeup in the world that could ever look so authentically, intrinsically horrifying as the scene laid out before me.

My eyes were stuck on the knife. I couldn't tear them away. I began to shake, great trembles hijacking my central nervous system, rocking through me like mini-earthquakes. Looking back on the moment, I'd question why I didn't immediately pull my phone from the thigh pocket of my yoga pants and call the police. I suppose I was in a good deal of shock. At the time, though, there was no rational thought commanding my actions as I took a terrified shuffle closer to the tomb, so I could finally see the poor woman's face.

When I did, my mind shorted into a drone of static, like a television with crossed wiring. It wasn't just her skin, which was pale as the stone on which she lay, or her blueish lips, still parted from her final breath. It was the fact that... I knew her. I knew those owlish glasses, recognized that sleek white hair. I'd seen them only a few days ago, moving around the garden beds of her front yard.

I was staring at a Eliza Proctor.

"Oh my god," I whispered.

"Oh my god!" someone yelled from somewhere behind me. "*OH MY GOD!*"

I heard the sound of running footsteps. Wrenching my eyes away from Eliza, I managed to turn around in time to see two female dog-walkers in workout attire approaching with a pair of leashed golden retrievers. The dogs were bounding at me, eager to make a new friend. The owners looked less thrilled to meet me. In fact, their expressions were contorted in utter horror as they looked from me to the lifeless body I'd been looming over, much like a criminal caught red-handed, and back again.

"What have you done?" one of the women cried, backpedalling a few steps, as though I was a knife-wielding maniac about to attack her. The once-enthusiastic dogs, following their owner's lead, shifted into protective stances and began to growl at me when I took a few shaky steps toward them.

"Stay where you are!" The other woman fumbled in her fanny-pack and pulled out a small canister. "Don't come any closer! I have pepper spray and I'm not afraid to use it!"

"It's not what you think!" I held up my hands helplessly. "It wasn't me!"

The woman merely lifted the canister, finger poised on the top. (Considering that she was accusing *me* of being a psychopath, she seemed a little too excited by the prospect of dousing me with it.)

The other woman had already whipped out her phone. I could hear her shouting hysterically into the receiver as they both turned and ran away from me, their dogs galloping after them.

"Yes, we need police! Please, come quickly! We've just witnessed a murder at Charter Street Cemetery!"

Hellfire and brimstone.

I sat on the grass with my knees pulled up to my chest, leaning back against the fence on the outer perimeter of the cemetery. My back was to the crime scene, but I knew if I turned to peer through the wrought iron rungs, I'd see a whole flock of forensics investigators moving around the tomb where Eliza's body lay. Policemen in starched navy Salem PD uniforms were cordoning off the entire area with bright yellow tape, but that hadn't stopped a crowd of curious onlookers from gathering in the adjacent alleyway. Some of them were snapping pictures. Many of them were staring at me with naked curiosity.

What's with the redhead sitting inside the crime scene?

A sharp siren bleated from the main street. The crowd parted long enough to allow an unmarked police cruiser to nose up the narrow alleyway that abutted the cemetery. Through the windshield, I recognized Detective Caden Hightower, looking solemn as he parked, shut his engine, and ambled out of the vehicle. His intense eyes never shifted away from me as he approached, dropping down into a crouch less than a foot away, effectively shielding me from the onlookers with his body. His handsome face was creased with concern.

"Gwendolyn," he greeted gently.

"Detective." I tried a smile, but couldn't quite manage it. "How's your day going?"

"Better than yours, from the looks of it." His gaze moved behind me, to the graveyard. "Care to tell me what happened here?"

"I... I don't know."

"Two dog-walkers who called this in said they saw you standing over the body."

"That's true, I was. But I didn't kill her! I swear, I didn't!" A note of panic threaded through my words. "She was like that when I got here!"

He scanned me up and down, taking in my zip-up sports bra, fitted yoga pants, and sneakers. "Why were you here in the first place?"

"I'd just finished my morning run, and was stretching—"

"You stretch in a graveyard?"

I shrugged at his doubtful tone. I liked graveyards. I always had. So had Aunt Colette. When I was a kid, she'd taken me to historical burial grounds all up and down the Massachusetts coastline on summer days when the shop was closed for business. She'd pack a picnic basket full of sandwiches, spread out a blanket on the grass, and lay flat on her back, staring straight up at the sky, completely unbothered by the thought of long-dead Pilgrims entombed beneath us.

Whenever life gets too big to hold in your hands, plant your feet on old ground, she told me once, after my brand new bike got run over by a delivery truck and I convinced myself she was going to send me away from Salem forever in punishment for my carelessness. *These gravestones have stood for three centuries, kiddo. They'll probably stand another three after this — long after you and me are nothing but dust. You want to know a secret? No one remembers any of the crap you did wrong or any of the mistakes you made when you're nothing but a name on an old stone.*

Stop worrying so much.

Live your life.

I wished she was here. I could've used some of her sage wisdom right about now.

"Gwendolyn," Caden prompted, snapping me out of my thoughts.

"Yes, I like to stretch in the graveyard. It's peaceful here. Usually. When there aren't dead bodies lying around with knives jutting out of their chest cavities." A semi-hysterical giggle caught in my throat. I instantly swallowed it down with an embarrassed gasp. "Goddess, that's not funny. I apologize. I don't know why I said that. I didn't mean to be so... flippant."

Cade's kind expression didn't even flicker. "You're in shock. You've experienced a trauma. It's quite all right. Normal, even."

Jeeze, he was nice. Suddenly, I had the overpowering urge to throw myself into his arms and weep like a child while he pet my hair in soothing strokes. I managed not to humiliate myself further by doing so, but there was no holding back the flood of emotions. My tears began to flow, and once they started, there was no stopping them.

"Sorry. Ignore me," I said idiotically, wiping at my face. It was useless — the tears were a torrent. "I'm just really freaked out, you know? I was walking down the path toward the gate, turned around a bend, and then... there she was. At first I didn't even realize it was a real body. I thought—" I sniffled hard, trying to contain my sob. "I thought it was a stupid p-p-prank. I didn't even r-r-ealize—" My hiccups grew more frequent — and more pathetic — as I blubbered. I squeezed my eyes closed, trying to stem the weeping, but it did little good. "—that she was d-d-dead until I saw her f-f-f-face."

My hiccup was smothered by the fabric of Cade's shirt as he reached out and pulled me into his arms. He was warm and solid and right then, I desperately needed something to hold onto, something to keep me from shattering into a zillion pieces.

"Shh," he whispered into my hair, cupping his hand at the nape of my neck. "It's okay, Gwen. You're okay."

I cried, gripping the lapels of his blazer with both hands, burying my face in his strong collarbone, allowing him to hold me close. Normally, such a public show of emotion would've been grounds for changing my identity, fleeing the state, and running off in the night, never to return. But right now, I didn't have a choice in the matter. There was something about Caden Hightower that made me feel safe enough to be completely vulnerable — even in front of a crowd of gawking strangers.

I'm not certain how long we stayed like that. Long enough for my tears to slow from ragged sobs, for the shaking of my body to subside. Only when my mind cleared did I become aware — *highly* aware — of our position. Cade's arms were locked tight around my body. I was half-sitting in his lap. His head was bowed, his lips were pressed against my temple. It felt good. Great, actually. Beneath those fitted button downs and basic khakis, the silver fox detective was packing some serious muscle.

I tilted back my head to meet his gaze. His blue eyes were so bright, so warm, a Caribbean sea soothing away all my jagged emotions. I opened my mouth to say something to him. I hadn't even fully decided what that something would be — an apology, a thank you, yet another plea concerning my innocence — but I never got the chance, seeing as someone else spoke first.

"Isn't this cosy."

I practically vaulted out of Cade's arms at the low, clipped voice that rolled across the cordoned-off section of cobblestones. My head whipped around to see Graham ambling toward us with long strides. His Bronco was parked behind Cade's SUV, apparently having had no trouble bypassing the mass of rubber-neckers still gathering on the narrow street. I'd been so over-wrought, I hadn't even heard him pull up.

"Graves," Cade said, sounding annoyed. "Wasn't expecting you just yet."

"Why's that?" Graham's gaze cut to the graveyard, where a photographer was snapping pictures of the scene.

"Not sure it's connected to your investigation," Cade informed him. "Which means it doesn't concern you."

"If it concerns Gwen, it concerns me," Graham fired back without missing a beat.

My whole body went solid at this statement. He said it in a cold, unflinching tone, his manner completely detached, but heat bloomed through me regardless. I stared up at his face, but he wasn't looking at me. He kept his gaze on the graveyard — even as he said, "You two plan to sit there and cuddle all day or are we going to sort out a crime scene?"

With a rattle of displeasure that shook his broad chest, the detective helped me to my feet. My knees faltered for a moment, threatening to give way, but he steadied me with a steely arm around my waist. The pads of his fingers dug into the slice of bare skin between my leggings and sports bra as he plastered me against his side.

"You good?" Cade whispered, head tilted down to me.

"Good," I echoed, lying through my teeth. I was so *not* good it wasn't even funny.

Cade didn't release me. His head lifted back to look at Graham. I did the same, and the moment I did, found myself ensnared by a frosty green gaze. It was a look I knew well. *Captain Cold*, my old nemesis. No trace of the man I'd gotten glimpses of beneath the ice, these past few weeks. It took all my remaining strength — and, honestly, there wasn't much of it left — to keep from shivering. We stared at one another for a small eternity before Cade cleared his throat and Graham jerked his eyes away from me.

"I haven't had a chance to see for myself. I only got here a few minutes before you did, Graves, and I was—"

"Occupied," Graham growled. "Yeah. Saw that."

I was still hauled up against Cade's side, so I felt him suck in a deep breath long before I heard it leave his mouth in a sharp gust. "Preliminary assessment from the forensics guys indicates she was likely killed elsewhere, then brought here and intentionally staged. You're free to look around when I do, form your own judgments on what you see."

"I always do," Graham returned, sounding distinctly unhappy but not entirely surprised by this news.

I, however, was surprised. My eyes went wide. "Staged? She was *staged* here?"

"Looks that way, honey," Cade said gently.

"Why?" I nearly started crying again. "Why would someone do that? What possible purpose could that serve, except—"

My words choked off into silence as emotion won the battle over coherence. I tilted my head up toward the sky, trying to banish the impending tears. I would not cry, not again. I was stronger than that.

Right.

Cade loosened his hold on my waist — not much, just enough to turn and look fully down into my face. "Gwendolyn, why don't you go wait in my car?" he asked, his blue eyes as gentle as his tone. "You don't need to hear this shit, honey. I'll come get you after I'm done here."

"I'm okay," I assured him, though I was anything but. I didn't want to wait in the car. I wanted to know what was going on with Mrs. Proctor — especially if I was about to be labeled the prime suspect in her murder. "We both know I'll have to hear all of this stuff eventually, Detective. I might as well get it over with as fast as possible."

He frowned, an indecisive look stealing across his features as he studied me for a long moment. Whatever he saw must've been enough to convince him I could hack it, because eventually he turned back to Graham.

"You're tagging along, I presume?"

Graham didn't respond except to growl incomprehensibly, "One more *honey* and we've got problems, Hightower."

For some reason, I didn't get the sense he was calling the

detective an endearment. The men traded a loaded glance, communicating something they didn't feel the need to share with me.

Cade shook his head. "Stay focused, Graves."

"Not my focus I'm worried about." Graham's jaw clenched as his eyes moved again to Mrs. Proctor, who was was now hidden from view behind some portable privacy screens the crime scene squad was setting up at the perimeter of the graveyard, blocking the view from the street. "If she was staged, that fits the pattern."

Cade expelled another sharp breath. "We don't know for sure—"

"Oh, fuck off, Hightower. What do you want, a handwritten confession from the perps? Can't connect the dots without construction paper and a pack of crayons at your disposal?"

"I know your main form of transportation is jumping to conclusions, Graves, but some of us are duty bound to follow the letter of the law," the detective responded in a stern tone I'd never heard from him before. "I'm not prepared to declare this open-and-shut before I've had a chance to go through the scene, inch by inch. You have to give me a few days."

"And in the meantime?" Graham's unhappy eyes flickered to me. It lasted less than a heartbeat before his gaze jerked back to Cade. "We both know they did this for her. Left the body here, specifically, for her to find. We both know what that means. And we both know they won't bother with a second warning."

I tensed.

Beside me, so did Cade. "We don't know anything, yet."

"For fuck's sake, Hightower—"

"Look, what do you expect me to do, Graves? Put her under twenty-four hour surveillance on no more than a hunch? Take her into protective custody?"

"For starters." Graham paused, glowering. "I've already got a man on her. Hourly drive-bys of her house during the night.

Front entrance of the shop is now wired with surveillance, so is the alleyway door."

I felt my eyes widen. This was news to me. Then again, I *had* been feeling like someone was stalking me. I was oddly happy to know it wasn't all deluded paranoia I'd fabricated in my head. Still...

Cameras on the store exits?

Hourly drive-bys?

That felt... extreme.

Excessive.

Until my mind filled with a vision of Eliza's dead corpse and, just like that, Graham's actions no longer felt extreme or excessive. They felt very, very necessary.

"She's covered, then," Cade pointed out.

Graham's eyes were again on the cemetery. "Not covered enough. You have a full force at your disposal, funded by Salem citizens you're meant to protect. Use it. Protect her."

Cade finally released me, but only so he could run an exasperated hand through his thick, silver-streaked hair. "Right now, our priority is on identifying the victim. That'll take some time. After that, we can talk about our next steps in—"

"It won't," I blurted without thinking. "Take time, that is. Her name is Elizabeth Proctor."

Both men's heads snapped in my direction. I instantly wanted to evaporate.

Why hadn't I just kept my mouth shut?

"Gwendolyn," Cade said slowly, turning his body fully toward mine. "You know the victim? Personally?"

"Um." I swallowed hard, trying not to show the panic that was clawing its way up my throat, blocking off my air flow. "She's my neighbor. *Was* my neighbor."

"Why didn't you mention that straight away?"

"You didn't ask."

Cade's bright blue eyes narrowed, for the first time since I'd met him losing some of their trademark warmth as they beheld me. In fact, if I didn't know better, I'd say he was regarding me with the same shrewd suspicion he used on criminals in the interrogation room, the intensity cutting as a blade. I didn't blame him. I wasn't so obtuse that I couldn't see how odd all of this looked to an outside observer. How coincidental. Even *I* would think I was guilty, seeing the scene from a birds' eye view.

"When did you last see her alive?" Cade asked.

"Yesterday. Wait, no — the day before yesterday."

"Which was it? Yesterday or the day before?"

Fighting off a shiver, I wrapped my arms around my torso and hugged myself to keep warm. My bare arms and exposed midriff might've been fine while I was running, but my core temperature had long since returned to normal. I was officially freezing. "The day before," I said firmly. "Our front yards abut. We bumped into one another in the morning. She was raking the leaves from her garden beds."

"Did you speak to her?"

My mind spiraled back two days, to Friday morning. I'd been in a rush, running late to get to the store after a sleepless night of tossing and turning. I'd bumped into the terrible trio — better known as Eliza, Sally, and Agatha — as soon as I stepped out into the sun-drenched October day. They were gathered by the fence that divided Eliza's property from mine, standing in the freshly-raked garden beds. Each of them was chanting something, a low incantation I couldn't quite make out, and holding a jar of white crystalline powder.

I'd been momentarily terrified I was about to receive another magic mickey and wind up strapped to a chair in a basement... until I realized the substance in their jars was not shimmery gray, like my last witchy-roofie experience, and that they were not aiming it anywhere near me but, instead, sprinkling a thick perimeter of it around the property line.

"Don't worry, Gwendolyn," Eliza had called, sounding amused by the paranoid look on my face as I hastened toward the gate. "Only salt."

I didn't stop walking, but I did stumble a bit at her announcement. Salt. A common practice for protection when placed in a line around one's home. I knew from all my occult readings, as well as witnessing Aunt Colette's own traditions, that many witches saw it as a first line of defense against unwanted energies, unwelcome spirits, and uninvited guests.

"You think you need protection from *me*?" I'd muttered, reaching for the gate handle. "That's a laugh."

Eliza's voice carried after me. "The protection is not for us."

Sure enough, as I stepped through the gate, my feet were confronted with a thick line of white crystals that lined the sidewalk along the entire front of my property. I had no doubt, if I walked into Dan and Rich's yard, I'd find a similar line bounding the other side of my fence. Probably all along the back yard, as well.

They were protecting me.

I'd spun around to stare at the three woman, not sure what to say. This surely didn't make up for them kidnapping me, but I couldn't help it — my heart softened a bit at the thought.

"You're still keeping me safe?" I'd asked, brows high. "Even though you're angry at me for not leaving town like you wanted?"

Sally had nodded firmly. "Someone has to, child."

"Not that you deserve it," Agatha had muttered.

"When the Heretics strike, The Bay Colony Coven will be ready," Eliza had added, her voice calm and measured, a direct contradiction to her fierce words. "See that you are as well, Gwendolyn. There is only so much we can help from a distance.

You must be on your guard. Time grows short. And enemies may be far closer than you think."

I'd nodded, latched my gate, and rushed to the store without another word. That was the last time I saw Eliza Proctor — the last time I saw her alive, anyway.

"Gwendolyn?"

Cade's low, prompting voice snapped me back to the present. I swallowed hard and shook off the memories cobwebbed across my mind.

"No, we didn't really speak, just called our typical good morning greetings. I was running late for work, I didn't have time to chitchat."

His watchful eyes moved over my features, studying me with an intentness that made my chest tighten with nerves. He didn't look like he fully believed I was telling him the whole story — probably because I *wasn't*, and he was a smart guy. I might not be smart, but I was wise enough to know that telling the truth right now wouldn't do me any favors. In fact, I was pretty sure spilling the whole twisted saga would result in one thing and one thing only — me, locked away in a cell for the foreseeable future, wearing an orange jumpsuit (that, I shuddered to think, would clash abominably with my hair color), trying to make a bunch of straight-laced, no-nonsense cops understand that just because I did indeed have motive for revenge against Eliza Proctor, seeing as she'd kidnapped me and tried to run me out of town, I wouldn't ever in my wildest dreams actually hurt a little old lady. Certainly not with something so gruesome as an occult knife through the heart.

These panicked thoughts careened around my brain as the silver fox detective studied me, setting off alarm bells as they ricocheted off the inside of my skull. An unhappy line appeared between Cade's dark brows as they furrowed inward.

"Gwendolyn..." he pressed, looking grim.

"Enough, Hightower." Graham's voice cut in sharply. "This isn't the time."

Cade's jaw tightened, but he nodded and glanced away from me. Blowing out a long breath, he steered his eyes toward the graveyard. "Let's get this done, then."

Graham appeared before me, closing the distance between us in a blink. I took one look at his stony expression and knew that his anger was burning perilously close to the surface. Still, I made not a peep as he shrugged out of the wickedly cool, wickedly faded leather jacket he was wearing and dropped it around my bare shoulders. It settled against my skin, still warm from the heat of his body and smelling faintly like him, spicy and woodsy. There was something so heartrending about the gesture, I found myself fighting the urge to cry again, my eyes prickling precariously as they stared into his.

"Graham," I whispered brokenly, not knowing what to say to him. Not knowing whether to hurl myself into his arms or turn on a heel and run. "I don't— I'm—"

"Not here. Not now," he cut me off. His large hand found mine beneath the jacket that shrouded me, fingers twining so tight I thought my bones would turn to dust in his grip. "Later."

With that slightly ominous vow hanging in the air, he started walking after the detective, towing me along at his side. Lacking any other choice in the matter, I followed him into the graveyard.

CHAPTER NINETEEN

I should've been a tennis player. Love means nothing to me.
— Gwen Goode, contemplating a different career path

I had many things in life to be thankful for but, on that particular morning, I was most thankful that hadn't eaten breakfast before my run. Because if I had, after walking through the cemetery crime scene, keeping close to Graham's side the entire time, it might've come straight back up.

Earlier, when I'd first spotted Eliza, I was in a state of shock, my system barely processing the gruesome sight before me. My second viewing — during which I saw not only Eliza's body, but the symbols traced into the grass and the warning message spelled in dried, bloody letters across the tomb on which she was splayed — was infinitely worse. So much worse, in fact, I began to sway on my feet as the world went black around the edges of my vision.

I promptly found myself swooped up into Graham's unyielding arms, one beneath my knees, the other around my shoulders. I'd begun to protest as he carried me away from the crypt, straight to his Bronco, but one fleeting glance at his expression had me clamping my lips shut and swallowing down my words.

"*Stay*," was all he'd clipped after depositing me into his passenger seat, slamming the door, and bleeping the locks. As if I was going to run away. Run? I could barely stand, let alone run.

He'd stalked straight back into the cemetery, disappearing behind the makeshift privacy screens, not returning for nearly a half hour — during which time I'd made the executive decision to keep the The Gallows closed for the day. I texted Hetti that I had a personal emergency and dispatched her to put a sign up in the front window explaining that we'd be back to business on Tuesday morning. The barista, never one for emotional displays, didn't demand an explanation; she merely did as I asked without pushback, not ten minutes later sending a picture of the shop's front door, where a piece of printer paper bearing several words in her bold, chunky handwriting was taped against the glass.

C U NEXT TUESDAY

Not the nicest missive to our shunned customers, but I had bigger things on my plate than politeness. Namely, scrubbing the memory of Eliza's lifeless body from my retinas, where it seemed indelibly scored, and clearing my name of a potential murder charge. I had a feeling Cade wanted to bring me down to the station — actually, it was more than a feeling, seeing as when he and Graham emerged from the cemetery and marched back toward the Bronco, they were engaged in what could only be described as a battle of wills. Cade gestured more than once toward the Bronco — toward me — and his handsome face was set in a seriously unhappy frown as he listened to whatever Graham was saying. I was no lip reader, but I'd stake my right kidney that the words, '*She's not going anywhere with you, Hightower,*' left the uncompromising line of Graham's mouth, along with a few choice expletives not fit to print.

Whatever he said, it was effective. Detective Hightower shot one last dark look at me through the windshield, then stormed toward his unmarked cruiser. He'd no sooner turned his back when Graham slid into the driver's seat. He didn't say a word as he started the engine, immediately punching buttons on his steering wheel to dial a number at the top of his contacts list. The Bronco rolled slowly after Cade's cruiser — which was flashing its lights to encourage the lingering crowd to disperse — as ringing filled the cab.

After just two short rings it connected. A smooth feminine voice greeted, "Gravewatch Securities, this is Brianne speaking. How many I help you today?"

I stiffened a bit, a vision of the perfect blonde receptionist in her perfectly coordinated outfit flashing in my mind. Goddess, even her phone voice sounded polished. I caught myself wondering if she and Graham had ever explored a relationship outside the bounds of employer-employee, and quickly banished the thought to the dark recesses of my brain. What was I, jealous? How ridiculous.

"It's me," Graham said by way of greeting.

"Graham." Brianne's voice warmed noticeably as she recognized his deep rasp. I tried not to clench my teeth. "What do you need, sir?"

"Something's come up. Unexpected, but priority. I need you to shuffle some of my other shit around, and help put out any new fires that crop up while I'm dealing with this."

"Anything," she agreed instantly. Breathlessly. "Anything you need, I'm on it."

I'll bet.

I rolled my eyes as I looked out my window. I was getting the distinct impression that Brianne's favorite job benefit was watching Graham's rock hard ass as he strolled out the front doors of Gravewatch every afternoon. Not that it was any of my business who stared at his — annoyingly fine — ass. An ass I had caught myself staring at on more than one occasion in the past, before I remembered my sanity and yanked my eyes up to safer targets.

"Holden and Hunter should be inbound this afternoon. They've been keeping eyes on the O'Banion situation, finally got a lead on our target this morning," Graham informed Brianne. "If that lead pans out, tell them to use the holding cell. I don't want the exchange going down until I've had a chance for my own face to face."

I'd gone still at the word O'Banion, my head whipping in Graham's direction. He didn't even look at me, focused on guiding the Bronco down the final stretch of the narrow side street, then turning out onto the main drag.

"Call Sawyer," he continued. "He pulled a surveillance shift last night, but he'll come back in. Tell him I need a full sweep of the Old Burying Point area — traffic cameras on Charter Street, exterior shop and restaurant CCTV, the works. I want all of it analyzed with a fucking fine-tooth comb, along with the rest of her running route. I want to know if there were any other surprises left for her that we missed, or if these fucks were dumb enough to slip up and show their faces."

My brows raised. I had a creeping feeling I was the subject of Sawyer's latest surveillance gig. Normally, this would've pissed me off but, seeing as not one hour ago I'd come face to face with a dead body, I let it slide.

"Welles is in New Hampshire finalizing shit with the Feds,"

Graham went on. "But he'll be back by tonight. Loop him in with Sawyer, it'll go quicker with two sets of eyes."

I could hear the scratch of a pen — Brianne jotting down notes. When the scratching stopped, she asked, "And Kier? Is he still after that skip?"

"Last I heard — and last I heard was too fucking long ago." A current of displeasure entered Graham's clipped voice. "Call him, get a status report. Soon as you can. He doesn't answer, you ping his phone. We all know Kier can handle his shit, but we also know how he gets when he's off the grid. Especially when he's after a skip with this sort of rap sheet. I have too much on my plate to be worried about him crossing lines we can't walk back. I want a lock on his location by end-of-day. Alert the boys we may need to reel him in."

I stared at the man seated beside me, my mind slowly turning over the names of his men. Holden, Hunter, Sawyer, Welles, Kier. Hot names, no doubt fitting a legion of hot, veritable badasses under his command. I'd known, of course, that Graham ran a successful operation. I'd seen him in action, gun in hand. Hell, I'd even been to his offices, seen the sleek Gravewatch reception area and prime views from his cushy conference room. But it was something rather different to witness him barking orders, issuing tasks, steering the fates of a whole company with what seemed like ease and skill.

"Consider it handled. I'll get right on it, sir," Brianne assured him, her voice even warmer and breathier over the line. "Do you require any assistance with this new priority issue you're dealing with?"

We came to a stop at a red light. Graham's eyes moved to me. They were glittering with sudden, unexpected heat. "No. This is a one-man job."

I gulped.

What the hell did that mean?

"Will require all my focus for the rest of the day," he continued, still staring at me. "Probably all night."

My stomach pitched nervously.

Um...

Graham's gaze slid down my body, which was still engulfed in the large leather jacket but, as he looked at me, I felt like he could see straight through it to the fitted spandex running outfit I had on underneath. It took all my effort not to squirm in my seat.

"My hands," he informed Brianne, his eyes moving back to mine. "Will definitely be full."

My stomach dropped straight out the floor of the Bronco.

The car behind us beeped as the light changed over from red to green. Graham tore his attention from me and fixed it back where it belonged, on the road. My heart was pounding hard, pulse roaring between my ears as we began to drive again.

When Brianne spoke, I jumped. I'd been in such a momentary daze, I'd forgotten she was still on the line.

"Understood, sir. But if you need anything else — *anything* — I'm at your full disposal."

Anything, Brianne? I thought scathingly. *Really? Anything at all? Like, perhaps, a blow job at his desk? A quickie on the conference room table? A tutorial on the creative uses of his handcuff collection?*

I gritted my teeth, annoyed at myself. I'd never been jealous in my life over a man. I was not a jealous person. I didn't *do* jealous. The way I saw it, if a man's eyes — or hands, or other parts — began to wander, the best course of action was to let him keep on wandering, straight out of your life.

Even when I'd been cheated on by ex-boyfriends, I'd hardly batted an eye, let alone allowed the notorious green-eyed monster to rear her ugly head. And yet... here I was. Positively *green* as I contemplated a million unhinged, irrational scenarios between Graham and his employee.

I needed to get a grip.

"Appreciate it," Graham thanked her professionally.

Watching from the corner of my eye, I saw his thumb moving toward the disconnect button.

"Goodbye, sir," Brianne breathed into her receiver.

"Bye, Brianne!" I couldn't help myself from chirping, my voice falsely bright. "Have a *super* day!"

Graham punched a button to disconnect the call. I felt his eyes slide to my face and, after hauling in a deep breath, I forced myself to glance over at him. He looked like he was attempting to swallow down a laugh, his lips fighting a twitch.

"What?" I snapped, heat rising to my cheeks.

"I didn't say a word," he murmured, turning back to the steering wheel. But he didn't need to say a word — the quick, irrepressible grin he flashed said it all.

Hellfire.

My fingernails bit into the palms of my hands as I faced the windshield. I didn't ask where we were going — honestly, I was just happy it wasn't an interrogation room at the local precinct — and wasn't altogether surprised when Graham turned onto Pickering Wharf. When we passed by the front of his building, I (barely) resisted the urge to crane my neck to see if I could spot Brianne sitting at her desk, no doubt doodling *Mrs. Brianne Graves* on her notepad.

He pulled around the back, hit the button on his visor to open the garage door, and parked in the empty bay. The motorcycle and SUV were both missing from their spots. I'd barely removed my seatbelt, but Graham was out of the Bronco, rounding the hood, yanking open my door. He grabbed my hand and dragged me out, ignoring my soft screech of alarm as my sneakers collided with the concrete. For once, I was thankful I wasn't in heels.

Biting my lip to keep my commentary contained, I watched

him punch in the code to unlock the door, then allowed him to drag me up the stairs to his loft. It was just as I remembered, all warm camel and soft leather, art and books, high beamed ceilings and exposed brick walls.

Graham led me straight into the kitchen area, dropping my hand so he could shove me — yes, *shove* me — up onto a stool. I glared at him as he walked around to the opposite side of the kitchen island, so there were several feet of butcher block between us. But as soon as I saw his intense expression, my glare slipped right off my face and I found myself grateful for the distance.

He looked at me for a long, long time, a kaleidoscope of emotions moving over his features. Fury, frustration, irritation, desire. That last one hit me the hardest, a southpaw straight between the ribs. Eventually, he smoothed his expression clear, blew out a breath, and planted his hands against the butcher block.

I cleared my throat lightly. "Graham—"

"Don't," he cut me off. "So help me god, Gwen, my self-control is hanging by a fucking thread. If you throw even one sassy little line at me right now, if you try to cute your way out of this instead of telling me the goddamned truth for once in your fucking life... that thread is going to snap."

I didn't think I wanted to see Graham's control snap.

Then again...

My teeth sank into my bottom lip. "I do not cute my way out of things," I told him stiffly.

His hands flexed against the countertop so hard, the tips of his fingers turned white. "Gwendolyn."

"Um..." I swallowed, but my mouth was suddenly dry. "Okay. I won't be purposefully cute. Though, I do reserve the right to be cute by accident. Sometimes, I can't control it. Sometimes, it just slips out."

He stared at me for another long beat, then jerked a hand though his hair, mussing it instantly as he muttered a low, frustrated, *"Christ."* His chest expanded as he hauled in another breath, then pinned me with a look that stole all the air, every bit of it, straight out of my lungs.

"You've been lying to me," he began, blunt as ever. "I've been letting you because, frankly, you're a shit liar, and I figured none of what you were lying about posed any real danger. That was my fuck up. Should've pushed you harder from the start. Now, I'm pushing."

I was smarting a bit over the *shit liar* comment, but managed not to retort.

"You and I are going to have an honest conversation about what's been going on. Warning you right now, Gwen, this conversation can go one of two ways." He took another slow, rattling breath and I got the sense he was fighting to keep his tone steady. "First way? We sit here, drink coffee, and you spill. Everything. All of it. Anything I want to know, even if you think it's not important."

"And the second?" I asked, my voice barely audible.

"Second way, you decide to withhold information — information I need so I have a full picture of what's going on around you, information I need to keep you safe moving forward, seeing as a woman of your acquaintance was left practically fucking gift-wrapped for you to find on your run this morning, information I should've had from the fucking start so maybe I could've prevented that from happening or, at the very least, prevented you from seeing that shit..." He shook his head. "Shit that's going to make it even harder for you to sleep at night when we both know you've got enough fucking issues in that department..."

I swallowed hard.

"You decide to withhold any of that information, you even *think* about withholding any of that information, and I will toss you over my shoulder, take you to my bed, tear off your clothes, and quite literally fuck the truth out of you. And babe?" He leaned in, hands planting back on the countertop, and glared at me, his eyes narrowed to emerald slits. "I will enjoy it."

I nearly fell off my stool. I was no longer breathing, my lungs refusing to pump air in or out. My throat was closing with a lump of emotion. I wasn't sure if it was sheer, instinctual panic or pure, animalistic attraction. Judging by the heat pooling between my legs, the pulsing ache of need his words set off inside me, I was leaning toward the latter.

Graham quirked one dark brow, as if to ask, *Well? Which option will it be?*

Forcing a gulp of oxygen into my lungs, I pressed my thighs together hard enough to stop circulation to my toes and whispered, "I'll tell you the truth."

Something flickered in the depths of Graham's eyes, there and gone so fast I couldn't be sure what it was... but it looked a hell of a lot like disappointment. He turned away and flipped on the coffee machine to brew a fresh pot.

"Let's start with Elizabeth Proctor," he said, his voice carefully empty of the gritty desire it held only a moment before.

I nodded even though he wasn't looking at me, he was occupied retrieving two mugs from his cabinet. With no other option — okay, that wasn't *exactly* true, but I was pointedly not thinking too hard about the other option Graham had spelled out, which involved him screwing my brains out until I was physically incapable of deception — I began to speak in a soft, tremulous voice that sounded nothing like my own.

"Eliza was my neighbor. She lived in the Victorian house next door to Aunt Colette for as long as I can remember. When my aunt was alive, they were good friends." I paused. "She was also a witch."

Graham paused, grip tightening on the mugs. "A witch."

Goddess, he was going to have a field day with this. The man loathed the supernatural, scorned anyone who considered themselves a true believer. I could only imagine what he'd think about the story I had to share. But I forced myself to keep talking.

"Eliza and my aunt were both members of the same group of Wiccans. They call themselves the Bay Colony Coven. And Aunt Colette... I guess she was sort of like their head honcho, before she died. Their High Priestess."

"You guess?"

"I didn't know about any of this until the other night," I whispered, wincing as I prepared for the next part of the story — one I knew would not please the man standing across from me. "Until... Eliza and two of the other witches in that coven... sort of... kidnapped me."

Graham's hands grew so tight on the mugs, I was somewhat concerned the stoneware would shatter to pieces. He glared at me, eyes dark with barely leashed fury.

I forced myself to carry on despite the intimidating wrath pouring off him, thickening the air between us. "I know I told you I didn't see anything in the alley, or when I woke up in the basement. I'm sorry, Graham, I truly am, but I lied."

"Why?" he gritted out, teeth clenched.

"You were so pissed off, wanting to exact revenge on the people who took me... I was afraid if I told you what really happened that night, you'd go after them. I didn't have the heart to get three octogenarians into serious trouble. Not when they didn't mean any real harm. They only did it to keep me safe."

"We'll circle back to you thinking I'd actually go after three little old ladies on a quest for revenge," he said slowly, sounding ticked off by the idea. "For now, explain to me how, exactly, kidnapping someone is equated to keeping them safe in that fucked up head of yours?"

My tempter flared, but I tamped it down. "The Bay Colony

coven wants me out of town. When they kidnapped me, they told me to close up the shop, sell the house, and leave Salem forever."

Graham's eyes flashed. "*What?*"

"Yeah. They weren't too pleased when I told them I had no intention of going anywhere."

Some of the intensity bled out of his eyes. He gestured for me to continue.

"They want me gone for my own safety, but also for theirs. They're convinced that, as the only living descendant of their former High Priestess, my blood is the key to unlocking a curse they laid on a sept of other witches, ages ago. Dark witches. They call them Heretics. I don't know specifics but, whatever witchy woo-woo they're into, I'm guessing it's a fair bit more taboo than dancing naked under the light of a full moon or sprinkling cinnamon on their stoops for good luck." I paused, pulling in another breath. "According to Eliza, Agatha, and Sally—"

Graham shook his head, amused despite his deep frustration. "*Christ.*"

"—these dark witches, the Heretics, are the ones responsible for the animal sacrifices that have been popping up all over town. They think they're gearing up for something else. Something... bigger."

All humor faded instantly from Graham's expression. His eyes raked over me. "You. They're coming for you."

"I..." I shrugged, trying not to let my voice shake. "Yeah. They're coming for me."

A curse exploded from his mouth, loud enough to make me flinch. "And you didn't figure I needed to know any of this shit? Jesus, Gwen! I knew you were reckless with your safety, but this—"

"I didn't take it all that seriously! Not until today." My voice wobbled, regardless of my efforts at steadiness. "Not until I saw

Eliza lying there on that crypt, stabbed through the heart with an occult blade." I sank my teeth into my lip, hard enough to tear the skin. "They've been watching me. They knew I'd stop there to stretch after my run. They wanted me to find her like that. That's why they left that message in the blood."

An image of the crypt beneath Eliza's corpse, the stone streaked with bloody letters, filtered into my mind, and I fought off tears with rapid blinks.

"*Tu es proximus,*" I murmured. "It's Latin. It means—"

"You are next," Graham finished for me. His face was set like stone when I looked across the island at him.

"I swear, if I'd thought for one minute that Eliza, Sally, and Agatha were right, that I was actually in danger... I would've done as they said. I would've left town. I would have..." I trailed off abruptly as another thought — a new one, and a seriously unpleasant one at that — snaked its way into my head. There was a brief moment of silence, only the faint gurgle of the coffee machine as it neared the end of its brew cycle to disrupt my troubled mind, which was tripping over itself, struggling to process the realization I'd just reached.

"Gwen," Graham called softly, heading for me as he sensed my gathering panic.

"Oh my god," I whispered, feeling the world tilt beneath me. Horror slammed into my chest like a sledgehammer, overriding every other emotion. "*Oh my god.*"

Sliding to my feet, I yanked my arms out of Graham's leather coat and dropped it on the stool I'd just vacated. Without even looking at him, I sped for the door. I needed to get the fuck out of here. I needed to go home, pack my shit, get in the car, and *go*.

Graham's arm hooked around my waist, stopping me before I made it past the kitchen.

"Where are you going, Gwen?" His voice was uncharacteristically gentle.

I blinked rapidly, my breaths coming out so fast I was practically hyperventilating. "I have to go," I told him, the words strangled with emotion as I struggled against his hold. No use — his arm was a steel band, unshakable. "I have to get out of town, right now, before anyone else gets hurt."

"You're not going anywhere."

My head tipped back and my gaze went up, up, up — passing the collar of his t-shirt, sliding up the tan column of his throat, bypassing his razor-sharp jawline, tracing the proud bridge of his nose, eventually finding his eyes. They were so soft as they met mine. Almost...

Tender.

It was a look I'd never seen before from Graham, not in all the years I'd known him, and it broke something wide open inside me. I felt a crack in the foundations of the walls I kept so close around my heart, in the shields I refused to ever let fall. I stood there in the circle of his arms, shaking like a leaf, heart hammering, and allowed my wild eyes to pool with the tears I'd been fighting since I realized what I'd done.

"She's dead because of me," I croaked, my voice shattered. "They killed her because of me."

"No, Gwen." Graham's reply was firm. "That's not true."

"She told me to go. She told me something bad was coming. She told me danger was close — closer than I could ever expect." I felt the hot tears sliding down my cheeks, dripping off my chin, a stream of salt and grief I could not stop, not even if I tried. "I didn't listen. Why didn't I listen? Why didn't I go? Why didn't I leave town, like they asked?"

"This is your home," he reminded me, shaking me lightly.

"It doesn't matter! It was Eliza's home too, and she's dead! They killed her!" A crack split my voice again as devastation sluiced through me, unrelenting. "*I* killed her! I'm just as culpable as the person who drove that knife through her heart!"

Graham's arms vanished from my waist, but only so he could grab my face between his hands. The callused pads of his fingers moved swiftly beneath my eyes, wiping the endless flood of tears away as soon as they materialized, as if he might stem the flow if he kept at it long enough. I felt soft pressure at the hinge of my jaw as he tilted my face up to look into his. Leaning down, he rested his forehead against mine.

We were close enough to share the same breath, close enough — under normal circumstances — to make my heart palpitate with a heady mix of trepidation and anticipation as I prepared to put some necessary distance between us. But right then, the last thing I wanted was distance. I had no strength left to bolt. I had no energy left to fight — not against him, not against myself, not against my own feelings. Not when he was there, right there, holding me together even as I felt myself coming apart at the seams.

He was strong.

He was steady.

He was... *Graham.*

My Graham. My light in the dark, my hope for better days. And in that moment... I could really use some freaking hope.

I didn't think twice about it. I didn't let myself think at all. I just acted — pushing up onto my toes, I planted my mouth against his. He froze, going totally still. I felt his soft intake of air, felt the surprised jolt that shook his whole body like a volt of raw electricity. His hands tightened on the sides of my face and, for a split second, I thought he was going to set me back on my heels, pushing me away with placating words.

Until he groaned and kissed me back, his mouth melting against mine, somehow soft and hard at the same time, gentle but firm. I slid my hands up his sides, under his t-shirt, feeling warm skin and hard muscle, and he pulled back an inch.

"Gwen, you're upset. Maybe—"

"Please," I whispered.

Hell, I begged. I could hear the desperation in my own voice, that one word so full of longing it was impossible to deny. And he didn't. Not for another second. His mouth slammed back down on mine, all traces of soft and gentle gone, replaced by fierce and wild. His tongue spiked inside my mouth, tasting me like he'd been dying for it, and I moaned, it felt so damn good.

I pushed at his t-shirt, impatient for more skin, and he was all too happy to help. Reaching one arm behind his collar, he broke our mouths apart only long enough to whip the shirt over his head and toss it aside. I didn't watch to see where it landed. I couldn't — his head came immediately back down, lips claiming mine in a bruising kiss that made me gasp. His hands found my waist, sliding along the bare skin between my sports bra and fitted yoga pants, and I shivered at the sensation.

He felt the shudder of pure desire tremble through me and a growl moved in his throat as his searching hands divided paths, one circling around to the small of my back, the other sliding upward to palm my breast. My nipples were hard from the arousal that thrummed through my bloodstream like a potent drug. Even through the thick spandex fabric, his fingers felt utterly fantastic.

I wound my hands around his neck, kissing him deeper as he worked my nipple, tracing the rigid peak, then tugging sharply on it in a way that left me gasping and clutching at his shoulders to keep from falling off balance. My knees nearly gave out beneath me when he rolled his fingers, toying with me expertly. His mouth left mine to lave my neck, his tongue exploring the sensitive skin beneath the hollow of my ear in a way that made my breath catch.

"Fair's fair," he muttered against the sensitive lobe of my ear, fingers poised at the zipper at the front of my sports bra. In one smooth tug he pulled it down, baring my breasts to him. The straps slid over my shoulders, the bra falling to my feet as I arched my back. I felt the kiss of air against my nipples a second before Graham bent down to capture one in his mouth. I nearly screamed as his tongue circled; I *did* scream when his teeth clamped down and tugged sharply, sending a shot of arousal straight down to my clit.

Shoving my hands into his hair, I held him close as he worked one breast, then the other, driving me wild with lashes of his tongue. His hands found the elastic waistline of my yoga pants and, *whoosh*, like magic, they disappeared down my legs, tangling on my running shoes. His mouth left its dizzying task as he fell to his knees and jerked the sneakers off my feet, one after another, then tossed them clear across the room. My pants followed an instant later, leaving me in nothing but my white cotton thong.

On his knees, he looked up at me, hands sliding up the bare skin of my legs, landing at my hips. His eyes were burning with so much passion, I lost my breath. His voice was sandpaper, rough with grit.

"You are so fucking gorgeous, Gwendolyn, it almost hurts to look at you."

My lips parted on a sigh. *Graham "Lifeguard God" Graves thought I was gorgeous.* Somewhere deep inside me, a gawky, gingery, preteen girl was doing cartwheels of joy.

He got to his feet, barely giving me time to blink before he stooped again and swung me up into his arms, sliding one under my knees so I was cradled against the warm skin of his chest. He stalked toward the sleeping alcove, wearing nothing but his jeans and motorcycle boots, each step making my heart pound a little harder.

Was I really about to do this?

He tossed me onto his king-sized bed without preamble. I bounced as I landed and I saw his eyes on my bare breasts, glowing bright with need as he reached for the button of his jeans.

Hell yes, I was about to do this.

I got on my knees and crawled toward the edge of the bed, toward him, unable to tear my eyes from his as they worked the zipper. He shoved down his jeans, bringing his underwear along for the ride. His cock sprang free, already fully erect, and I felt a lightning bolt of pure feminine appreciation strike directly between my thighs. Seeing Graham in all his glory for the first time — and there was a *lot* of him to see — stole every thought from my head. (Well, every thought except *holy-shit-I-need-him-inside-me-right-this-freaking-instant-or-I-may-die-of-unfulfilled-desire.*)

"You on the pill?" Graham asked, eyes so hot on mine I thought I'd have third degree burns as he leaned over me on the bed. His left hand planted against the mattress as his right slid beneath my pony tail and wrapped around the back of my neck. I felt his thumb brush my pulse point, which was thundering madly.

"Yes," I breathed, craning my head back, offering him my lips.

He took them, his mouth greedy and demanding, his kiss nearly bruising as he moved us deeper onto the bed. His hand left my neck and, a second later, I felt a sharp tug at the crown of my head. My hair tumbled free of its tie, auburn locks cascading down in a cloud of waves around my head and shoulders. Graham growled as his hands slid into it, fisting in the length.

"God, this hair. I dream about this hair. Sliding against my pillow. Falling over your skin." He palmed my breast with his other hand, his touch urgent. "Looks like fire, feels like silk."

My lips were at his neck, his collarbone, his jaw — kissing everywhere I could reach. My hands were on a quest of their own, skating down the ridges of his abdomen, feeling the coarse brush of hair that led in a path straight downward. Graham hissed out a gust of air as my hand closed around his cock, circling the thick shaft with my fingers. He was so hard it made my mouth water.

I tried to stroke him, but he didn't let me get more than a few touches in before his hand left my hair and planted itself on my chest. He pushed me back, flattening my body against the duvet. His fingers hooked in my thong and again, with another blink-and-you-miss-it *whoosh*, he'd whipped it down my legs and tossed it away. His strong hands closed over my ankles, jerking my thighs apart, exposing the most intimate part of me.

For a moment I was tempted to shy away, but when I saw the raw look on his face, the ragged hunger that smoldered in the depths of his eyes... I couldn't even breathe, let alone hide from his line of sight. And I found, the longer he looked at me, the less I wanted to. Under his gaze, I felt just as gorgeous as he told me I was.

"Are you going to stare at me all day, or are you going to fuck me?" I whispered.

With a rattle of desire deep in his chest, he lunged forward, one forearm planting in the mattress beside my head to take the brunt of his weight, the other hand sliding between my legs. His finger hit its target the same moment his mouth claimed mine, sending a blinding pulse of pure lust through me. Hands on his ass, I urged him closer, craving maximum skin contact. He resisted, keeping most of his weight off me, and refused to let me pleasure him back even as he worked me with his mouth and with his fingers. His cock was hard as steel against my thigh, a heavy weight that stole all my focus.

I needed him.

Now.

"Graham," I pleaded, writhing beneath him.

"What do you want, Gwen?"

I didn't hesitate. "You."

His finger circled again, a delicious roll that made my bones quake down to the marrow. "How much?"

"So much it hurts."

The tension slowly ramped up, need burning inside me until he'd stoked the flames to such an inferno, I thought I was going to come just from his fingers. As if he sensed how near I was, he pulled back right before I reached the point of combustion.

"Graham," I cried at the loss, jerking my hips as desire coursed through me. I wanted his fingers back, his mouth back. "No! Don't stop."

"Patience, baby." He chuckled — *pure evil!* — and I felt him move between my hips, felt the head of his thick, throbbing shaft poised at my entrance. "We're coming together this time."

My eyes, which had fallen mostly closed, opened fully. I looked up into his, the green so molten it was hard to believe he'd ever looked at me with anything resembling coldness. Whatever expression he saw on my face made his own contort into something so hot, so untempered, my desire ratcheted up yet another notch.

The head of his shaft nosed inside me, so big he stretched my anatomy to its limits. I whimpered in a heady combo of pleasure-pain that was so good, it defied all description.

"Graham," I begged as he inched inside with excruciating slowness, my fingernails digging into the smooth skin of his back. "*Please.*"

"Too fast and I might hurt you, baby."

"I don't care if you hurt me, just fuck me!"

I saw a flash of his dark grin. And then, not needing to be told twice, he slammed inside, filling me to the hilt, so deep it was a shock to the senses. The sensation of fullness was nearly more than I could take, but in the best sort of way imaginable. I bowed up off the bed, feeling practically split in two, but Graham's hand had a steady lock on my hip. He began to pound into me, groaning as he found a rhythm. I couldn't swallow down my own sounds of ecstasy as my eager body pushed up to meet him, thrust for thrust, until he was driving into me with such bruising ferocity neither of us could properly draw breath.

Pure pleasure had me in its grasp. I felt it in the building tempo deep within my core, in the telltale tightening of my limbs as they wound around his body. I couldn't hold back. It was coming.

I was coming.

"Baby, I'm—" I gasped against his mouth. "I'm—"

"Not yet," he growled back, hips pinioning me harder, faster. "Together."

The waves of passion were rising higher and higher, swamping me, dragging me under a bit deeper with every passing second. I knew Graham was close too. I could feel his ragged breaths on my lips, could see the thunderous rate of his pulse in the vein that corded up his neck.

"Fuck, Gwen," he groaned, grinding his hips harder against me. "*Fuck*, you feel unbelievable."

"Graham—"

His mouth hit mine, stealing the rest of my words, stealing my breath, stealing my sense of the rest of the world. All that was left was him, moving inside me, driving me to a height I'd never felt before. And when I hit that precipice, when my muscles clenched and my legs wrapped tighter around his back, holding him as close as physically possible, when the final shred of control slipped through my fingers and burst into flames... I combusted into pure, undiluted desire. And he was right there with me, spark for spark, flame for flame, heartbeat for heartbeat, coming in sync, just as he'd demanded.

Bossy and alpha, even in the throes.

He slammed home, planting himself deep as he exploded

344

into me. I scream-sobbed into his mouth, so overcome by the sensations flowing through me I couldn't be silent, even if I tried. My orgasm crashed into me and it was *huge*. Massive. The biggest I'd ever felt by a mile, and so potent I thought my nerve endings would immolate. Graham roared with his own release, my name on his lips as his hips jerked over and over, until he was totally spent.

It took a while for us to come down from the high. A long while. Even as the aftershocks moved through me, I kept my legs looped around his hips, my arms around his back, wanting to keep him as close as possible. Delaying the inevitable moment of separation as long as I could.

He lay on top of me, his punishing thrusts slowing to lazy, soft slides that made my over-sensitized insides tremble and my breaths hitch inside my throat. When his hand lifted to trace the slope of my jawline, his eyes soft and warm as they stared down into mine, I stopped breathing altogether.

"Worth the wait, baby," he murmured, brushing his lips against mine with such sweetness, my eyes filled with tears. "Worth every fucking second. Worth a whole fucking lifetime."

CHAPTER TWENTY

She's so flaky, her nickname should be croissant.
- Gwen Goode, trying to make plans

I sat in Graham's glorious pedestal bathtub, the warm water flowing over my breasts, leaning back against the man himself. His long legs barely fit, even with his knees cocked up. I was settled between them, feeling boneless and utterly relaxed as his strong hands worked at the muscles in my shoulders.

After we'd fucked in his bed, I'd let him carry me to the shower where he'd taken his time lathering up a loofah with luxurious smelling shower gel and washing every square inch of my body, his hands slippery as they moved over my skin beneath the hot water. He showed a bit of extra dedication to cleaning between my legs, eventually abandoning the loofah altogether in order to delve his tongue against my cleft as his fingers rolled on my clit.

His mouth was so skilled, it took me an embarrassingly short time to reach climax — something I did moaning his name, clutching his hair as the rainfall shower-head coursed down on us both. Fair play worked both ways, though. It was my turn with the loofah, and my turn to do something I'd been thinking about for years. Dropping to my knees, I took him in my mouth, more than a little bit delighted to finally have the opportunity to feel all that was Graham between my lips, to look up and see him coming undone from just the stroke of my tongue and the pump of my hands. I nearly came again, seeing that look on his face as he fucked mine.

He didn't let me finish him with my mouth, though. He'd yanked me up and lifted me into his arms, his hands cupped firmly at my ass as he pinned me against his expensive, imported tile wall, and proceeded to screw my brains out. Thus, delivering my third orgasm of the day and sending me to an alternate plane of existence, where things like Heretics and dark sacrifices and horrific murders did not exist and never would.

Now, we were in his tub. Graham's hands were moving over my skin, not seeking any sort of gratification, just lazy strokes that felt indescribably good. I turned my head to rest it in the hollow of his neck, my forehead planted firmly against his pulse point, absorbing its slow drum beat against my skin.

"How are you feeling, gorgeous?"

I snuggled closer, loving the slide of my bare skin against his beneath the bathwater. "So good, it should be illegal."

He smiled — I knew because I felt it against my hair, where his mouth was currently pressed. "You better be, after three orgasms."

"Is that, perchance, arrogance I detect in your tone, Graham Graves?"

"Told you before, told you a dozen times — it's not arrogance if I'm right. It's just fact."

Normally, I would've scowled at him. Seeing as my bones were made of gelatin from the aforementioned orgasms, I settled for a heavy sigh.

"Can we stay in this bathtub forever?"

His smile widened, moving against my temple. "You're a prune already, baby. Any longer in here, they'll bottle you into juice and slap you on the breakfast menu at a retirement home."

I giggled, knowing he was right, but not moving an inch. I wanted to stay right there, in that moment, for the rest of time. Unfortunately, the water eventually grew intolerably cold and Graham led me out, wrapping my body in one of his big, fluffy towels, taking pains to wipe every droplet of moisture from my skin with such dedication, you'd think I was the Wicked Witch of the West, about to dissolve into green smoke if exposed to a single molecule of water.

My lips twitched as I thought about the *The Wizard of Oz*. Not long ago, the only thing Graham Graves ever called me was Glinda — and in a mean, mocking voice, at that. Not Gwendolyn or Gwen or babe or baby or, my favorite of all, gorgeous.

"What are you smiling about?" he asked, narrowing his eyes on my mouth. His lush hair was damp, sticking up several directions after he'd vigorously shaken it like a dog, sending droplets sailing everywhere. The sharp v-cut of his abs disappeared into the towel he'd slung around his hips. It was a good look. Beyond good, actually. It was a *hot* look. Made even more hot by my intimate knowledge of what lay beneath said towel.

"Gwen."

I jolted out of my mini-daze of lustful thoughts and focused on his face. "Are four orgasms not enough to smile about?"

His eyes glittered. "By my count, only gave you three, babe."

I dropped my towel to the floor, watching with triumph as his eyes dilated to pricks of lust as they swept the length of my naked form. Stepping toward him, I traced a line down his stomach with the tip of my index finger, following the line of hair downward, feeling his muscles contract as he sucked in a sharp breath.

"Three *so far,*" I whispered, catching his mouth with mine, feeling his arms wrap around me as he hauled me against him, skin to skin. I felt his cock swelling against my thigh beneath his towel and couldn't help grinning as I whispered, "But I'm thinking you're about to change that."

HOURS LATER, we were tangled together on Graham's sofa, my body sprawled mostly on top of his, watching the fire crackle in his fireplace. It was nearly dusk, the sun slanting toward the horizon, bathing the harbor in mellow shades of amber and gold. Graham's hands were in my hair — which, by the way, was out to *there*, given I'd let it air dry after our bath. (And after rolling around in Graham's bed while earning my highly anticipated fourth *O* of the day.)

We'd finally drunk the coffee Graham brewed earlier while he'd made us lunch. Nothing fancy, but he was well stocked with fresh bread from the bakery around the corner, plenty of cold cuts, and condiments galore. After sliding my sandwich in front of me, he retrieved a bag of Cape Cod kettle-cooked potato chips from his cupboard and my eyes widened in delight.

"I love those!" I exclaimed. "They're my favorite."

"I know," he said, dumping a healthy handful on my plate. He skimmed his lips along my jawline, then turned to his sandwich and dug in. I, however, froze, momentarily stunned by the chips on my plate.

I know, he'd said.

Because he did. He knew what chips I liked, and how I took my coffee. He knew I preferred turkey over ham, and mayo over mustard. He knew I wasn't a big fan of anything with too much spice, because I was a weakling when it came to hot sauce and had expressed this at nearly every meal we'd both attended for the past few months.

He knew me.

This was sweet, but it was also strange. This was uncharted territory for me. In the past, I'd never been intimate with a man I'd been friends with (okay, *friends* might be a stretch... but... a man I knew as well as Graham) prior to sleeping with him. Previous guys didn't know my chip preferences after a few rounds between the sheets. Actually, previous guys didn't know my chip preferences *ever*. Most guys didn't pay attention to that sort of detail, in my experience.

Graham, it would appear, paid attention.

Close attention.

I found myself the subject of said attention all throughout lunch. We sat near to one another, our stools pulled together, our thighs brushing, elbows bonking as we lifted our sandwiches to our mouths and sipped our coffee. And it probably should've freaked me out, made me duck for cover, sent me running to the hills. But... it didn't.

Maybe it was the four orgasms. Maybe it was the belly full of my favorite potato chips. Maybe it was just being near Graham, my drug of choice, drinking my fill of him until my soul was near to bursting. Whatever the reason, I was feeling exceptionally mellow.

Now, I snuggled closer to his warmth, my half-lidded eyes on the fire, feeling sated and exhausted in the best sort of way.

"You're sweet when you're sleepy," Graham whispered, trailing a finger through the curls at the side of my head, tracing the delicate shell of my ear. "Never seen you so quiet."

I turned my chin where it was planted on his chest so I could meet his eyes. "I'm always sweet. Everyone else says so. It's you who brings out the snark in me."

One dark brow quirked up. "That so?"

"Yep."

"Gotta tell you, baby, if you're waiting for an apology on that front... don't. I like your snark. Can't say I'm sorry for spurring it."

"You," I informed him, trying — *failing* — to sound uppity. "Are annoying."

"Uh huh. Try to remember that the next time you're screaming my name, begging for me to—"

Whipping my hand up to his face, I placed it over his mouth and drowned out the rest of his words.

He licked my palm.

"*Hey!*" I yanked my hand away and wiped the saliva on his couch cushion. "Don't lick me!"

His eyes glittered with heat. "You didn't mind me licking you earlier."

This was true. In fact, just the memory of his mouth between my legs was enough to inspire a mini mental daze — one I only jolted out of when I felt his subdued laughter rumbling his body beneath mine.

"Are you, perchance, laughing at me Graham Graves?"

"Yeah, gorgeous." He was smiling as his neck arched and he claimed my mouth in a searing kiss that had my head spinning by the time he released me. "No one makes me laugh like you do, Gwen."

I stilled at the seriousness of his tone. "Really?"

"Really. One of the things I like best about you."

"Oh," I said lamely, feeling emotional for no reason at all.

"That," he continued. "And your fucking fantastic heart-shaped ass. Plus those legs of yours, so long I swear they could loop around me twice when I'm buried deep inside you."

"Anything else?" I asked wryly, not sure whether to be complimented or insulted by his blatant objectification.

"Your hair. God, your hair. So thick, so soft. Next time you suck me off, baby, we aren't doing it in the shower. I want to feel that silk falling all around me when I'm in your mouth."

The mouth in question went utterly dry. I attempted a swallow, trying not to succumb to the furl of pleasure his words unearthed inside me. "Right. Um. Glad to know my body lives up to expectation."

"Expectation? No. *Fantasy* would be closer." His eyes were still glittery with heat. "Don't act like you don't like my body, too. Earlier, when you had my cock in your hands, you said I was the biggest—"

I slapped my hand over his mouth again, shooting him a warning glare. "Nobody likes a braggart!"

His grin against my palm was enough to make my heart turn over. When I pulled my hand away, he gazed into my face for a long time with thoughts working in his eyes, searching for an answer to a question he'd never got around to asking.

"What?" I whispered when I couldn't take it anymore. "Why are you looking at me like that?"

With a start, his expression locked down, whatever he'd been thinking vanishing behind a mask instantly. Eyes carefully guarded, his smile was still sweet as he leaned in to nuzzle my neck. "You want to sleep here or in my bed?"

My body tensed. "Graham..."

"What?"

"I can't stay."

At my tone as well as my sudden tension, he pulled back from my neck, staring at me with both brows raised. His body had gone tense, too.

"You know I can't stay here," I whispered, not wanting to hurt him but needing to be honest. "I don't sleep with other people."

He stared at me some more.

"I *can't* sleep with other people," I stressed. "You know this about me."

The staring continued.

"I need to be home, in my own bed."

More staring.

A hint of anger — an emotion I was highly familiar with when it came to Graham Graves — stirred to life inside me. It was faint, a mere trickle beneath the riptide of passion I'd been riding all day, but it was there. "Graham, I mean it. I'm worn out. I need you to take me home."

"Can't do that."

My eyes narrowed and I pushed up on his chest, rising into a seated position on the sofa, the hint of anger strengthening into something more tangible. "Well, I'm not staying here."

"You are," he countered straight away.

Okay, the anger was more than tangible, now. Sliding off him completely, I gained my feet and paced several strides away from the couch so I could effectively glare down at him. This effort was undermined only slightly by the fact that I was naked as a jaybird.

"What do you mean, *I am*?" I yelled. "I just said *I'm not* and, last I checked, I'm a grown woman who makes her own decisions!"

Graham sighed, ab muscles curling as he knifed up into an upright position and planted his bare feet on the rug. He too, I might add, was naked as a jaybird.

"I see sleepy, sweet Gwen has left the building," he muttered.

"Sleepy, sweet Gwen doesn't stick around for autocratic, overbearing Graham!"

His eyes flashed, not with humor or desire but with something I was far more accustomed to seeing when he directed them at me — irritation. "You might not want to stay here tonight, but I frankly don't give a fuck about your hangups. Your neighbor was killed today. You're a goddamned target. You're staying put. Get used to it."

The reminder of Eliza admittedly took a little bit of the wind out of my sails, but truth be told I was more fixated on his other comment.

"My hangups?" I repeated, voice shaking with outrage. "*Hangups?*"

He nodded. "Yeah. Your hangups. Something wrong with your hearing?"

"Screw you!" I snarled at him, so furious I could barely breathe. "You have no right to talk about me like that! You have no idea — no *freaking* idea — what I've been through or where I'm coming from, and you certainly have no right to judge me for it!"

"No right? *No right?*" He took two steps toward me, his face a dark storm of rage. "You forget — *I know you, Gwen.* I'm not some guy you met at a bar who took you home for a quick fuck. I know all about your mind — how it works, how it tells you no one is safe, no one can be trusted. How it tells you to keep the world far, far outside those walls you've built up."

I flinched, but he kept going.

"You live in a house you're afraid to decorate, you date men you're unwilling to give your heart, and you push away anyone who tries to change that. But you know what, babe? The only person you punish in the end for all that effort? That'd be *you*."

My heart squeezed, the pain of it crippling. I fought tears, wishing he'd stop. Wishing I was weak enough to *beg* him to stop. But I wasn't raised in a trailer park with an abusive mother for nothing. If I knew one thing, it was how to stand there and take a verbal lashing.

Graham leaned in, hands planting on his hips as he leveled me with a lethal look that cut me to the bone. "You want to go home to that big empty house to cloister yourself away in your perfectly designed bedroom sanctuary, where you can shut out all the chaos? You want to seal yourself off from the world and act like there's nothing out there that can hurt you? Too bad, baby. You're in the real world now. This, here with me today — *this* was the real world." He pointed from his chest to mine, from his heart to mine. "You felt it, I know you did. And I'm not letting you slip back behind your defenses just because you're running scared."

I stared at him for a long time. We were both breathing hard, like we'd run a marathon. I wanted to close the gap between us, I truly did. I wanted to hurl myself across the distance into his arms, to feel the heat of his body all around me, moving inside me, turning me inside out one touch at a time. But his words shifted around inside my head, a haunting refrain I couldn't shut out, no matter how I tried.

You live in a house you're afraid to decorate, you date men you're unwilling to give your heart, and you push away anyone who tries to change that.

It hurt like hell, knowing that's what he saw when he looked at me. Damage. Hangups. Issues. Trauma. Even if it was the truth, I hated the reminder. It cut me, cut me deeply.

Actually...

It pretty much crushed me.

My expression iced over. My eyes went dead, all the joy and light and happiness I'd been brimming with for the past few hours draining out in a great slide, leaving nothing but the hollow ache of agony behind.

Stiff as a board, I turned my back on Graham and began the humiliating task of retrieving my clothes from the various corners of the loft where they were strewn. As I was jerking up my yoga pants, I felt his heat close behind me. His hands settled at my hips as I zipped my sports bra closed, but I jerked out of his grip with so much rage, I stumbled off balance and had to catch myself against the kitchen island.

"You say you know me, huh?" I whirled around to face him. A tear snaked down my cheek and I brushed it away, furious at myself for revealing how shattered I was by his words. "Then you should know — anyone who talks to me like that is dead to me. *Dead. To. Me.* You want references? Call my exes. Call my mother. Ask them the last time I spoke to them. Ask them if I went back for a second helping after they'd hurt me like you just did."

"Gwen—"

"No, Graham. This? Today? It wasn't the real world, it was an *escape* from the world. I saw something awful and I fell apart in the aftermath, torn up with guilt for my part in it, heartsick for failing to prevent that horror from coming to pass. You were there to hold me together. That's it. I needed someone, and you were there."

He looked beyond pissed, his jaw clenched tight. "Gwendolyn—"

"But," I sallied forth. "As you were so happy to remind me, I can't *cloister myself away* and *pretend the real world doesn't exist*—"

He had the good grace to flinch, at that.

"—so, I'll be going home, now. I have doors that lock and the phone number of an extremely attractive local detective on speed dial. You yourself told me I have a net of surveillance watching my every move. I'll be just fine. I don't need to stay in your bed to be safe. In fact, knowing how you chew up and spit out the women you sleep with, I'm pretty sure that's the last place on earth I'd *ever* be safe."

He stared at me, eyes moving over my face, hands curled into fists at his sides, looking for all the world like he wanted to reach out and yank me into his arms. Despite all my claims to the contrary, there was a part of me that wished he would — wished for it so badly, it was difficult to hold on to my anger.

Thankfully, for both our sakes, he didn't.

"I'll take you home," he said finally, his voice stripped bare.

He turned away, searching for his own clothes, and the hollow ache inside my chest grew into a chasm that threatened to swallow me whole.

"A<small>RE</small> you sure you don't want me to stay over?" Flo asked, scrunching her nose at me. "I know you aren't a slumber party sort of gal, but I'm happy to crash on the floor. No spooning required."

"I'm sure," I told her for the tenth time.

"But you shouldn't be alone after a day like—"

"Flo." I settled my hands on her shoulders, squeezing through the fabric of her jacket, and spun her around on the shallow stoop at the front of my house. "*Go.*"

"Okay, okay," she grumbled, jogging down my steps to the front gate where Desmond was waiting for her. Even in the dark, I could see how he held the gate open for her to slip though, how his hand reached out to engulf hers. He sent me a quick wave as he dragged his pouting girlfriend to their hatchback.

Once they were gone, I locked up and leaned back against the front door. It felt blessedly solid under my spine, a marked change from everything else in my life. The very ground beneath my feet felt shaky, as though at any moment I'd take one wrong step and the earth would crumble, sending me into a plummeting free fall.

It had been a long day.

I snorted, pressing my eyes closed.

Understatement of the century.

After our blowout, Graham had driven me home in utter silence. He didn't speak to me, didn't touch me, didn't even look at me. I knew this new wedge between us was partly my fault — okay, *mostly* my fault — but I wasn't willing to bridge the gap. Neither was Graham, seeing as he remained silent even as he pulled to a stop outside my house, climbed out, went inside (using *his* key, I might add, probably just to piss me off), checked the house for threats, and left without so much as a *thanks for the orgasms*, locking up soundly behind him as he went. Then, with the roar of the Bronco's engine, he was gone.

I waited an appropriate amount of time to burst into tears. (Read: approximately zero-point-two seconds after his engine faded from earshot.) Then, because I was Gwendolyn *Freaking* Goode, not a lame crybaby loser brought to her knees by a guy, even when that guy was Graham, I forced myself to get it together. I took a shower (trying really, really hard not to remember the last shower I'd taken), dried my hair into shiny, bouncing waves, dabbed on enough makeup to feel human, then donned my outfit armor. (*Outfit Armor: Home Edition* though, which meant sheepskin L.L. Bean moccasins instead of heels, a silk lounge set in a pale ivory shade instead of a dress, and an extra cozy, extra long, open-faced cardigan with a deep hood I could pull up over my head when I felt like going full couch-potato mode instead of a stylish cropped moto jacket.)

I looked in the mirror and nodded at my reflection in approval. I looked like me. Cool, calm, in control. Unfortunately, I didn't *feel* like me. The poised woman reflected in the mirror was just that — a reflection. A mirage. Beneath the surface, my emotions were a scattered mess. My heart physically hurt, panging painfully with every beat.

It was late, well past dinnertime, but I'd called Flo anyway and illuminated the *emergency girl's night* beacon. Fifteen minutes later, she was waving Desmond off from the front stoop as I held the door open for her. She took one look at my face, reached into her bag, and yanked out a bottle of tequila. Patrón. The good stuff. I took one look at the tequila in my best friend's hands and promptly burst into tears yet again, shattering all my efforts at looking cool and composed and unaffected in an instant.

It must be said, Florence Lambert had a lot of great traits. She was an excellent parallel parker. She never quibbled over splitting the check exactly in half to avoid doing math, even if one of our entrees cost slightly more. She was a great teacher, the kind who genuinely cared about her students and painstakingly nurtured their progress. She laughed at my dumb jokes even when they weren't funny. And she was always up for pretty much anything, be it last minute tickets to a Fleetwood Mac reunion concert or a spa weekend in the Berkshires or a stakeout at the home of a psychic employee on the run from a local Irish crime family.

But her best trait of all was that she never judged. She never had, not from the first moment we met, back before I learned how to dress in a way that flattered my body type and didn't yet know the difference between CheezWhiz and charcuterie. Sure, she made her opinions known, she spoke her mind, she never pandered to me... but she was unfailingly in my corner, no matter what, even when our mindsets clashed.

Which is why I walked her straight into the kitchen, located two shot glasses, and poured us each a healthy dose of Patrón without preamble. By the time I slid a brimming shot in front of her, Flo was already settled on her stool, sprinkling salt from my sleek glass shaker on the side of her fist. Once I'd done the same, we salt-licked, lifted our glasses high, clinked them together, and said, as was our custom, in perfect unison, "Down the hatch!"

The tequila was still burning a fiery path down my esophagus when I blurted out, "Graham and I slept together."

Flo stared at me for a beat, her throat still working to swallow the shot. Nodding, she reached for the bottle, doled out another round, and threw it back without waiting long enough for me to even lift mine from the counter.

"*Hoo-bah!*" She blinked hard, then focused fully on me. "Okay. I'm ready. Hit me with it."

I threw back my own shot, relishing the burn. Then I did as she commanded. I unloaded everything on her. The whole, devastating drama, start to finish, from finding my neighbor very, very dead in a graveyard to getting very, very naked with Graham in his loft afterwards, resulting in four of the best orgasms of my life. I didn't skimp over the details. (Though, admittedly, some of the details required us to pause for another round of tequila shots, such was their nature.)

By the time I was done, we were both crying, the bottle was well on its way to empty, and my broken heart, though still broken, felt marginally less burdened. I wasn't sure if this was a result of venting or consuming six mind-numbing shots of tequila. Whatever the reason, I wasn't about to quibble.

Flo, being Flo, did not judge harshly or foist upon me any unsolicited advice. She did, however, gather me into her arms and hug me until the sobs that were closing off my airway stopped posing a threat to my longevity. We sat for a long time, both a little bit drunk, swaying lightly on our stools with our hands clasped tight.

"I just can't believe it's over before it really even had a chance to start," I whispered eventually, trying very hard not to start crying again now that the tears were finally under control.

"Gwennie," she said eventually, hiccuping lightly. "It's not over until opera."

"Opera?"

"You know. Fat lady, singing." She shrugged. Her chocolate brown eyes were a hazy mix of intoxication and unconditional love as they peered into mine. "I might not know how all this is going to shake out, but I know you and I know Graham. You are the two stubbornest individuals to ever walk the earth — especially when you care about something. And you both care about this too much to let it fall apart over one disagreement. This isn't the end for the two of you. Not if you don't *let* it be."

I clung to the fragile thread of hope in those words now that she was gone and I was once again alone in my big, drafty, empty house. She'd wanted to stay, but it was nearly midnight she had to haul her hungover ass into a classroom bright and early the next day. I, thankfully, could sleep in, since The Gallows was closed on Mondays. I planned to shut off my phone, lock my doors, and stay in bed all day, not moving a muscle except to tap my index finger against the Kindle screen.

Proving Graham right, an annoying voice whispered from the back of my mind.

I ignored the voice, gritting my teeth as I walked into the kitchen to turn off the lights and shove the cork back in the nearly empty tequila bottle. I was weaving a bit, the effects of the alcohol still pounding through my bloodstream as I made my way upstairs to my bedroom. Halfway up the staircase, a familiar sound from the front door made me freeze with one foot poised mid-step.

The deadbolt.

It slid open with a low clunk as someone turned a key in the lock. Swallowing hard, I spun around — a bit too quickly, given my tequila-drenched senses. My hand clutched the bannister so I wouldn't fall down the stairs as I watched the door swing open into the dark entryway. A shadowy figure walked through it, moving in total silence. Seeing as there was only one person, myself not included, who had that key in his possession, it wasn't difficult to guess the identity of my unexpected nocturnal visitor.

As to why he was here?

I had no earthly idea.

CHAPTER TWENTY-ONE

A man shouldn't care about your 'body count' unless you're secretly a serial killer.
— Gwen Goode, refusing to kiss and tell

My heart stumbled in my chest as I listened to Graham quietly locking the door, as I heard his muted footsteps carrying him deeper into the foyer. I told myself to move. To run upstairs and hide in my bedroom like a coward. But I was still standing there, frozen, when his hand located the switch and light flooded the room. I blinked against the sudden brightness.

When my eyes adjusted, they instantly locked on Graham's. He was standing at the bottom of the stairs, wearing his typical getup of boots, dark wash jeans, and a leather jacket, and looking up at me with an expression I couldn't for the life of me decode. The strap of a leather duffle dangled from one of his broad shoulders. In his left hand, he held a set of keys; in his right, what appeared to be a bundled sleeping bag, the kind you'd take on a camping trip.

"What are you doing here?"

He didn't answer my whispered question. He set down the duffle and sleeping bag, shoved the keys into the pocket of his jacket, and began to climb. I watched him coming at me, my hand tightening on the railing to hold my ground, eyes never shifting away from his.

"Graham, I asked what you—"

"Sleeping here," he informed me, coming to a stop on the step below mine. With our natural height difference, this put us almost perfectly at eye level.

"What?" I breathed.

"You can't sleep at my place. So, I'll sleep here."

"Here?"

"There are about a dozen empty rooms to choose from. I'll be far enough away to give you your space, let you get some rest in peace. Close enough to cover you if anyone makes a move."

"We..." I said weakly, holding tighter to the railing. "We're in a fight."

"Don't give a shit," he clipped back.

"You don't give a shit?"

"Nope. Not one shit." His eyes narrowed dangerously. "You want to be pissed at me, be pissed. Hell, I'm pretty fucking pissed at you, too. But I'm here. Told you before, I'm not letting you run from this. That goes both ways. Means I don't run either, even when you're a bitch."

"Did you just call me a bitch?"

"Yeah, because you're being one."

"And you're a dick!"

"I can be, yeah. Especially when you piss me off, which you're liable to do seeing as you've got a temper and can be stubborn as hell when you set your mind to it."

"I do not have a temper!" I yelled, directly contradicting my own words as anger coursed through me in a hot current.

"Babe, you're a redhead," he said, as if this explained everything. "You've got a temper. So do I. We're naturally going to butt heads. Luckily, I'm guessing the makeup sex will be off the charts, seeing as regular sex is already fucking dynamite, so I don't foresee that being too much of an issue longterm."

I blinked, momentarily dazed by the intriguing concept of makeup sex with Graham. Then, scowling, I forced myself to focus on being pissed at him. "Longterm? We can't even make it *one day* without fighting!"

"Then stop fighting with me."

My head nearly exploded off my shoulders. "You're unbelievable!"

"Maybe. Or, maybe you're so used to people fucking you over, you can't see what we've got is worth fighting for. Maybe you're so braced for getting hurt, you're determined to keep me at arm's length like the parade of guys who came before me."

"*Parade?* There weren't that many guys!"

"Even one was enough," he gritted out, jaw locked tight, as though the memory of me with other men caused him physical pain. "Point is, I'm not them. Don't treat me like one of them. Definitely don't expect me to respond to your bullshit like one of them. You push me away, I'm telling you right now, I'm not going."

Goddess, he was so damned bossy.

I ground my teeth together, probably removing a year's worth of enamel in the process. My voice came out shaky with anger — and possibly just a bit of anxiety. "You act like I don't have my reasons for holding you at arm's length."

"Name one."

"Okay, fine. When I first got back to town, if you remember, you didn't exactly throw out the welcoming committee. I walked into The Witches Brew and heard you talking about me, about my store, about my Aunt Colette. You said you'd rather *stick your dick in a doorway* than ever get involved with a girl like me!"

The silence was stormy. As was his voice. "Are you fucking kidding me?"

"No, Graham, I am not fucking kidding you!"

"You're still holding on to that shit? After everything?"

"That *shit*, as you call it, happens to matter to me. And I don't hear you apologizing!"

He scoffed. Actually scoffed, like I was being ridiculous. "You don't want an apology, Gwen."

"Spoken like a man who refuses to give one!"

"Two years ago, I made one offhand comment — one you were never supposed to hear, one that didn't even mean anything, seeing as I was standing in a bar shooting the shit with my friends, not giving a sworn statement on my thoughts and feelings in a court of law. You've been nursing a grudge ever since."

My mouth opened to retort, but he kept right on talking.

"You aren't mad about what I said. You're using that grudge as an excuse to keep me from getting in there." His hand came up to press flat against my heart, one finger sliding along the bare skin of my clavicle bone above my tank top. "But, babe... like it or not, I'm getting in there. I can see it happening, bit by bit. And guess what? I fucking like it in there. I like it a lot. So, you'd better get used to it, because I'm not backing off and I'm not running out. You and me, we're going to ride this wave together and see where it goes."

Panic was rising inside me, despite my attempts to quash it. I locked my knees to keep from running scared. To cover my blinding terror, I said in an uppity voice, "I suppose I don't get any say in this."

"No, you don't," Graham agreed instantly. "Not when *your*

say involves you ignoring my existence or running for cover or pretending there's nothing happening between us, when we both know I could have you flat on your back, screaming my name, begging me to let you come about five seconds after I put my hands on you."

I narrowed my eyes at him. "Have I ever told you you're arrogant?"

"You've mentioned it."

I scowled at him, but it was halfhearted at best. I was too drunk and too tired to execute a glare with any sort of real wrath behind it. And his words, while completely overbearing, were unfortunately also accurate.

"Fight over," he declared. His green eyes glittered as anger dissolved into something else — something that made my breath halt. "Makeup time."

Caught up in thoughts of making up with Graham in a variety of creative ways, I swayed a bit on my feet. "Um..."

He scanned me up and down. "You drunk?"

"No," I lied.

"Yeah, you're drunk." He leaned in, so we were only a few inches apart. "Watched Flo stumbled out of here a few minutes ago. Des could barely get her ass in the car, she was weaving so much, belting show tunes at the top of her lungs."

"You—" I bit my lip. "You watched...?"

"Been parked on the street for the past three hours, Gwen."

My teeth sank harder into my lip. Suddenly, I found myself on the brink of tears. "Oh."

He stared at me. He wasn't touching me, but his eyes were like a physical weight on my skin.

"Why?" I asked, the word cracking in my throat.

"Gwen..." He shook his head, voice softening a shade. "You know why."

I did know why. He was keeping me safe. Keeping an eye on me, even after the way we'd left things.

You don't run.

I don't run, either.

The urge to cry grew stronger, pricking at the back of my eyes.

"How drunk are you?" he asked, watching me closely.

"On a scale of one to wasted?"

"Not sure that scale is scientifically correct, but yeah. On a scale of one to wasted, where are you falling right now?"

"Why?" I asked.

"Because I want to fuck you, baby, but I'm not going to do it if you're totally blitzed."

Hellfire.

My eyes widened, my breath caught, and a volt of pure, undiluted lust shot straight between my legs. "I'm thinking..." I whispered, heart thudding against my ribs. "I'm not that drunk. Suddenly... feeling remarkably sober."

"Thank fuck," Graham grunted.

Then, so fast I didn't even see him move, I was jerked off my feet into his arms. His mouth crashed down onto mine, kissing me hard, his lips a bruising assault that I welcomed with every fiber of my being. His hands found my ass, lifting me firmly against him, and I threw all my limbs around his frame, legs wrapping around his waist, arms winding around his neck. He never stopped kissing me as he carried me up the stairs, down the hall, and into my dark bedroom.

I SLEPT LIKE THE DEAD. (I suppose half a bottle of tequila and oodles of mind-boggling sex will do that to a girl.) When I woke, I stared in disbelief at the clock on my bedside table, which proclaimed 10:34AM, certain I was reading it wrong. I hadn't slept past ten since...

Come to think of it, I'd *never* slept past ten.

Looking around my empty room, I saw Graham's jeans were gone from the floor where he'd left them last night. He'd taken them with him when he went to sleep in the room down the hall, leaving me in a state of post-orgasmic bliss so complete, I could barely lift my head to kiss him goodbye. His t-shirt, however, was still crumpled in a ball beside my dresser. I slipped it over my head before I wandered into the bathroom, enjoying the faint smell of him that lingered on the fabric as I used the facilities, brushed my teeth, and dragged on a pair of fresh panties.

Barefoot, I made my way downstairs in search of coffee and Graham — not necessarily in that order. I found him almost immediately, following a strange grating sound through the empty echo-chamber that was my house all the way to the unfurnished dining room that adjoined the kitchen. I froze on the threshold, eyes widening at the sight that greeted me. Graham, barefoot and shirtless, the top button of his jeans left undone, his hair messier than usual, his big hands working a flat chisel as he peeled away a large chunk of Aunt Colette's horrendous, orange floral wallpaper.

I'd begun to strip down the walls in here ages ago but, when the project proved far more labor intensive than I'd anticipated, I'd given up almost before I'd begun, removing only a narrow section beside the fireplace. For months, I'd been walking past this room, grimacing at my unfinished work — as well as the genuinely putrid floral pattern — and feeling guilty for abandoning it. Hell, just last night as I sat drinking tequila with Flo, I'd told myself I would get back to it as soon as the high season ended and life calmed down a bit.

But now, like magic, ninety-nine percent of the walls were bare down to the plaster. Graham was hard at work on that final one percent, peeling slowly but steadily so it came down in one clean piece. How he managed that, I have no idea — when I'd tried, it all came apart in tattered fistfuls. Then again, Graham seemed incapable of doing anything incompetently.

He dropped the final section of the orange monstrosity to the floor and turned in a slow circle to inspect his handiwork. When his gaze moved past the threshold, they jerked to a stop as they caught on me.

"Babe."

I came unglued from the doorjamb where I'd been leaning. "You took down my wallpaper."

He stayed still as he watched me walk toward him, his eyes lit with an uncharacteristic wariness. "Yeah. You mind?"

"*Mind?*" I snorted and shook my head. "Why would I mind? Do you have any idea how many months I've been staring at that ugly wallpaper, wishing it would magically strip itself? I always loved how Aunt Colette was a groovy hippie chick, but her decor style was stuck in the '70s in a very big way."

I watched him relax, lips twitching. "Wasn't sure if I was messing up whatever grand home-reno plans you've got up your sleeve."

"Nope, just never got around to finishing. Now, I guess I don't have to." I stopped in front of him, sliding my hands along his bare waist and tilting my head back to look up at him. "Thank you."

He didn't touch me, seeing as his hands were caked in wallpaper paste, but his lips descended to claim mine in a light, brief kiss that I wished lasted about ten times as long.

"You're welcome," he murmured, pulling back to examine me. "You sleep okay?"

"It's almost *eleven*. If I slept any better, I think it would be considered a coma."

He chuckled.

"How about you? I feel guilty, it must've been uncomfortable on the floor in your sleeping bag..." My nose scrunched as my conscience nagged at me. "And the house gets so cold at night—"

"I've slept worse places. Trust me."

"But—"

"Baby, pick your battles."

With a soft sigh, I let it go. "I need coffee."

"There should still be some left." Graham jerked his chin toward the kitchen and started herding me in that direction. "Made it when I woke up. 'Course, that was about five hours ago, so you might want to brew a fresh pot."

He was teasing me, his tone light and warm in a way I'd never heard before. I scowled playfully at him as I stomped to the cupboards, yanked down a mug, and fixed myself a steaming cup with a dollop of milk.

Graham went the sink to wash off the gooey residue. As soon as he'd dried his hands, he came straight to me. Grabbing the coffee mug right out of my hand, he set it aside and lifted me up onto the kitchen island. I gasped in surprise as he moved between my thighs and pulled me up against him, full frontal. His lips hit mine, giving me the sort of all-consuming kiss I was coming to expect from Graham, the kind that held nothing back and demanded I do the same in return.

"There," he said, voice rough but satisfied when he finally broke away. "That's a real good morning kiss."

He could say that again. I was plastered to his front, panting hard, unable to form words. His lips moved to my neck, nuzzling as his hands moved under my shirt to caress the small of my back.

"You look good in my clothes, babe."

"Mmm?"

"Better out of them," he added, dragging his lips along my

jawline. Things were just starting to heat up when I heard the dreaded buzz of his cellphone in his back pocket. He backed away with a reluctant sigh, leaning against the counter across from me as he fished out his phone and scowled down at the screen.

"Better be good," he thundered lowly as soon as he had it at his ear. His eyes roved over my bare legs as he listened to whatever the person on the other line was saying. I used the momentary time-out to sip my coffee and let my eyes do some roving of their own, trying to wrap my head around the fact that Graham Graves was barefoot and shirtless in my kitchen on a Monday morning. No matter how hard I tried, it was difficult to convince myself I hadn't stepped into an alternate universe overnight.

"No," Graham said into the phone, pinching the bridge of his nose. "No, I want you to wait for me. I'll be there in a half hour." He paused. "Because I'm your boss. You don't get free rein to run shit without my go-ahead just because we share a gene pool."

My brows arched up toward my forehead. Was he talking to one the twins?

"Holden, I can't make this any clearer," he said, confirming my suspicions. "I don't give a fuck that you and Hunter are chomping at the bit. You can wait until I get there. Warning you now, you don't wait, there'll be repercussions. How do you feel about desk duty in the surveillance room every night for the next month?" He paused again. "Yeah. Thought so. See you in thirty."

Disconnecting the call, he immediately moved back to me. His hands came up to cup my face and his lips brushed over mine, featherlight.

"Sorry, gorgeous. Gotta go. Can I use your shower?"

"Of course. Use the master, off my bedroom." The downstairs bathroom wasn't renovated, its hardware old and in need of replacing, its tile walls cracked and dated. I paused, not wanting to pry but deeply curious. "Everything okay at work?"

He nodded, but I couldn't help wondering if he was telling the truth. His expression was serious, his eyes were alert. "Nothing we can't handle, nothing we weren't expecting. We have..." He hesitated a beat. "Someone in custody in the holding room at Gravewatch. I need to get over there before my twin brothers go off half-cocked and do something that'll piss me off."

"Do they usually go off half-cocked?"

"Let's just say, Hunter and Holden aren't known for their delicate touch. They're both twice as smart as me but about half as patient."

This, I found hard to believe.

Graham must've seen the doubtful look on my face, because his lips twitched. "You think I'm hot-headed and high-handed? Be grateful you haven't met the twins yet."

Yet.

Those three little letters sent a nervous, happy flutter through my stomach.

"They're very good at what they do," he went on. "They've been working for me a while, and they both have a shitload of experience in the field from before they came on board at Gravewatch. I know I should back off. Still, no matter how good they are... I spent years watching them do stupid teenage shit. Past fuck ups carry weight against present potential, whether they like it or not." He paused and an undeniable thread of pride wound into his words. "The stubborn bastards seem to thrive on the challenge of proving me wrong, though."

I'd never heard Graham talk about his siblings before, not in any sort of depth. Seeing him in big brother mode unleashed another happy, fuzzy flutter in my gut.

"*Overprotective* is in the firstborn job description," I said softly. "You're looking out for them."

"As much as they'll let me, yeah." He blew out a breath. "They're grown men, not teenage hellions anymore. I trust them

— they wouldn't be on my payroll if I didn't — but that doesn't mean I don't call them on their bullshit and keep an eye on them whenever I can. They've got some darkness they need to work through. Not pushing them to do it before they're ready, but not letting them bury it deep, either."

That was pure Graham. Pushy, but only when he knew you could handle it. *I'm a patient man*, he'd told me once. I knew now, from firsthand experience, that he wasn't lying. Just as I knew his twin brothers were in good hands whenever their big brother decided they were ready for a push out of the darkness, into the light.

I smiled at him as that warm, fuzzy feeling inside me expanded exponentially. His eyes watched my lips as they curled up at the corners, like he was memorizing the sight. And the expression on his face...

I gulped.

Boy, was I ever in trouble.

"Much as it pains me," he murmured. "I really do have to go."

"I know you do."

He didn't move. Only his eyes shifted up to mine, and they were suddenly very serious. "Stay here. Doors locked at all times. Don't open them for anyone. Don't go on a run."

"I wasn't planning on it, bossy," I informed him, rolling my eyes. "In fact, I burned so many calories with you in the past twenty-four hours, I may never run again."

His lips twitched. "I'll be back tonight. You need something urgently in the meantime, you've got my number. If I don't answer, call the office. Brianne will track me down."

Oh, I bet she will.

"I'll bring dinner if I finish up early enough. You want takeout from Ledger?"

"Yes," I said instantly, all sour, secretarial-related feelings vanishing. I freaking *loved* Ledger. We'd all gone there last winter for Desmond's birthday dinner, and again in the spring for Florence's. "I want—"

"The mushroom campanelle," he finished for me. "I remember."

He *would* remember.

He remembered everything.

My throat felt tight, too tight to speak, so I just leaned forward and pressed my lips to his instead, letting my kiss say everything I couldn't find the words for. Graham kissed me back, his hands in my hair and his tongue in my mouth, until I was more than a little hot and bothered, digging my thighs into his hips, squirming against his chest, reaching for the zipper of his jeans.

He stepped deftly out of reach, earning my darkest glower in return.

"Sorry, babe." He grinned, the smug jerk. "Not starting something I can't finish."

With playful tap to the tip of my nose, he was gone, rushing upstairs to get in the shower, then heading out into the world of alpha male badassery to handle goddess only knew what. I sipped my coffee, which had long since gone cold, and tried to regulate my breathing — a process that took the full duration of his shower, seeing as every time I thought about him up there, naked and dripping wet, my airway closed up again.

Hellfire.

I was in trouble, all right.

Deep.

I WAS ANTSY ALL DAY, brimming with nervous energy I couldn't seem to dispel no matter how I tried. The clock ticked with painful slowness, minutes dragging by like hours, hours slogging by like days. I told myself I wasn't waiting for Graham to come back, but my lies weren't very convincing.

I'd spent several hours cleaning up the mess in the living room, shoving sections of discarded wallpaper into trash bags and hauling them into the bins in the garage, then sweeping the hardwood floors clean of dust and grime. When I was finished, I looked around at the bare walls, a blank canvas ready for me to bring to life, and was hit with an almost uncontrollable urge to drive to the nearest hardware store to purchase paint samples. (A deep blue shade would look stunning against the warm wood of the fireplace mantle... but something in the green family might work too...) Since I'd promised Graham I wouldn't leave the house, I suppressed this urge.

Flo called to check in on me during her lunch hour. She wasn't able to talk long, seeing as she was in a staff break room surrounded by fellow elementary school teachers, but I gave her the general gist of what had happened after she left the night before. She shrieked her joy into the phone so loud, it was a miracle my eardrum didn't rupture.

"This calls for celebratory drinks at The Witches Brew," she told me. "The four of us, tomorrow night. Our first official double date!"

"Flo—" I'd started to protest.

"See you both at eight!"

She disconnected before I could get another word in. Typical Flo. I wondered if Graham would ease my house arrest long enough for a few rounds with friends. Somehow, I doubted it. He was taking this *keep-Gwen-safe* business seriously.

I'd seen the unmarked SUV looping down my block a handful of times throughout the day. The windows were too tinted to tell whether it was a cop making the rounds or one of the Grave-watch men. Frankly, I didn't much care who it was, I was just happy to see them cruising past. Yesterday, with all that happened, I hadn't had much time to properly process Eliza's murder — or what it might mean for me. I thought about the message her killers had written in her blood on the side of the tomb.

TU ES PROXIMUS

You are next.

It was the Heretics. It had to be. It was a perfect match for the first message they'd left in my back alley. It was washed away weeks ago, but I could still see it burned into my mind, like a brand I'd never be able to remove.

RESURGEMUS

We shall rise again.

Their verb tense was worrisome. Not "we have risen" but "we shall rise." Not past but *future.* There was still more to come. Another sacrifice, another ritual. And if the Bay Colony Coven ladies were right, if I was their intended final target...

A memory of Eliza's body — stabbed through the heart, left on display in a graveyard like a macabre spectacle — drifted through my head and a shiver of fear moved down my spine, settling in the pit of my stomach like a ball of lead. I had no appetite, which was probably a good thing since Graham texted me around dinnertime, informing me that his situation at work was taking longer than excepted. Takeout night would have to be a raincheck.

Won't be back until late, he'd messaged. *Eat dinner without me. When I get there, I'll eat you for dessert.*

That dark promise had me determined to stay awake until he arrived, no matter how tired I was or how late the hour crept. But I was fighting an uphill battle — and losing. My mind was exhausted from running in circles all day. So, at eleven, fighting a yawn, I double checked the locks one last time, stripped off all my clothes, and climbed into bed with my Kindle to read until Graham got back.

I'd only made it a handful of pages into my book — poor Lady Scarlett was pregnant with Captain Tristan's baby, but the mutineering crew was about to make her walk the plank in shark infested waters — before exhaustion took hold of me and I fell fast asleep.

MY ALARM BEGAN TO CHIRP, bringing me out of a fitful doze. I'd been dreaming of Pirate Kings and bloody pentagrams, slaughtered animals and ornate knives. I looked around my bedroom in confusion, blinking away the remnants of slumber. No signs of Graham anywhere. I'd fallen asleep reading and, if he'd come in when he got back, he hadn't bothered to wake me.

A current of displeasure frazzled through my nerve endings. Truth was, I missed him. It had been barely a day, and I missed him.

Gaia above.

How quickly I'd become addicted to the man. Rolling my eyes at myself, feeling like the ultimate lovesick idiot, I commenced with my typical morning bathroom routine, taking extra care to slather on moisturizer. The New England weather was getting colder with each passing day, and the blustery October winds were prone to chafing my cheeks. I pulled on my best attempt at outfit armor, given that I was rushing twice my normal speed — wool tights, suede boots, flowy skirt, corset-style blouse, handmade wooden jewelry I'd found in a funky boutique up in Newburyport last summer — and styled my hair in record time. By the time I hit the hallway, I was ready to tackle the day.

It was nearly eight. I needed to get to the store. There were a bucketload of things to tackle before we opened, especially with our unexpected Sunday closure. But when I peered into the room down the hall where Graham had taken to crashing — the sun-

378

drenched one I'd always envisioned as my home library — I saw he was still fast asleep. His big body barely fit within the confines of his sleeping bag. Even with the spare pillows I'd given him from my bed, he looked deeply uncomfortable, a furrow marring his unconscious brow.

I swallowed a pang of guilt as I crept by, for the first time in my adult life seriously regretting my sleeping hangups as I made my way downstairs and started brewing a pot of coffee. Whether I wanted to admit it or not, Graham had been right the other day — my issues were really only punishing *me* in the long run. It was my fault we weren't able to spend the night cuddled together in my bed, like a normal couple just starting out.

Not that we were a couple.

I wasn't sure what we were. Graham had implied there was an "us" but we hadn't really defined anything. Was he my boyfriend? Friend with (mind-blowing) benefits? I had no idea, and I definitely wasn't going to be the one to bring it up. Not unless forced by trained interrogators in a dark room, my fingernails pulled out with systematic violence by the roots. (Maybe not even then.)

I was halfway through my second cup of coffee when a warm arm slid around my midsection and I was pulled back against a solid chest.

"You didn't wake me," Graham rumbled into my ear, his voice still rough with sleep.

"I could accuse you of the same thing." I turned on my stool to narrow my eyes at him. "I was looking forward to *dessert*, Graham."

His lips twitched as they brushed against mine. "Didn't get back until past midnight. I poked my head into your room, but you were out like a light. Couldn't bring myself to wake you." He paused briefly, brows creasing. "Also... wasn't sure you'd want me to. I know you don't particularly enjoy the idea of anyone coming into your space when you're asleep."

That was so considerate, all my annoyance instantly evaporated.

"Why are you dressed?" he asked, eyes flickering down my form, taking in my outfit.

"Um... because I have work?"

"You're not going to work."

Just like that, my annoyance was back. "Excuse me? It sounded like you said I wasn't going to work."

"Seems you heard me just fine."

"Graham," I said, striving for a patient tone. "I have to go to work. I have to open the store."

"You don't, actually. You're the owner. You make the hours. What are you going to do, fire yourself?"

"If I don't open, I lose business. I can't afford to lose business. Not during high season. These next few weeks are the busiest of the entire year. The profits we make in October keep the lights on for all the other months."

"And what good is having a business if you're not alive to run it?"

I rocked back, startled by the severity of his statement.

Graham planted his hands on the counter, bracketing me within his arms. "Babe, what part of Eliza Proctor dying a gruesome death at the hands of these freaks didn't sink into that fucking head of yours?"

"Trust me, it sank in. It sank in so deep, it's giving me nightmares. I know what's at stake." I stared into his eyes and, reminding myself his bossiness was born of a need to protect me, I brought my hands up to lay against his chest. "But I also know you're going to keep me safe and breathing, no matter who comes at me."

Something flickered in his eyes, a flash of an emotion that

was there and gone so fast I couldn't decipher it. "You trust me to keep you safe?"

"Of course I do," I said instantly. "You're Graham Freaking Graves."

A heartbeat later, I found myself crushed up against his chest, his arms around me, his heart thundering beneath my ear as it pressed against his bare skin. I could barely breathe, he was holding me so tight.

"I take you straight there, I bring you straight home," he muttered, mouth at my temple. "No detours. If I can't be there, one of my boys will bring you."

I nodded and wheezed, "Okay."

"There are cameras on all the exits so we can monitor who comes and goes. That said, the nature of your work, you're dealing with strangers all day."

"Customers," I corrected.

"Strangers," he countered firmly. "You need to be mindful. I know you like people to feel at home, settle in, and nurse free coffee refills for six goddamn hours, but you need to take note of anyone who lingers too long or starts acting strange."

"It's Salem. Everyone acts pretty strange."

A low rattle of displeasure vibrated through his chest and his arms tightened even more, compressing my ribcage. "Got a bad feeling about this shit, Gwen. Don't like sending you out into danger when I've got a bad feeling and precisely zero leads."

"Can't... breathe..." I wheezed, only half joking.

His arms loosened marginally. "My boys are scanning through CCTV footage around the cemetery, trying to catch a glimpse of whoever left Proctor's body there. I'll meet with High-tower later today, get the official rundown of the crime scene. With any luck, they'll find a set of prints on that knife. Give us a direction to run, at the very least. In the meantime, just promise me you won't do anything stupid."

"When do I ever do anything stupid?"

"You really want me to answer that?" He snorted in amusement, sounding far less tense. "Need I remind you that just a few days ago, you and Florence pulled a Thelma and Louise, nearly getting yourselves shot up by Mickey O'Banion and your crazy-ass psychic?"

Not to mention our eyes gouged out by a fortune-telling parrot. But he didn't need to know about that part.

Feigning anger, I smacked him on the arm. "You know, just for that comment, *you* get to be the one to explain to Flo that we can't meet her and Desmond for drinks at The Witches Brew tonight for our first so-called *double date.*"

Graham stilled, his body going solid as a rock against mine. My mouth gaped open as I realized what I'd just said. I immediately tried to walk it back.

"Not that we're, well, *dating* or anything. It was just something Flo said on the phone yesterday."

He stared at me, expression unreadable.

"You know Flo," I prattled on nervously. "Always ten steps ahead of herself when she's excited about something."

He was still staring at me.

"Anyway, I definitely didn't mean for it to sound like— I guess, I didn't mean to imply that—"

"You told Flo about us?" he cut me off, his voice a deep rasp.

"Um." I swallowed hard. "Yeah. Sorry, should I not have—"

"Don't apologize."

"W-what?"

"I'm glad you told her."

"You are?"

He nodded. "Fucking thrilled, baby."

My eyes felt huge in my face, wide as saucers. But I could see by his gentle, unguarded expression that he wasn't lying.

Graham was indeed happy I'd spilled the beans to my best friend about us.

Us.

There was an us.

It was official.

"I wasn't sure you wanted people to know," I whispered, my mind spinning a million directions at once. "I didn't want to—"

"Gwen," he clipped.

"What?"

"Shut up."

I shut up.

Mostly because, at that moment, he kissed me, which gave me no other choice in the matter.

CHAPTER TWENTY-TWO

You were my cup of tea.
(I drink coffee now.)
- Gwen Goode, caffeinating

"Whoa. Your aura is so stormy, they're going to put out a Nor'Easter watch for the entire Eastern Seaboard."

Hetti's statement greeted me the moment I stepped through the front door of The Gallows. It was just past 9AM, which meant I was officially late — thanks to a certain bossy alpha male.

Flipping the CLOSED sign to OPEN, I heaved a sigh and allowed the door to swing shut. Hetti came out from behind the espresso bar, making several more comments about the dark color of my supposed aura as she examined me.

This was not surprising.

Graham and I had another tiff as he drove me to work — mostly because he was being high-handed again. Before he dropped me off, he'd informed me of his plans to track down Sally and Agatha to ask them some questions about my kidnapping and their suspicions regarding the Heretics' next move. I'd told him to leave them the hell alone, seeing as their friend had just been murdered. They deserved some time to grieve in peace. The last thing they needed was a squad of Gravewatch badasses descending upon them like locusts, demanding information at gunpoint. Besides, they'd already told me they'd never trust law enforcement to handle the Heretics. If anyone was going to talk to them, I thought it should be me.

Graham, unsurprisingly, disagreed.

Ignoring the NO ENTRY signs like they didn't apply to him, he'd driven the Bronco right up onto the pedestrian-only mall downtown, pulling to a stop outside the front door of the shop to make sure I got in safely. This was equal parts exasperating and considerate. Since I was already annoyed with him, I chose to see it as mostly the former.

I'd shot him a dark glare and moved to get out of the passenger seat. My hand hadn't even hit the door handle when I found myself tagged around the back of the neck by a large, warm hand and hauled bodily across the cab, onto his lap. My screech of surprise was drowned out by Graham's mouth, which caught mine in a searing kiss that was so thorough, it turned my bones to water. Feeling me go totally limp in his arms, he'd grinned at me, green eyes simmering with heat.

"Wish I'd known two years ago I could kiss the bitchiness out of you."

"Excuse me?"

"Would've spared me a lot of nights with blue balls, babe."

My eyes narrowed. "You're going to be experiencing them again tonight if you keep being an ass."

In lieu of a response, he kissed me again. When he was done,

I was unable to remember my own name let alone my train of thought, effectively reduced to a puddle of lust in his lap.

"Don't make threats you can't carry out, baby," he whispered, sounding just as turned on as I was, but also highly amused. "We both know tonight, I'm in your bed."

"Whatever," I snapped halfheartedly, jerking out of his arms. "I need to get to work."

He let me go, eyes hot on my body as I shifted my skirt back into its proper place, adjusted my corset-style blouse, and hopped out. It took monumental effort not to glance back at the Bronco before I scurried into the shop. It wasn't until I'd stepped inside that I realized he'd completely manipulated me, his kiss dizzying my head so much I'd lost track of our argument about Sally and Agatha.

Goddess, the man was infuriating.

"Not to make your morning worse or anything..." Hetti's voice snapped me into the present. I brought my focus back to her, watching as she tucked a lock of purple hair behind one ear.

"That detective is here again," she continued hesitantly. "He's waiting for you in your office. And, boss, he does *not* look happy. His aura is even darker than yours."

Given the way things had been going lately, I didn't think this boded well for me. "Did he say why he's here?"

Her voice dropped to a reluctant whisper. "No. But..."

"But *what*, Hetti?"

"Well... you know that dead body they found? The one with... uh... the knife through the heart?" Her eyes darted away, unable to meet mine as she continued reluctantly, "I'm pretty sure they think you're the one who stuck it there."

Hellfire.

"We have to stop meeting like this," I joked lamely as Caden Hightower settled in at the interrogation room table. He pushed a styrofoam cup of muddy brown coffee across the metal surface that divided us. I took it to be polite, with no intention of drinking its contents.

Caden didn't even crack a smile, which was the third indication something was very, very wrong. (The first indication being him waiting for me at The Gallows with a search warrant in hand, the second being him immediately insisting I come with him down to the station.)

"Gwendolyn. Thanks again for coming."

"You didn't give me all that much choice, Detective." I swallowed hard, grip tightening on the coffee cup. I hadn't been thrilled about leaving Hetti alone to handle the store but I figured I'd be even *less* thrilled about being slapped in handcuffs, so I didn't put up too much fuss.

"The things I need to discuss with you are part of the official investigation," Caden informed me in a calm, measured tone. "It's better to do it here."

My eyes skittered up to the ceiling camera in the corner of the room. The red light was on, a constant reminder this conversation was being recorded. "Do I need a lawyer?"

His blue eyes were steady on mine. "You aren't under arrest. We aren't bringing any charges against you at this time. But you're entitled to representation if you feel you need it."

"I don't have anything to hide," I told him, hoping it wasn't a lie.

"Then, let's proceed." He reached into a box on the floor beside his chair and pulled out a clear plastic bag marked EVIDENCE in bold black font across the seal. "Do you recognize this?"

I stared at the knife inside the bag. The last time I'd seen it, it was embedded in Eliza's chest. Throat too tight to speak, I nodded my assent.

"This is the murder weapon that killed Elizabeth Proctor," Caden continued, placing the bag flat on the table between us. I couldn't tear my eyes away from it. There was a dark crusting of dried blood on the blade. "Our forensics guys dusted it for prints. They managed to pick up a set off the handle. We ran them through the system. Long shot. But we got a hit."

My eyes jerked up to his. "That's — that's good news, isn't it?"

Caden didn't look like he thought it was good news. His mouth was flat, no signs of a smile anywhere to be seen. "The set of prints we found, Gwendolyn... they're yours."

I jolted back in my seat, metal slamming into my spine. "*Mine?*"

He nodded stiffly.

"But that's... that's impossible!" I felt all the blood draining out of my face. "There must be some mistake..."

Okay, so, technically it wasn't *impossible*. My prints were in the system — courtesy of my adoring mother, who had me arrested when I was seventeen for breaking into our trailer. I was mostly moved out by that point, but I'd (foolishly) returned to New Jersey to retrieve the last of my belongings before I left for my first semester of college. I didn't have much worth taking — most of my stuff was already in Salem — but I'd wanted the silver charm necklace Aunt Colette gave me for my sweet sixteen.

Little did I know, Mommy Dearest had long since pawned it for cash. When I confronted her about it, she called the cops on me. I'd been summarily cuffed, shoved into a cruiser, and processed down at the local precinct before the police chief realized I was a minor and let me go.

I hadn't seen my mother since.

I didn't have a criminal record. I'd never been charged with anything. But apparently my prints were still accessible to anyone with a badge and a search engine. How's that for *justice?*

Detective Hightower's head tipped to one side as he examined me, his handsome face solemn. "While I was waiting for you to arrive this morning, I had a chance to look around your shop." He hesitated briefly. "Were you aware there's a dagger missing from the display case in your back room?"

"*What?*"

"The empty sheath is still there. There was even a little cardstock sign by its holder explaining the history of the weapon, the occult practices it's been used in over the centuries. Hope you don't mind, I took the liberty..."

Caden reached down and pulled out a second, much smaller evidence bag. It contained a tiny handwritten placard covered in Aunt Colette's familiar sloping script. I must've seen it a thousand times over the years, but I'd never really taken the time to study it closely before.

Athamé dagger — unknown pagan origin, circa 1500s. A ceremonial, double-edged blade traditionally used to direct mystical energy during a blood sacrifice.

Beside the description, there was a sketch of the occult knife, sharp lines of ink depicting its curved, engraved handle, along with the distinctive pentagram at the base.

"Gwendolyn... can you explain how a knife from your shop, bearing your fingerprints, came to be embedded in the chest of Elizabeth Proctor?"

"I..." I cleared my throat, trying to remain calm. "I have no idea."

"What was your relationship to the victim?"

"I told you already, she was my neighbor."

"And were things always *neighborly* between you?"

"What do you mean by that?"

"We spoke to some of the other people who live on your

street. They implied things weren't always entirely friendly between you and Mrs. Proctor. They specifically mentioned an incident last week. It seems they witnessed you two engaged in some sort of heated disagreement?"

Hellfire.

Dan and Rich had totally narced on me!

"According to our sources," Caden continued. "Mrs. Proctor was seriously shaken up by the altercation. Needed a cup of tea to calm down afterward."

"It wasn't an altercation," I insisted.

"What was it then?"

"A minor tiff. *Minor*," I stressed.

"Over?"

"I can't even remember, that's how minor it was," I lied. My heart was beginning to race and my palms were feeling sweaty. I fought the urge to pull them into my lap, not wanting to appear fidgety. (Everyone knew only guilty people fidgeted.)

"The coroner estimates Proctor's time of death at around 10PM the night before you found her body." He paused. "What were you doing on Saturday evening?"

"Inventory at the store. I had a big delivery, it took hours to unload it all."

"Until when, exactly?"

"I don't know. Late. I didn't really keep track."

"Alone?"

"Yes." I sucked in a deep breath. "Are you accusing me of something, Detective?"

"Just trying to get a full picture of what went on around the time of Elizabeth Proctor's death."

"You can't seriously believe I had anything to do with it!" I blurted.

He leveled me with a solemn look. "Gwendolyn... I wouldn't be doing my job if I didn't at least consider the possibility of your involvement. Not only were you in possession of the murder weapon, you were found standing over the body. You have no alibi and were seen fighting with the victim mere days before her death."

I had to admit, when he spelled it out like that, even *I* thought I sounded guilty.

Stone-faced, he stared at me for a long time. I stared back, knowing anything I told him would only make me appear guiltier in his eyes. What sort of salt-of-the-earth, straight-laced cop from Baltimore, of all places, would buy into a twisted tale about witch covens and blood feuds?

"If you don't come clean with me, I can't help you." His voice dropped lower, nearly to a whisper. "I can't protect you."

I swallowed hard, struggling not to fold. I didn't want to lie to him. I respected the man. And I liked him. *A lot.* In fact, since the first moment I'd met Detective Caden Hightower, I'd thought he was pretty damn close to perfect. If not for Graham staking irrefutable claim to my heart, I'd probably be halfway in love with him.

He was so unguardedly handsome, so full of warmth and kindness, it would be hard for any girl *not* to fall in love with him. And yet, looking at him now, I saw a different side to him beneath that gentlemanly exterior. An undercurrent of unflinching steel. The kind I supposed you'd need to hack it as a homicide detective.

"I think..." I took a deep breath. "I think I might want that lawyer after all."

"You're not being arrested, Gwendolyn. Not today, anyway," he informed me — doing approximately *nothing* to soothe my ragged nerves. "Level with me, here."

I shook my head back and forth. My mind was spinning so fast, I could barely think straight. "Someone is setting me up. That's the only explanation for all of this."

"Why would someone want to frame you for murder, Gwendolyn?"

"I have no idea!"

"Who would do something like that?"

"I don't know! Maybe the same people who are leaving animal sacrifices all over town?"

Cade reached to the opposite side of the table where a manila folder sat waiting, and flipped it open in front of me. I'd seen the contents before, the last time I'd sat in this chair — a stack of glossy pictures depicting the Heretics' sinister activities — but felt my stomach roil anyway as the bloody symbols and severed parts assailed my eyes. In addition to the original photos, they'd added snapshots of the slaughtered donkey from my alleyway.

"We have no concrete evidence that these—" He tapped a finger against the top photograph. "—have anything to do with Elizabeth Proctor's murder. Nothing ties the two together. Except *you*, Gwendolyn."

My eyes shifted from the gruesome photograph to the other side of the folder. Tucked halfway in the flap there was a paper map of the city limits, printed in black and white. Someone had drawn small Xs in red marker at the spots where the animals were discovered. One at The Gallows, another down by Bertram Field, a third by the dog park near the river, a fourth by the community garden at Palmer Cove, a fifth up at Gallows Hill.

It was all so random.

Random places.

Random times.

Unless...

The breath caught in my throat.

"What?" Cade called softly, drawing my gaze to his face. "What is it?"

"Probably nothing."

"I'll decide if it's nothing, Gwendolyn."

"The sacrifices... they were all found several weeks apart, right?"

He nodded.

"The lunar calendar," I whispered, mind working double time as I turned over possibilities. "It would make sense. If the people doing this are pagan..."

"Gwendolyn," Cade prompted impatiently. "Explain."

I grabbed the map from the folder and stared down at the red Xs. I tapped my pointer against the one by the dog park. "This one was first, right?"

"Yes. The cat."

"When did you find it?"

Cade consulted his notes. "Late March."

"Ostara," I whispered, barely waiting a beat before I planted my finger on the next X, the one down at Palmer Cove. "And this one? When?"

"Early May."

"Beltane."

"Gwendolyn—"

My finger drifted to the X at Gallows Hill. "When did you find the goat here?"

"End of June. Look, what is this all about?"

I jerked my gaze up from the map to meet his. I knew I was wild-eyed, but I was so caught up in my discovery, I didn't care (*much*) if he thought I was crazy. "I should've realized before — what they were doing. But when you first told me about this, I was so freaked out by the dead animals in those photographs, I didn't even pause to consider the timeline."

His brows were high on his forehead. "The timeline?"

"The sacrifices are happening in alignment with the lunar calendar. It makes sense — many pagans derive power from celestial events. Full moons, solar eclipses, solstices, equinoxes." I jammed my finger down at the map. "The cat was found right around Ostara, also known as the spring equinox. The rooster was Beltane, which is May Eve. The goat would be Litha, the summer solstice. The pig lines up with Lughnasadh, sometimes called First Harvest. And the donkey at my store a couple weeks ago..." I sucked in a breath. "Mabon. The autumn equinox. Goddess, I should've realized sooner."

Caden Hightower looked at the map, his expression a mix of confusion and disbelief. When his eyes lifted to mine, there was an intensity in their depths that made me nervous. "What's next?"

"Pardon?" I asked, confused.

"Next on the lunar calendar. What's the next big celestial even these pagans would pick for their sacrifice?"

My blood ran cold. "Samhain."

"And when's that, exactly?"

"Halloween," I whispered, my voice thready. "It's on Halloween."

I sucked down a large gulp of Bordeaux, closing my eyes as the music washed over me, loud enough to rattle my bones. The band onstage was midway through a kickass rock cover of *Cosmic Love* by Florence + The Machine, one of my all-time favorite songs. I was smooshed in a back booth at The Witches Brew, Graham's warm body pressed close beside me on the padded bench seat. He had one arm slung around the back of the booth, his hand drawing lazy circles on the bare skin of my shoulder. His other loosely gripped a draft of beer.

"You know, I was thinking," Florence shouted from across the table where she and Desmond were sitting, straining to be heard over the rollicking chorus. "If they send you away for life, Gwennie, can I have the Thunderbird?"

My eyes cracked open so I could properly scowl at her.

She winked at me. Then, a dreamy look moved across her face as she spotted Graham's hand on my shoulder. She practically shimmied in her seat, thrilled beyond words that we were on a *double date* with our men.

"Gwen isn't going anywhere," Desmond said firmly, sipping his beer. "She's innocent. Only a matter of time before the police figure that out."

It wasn't the police I was worried about. Hell, if they locked me up, at least I'd be safe behind bars where the Heretics couldn't get to me. Fear stirred to the surface and, despite my efforts to quell it, I trembled. Feeling it, Graham tightened his grip on my shoulders and ducked his head close to my ear.

"You okay?" he asked, voice a low murmur.

I nodded, even though I wasn't. Not really. I'd felt shaky and tense ever since I shared my worrisome theory with Detective Hightower this morning. We'd had only moments to discuss it in depth before the interrogation door flew open with a bang.

"You've got to be shitting me," a voice growled from the threshold.

Graham.

I'd been stunned to see him. Detective Hightower, on the other hand, seemed not at all surprised by his abrupt arrival.

"Graves. Surprised it took you so long."

"Tell me I am not seeing what I think I'm seeing." His eyes flashed to me for a split second. "Tell me you are not questioning my woman as a suspect in a homicide without proper representation?"

I jolted at the words *my woman*, startled to hear myself described as such.

Cade glanced at me, frowning. "You his, now?"

I opened my mouth to proclaim that I wasn't his — that I

wasn't *anyone's* thank you very much — but Graham beat me to the punch.

"Gwendolyn is mine. She's been mine a while, you just haven't wanted to accept that." Graham's voice was scathing. "That ends now. You are not pulling any more of this shit without my knowledge. No more ambushing her at work, no more chats down at the station unless I'm sitting next to her. If I hear otherwise..."

The tension in the small room mounted to scary levels as the threat dangled between them, unspoken. The air grew so thick with testosterone, I could barely breathe.

Cade's jaw was clenched with carefully-contained rage. "She said she had nothing to hide and, like it or not, I'm doing my due diligence—"

"Oh, piss up a rope, Hightower. She's not a suspect here, no matter what the evidence says. Treating her like one doesn't make you a good cop, it makes you a fucking sheep." Graham held out a hand to me, never shifting his burning gaze from the detective. "Come on, Gwen. We're leaving."

Normally I would protest at being summoned like a dog, but in this particular case I didn't hesitate. I pushed to my feet and hauled ass to his side, making not a peep of protest as his hand enveloped mine in a bone-crushing grip.

"I'm not finished with her," Cade said, rising from his chair.

"You are." Graham's tone brooked no room for argument. "You need a follow up, call my attorneys. As of this moment, they represent her."

With little other choice, Cade had watched us go. He hadn't looked happy about it. As for Graham, he wasn't happy either. Not when he drove me back to the store, not when I dragged him into the back office to tell him about the missing knife in my display cabinet, and definitely not when I'd voiced my theories regarding the animal sacrifices. By the time I was finished talking, his jaw was ticking like a bomb set to explode.

"Whatever they're planning will most likely happen on Halloween, then."

I'd nodded, at a loss for words.

"Not even three weeks away," he'd muttered, running his hands through his hair. "Christ. Certainly puts a clock on things."

"In a way, this is good," I'd said, trying to look on the bright side. "Now, we know I'm safe. We can stop constantly looking over our shoulders for a little while. At least... until Halloween."

When they sacrifice me on an altar of blood.

Graham did not look like he agreed with my assessment that this was good. Graham, in fact, looked so off-the-charts pissed, it was somewhat surprising he didn't explode out of his skin like the Incredible Hulk in a fit of uncontrollable rage. But, with a series of deep breaths, he'd managed to rein it in, only to yank me into his arms to lay a hot, lip-bruising kiss on me, after which point he muttered, "Do not leave the store until I come back to pick you up." Then, he turned on his cool-as-shit motorcycle boots and stormed out.

I'd worked the rest of the day — which was remarkably hectic for a Tuesday — at Hetti's side, playing backup barista, cleaning tables, rinsing dirty mugs, chatting with customers, and ringing in sales until the near-constant chime of the cash register was giving me a headache. It was wall-to-wall customers. The espresso machine never stopped steaming, books and baubles were flying off the shelves faster than we could restock them. Even the citrine was moving, which I considered a bonafide miracle. Both Hetti and I were dead on our feet by the time we flipped the door sign to CLOSED.

Graham showed up to collect me a few minutes later. I thought he was going to take me home when I finished my nightly cleaning routine, but he surprised me by driving across town to The Witches Brew. When we'd walked in, Flo and Des were already seated at a snug booth in the back, sipping drinks. Both of them grinned wide at the sight of us, hand in hand. They'd barely stopped grinning in the thirty minutes since — the pointed exception to their buoyant moods being the moment I filled them in on my morning visit to the Salem Police Station, as well as my current status as Suspect Numero Uno in the investigation into Eliza Proctor's untimely demise.

"Gwennie!" Flo shouted to be heard over the music — a badass version of *Supernatural* by Barns Courtney, featuring a head-banging drum solo. "Does all of this mean our Halloween plans are off?"

"No tricks or treats for me this year," I replied morosely. "Graham says I have to stay under lock and key until the Heretics situation is handled."

She scowled at the man beside me. "Get a move on, will you?"

"Working on it," was his terse reply.

I stifled a giggle.

"These Heretics are seriously *the worst*," Flo muttered grumpily. "It's one thing to threaten your life. It's another to derail our party!"

She was not wrong. Disappointment shot through me at the thought of missing Florence and Desmond's annual All Hallow's Eve Bacchanalia. Last year, it had been a massive affair complete with costumes, decorations, and deadly-strong, ruby red party punch they served out of a ginormous plastic cauldron in the kitchen. We'd had epic plans to make this second incarnation even better than its predecessor. (Namely, with a skeleton-themed meat and cheese centerpiece we intended to introduce as our c*har-spook-erie* board.)

Flo liked to invite everyone she'd ever met to her Halloween bash — old high school buddies, the fellow teachers at her elementary school, Desmond's university coworkers, even strangers she met in line at the grocery store while shopping for party snacks. Last year, the cops were called on us around midnight. (Hello, noise violation.) Most people would've taken this as a sign to shut things down. Not Flo. She'd cranked her spooky playlist down to an only-slightly-less earsplitting decibel and continued to carouse through the night.

"I can't be Velma without a Daphne!" Flo cried. "They're a package deal."

I shrugged. "Sorry, Flo."

We'd picked out costumes ages ago — Daphne and Velma from *Scooby Doo* — and painstakingly thrifted our outfits from secondhand stores.

"Velma and Daphne?" Graham asked, sounding amused as he looked across at Desmond. "Let me guess... Fred?"

I turned to him. "You're just upset because no one asked you to be Shaggy. *Psh.* As if you could pull it off."

"Not sure that's the insult you intended it to be, babe," he returned, grinning.

My eyes narrowed. Last year, Graham hadn't even bothered with a costume. He'd just appeared for a few hours in his standard jeans-boots-jacket combo along with the girl he was seeing at the time — a seriously stunning blonde named Madison, who was dressed loosely as an angel. I say *loosely* because she was only wearing white lingerie, thigh-high go-go boots, and a set of feathery wings that did not hang low enough to obscure her perfectly toned asscheeks.

For the record, Flo and I went as matching minions from *Despicable Me*. I had a wedgie all night from the suspenders and it took days to get off all the yellow grease paint. (I regret nothing.)

"Let me guess!" I poked Graham lightly in the chest. "You

plan on going as an arrogant, bossy, annoyingly-good-in-bed bounty hunter badass?"

He grinned wider. "Not sure that's the insult you intended it to be either, babe."

I rolled my eyes. He was so irritating. And unfairly sexy. Especially when he curled his arm around my shoulders and dragged me up against his chest so he could brush his lips against mine.

"Jeeze, could you two be any cuter?" Florence sighed dreamily. "Aren't they cute, Des, honey?"

Desmond, dutiful as ever, echoed, "They're cute, Flo."

"Remember when we were like that? Unable to keep our hands off each other?"

"Honey, you jumped me in the shower this morning," he reminded her softly. "I wouldn't exactly say our spark is gone."

Flo giggled. "Right."

As we broke apart from the kiss, Graham and I exchanged a lingering glance that had me squirming in my seat. His hand left his beer glass and slipped beneath the table to curl around my thigh. "You about finished with that drink?"

"Um..." I gulped and glanced at my wine glass. It was still quite full. "Not really."

His hand bunched in the fabric of my skirt. "Too bad, baby. Haven't been inside you even once today. Starting to go into withdrawal."

Without looking away from the mesmerizing heat of his eyes, I flung out my hand, grabbed my wine glass, pulled it to my lips, and took a hefty gulp. When I swallowed, Graham was grinning wider than I'd ever seen before.

WE SAT IN MY BED, Graham dressed only in his boxers, me in his t-shirt, eating Chinese takeout straight out of the containers.

It was late, hours after we'd gotten home from The Witches Brew after parting with Florence and Desmond, and I was still riding a post-orgasmic high, courtesy of one Graham *Freaking* Graves.

"What's your middle name?" I asked around a mouthful of egg roll, suddenly curious.

He froze with the chopsticks poised halfway to his mouth, his shrimp dumpling suspended mid-air. "Why?"

"Just curious, I guess."

His brows shot up in question. "*Curious.*"

"What?" I asked, feeling self-conscious. "Can't I be curious about you?"

He set down his chopsticks, abandoning his dumpling in its container, and turned fully to face me.

"Oh no," I exclaimed, holding up my chopsticks in the shape of a cross, like a priest warding off a demon. "That's your *have-a-serious-discussion-with-Gwendolyn* face."

He laughed. It was a good laugh. My whole stomach turned to butterflies at just the sound of it. (I don't even want to tell you what happened to other parts of me.)

"Seriously, Graham, we've entered the *excellent-food-after-excellent-sex* portion of the evening. I don't have the mental capacity for a serious discussion."

"Relax. I'm not going to attempt a rational conversation with you. I know better by now."

Rude!

His lips twitched at my lethal glare. "I was just surprised."

"Surprised?" My brows lifted. "Why?"

"You've never asked me a question before. Not outright anyway, not without a reason behind it. That was the first time you've ever wanted to know something about me just because it means something to you to know it." He leaned forward and kissed me, a light brush that promised more. "I like that, baby.

Like you being curious about me. Like you wanting more instead of running away."

"Oh." I tried to breathe steadily, but I'm pretty sure I failed. In fact, I'm pretty sure I was hyperventilating.

"It's Seaton by the way," Graham continued conversationally, picking up his dumpling again.

"W-what?" I asked, feeling dazed.

"My middle name. It's Seaton."

"Seaton," I repeated, lifting my egg roll back to my mouth. "Graham Seaton Graves. Sounds rich."

"Babe. I *am* rich."

I choked on the bite of egg roll. "Excuse me?"

"I'm rich. Rolling in it."

My eyes bugged out of my head. I could only repeat, "*Excuse me?*"

"Not sure what part of this you're struggling to comprehend."

"Um, maybe the fact that you just announced your lofty financial status like it's nothing of consequence."

"Because it isn't." He was staring at me like I was the crazy one in this scenario — which was *clearly* not the case. "It's just money. It doesn't matter."

"Spoken like someone who grew up with it."

"Yeah, can't fight you there. My family was well-off. But I haven't taken a dime from them. Earned a full ride to Harvard with a football scholarship. Haven't touched the trust fund my parents set up for me, mostly 'cause that comes with strings attached, strings I have no interest in. Everything I have, I earned. Not saying I'm a billionaire, but I make enough to keep my men well compensated. I have enough socked away to retire on a white sand beach somewhere warm whenever the time comes that I get bored of fixing other people's problems. I own my loft. Own the whole Gravewatch building, in fact."

My eyes were wide. Overwhelmed by the font of information, I could only manage to murmur, "You want to retire to a white sand beach?"

He nodded. "Ever been to the British Virgin Islands?"

"Never been south of the Jersey turnpike."

"Babe." He shook his head in disgust. "That's just sad."

"I'll add it to the bucket list. If you're lucky, I'll send you a postcard from the beach — right after I apply for a passport and save enough money for a plane ticket, that is."

"No point sending me a postcard, seeing as I'll be sitting on that beach next to you," he informed me. "But if you want to waste the postage, it's no skin off my back."

I sucked in a sharp breath at the thought of vacationing with him. It was a good thought. So good, I forced myself to change the subject, for fear I'd blurt out something truly idiotic. (Something regarding a decades-old fantasy about Graham Graves in a bright red lifeguard suit.)

"Did you know I own The Gallows building?" I asked, tilting my head to the side. "There's an apartment upstairs. Aunt Colette used to rent it out a million years ago, but I haven't been up there in ages. Probably not since she died. If business ever turns bad, I guess I could renovate it, find a tenant to bring in some extra income."

He was silent for a long beat. When he spoke, his voice was soft. "You okay now, though? Financially?"

"I'm okay. I'm *solid*, even, which is something I'm not really used to being. This house is paid for, so I don't have a mortgage. Just taxes — which are admittedly a bitch, but I manage. Same goes for the store. I have some overhead in terms of inventory, plus I have to pay Hetti a big enough salary to put up with me... But business has been good. More than good, actually. The other day, I put up a listing for a part-timer on a few websites. It wouldn't hurt to have a backup barista, someone to cover when I get tied up or Hetti needs time off."

"That's great, baby."

The pride in his voice made my throat feel tight. "Thanks."

"Promise me one thing."

"What?"

"Before you hire anyone, you give me their name. First and last. Let me check them out." A crease furrowed between his brows. "Can't have just anyone lurking around. Not planning a repeat of the Zelda situation. You get me?"

"I get you," I whispered around the sudden lump of emotion blocking my airway. Since my aunt died, no one had ever tried to take care of me. No one had been there to watch my back, spotted me when I was liable to stumble. It was a good feeling.

Scratch that, it was a freaking *great* feeling.

"I suppose I should start looking for a new psychic, too." I shrugged, digging through the lo mein carton for a shrimp. "Seeing as Madame Zelda has yet to reappear. I'm losing potential business every day she's gone."

Graham was silent.

"Has there been any sign of her? I've been so focused on Eliza's murder, I forgot to ask you what's going on with the O'Banions these days."

He blew out a long breath, set down his chopsticks again, and ran a hand through his hair. "Fuck."

My brows shot up as unease rippled through me. "What?"

"I've been wondering when you were going to ask me about this shit. Was hoping for a few more days' reprieve."

"Why?" I asked, instantly suspicious. "What's going on?"

"Nothing you need to know about."

"Graham!"

"You've got enough on your mind, I don't want to pile on any more."

"You know where she is, don't you?"

His brows furrowed deeper and he repeated, "*Fuck.*"

"You have to tell me."

"Technically, I don't. You aren't the client. Your involvement in this is nonexistent, in my opinion."

"Well, in *my* opinion, you hiding information from me makes you a total jerk!"

"Oh no, how will I live with myself, knowing you think I'm a jerk?" he drawled, sarcasm thick. "News flash, babe, you've thought I was a jerk for years. Doesn't bother me. Sure as shit doesn't mean I'm letting you get involved in Zelda's clusterfuck."

My temper was gaining steam. "I'm already involved!"

"And you're not getting *more* involved."

"If you don't tell me, I'll be forced to go around you and find out myself. I'll call Flo, we'll get in the Thunderbird... Thelma and Louise, the sequel."

He shook his head back and forth, looking like he wanted to shake some sense into me. "You're a pain in my ass, you know what?"

"Sure. Whatever." My smile was saccharine sweet. "Spill the beans, Graves. Where's Zelda hiding?"

"She's not hiding anywhere." He paused, exhaling sharply. "We have her in the holding room at Gravewatch."

"*What!?*"

I stared at him in disbelief. Yesterday morning, when he'd mentioned the urgent situation at work, he'd let it slip they had *someone* in custody. He conveniently never mentioned it was my missing psychic! I couldn't help wondering what other truths he'd omitted as I gaped at him, awaiting an explanation.

"The twins tracked her down," he informed me. "She was halfway to New Hampshire, hiding out at a shitty motel off the side of the highway. They convinced her to come back to town with them."

"Convinced her how?"

He paused. "Creatively."

"I can't believe you didn't tell me this."

"Babe, it was need-to-know."

"And?"

"You didn't need to know."

My temper had, by this point, gathered so much steam, I feared my ears would soon begin to whistle like a boiling tea kettle. "You were hoping I wouldn't *ever* know," I hissed, a note of accusation coloring my tone. "You were hoping... what, exactly? That I'd develop a timely case of amnesia? That I'd just forget all about Madame Zelda? That I wouldn't notice when a story hit the papers about the middle aged woman found dead in the dumpster behind The Banshee?"

"Babe, I'm sure the O'Banions wouldn't dump the body behind their own bar. Not the brightest bulbs, I admit, but even they know better than that."

"This is not a joke! This is a mess!"

"Fully fucking aware of that, Gwen." His own temper lashed out, sudden as a whip. "Christ, you think I wanted to get involved in any of this shit? Trust me, it's not my policy to take on a whack-job client like Mickey O'Banion or any of his three brothers, seeing as they're all batshit insane — a genetic trait that only seems to get stronger with each incarnation."

"You didn't have to take the case!"

"I wasn't planning on it!" he clipped. "Not until I realized you were caught up in the middle of it."

I flinched in surprise.

He kept going. "I already have more business than I can handle. Didn't need one more fucking thing on my plate. My plate is full as it is. I have a man out of state after a skip wanted for felony assault and battery. Another finishing up an assignment with the Feds, an assignment that I had to delegate —

something, I might add, I *never* fucking do — so I could get back here and keep your ass out of hot water. My other men are scrambling to juggle all our local clients while taking on the monumental goddamn task of surveilling your every move, so we can hunt down the fuckers who are closing in on you before Halloween rolls around. The absolute *last* thing I need is to be chasing down an ex-con psychic and her talking parrot, or brokering deals with the likes of Mickey O'Banion."

My temper had sputtered out as he spoke, evaporating beneath the realization that he'd gotten tangled in a web of criminals for *my* sake. Not just him, either. He'd gotten his men tangled too, when they undoubtedly had far more important things to which they should be dedicating their not-inconsiderable skills. Graham was working overtime, spreading his resources thin, just to keep me safe.

Humbled beyond the powers of speech, I could only manage to murmur a soft, "Oh..."

"Yeah." His brows furrowed as he scowled at me. "*Oh.*"

"What about the stolen jewelry?"

"Didn't have it on her. Best guess? She fenced it somewhere along the way when she headed north. We're attempting to find out where. So far, she hasn't felt inclined to share." His green stare grew hard, a familiar uncompromising light shining on the surface of his irises. "Luckily, one of my men — Welles — specializes in intel extraction. He'll get it out of her eventually."

"He's not going to beat it out of her, is he?"

Graham's lips twitched when he heard the alarm in my voice. "Not in the torture business, babe. Welles has a way of finding people's weak spots, and applying pressure as necessary." He paused. "That's figurative weak spots, not literal, just to be clear."

"Don't make fun of me! This stuff isn't exactly in my typical wheelhouse. I'm still trying to wrap my mind around the fact that you've got my former employee imprisoned in your office."

"It's not like it's a cell with bars and a stone pallet. She has a bed, she has a bathroom, she has a fucking television for god's sake. Compared to the fleabag motel she was holed up in, it's an upgrade." He shot me an unreadable look. "Going to need it fumigated after she's gone. That bird of hers stinks to high heaven."

This wasn't a lie. I'd had the distinct displeasure of meeting — and smelling — Hecate once. And once was enough.

"I want to see Zelda," I declared, collecting the empty takeout cartons and discarding them in the trash can across the room.

"No."

"Just *no*? Flat out? We can't even discuss it?"

"Nope."

"Even maximum security prison has visitation," I pointed out

"Gravewatch doesn't."

I stared at him for a moment, studying the unyielding set to his features, then shrugged. "We'll circle back to this at a later date."

He shook his head in exasperation. "Gwen—"

"So," I said, quickly changing the subject as I walked back to rejoin him on the bed. "Once you figure out where she's stashed or pawned the jewels... what's the plan? You're not going to hand her over to the O'Banions, are you?"

"When we get the jewelry back, we'll arrange a meet with the O'Banion boys. We hand it over, the debt is cleared, Zelda splits town before they can seek retribution... and we hope like hell Mickey and his brothers don't get it in their heads to chase her down just for sport." He paused. "Either way, she's out of Salem, out of our lives, for good. Our involvement ends there."

"And if she doesn't want to leave? What then?"

"Too bad for her." He shrugged. "Zelda made her bed, Gwen.

You can't save her. You've already done far more than she deserves, bringing me and my boys in on her behalf."

"But—"

"You think Mary O'Banion is the only little old lady she's conned out of her precious jewels? You think there isn't a trail of stolen inheritances stretching from Salem to Providence and back? Jennifer H. Custer has been operating her Madame Zelda scheme for a while. Only difference is, this time she picked the wrong mark." He reached out and ran his fingertips along my cheekbone. "I know you've got a bleeding heart hidden under all your sass, baby, but I personally don't have a whole lot of sympathy where that charlatan is concerned. If I had my way, she'd already be rotting in a jail cell."

I leaned my head into his touch, sighing contentedly as he stroked my skin. "Graham?"

"Yeah?"

"Thanks for doing all this for me."

He was silent for a long beat, just staring at his thumb as it moved back and forth on my cheek. "You don't have to thank me, Gwen."

"Why?"

"Not keeping you safe for your sake. Keeping you safe for mine." His eyes were intense. "If anything happened to you..."

"Nothing is going to happen to me."

In a flash he'd pulled me onto his lap, settling back against my headboard with his arms wound tight around me. I could feel the tension thrumming through him. His chest moved rapidly as he struggled to regulate his ragged breathing. His lips hit my hair and his voice, when he spoke, was almost inaudible. "What are the odds I could convince you to leave town until all this blows over? Spend Halloween with me on a beach in Virgin Gorda. We'll drink rum, fuck in the sand, fall asleep under the stars..."

"Sounds like a dream," I whispered.

"Say the word, I'll make it a reality."

I tilted my head up to look into his eyes and felt my breath hitch in my throat. They were deadly serious. He wasn't joking at all. I knew, if I so much as nodded, he'd have two tickets to paradise booked within the hour.

It took every shred of responsibility I possessed to murmur, "Let's go for Thanksgiving instead."

His eyes filtered through several intense emotions — none of which was surprise. He'd known I'd never agree to leave. He'd asked anyway.

Pure Graham.

"I could do Thanksgiving," he said softly.

"You wouldn't miss it?"

"Dry turkey and family squabbles or you in a bikini and an overwater bungalow?" He shook his head, like I was an idiot. "Babe. No contest."

I swallowed hard, trying not to start blubbering.

"Make sure you look good tomorrow, Gwen."

"Don't I always?"

"Yeah. I just don't want you bitching at me for the next ten years that your hair isn't the way you like it in your passport photo." He kissed my temple, his lips warm and soft, and his voice was a mere whisper. "First thing tomorrow, before work, we're crossing that off the list. The sooner we can hit that beach, the better."

CHAPTER TWENTY-THREE

Yeah, I do marathons.
Mostly on HBO.
- Gwen Goode, binge-watching

"Justice is a double-edged sword!" Hecate shrieked, black tongue jutting from between her beak. *"Double-edged sword!"*

"She loathes the cage," Zelda said, drawing my gaze back to her. "But my captors insist upon it."

We were seated at the small folding table inside the holding room at Gravewatch. It had taken four full days of creative persuasion (by *creative* I mostly meant *naked*) but Graham had finally caved and agreed to a brief visit with my former psychic. I had a feeling this decision was, at least in part, because Zelda was being unnaturally stubborn, refusing to reveal where she'd stashed the stolen jewelry.

Graham was frustrated. His men were frustrated. Hell, *I* was frustrated. Still, I strove for a light, unbothered tone. "How are you doing, Zelda? Do you need anything?"

"Besides a pack of cigarettes, an orgasm, and my freedom, you mean?"

I loosed an involuntary snort of amusement.

"I assume I have you to thank for my continued internment here?"

My amusement faded. "Actually, you can thank *yourself*, Zelda. You're the reason you're here. And if the O'Banions find you before they get their possessions back, you'll be wishing for the safety of this room."

"*Beware the hierophant!*" Hecate squawked.

She stared at me, her cloudy blue eyes brimming with resentment. She was clad in a pale pink caftan, a matching turban poised atop her head. She'd made a halfhearted attempt at makeup, lining her brows with dark pencil and coating her lips in a thick, cakey layer of plum colored lipstick.

"Did they send you in here to make me talk, Gwendolyn? If so, you can save your breath. I'm not telling you a damn thing. After the way they've treated me? Those *twins*." She hissed out the word like a curse. "Devils, the both of them! And you're the one who sicced them on me!"

I glanced briefly at the camera mounted above the door. We were being monitored by live video feed in the control room down the hall, just in case Zelda pulled any funny business. Not that she could. The room was stripped to the barest of bones, with a partitioned bathroom area, a bed frame, two-person table, and a flatscreen bolted to the wall. It was completely devoid of art and color. Beige tile on the floors, beige paint on the walls. It didn't even have a window.

"I'm sorry you feel that way, Zelda," I forced myself to say.

"You aren't sorry, you entitled little brat. You're just as conniving and self-serving as the rest of them." She spat at the floor, a disgusting gob of translucent saliva splattering against the smooth tile scant inches from my boot. "All of this is your fault."

My spine snapped ramrod straight. "Excuse me?"

"You heard me. You're to blame! I had a plan. I was going to disappear, start over fresh somewhere. Instead, thanks to you, I'm rotting in this room while Mickey and his brothers circle closer. As far as I'm concerned, if they make trouble for you in the process, it's no more than you deserve. "

My veins burned with indignation, but I kept my voice casual. "You know, you're right. It *is* my fault you're here, Zelda. Or, should I call you Jennifer? That's your name, isn't it? Jennifer H. Custer. A conwoman. A fraud."

She scowled, her penciled brows furrowing.

I kept going. "I guess it doesn't really matter what I call you. The point is, you're not who I thought you were. Because I thought you were my friend. I thought you were my business associate. I thought you could be trusted. That's the only reason I dragged the men here at Gravewatch into this mess in the first place. I thought I was *helping you.*"

The skin around her lips pulled tight as a drawstring purse, deep smoker's grooves feathering the skin.

"Ever since I made it clear that I didn't want anything bad to happen to a friend of mine, the men in this office have been busting their asses to make sure you're protected," I continued. "Brokering a deal on your behalf with the O'Banions — *the freaking O'Banions!* — to ensure you can walk away from this mess you've created without a Mickey-shaped shadow for the rest of your days."

Zelda was beginning to look a little nervous.

I pushed my chair back from the table and got to my feet. "You know what? I made a mistake, putting myself out there for you. I thought you were worth saving, but I see now that we don't mean anything to one another. So, I'm going to give you exactly what you want." I paused, for maximum effect, planting my hands on the table to look her dead in the face. "Your freedom."

Shock registered in her cloudy blue eyes.

I glanced at the camera and bluffed for all I was worth. "Boys? I changed my mind. Call the O'Banions. Tell them they can have her."

She paled, eyes darting from me to the camera and back again. "*What are you doing?!*"

"Exactly what you wanted. Letting you go. I'm sure the O'Banion boys will be thrilled to see you."

"You wouldn't!"

"An entitled little brat like me?" I grinned. "Oh, I think I would."

"Gwendolyn!" she hissed. "Get back here!"

"No," I called over my shoulder, heading for the door. "No, I don't think so."

"I'll tell you where the jewelry is!"

I froze with my hand on the knob. When I glanced back at her, she was slumped in her chair, the picture of defeat, her turban tilting precariously to one side.

"I'll tell you," she whimpered, putting her head in her hands. "Just... please. Don't give me to Mickey."

"*Fortune favors the bold!*" Hecate cried, rattling her cage with sharp claws. "*Fortune favors the bold!*"

Damn straight, it did.

I sat in the Gravewatch surveillance room, spinning around on the office chair. The space was impressively high tech, with two tiered levels of computers facing a large bank of monitors that took up one entire wall, showing a wide variety of video feeds. I felt like a secret agent, about to receive the codes for a highly classified mission.

Graham's hands settled on the backrest of my chair, halting my aimless spinning. He crouched down before me, eyes lit with amusement.

"Ready to go?"

I shook my head, eyes on the monitors over his shoulder. One of them showed the inside of a dimly lit, somewhat dingy bar. A bar, I'd since learned, was none other than The Banshee, home base for the O'Banion family. How Graham and his boys managed to get eyes inside without being caught was a mystery. A mystery I very much wanted to solve, but had thus far gotten no details about. In the face of my best pleading puppy dog expression, Graham had merely leveled me with his standard no-nonsense look and said, "Need-to-know, babe."

Whatever.

"We can't leave," I insisted now. "What if something exciting happens?"

Sawyer, the mega-muscular, blue eyed, blond haired badass sitting at the main computer console, scoffed under his breath. It was clear he didn't find surveillance duty as thrilling as I did. In fact, the bored-to-death look on his face suggested he'd much rather be out hunting down bond skips or dodging bullets than sitting there, waiting for something to happen.

Graham sighed and ran a hand through his hair. "You want to stay here for the rest of eternity or you want dinner?"

"Here for eternity," I replied instantly.

"Gwen."

"You take all this—" I gestured around. "—for granted! You're totally desensitized to the coolness factor."

Sawyer scoffed again.

"Somehow, I'll survive," Graham drawled.

"*Fine.* Feed me if you must." I allowed him to drag me to my feet. "You'll let me come back though, right? Soon? I want to meet the rest of the guys."

So far, I'd only met the (mostly silent, occasionally scoffing) Sawyer and (somewhat chattier, but definitely not verbose) Welles. Welles was a brunet behemoth with a killer man bun, wicked facial hair, and eyes so bright hazel they were almost gold. I'd barely been able to form words when he closed his massive hand around mine in greeting — and held on a beat too long for Graham's liking, judging by the scary, deep, growly sound he made before reclaiming me with a firm arm around my shoulders. If I was Welles, I would've been intimidated. But Welles had just winked at me as I was dragged away, looking completely unaffected by his disapproving boss.

I could see him now on the monitors. He was in the holding room with Zelda, getting specifics about the location of the stolen jewelry. According to her twisted tale of woe — which she'd unloaded on me about twenty seconds after I threatened to walk out — she'd known she'd never be able to fence the priceless gems anywhere local. Not with the O'Banions watching her every move. So, she'd boxed them up and shipped them to a tiny town somewhere in the boondocks of central Maine, where her sister lived, with plans to drive up there and collect them in a few weeks once things cooled down a bit. That being said, she wasn't exactly tickled pink when the twins had burst into her motel room and brought her back to town.

Graham led me — dragging my heels the whole way — out of the surveillance room and down the hallway in the opposite direction of the reception area, where perfectly poised Brianne was no doubt sitting, fielding phone calls in her most soothing phone voice. A steel exit door with an access panel brought us into the garage bay where Graham's Bronco was parked. The black SUV was missing from its spot, but the motorcycle was there.

"Is the Triumph yours?" I asked, eyeing the sleek bike.

"Nah. Sawyer rides."

"Oh." I stared at it, wondering what the badass blond would look like sitting astride all that chrome and black. My mouth felt suddenly dry.

"Gwen, baby, you're drooling," Graham remarked, punching in the door code for the stairs. "Just had these floors detailed, I'd prefer not to do it again."

I glowered at his broad shoulders all the way up into his loft.

Graham opened a bottle of wine and poured us each a glass. He set about making dinner while I wandered around his space, being nosy. (My offers to help slice and season were gently but firmly rebuffed.) In my wanderings, I discovered that Graham had even better taste than I'd originally given him credit for. (And I'd given him a lot of initial credit.)

His bookshelves were stuffed to bursting, an eclectic mix of genres. His bar cart was stocked with top shelf liquor and heavy crystal lowball glasses. His oversized abstract artwork collection was supplemented by a trio of personal photographs, hidden away on the low table behind his desk. I examined them each in turn, taking my time to study the images.

One showed Graham flanked by two slightly younger men that were mirror images of each other — Holden and Hunter, both dark haired and very nearly as ridiculously handsome as their older brother. It was the twins' high school graduation day, judging by the shiny caps and gowns they were wearing. All three of them were beaming at the camera. Though they were younger in the picture, there was no denying they were the same men I'd seen during shootout at Madame Zelda's apartment.

Fantastic.

That meant the twins had seen my eighty-five-point turn in

the Thunderbird. I certainly knew how to make a first impression, huh? If they were anything like their brother, I had a lot of teasing to look forward to in the future. I sighed and exchanged the frame for another.

The second photo was of Pickering Wharf, taken at sunset, the harbor bathed in red and yellow shades in the background, Gravewatch front and center in the foreground. I traced the shape of the building, feeling a happy flutter in my gut. Graham was proud of what he'd built, proud of the things he'd accomplished. I was proud of him, too.

The final photograph showed him as a tousle-haired little kid, no more than four or five years old, standing in front of a crouched man who looked so shockingly similar to Graham, I did a double take. His father. It had to be, the resemblance was undeniable. They were holding a fishing rod together, both sets of hands clutching the reel. And they were smiling.

I didn't know much about Graham's relationship with his parents but I'd inferred from a few pointed comments he'd made that they weren't exactly close-knit. I wondered what had happened to change them from that idyllic father and son fishing together to whatever fraught connection they currently maintained as I set the frame gently back on the shelf.

There were no photos of his mother anywhere to be seen. I filed that factoid away for further inspection and carried on with my snooping. Eventually, I located an old vinyl turntable tucked away in the back corner, with an orderly box of records underneath. I flipped through them, grinning when I saw one I liked, and put it on before I walked back to the kitchen area.

"*Listen to the wind bloooowwwww....*" Stevie and Lindsey started signing about breaking the chain.

"Fleetwood Mac?" Graham asked, watching me cross to him. His eyes were on my legs, which were on full display in my short sweater dress.

"*Best Of,* compilation album," I confirmed. I kept walking until I was right in front of him, set down my wine glass, and slid my hands around his waist.

"You done snooping?" he asked, voice warm.

I scrunched my nose. "I wasn't snooping, per se. I was... perusing."

"Babe. Snoop all you want. Nothing to hide."

"Well, in that case..." I jokingly made to vault out of his arms, but they tightened to steely bands, keeping me close. Smiling up at him, I asked, "What's for dinner?"

"Baked potatoes are in the oven, salmon's on deck. Brussels sprouts are steaming."

"What's for dessert?"

"I don't do dessert."

I scoffed. "That's *insane.*"

"No, that's why I have a six pack." He paused. "You like my six pack, if memory serves. Spent at least twenty minutes running your tongue down it last night before you su—"

"You know what?" I cut him off. "I've taken it under advisement. No dessert for you. I, however, will require something sweet to balance out the Brussels sprouts."

He chuckled. "You want dessert, we'll walk around the corner to Jaho for gelato later."

I crowed victoriously.

Chuckling again, he released me to check on the potatoes. I settled onto one of his stools, watching him move around his kitchen, trying not to totally freak out over the fact that we were doing this. Date night at Graham's loft, the picture of domestic bliss.

I'd never had this before. Not as a kid living with my mom, not with my offbeat hippie chick aunt, not living by myself, definitely not with any of the guys I'd dated. It was uncharted territory for me. But clearly not for Graham. He moved with total confidence, whipping together a gourmet meal with the same ease he handled a gun or steered his Bronco.

"When we head to your place tonight, remind me to bring my tool bag," he called over his shoulder as he stooped to slide the salmon onto the top rack of the oven.

I sipped my wine. "Why do you need your tool bag?"

"Your aunt had some basics in the garage, but half of them are so rusty and old they should go out with the trash."

"I'm... not following."

He finally turned to face me, taking a sip of his own wine. "My tools are better."

"Still not following."

"Gwen, babe, how do you expect me to build you bookshelves without my tools?"

I sucked in a sharp, audible breath. "*What?*"

"Last night you told me you always pictured the room I've been crashing in as your library." His brow furrowed in confusion. "You forget?"

No.

No, I hadn't forgotten.

I'd been half asleep, talking about nothing of consequence in the aftermath of several intense rounds between the sheets, my body and mind in a state of complete relaxation. Graham had peppered me with questions about the house, curious which room I wanted to tackle now that we'd finished the dining room. It had taken two days and two trips to the hardware store, but the walls were now a deep navy shade that made me shimmy with joy every time I walked past.

So much better than orange floral wallpaper.

I hadn't realized his postcoital questions would translate into immediate action. (I should've. This was Graham we were talking about, after all.) But it seemed he'd taken my sleepy musings about a home library — complete with built-in shelves, a rolling ladder, and a reading nook by the window — very seriously.

"You..." I swallowed, struggling to speak. "You're building me a library?"

"Assuming you still want one, yeah."

I promptly burst into tears.

Graham was there in less than a heartbeat, arms closing around me, pulling me into his chest. His hand stroked my hair as I sobbed against his t-shirt.

"Shhh, Gwen. Jesus, baby, what's wrong?"

Tilting my head back to meet his eyes, I knew my face was blotchy red from crying, but I didn't care. "*You!* You are what's wrong."

"I'm going to need a bit of elaboration."

"You're just... you're so..." I sobbed again, swallowing it down before it could escape, and pounded my balled fist against his heart. "You're so... so... *wonderful.*"

He stilled.

"And I need you to stop." I whimpered. "I need you to stop being considerate. Stop doing things for me. Stop being *you.* Because I won't be able to stand it if... I won't be able to get over it if... if..."

His fingers lifted to my cheek, wiping away my flowing tears. His voice was unbearably gentle. "If what, gorgeous?"

"If we end."

His body went solid against mine, every muscle locked tight. "Gwen..."

"This scares the shit out me," I confessed, the words thick with emotion. "You and me, when we're together? It's so good, it *terrifies me.* I don't know how to process it. I'm not good at this kind of thing. I've never really done this... longterm relationship stuff."

"I'm not the poster child for commitment myself," he pointed out softly.

"But you're good at it! Hellfire, you're practically living at my house. You took down my wallpaper. You bought me, like, thirty different shades of blue paint samples when I was being indecisive. You drive me everywhere I need to go. You cook me dinner. You hold my hand in public. And now you're *building me bookshelves!?*" My voice cracked, a ragged sound of pure panic. "It's too much. You're too much. You need to stop. Stop being so good to me. Because I'm going to get used to it. I'm going to start expecting it. And when it stops, I'm going to be totally, completely, screwed."

Graham's hands cupped my face, putting pressure on the hinge of my jaw so I had no choice but to meet his stare — which, I noticed, was deadly serious, no humor at all dancing in the green depths of his eyes.

"My turn to talk now," he said firmly.

"But—"

"My turn." He leaned forward, so his forehead was on mine. "Gwen, I know this scares you. I know you think you're going to get hurt if it ends. I know, even as far as we've come, you're still holding back, keeping me out of your heart because of some ingrained need for self-preservation. But you gotta know, baby... I meant it when I said I'm not going anywhere. I'm in this, just as deep as you are. So deep, I'm fucking drowning."

My breath hitched.

"I know you've got issues with trust," he continued. "I know you aren't used to letting people be there for you. But I am not your garbage exes and I'm not your selfish mom and I'm sure as shit not whatever deadbeat losers she dragged home when you were a kid. I'm not going to hurt you. I'm not going to fuck you over. I told you once before — you're safe with me. I stand by that statement, babe. I'd stake my fucking life on it."

Tears were pricking at the backs of my eyes. I blinked rapidly, afraid to let them fall, seeing as I'd only just gotten them to stop. His hands were still cradling my face, his thumbs circling my temples in soothing strokes.

"Babe..."

"It doesn't come easy," I whispered, my voice cracking. "The trust thing. It's not natural for me. My first instinct is to run for cover. To protect myself from any possible threat."

"To bolt," he said softly.

I nodded, my head moving in the span of his strong hands. I sucked in a gulp of air, trying desperately not to fall apart. "From now on, I'll... I'll try to ignore those instincts. I can't promise I'll be any good at it. But... I'll try."

"All I can ask," he murmured.

Then, his mouth came down to capture mine in a kiss so soft and so slow and so sweet, it stole my breath. It was a kiss like none I'd experienced before — a kiss that gave far more than it took, that shored me up inside until I no longer felt the waves of panic crashing through me, until the instinct to run screaming from the seriously scary things I was feeling for this man faded out into nothingness.

It was not explosively passionate — not an act of seduction, not foreplay used as a tool to get me into his bed for his own pleasure. This was a kiss entirely without intent. This kiss was a gift, just for me. And I took it. I took it all, everything he had to give me, all his strength and his solid warmth. I wound my hands up his body, twined them around his neck, pulled him closer, until we were pressed so tight together, I couldn't tell where he ended and I began.

"For the record," he told me when we finally broke apart. "The only reason I'm good at the relationship shit is because I'm doing it with you. I was shit at it with everyone else — a fact my exes would happily confirm."

"Graham…"

He'd barely let that emotional blow settle before he delivered another gut-punch. "And, babe, it will probably freak you out, seeing as you're you, but on your next day off, we're going shopping for furniture."

"Furniture?"

"You need a table for your dining room and a bed for your guest room. Tired of sleeping on your floor." He paused, glancing around. "You don't want to buy new shit, we'll bring my bed from here. I don't care."

I blinked in confusion. "But, if we take your bed from the loft, you won't have anywhere to sleep."

"Don't foresee sleeping at the loft much."

"Why?" I glanced around at the gorgeous space. "You love the loft. The loft is cool as hell. You have a vintage turntable. And a bar cart. Your shower is amazing. Your tub is even better. You have water views. You have cool art. You have a freaking Picasso print!"

"Not a print."

"What?"

"The Picasso." He shrugged. "Not a print."

"WHAT?!" I was surely hallucinating. "Please, for the love of all that is holy, tell me I have not been peeing in the presence of a real, actual Picasso painting."

"Technically, it's a sketch."

I stared at him.

"Basically a scribble."

I stared some more.

"Uncatalogued," he added.

The staring continued.

"Babe." He snapped his fingers in front of my face. "You still with me?"

"Nope." I shook my head to clear my bewilderment. "Still

trying to process the fact that you'd even consider leaving the loft when you have a freaking Picasso hanging on the wall of your bathroom when it really belongs in, like, I don't know. A museum. A hermetically sealed crypt. A vault at Gringotts."

"Not sure that last one is an actual option, but I like that you're concerned about the welfare of my art collection."

"Don't you joke with me, Graham Graves," I hissed. "I am not in a joking mood. I am in a freaking-the-heck-out mood."

"Gwen."

"What?!" I snapped.

"The loft might have all that shit, but it doesn't have you in it. And you count a hell of a lot more than all the rest." He heaved a martyred sigh, as though I was the one being ridiculous here. "The Picasso can hang on one of your walls — maybe in your library if there's room when I'm done building your shelves. The turntable can sit in your living room. And if you want, we'll put a pedestal tub in your downstairs bathroom when we renovate."

"When..." My voice was breathy with shock. "When... *we*... renovate?"

He simply nodded, then turned to pull out the baked potatoes with a pair of tongs and rotate the fish so it baked evenly.

"Graham," I said, panic infusing every syllable. "Correct me if I'm wrong... and I *must* be wrong, because the alternative is truly too unhinged to contemplate... but it sounds to me like... you think you're moving into my house."

He plunked the potatoes down on the counter, stabbed them with a fork to ensure they were done, then nabbed his wine and took another long sip. "Glad you're on board, babe."

"On board?" I screeched. "I'm not on board. I'm so far *off* board I'm like Jack in the movie *Titanic*."

He grinned.

It was an annoyingly good grin.

"I... this... you must be joking." I planted my hands on my

hips to give them something to do besides tear my hair out by the roots. "Tell me you're joking?"

"Not joking."

I was afraid of that.

The urge to bolt had never been stronger but, since I'd promised him I'd try not to do exactly that, I pushed it aside with brute force.

"You still freaking out?" he asked conversationally. Like we were discussing the weather.

"Yes," I hissed, teeth clenched. "I'm still freaking out. I plan on freaking out for the rest of time."

"Figured as much." He sipped his wine again, looking completely calm. "Let me know when you're done."

"Did you not hear what I said? *The rest of time.* That's when I'll be done."

"Uh huh."

"You can't move in," I informed him, feeling uppity in the face of his serenity. "We've been dating, like, five minutes."

"So?"

"So, that's not long enough to move in. That's not even long enough to call each other boyfriend and girlfriend. We haven't even had a proper date!"

He arched a dark brow. "You need labels for this?"

"No," I said, because, honestly, I didn't. "But—"

"As soon as your life isn't hanging in the balance, I'll make reservations." He narrowed his eyes at me. "Any more objections?"

"I.. It's..." I trailed off weakly. "It's too soon."

"Known you for years," he countered. "How is that too soon?"

"Two years is not exactly a lifetime. And most of those two years, if you recall, we were about as together as oil and vinegar."

That's when he hit me with the knockout, the southpaw, the

emotional blow to end all emotional blows. "Been a lot longer than two years, Firecracker, and you know it."

Firecracker.

The word rocked through me, sending me stumbling back into the counter. I caught myself on the edge just before I went down, gripping the butcher block so hard I thought my bones would snap. It took me a full minute to resume breathing, and another full minute after that to find the courage to lift my eyes up to his. He'd closed some of the distance between us while I had my silent panic attack and was now standing very still, arms crossed over his chest, watching me.

I croaked out a few words — the only ones I could manage. "You... you remember?"

"You thought I forgot?"

"Um..."

He shook his head and closed the gap between us, pulling me into his arms. His forehead came down on mine. "How could I ever forget you, Gwendolyn Goode? You're unforgettable. Always have been."

Goddess, I was going to need a lobotomy to get over this man.

I was breathing hard, nearly hyperventilating. "But... you never said anything."

"Neither did you." His voice gentled. "Figured you'd bring it up when you were ready."

My scoff was thick with incredulity. "You thought I'd casually broach the subject one day over tacos? That I'd blurt out, '*Hey, Graham, remember the gawky ginger kid who you saved from a sea urchin a million years ago? The one who used to stare at you with utter adoration every time she clapped eyes on you? The one who was constantly doing embarrassing shit whenever you looked her way? Yep! That was me!*' Seriously?"

"Not sure it would be over tacos, but, basically." He grinned at me. "*Utter adoration?*"

"You're annoying."

His grin didn't even waver. "Uh huh."

"I was young and naive!"

"Uh huh."

"I didn't know any better!"

"Uh huh."

"Oh, whatever," I snapped to cover my embarrassment. "You saved me from a sea urchin, did you really expect me not to develop a crush on you?"

"Nah. Sea urchins aside, every girl in town had a crush on me."

"Arrogant!"

"Maybe." His grin was so bright, it was blinding. "But you adore me. Utterly."

I rolled my eyes so hard I saw stars. I didn't retort, though. Mostly because... well... he was not wrong.

WE ATE dinner at Graham's loft — for the record, the salmon was Michelin-caliber — and afterward, since I was too full for gelato, he drove us back to my house. We didn't bother turning on the lights when we came in, moving directly upstairs to get ready for bed. It had been a long day. I was exhausted both physically and emotionally, especially after two glasses of wine and a delicious meal, not to mention several earth-shattering revelations courtesy of one Graham Seaton Graves.

He was quiet as he followed me up the stairs, then down the dark hallway toward my bedroom. He seemed to be in a contemplative mood, probably thinking about Madame Zelda's cache of stolen jewelry, sitting in a box somewhere up in the backwoods of Maine, or where he planned to hang his Picasso when he officially moved in. That's what I figured, anyway — until we stepped into my bedroom.

Snagging me around the waist with both arms, he spun me around. I didn't even have time to take a breath before his mouth hit mine. His kiss was hot, hungry, all consuming, and I suddenly realized he hadn't been planning a drive up to retrieve the O'Banions' property or pondering potential art placements.

Not even close.

Never breaking the kiss, his hands cupped my ass as he lifted me straight off my feet. My legs went around his waist and my arms wrapped around his neck as he walked me toward the bed. Planting a knee in the mattress, Graham flipped me onto it and came down on top of me, the delicious weight of his body setting off a tidal wave of desire in my veins.

I lost his weight and his heat for a moment as he shrugged out of his jacket and whipped off his t-shirt. He wasted no time in yanking off my boots, then peeling the clingy sweater dress up over my head and tossing it to a far corner of the room, leaving me only in a lacey, low-cut demi-bra and matching underwear.

"Fuck," he muttered, staring down at me in the lingerie. His breathing was uneven as his finger traced lightly over the peak of my right nipple, teasing it through the lace. "You particularly attached to this underwear, gorgeous?"

I loved when he called me gorgeous. I also, as it so happened, loved this underwear. It was from La Perla. It had cost a small fortune. It made my breasts and booty look fantastic. Hot as it would be for him to physically rip it off my body...

"Um," I breathed, sucking in a gasp as his fingers tugged sharply at my nipple. "Yes?"

"I'll buy you a new set," he muttered.

I didn't have time to protest before his body came back down on top of me and his mouth claimed mine again. Suddenly, I didn't care if he ripped my underwear. I wasn't even thinking about underwear. All my thoughts were caught up in Graham. His weight, his heat, his touch. He was like a drug, an addictive substance I could never get enough of, no matter how many hits I took, no matter how many fixes I got.

I reached for his chest, desperate to feel his warm, smooth skin beneath my fingers, but abruptly found my arms jerked up over my head, trapped in the confines of one of his large fists. I sucked in a breath, too surprised to fight against his grip as his weight pressed into me again, and too turned on to care as his lips landed on my neck. His mouth moved down the column of my throat, planting kisses against my skin, skimming a path of fire across my collarbone, licking lightly between the valley of my breasts.

He paused, lips lifting from my skin, and I made a small sound of protest, tilting my head to look down at him.

"Why did you stop?"

I caught a flash of white teeth in the dark as he grinned wolfishly in answer, then clamped down on my nipple through the lace. Gasping, I arched violently off the bed, pulling against his grip, which was still pinning my arms above my head. I wanted suddenly to touch him. To thread my fingers through his thick, dark hair and hold him close while his mouth did unspeakable things to my body.

Reading my mind, his hold finally disappeared. But before I could wind my arms around him, he'd slid out of reach, moving down to the end of the mattress. His fingers hooked in the waistband of my panties and, with one impatient tug, he yanked them down my legs and chucked them clear across the room, to join my dress. I gasped as a large hand circled each one of my ankles, yanking them apart. Baring me to him — completely.

"Christ, you're beautiful," Graham muttered, his burning gaze aimed directly between my legs. "I can't fucking wait to taste you. I'll never get enough."

I didn't even have time to catch my breath before my legs were jerked up over his shoulders, his head came down, and his mouth hit the target.

Hellfire.

Graham was good at everything, but he was especially good at this. I bit my lip to keep from screaming as he began to fuck me with his mouth. One of his hands spanned my ass, anchoring me firmly against his face, but the other found its way between my legs to join his mouth as he worked me over. He expertly thumbed my clit as his tongue speared deep inside me, gradually increasing his speed until I was bowing and squirming on the bed, lost in a sea of sensation. I felt the orgasm building, an unstoppable force that stole my breath and turned my bones to water.

"Hold still," Graham muttered, pulling back to bite my thigh, his teeth a sharp warning. "Or you don't get to finish."

"Please," I cried.

"Are you going to hold still like a good girl?"

"Y-yes."

"Say it."

"I'll be a good girl."

"Whose good girl?"

"Yours."

"Damn straight." He grinned. His lips were shining in the darkness, still wet. "*My* good girl."

His mouth dropped back between my legs, teeth scraping lightly over my hypersensitive center. That was all it took. I came, *hard*, the orgasm exploding through me, overriding all my senses. I think I actually may have blacked out for a moment, because by the time sanity returned, Graham was lying beside me, staring at my face in the dark. He wore a distinctly smug expression.

"Don't look so self-satisfied," I told him, still panting. "It's annoying."

"If anyone's satisfied here, it's you."

"Are you saying you're not satisfied?"

"On the contrary... hearing you admit you were mine was the most satisfied I've ever been."

Scowling, I made like I was going to get off the bed and storm away. Only, at the last second, I changed course, rolling to his side of the bed and straddling him instead. My elbows planted in the pillows on either side of his head. My hair fell around our faces in a thick curtain. I slowly lowered my body onto his. Through his jeans, he was hard as stone, the rigid length of him throbbing with need.

"Let's see if we can increase that satisfaction," I whispered, rubbing myself against his cock, slithering down his body until my face was level with his zipper. My teasing fingers found the button. "Shall we?"

With a growl, Graham yanked me back up, then flipped me over onto my back. His arms caged me in, his eyes glittered with heat. "Playtime is over. I need to fuck you now, Gwen."

"Patience is a virtue." I nipped at his earlobe with my teeth, sucking it slowly into my mouth. His whole frame shuddered in response, as though his control was hanging by the most precipitous of threads. "Don't make me beg."

"Gwen..."

"I want you in my mouth, baby," I breathed. "I want to play, just for a little bit."

He groaned and pressed against me, his cock throbbing as my hands worked his zipper down.

"Then, I want you to fuck me until I forget my own name," I continued. "I want you to fuck me until you forget yours, too."

"Christ," he muttered, rolling off me. For a panicked second, I thought he was going to walk away. A surge of heat rolled through me when I realized he was only shoving off his jeans.

"You can play later," he informed me as his cock sprang free, bossy as ever. "Right now, I'm going to bury myself inside you because, baby, watching you come just now, then hearing you beg to suck me off and fuck you into oblivion... that's about more than I can take without losing my fucking mind."

Wowza.

When he settled back between my legs, I gasped at the feeling of him with nothing to separate us. Hard, huge... and mine.

All mine.

"Firecracker," he said, his voice a low rasp of passion. "I don't care if you forget your own name. So long as you don't forget who you belong to."

I had no chance to comment on the deeply possessive comment before he thrust into me, sheathing himself to the hilt, filling me until I thought I might shatter in two. Frankly, from that point onward, I was in no state to care about his possessive streak. My mind went blank as he began to move, his hips thrusting long and hard and deep, driving me slowly toward the edge of euphoria.

I wrapped my arms and legs around him, holding my body to his, wishing I could disappear inside his skin. Fuse myself to him irreparably, so this moment would never disappear. So we would never disappear.

"God," Graham gasped, kissing me hard. "You feel so fucking amazing. Nothing in the world better than this. Right here. Inside you."

I kissed him back, unable to articulate everything I was feeling. It was all I could do to hold on as his pace increased to a pounding, punishing rhythm that made me dizzy with need. I could feel another orgasm building deep within my core as the hollow ache he'd created inside me filled up with passion once more.

"Gwen," he said, eyes locked with mine, the green bright enough to scald. "Come with me."

"Y-yes."

He drove deeper, so deep it bordered on painful, but in the best sort of way. My eyes pricked with tears, not from discomfort but from the sheer magnitude of what I was feeling. I was holding my breath, balanced on my tiptoes, standing on a tightrope, a hairsbreadth from plummeting into a swallowing abyss.

I could build a whole world around this feeling.

Around this passion.

Around this man.

The thought hit me the same moment my orgasm did.

"Are you there, baby?" Graham groaned.

"I'm there," I cried, clenching tighter around him as I fell off the tightrope, spiraling straight down into the depths of passion, a brilliant free-fall. And he followed me over — shouting my name as he climaxed, pouring into me, pump after pump, thrust after thrust, until my frazzled nerve endings were singing with hypersensitivity and my body felt wrung out, boneless and breathless and completely content in a way I'd never felt before.

Not once.

Not ever.

I could build my whole world around this man, I thought again as the aftershocks racked me. *I really could.*

My lips pressed against the skin of his chest, directly over his heart, which was beating just as fast as my own.

Maybe I already have.

AFTERWARD, we lay tangled together the dark, limbs wrapped tight around one another. Graham's lips rested at my temple, his breaths still ragged as his thudding heartbeat slowed back to a normal tempo. He pressed a kiss there, then began to detangle himself.

"It's late, baby," he whispered.

I recognized the start of what had become our goodnight ritual. He was getting ready to go sleep in the other room, leaving me alone to face the night in solitude. Respecting my boundaries, just as I'd requested.

All my life, I'd panicked at the thought of sleeping with someone else. But this time, in this instant, something inside me panicked at an entirely different reason. The thought of Graham getting out of my bed, walking down the hall to sleep alone on the cold, hard floor, suddenly seemed like the most unfathomable thing in the world.

Instead of letting him walk away from me, I sat up with him, pressed my bare breasts against his solid back, and wrapped my arms tight around his middle.

"Gwen?"

"Stay," I whispered against his skin.

His body tensed. "What?"

"Stay. I want you to stay."

There was a long pause. Even unable to see his face, I could tell he was fighting for control of his emotions, trying to get a hold on whatever feelings were raging inside him. When he spoke again, his voice was thicker than I'd ever heard it. "You sure, baby?"

"Please." I pressed a soft kiss to the blade of his shoulder, my words hushed. "Stay with me. Sleep with me. I don't want to spend seven hours of my day out of your arms, away from you, even if I'm unconscious. Not anymore. Not ever again."

I didn't need to tell him twice.

In a blink, he'd wrapped me in his embrace, rolling us onto our sides so we lay facing one another in the dark. With one finger, he reached up and tucked a loose tendril of hair behind my ear. There was a look on his face I'd never seen before. Something like wonderment. Something like... *love*. And, seeing it there, I didn't freak out. I didn't demand space. I didn't feel the urge to bolt.

I did, however, scoot closer, snuggling into his warmth. My eyes closed as his hand came up to cup the back of my head, holding me against him. And, with the steady beat of Graham's heart beneath my ear, I did something I never in a million years would've guessed was possible for a girl like me.

I fell asleep.

CHAPTER TWENTY-FOUR

Not today, Satan.
I'm free tomorrow, though.
- Gwen Goode, dealing with the devil

"That will be $6.66," I told the woman, glancing up from the cash register to slide her bag of bundled sage across the counter.

"Oh, I don't like that. *666*? Nope. Not today, Satan." She grabbed a handful of pocket-sized crystals from the basket on her left and plunked them down in front of me. "Better throw these in, too. In the name of the Lord."

I adjusted her total, accepted payment, and sent her on her way with a "See you on the other side!" The cash register was barely closed when another customer appeared before me.

"How's it hanging? Find everything you were looking for? Oh, a bottle of Flex on Your Ex! That's a good choice, he'll regret he ever let you go..."

And so it had gone all day.

All week, in fact.

It was ten days to Halloween and the store was slammed — wall to wall people drinking coffee, buying books, sniffing incense, asking about our extensive herb collection. The town's Haunted Happenings committee was projecting over a million visitors this October, smashing even last year's record of 900,000 — a statistic I didn't doubt in the slightest. Sales were so good, I'd been forced to place an emergency inventory order from our local suppliers. (We'd run out of to-go coffee cups on two separate occasions, a crisis that nearly caused a riot.) The hipsters and college kids who'd come to know The Gallows as a chill place to study or waste a few hours between classes were nowhere to be seen, temporarily supplanted by out-of-towners. I had no doubt that come November 1st they'd be back, abusing my free refills policy and camping out on my comfy armchairs.

Assuming I was still here, that is.

As the calendar counted down to Samhain, I grew more and more nervous, more and more paranoid. Even with video surveillance at the shop, drive-by security at the house, and Graham practically fused to my side during the hours I wasn't stuck behind a cash register, I felt like a hapless winged creature caught at the center of an invisible web — one that seemed to be tightening around me a bit more with each passing day. Somewhere in that web, there was a spider. I couldn't see it, but I could sure as hell sense it creeping closer, waiting patiently for the moment it would finally sink its venomous fangs into my flesh and suck me dry.

Shivering, I forced a smile as I turned to my next customer. "Welcome to The Gallows! I'm Gwen, your friendly neighborhood executioner. How can I help you today?"

Other than the small, *tiny*, concern that was my imminent demise, the rest of my life was sorting itself out rather nicely.

Things with Graham had never been better. He'd spent the past few days holed up in my soon-to-be library, tinkering, taking measurements, sketching out plans, and eventually disappearing to the hardware store for several hours, only to return with a metric ton of lumber strapped to the roof of his Bronco. I was under strict orders not to look inside the room until it was finished, which, according to my personal carpenter-slash-body-guard-slash-quasi-boyfriend, could take a couple of weeks. It was safe to say, the curiosity was effectively killing me. (Just what I needed — more threats of death looming overhead.)

My heart gave an unpleasant pang of longing at the thought of Graham. I hadn't seen him since yesterday morning. (Nearly thirty-six straight hours of deprivation! Not that I was counting, or anything.) He'd gone up to Maine to retrieve the O'Banions' stolen property from Jackie Custer, aka Madame Zelda's older sister, and evidently run into some snags. This didn't entirely surprise me, seeing as the Custer family gene pool skipped all the helpful, compliant traits in favor of sheer obstinance. However, he must've prevailed eventually, because the text I'd received from him this morning assured me he'd be back by tonight.

This was a relief, seeing as we had plans. *Fun* plans. Some might even call them *epic* plans. And I wasn't just talking about the party.

Florence had called a few days ago with the good news. She and Des had decided to move up their annual costume bash to tonight since we wouldn't be able to celebrate on the actual holi-day, on account of me being the target of bloodthirsty witches. I wasn't exactly sure how Graham intended to keep me safe on that fateful day... though I had a nagging suspicion it would involve a short stay in the holding cell at Gravewatch, under the watchful gaze of his legion of badasses. (Hopefully, Zelda was cool being the big spoon on the tiny twin bed.)

My costume was ready to go, waiting for me in a bag in the

back office so I could change the minute our last customer left and head straight to the townhouse. Florence needed help setting up the decorations, as well as supervision mixing the party punch. Last year, she'd made it so strong it was damn near toxic.

I fought the urge to check the clock for the hundredth time, knowing closing time was still several hours away. I wasn't sure if I was more excited for the party or for Graham to finally be back home. Probably the latter, if I was being honest with myself. Quite frankly, I missed him like hell. For a girl who'd never wanted to sleep with anyone else, *ever*, I'd grown rapidly accustomed to spending the night in Graham's strong arms, to waking up and seeing his face the instant my eyes peeled open. (I would also be remiss in failing to point out the undeniable merits of morning nookie.)

I didn't know what was wrong with me. It hadn't even been two full days. But even a few hours without seeing his grin, hearing his laugh, feeling his touch was difficult to endure. I was strung out as a junkie who'd gone too long without a fix, jonesing for a dose only he could deliver.

Goddess above. Get a grip, Gwendolyn!

I finished up with my customer — who purchased her body weight in crystals along with a stunning, vintage deck of tarot cards from the 1940s that cost more than my college tuition — and in the brief break between sales allowed my eyes to drift toward the front of the store where Holden and Hunter were camped out on my plush emerald sofa, glaring at everyone who stepped through the door.

The twins had been assigned to keep watch over me in Graham's absence. I'm sure they had more important things to do with their time than sit at The Gallows for two straight days. Even so, it was clear they took their orders seriously. The second I'd stepped out my front door yesterday morning, they'd appeared — an intimidating show of force in black leather, dark denim, and combat boots. I tried to memorize what they were wearing, since I couldn't tell them apart otherwise. They were truly identical, their faces a perfect mirror, from their sharp cheekbones to their thick lashes to the distinctive green flecks in their inky, intense eyes. I was glad I was so head-over-heels for their big brother because, *wowza*, if I'd been single, I would have been in serious trouble.

It had not escaped my notice that many of my female customers were lingering longer than strictly necessary this afternoon, nursing empty cappuccino cups, browsing the front table of books that just so happened to be closest to the sofa where Holden and Hunter were sprawled. Yesterday had been very much the same — a full fledged ogle-fest from open to close.

The twins, to their credit, did not indulge this blatant infatuation, or even seem to notice it. They kept their eyes peeled for potential threats, fielded occasional phone calls, and otherwise, kept silent and still on the sofa by my spooky window display. Between the two of them, they'd said approximately five words to me all day.

A terse '*Get in the car*' from Holden when I'd walked to the curb and firm '*No*' from Hunter when I'd offered to bring them one of Hetti's delicious caffeinated confections. (I guess they weren't pumpkin spice fans.) I tried not to take it personally. Sure, they were taciturn and intimidating as hell... but there was no denying they were also shockingly good for business. Half the XX chromosomes in Salem were currently wandering around my shop, finding excuses to hover — usually, in the form of unnecessary purchases.

The front door swung open for the thousandth time with a tinkle of bells and, as always, the twins went instantly on alert, their bodies tensing like snakes coiling in preparation to strike.

Two female forms glided inside. I knew from one glance they weren't here to peruse my goods or stare with undisguised longing at the men lounging in my cafe. Their black-on-black funeral attire, large brimmed hats, and tear-stained eyes gave them away in a heartbeat.

I stood rooted in place behind the mystical curiosities counter as they cut a path through the front section of the shop, descended down the two mahogany steps, and came to a stop before me.

"Agatha, Sally," I said in greeting, my throat thick. "I'm... It's... I'm glad to see you."

"Gwendolyn." Agatha's voice was stiff with formality and grief. "We're on our way to Eliza's viewing."

I'd heard the services were being held at a funeral parlor across town, with a burial to follow tomorrow morning at a nearby cemetery. It didn't feel appropriate to attend, given that I hadn't really known Elizabeth Proctor particularly well. There was also the small fact that, technically, I was still a person of interest in her murder. (Despite the Gravewatch surveillance footage that proved I'd been at the shop doing inventory during her estimated time of death, Detective Hightower had told me not to leave town until the investigation was complete.)

In any case, I thought it would be better for everyone if I paid my respects at the gravesite once she was buried and the crowds had dispersed. It had been weeks since I visited Aunt Colette's headstone, anyway. I was due to bring her some fresh calla lilies — her favorite — and fill her in on the insanity that was my life of late.

"I'm so sorry about Eliza. I know how close the three of you were..." I swallowed hard, my eyes moving from Agatha to Sally and back. "And I know you must blame me."

"We don't blame you, child," Sally murmured kindly. Her

eyes shone with unshed tears. "This feud belongs to the Bay Colony Coven. Don't take it on your shoulders."

"Eliza knew the risks," Agatha chimed in. "She chose to make herself known to an old enemy — one we made long before you ever came to town. We do not hold you responsible for what happened to her."

My heart clenched, a sharp squeeze inside my chest that made it difficult to breathe. I hadn't known how much I wanted their forgiveness until they gave it; hadn't realize how much I craved their absolution until it was handed to me.

"Thank you," I said, trying not to let my emotions get the best of me. "You don't know how much hearing that means to me."

"Just because we don't hold you responsible for what's happened doesn't mean you are free and clear. The Heretics are still out there. They will move against you — against all of us — sooner than you think."

"Samhain," I whispered, nodding. "I know. I thought about the past sacrifices and realized they must be following the lunar calendar."

They glanced at one another.

"Perhaps there is hope for you, yet," Agatha muttered grudgingly.

"Colette instilled in you the fundamentals, at the very least." Sally graced me with a tiny smile. "She would be happy to know you haven't entirely abandoned her teachings."

"I may not strictly believe in the witchy woo-woo, not the same way you do, but that doesn't mean I'm totally close-minded. Do you really think, after what happened to Eliza, that I'd question the danger the Heretics pose?"

They were silent. Clearly, they didn't have much faith in me after my previous pig-headedness when it came to this subject.

I swallowed down a heavy sigh. "I know I didn't take this

seriously when you first tried to warn me. But I promise I'm taking it seriously now. When Halloween arrives, I'll have ample protection to keep me out of their creepy little hands. You don't need to worry."

They exchanged another glance, conducting an entire conversation without a single word uttered aloud, the way only close friends could. I wondered if, in sixty years, Flo and I would still be talking with eye rolls and head tilts across crowded rooms. I sincerely hoped so.

"You must understand, Gwendolyn. Even if you don't believe in the *witchy woo-woo*, as you so affectionately refer to our sacred practices... the witchy woo-woo believes in you. The Heretics will do everything they can to reclaim the power they believe we bound fifty years ago, to unleash their dark revenge on the entire town in retribution for being cast out. And it is your Aunt Colette's blood — *your* blood — they need to do so. You are the key which will unlock the door to devastation."

"*Figures,*" I muttered lowly. A line of customers was forming behind Sally and Agatha, but I ignored it. "Look, ladies, I appreciate you coming here today. But like I told you, I am well protected."

"How?" Agatha sounded skeptical. "You have no power."

I pointed at the twins on the couch — only to realize they were no longer sitting there. Sometime during our confrontation, they'd crossed through the shop without my noticing. They now stood in silence several feet behind Agatha and Sally, looking every inch the bone-snapping, gun-toting badasses I'd promised. Muscular arms crossed over their chests, inky eyes intent, full attention trained on us as they shamelessly eavesdropped on every word we exchanged.

Agatha and Sally both gaped a little at my devastatingly handsome bodyguards.

"See?" My lips turned up at the corners. "Totally in good hands."

Agatha, with considerable effort, pulled her gaze back to mine. "Be that as it may... be careful. Eliza's loss was a harsh blow to our coven's collective strength — as the Heretics well know, which was why they targeted her in the first place. But we are not entirely depleted. Nor will we sit idly by on Samhain. We are gathering our forces. When the Heretics make their move, we will be ready to meet them in kind."

"We may not prevail, but we have a duty to try," Sally added. "For you. For Colette. For Eliza."

I stared at the two little old ladies, with their wrinkled cheeks and coiffed gray curls peeking out from their wide-brimmed hats, wondering what sort of forces they could possibly summon to effectively combat a sect of crazed killers with a penchant for bloody pentagrams. If I was thinking rationally, I might've said they were deluded. But, honestly, in that moment, all could think was that they were a heck of a lot braver than most people I'd ever met.

"We need to go, Sally," Agatha said. "We're going to be late for Eliza's viewing."

"Okay, okay," Sally muttered. But she didn't go. Instead, she took a step closer to the counter — making both twins tense — and pulled something from her pocketbook. "Here, Gwendolyn. Please, take this. It once belonged to your aunt. She would've wanted you to have it."

Before I could move a single inch, Sally leaned forward across the counter and slipped a thin silver chain over my head. I felt a warm weight settle against the bare skin between my breasts and, when I looked down at my cleavage, I saw a pale colored pendant shaped like a spike and engraved with strange symbols resting just above the plunging v-neck of my blouse.

"A bone shard from the first High Priestess of our coven," Sally explained, her voice barely a whisper. "For protection."

I wasn't sure how a necklace was supposed to protect me, but I didn't see the point in quibbling. Belatedly, my mind processed the first part of Sally's description. "Wait. I'm sorry — did you say *bone shard*? As in... from a *skeleton*?"

"Indeed." Sally was unruffled. "Chiseled from the femur of your own ancestor, Sarah Goode."

My brows rose. "The Sarah Goode killed during the Witch Trials?"

"The very same," Agatha said.

I lifted my hand to touch the pendant. The tip was remarkably sharp. The strange witchy sigils were etched deep into the bone. It reminded me of an ivory elephant tusk, carved with meticulous care. Creepy as it was, there was no denying it was beautifully crafted.

"Thank you," I forced myself to say as my hand closed around it. "For this. And... for keeping me safe. I wish..." I thought of Eliza and my eyes began to tingle. "I wish we'd met under different circumstances. I wish... a lot of things."

"Me too, dear," Sally whispered.

"Can't change the past. No use fretting over it," Agatha added.

"Maybe..." My voice was hesitant. "Maybe after Samhain, we could get together? Have tea, talk a bit. I'd love to hear more about Aunt Colette, Eliza, the whole coven. I'm sure you have stories."

"More than an afternoon's worth, child." Sally brightened visibly, her eyes twinkling. "I'll bake my cheesecake. With the raspberry preserve. And I'll teach you canasta. Have you ever played?"

I shook my head.

"Sally, you're terrible at canasta. You cheat!" Agatha glared at her friend, but there was no heat behind it. "If anyone's teaching her, it'll be me."

"You? Teach her?" Sally's eyes rolled. "You're so demented, you forget half the rules!"

"Better demented than deceitful!" Agatha retorted.

"For the last time, I do not cheat!" Sally cried, indignant. "Has it ever occurred to you I'm just a more advanced player?"

"Oh, you're advanced all right," Agatha muttered. "In *years*. On your last birthday, the candles were more expensive than the cake."

With effort, I managed to keep my giggles from bursting out. Instead, I cut in with a choked, "Don't you need to get going, ladies?"

"Oh, hell's bells!" Sally screeched. "Look at the time! Let's go, Ag, move it or lose it!" She glanced back at me briefly. "Be safe, Gwendolyn."

"We'll be in touch," Agatha grumbled, her voice far less stiff than when she'd first arrived. With that, she turned on a heel and headed for the exit.

Sally followed shortly in her wake, but not before she'd reached across the counter and clasped her hand around mine in a warm, maternal squeeze that made my heart clench. I watched them go, one hand clutching the bone pendant, the other planted against the display case in front of me, worried for their safety far more than my own. *They* didn't have a squad of badass Gravewatch men watching their six, after all.

When the front door shut behind them, I finally turned toward the twins. They were standing a handful of feet away, watching me with those all-consuming eyes that seemed to see straight into my soul. I gulped air in an effort not to backpedal away. The moment stretched on for a small infinity as I waited for them to say something — *anything* — that clued me in to their thoughts. Given the conversation they'd just overheard, I half-expected them to tell me I was a total nutcase.

"Graham has good taste," one of them, I still couldn't tell which, said finally, his deep rasp making me jump like a spooked horse.

Then, after that bomb-drop, they too turned and walked away from me, drawing the eyes of every woman in the shop as they did so. A collective feminine sigh of appreciation sounded from all sides as they settled their chiseled forms on the sofa at the front. With a sigh of my own, I glanced at my watch.

Barely noon.

It was going to be a long freaking day.

FIVE AND A HALF HOURS LATER, I was working in tandem with Hetti behind the espresso bar. She'd run completely out of milk, the demand was so high — and believe you me, the twins were *not* happy when I tasked one of them to run to the store around the corner for emergency supplies. Probably because I'd already asked them to go pick up our lunch order a few hours earlier at Life Alive, a vegetarian spot so delicious, I didn't even mind that it was health food. (This request had resulted in Hunter informing me he was, and I quote, 'Not a fucking errand boy.' Nonetheless, he'd stomped out and returned ten minutes later with my kale salad bowl, Hetti's sesame ginger wrap, and two vibrant green chlorophyll shots.)

It must be said, the matching glares the twins leveled at me on both occasions were enough to make me think they were regretting their earlier assessment about Graham's good taste in girlfriends.

"Twenty minutes till close," I muttered, stocking the last

carton of almond milk inside the fridge. "We can totally handle this. Right, Hetti?"

She, too, leveled a severe glare at me.

Whatever.

Her mood, already on a downward spiral, declined precipitously when the door bells chimed again, and yet another customer stepped up to the counter. I saw a flash of white and red stripes and braced myself for the booming voice I knew would undoubtedly follow.

"Ahoy down there, Gwendolyn!"

I popped up from behind the counter where I'd been crouched, slamming the fridge shut with my foot. "Hi, Peg-Leg Pete! How's it hanging?"

The pirate didn't answer. His gaze had already shifted away from me to stare with what could only be described as unadulterated adoration at my barista, as though he'd never seen anything in the entire universe so beautiful as a goth girl with bright purple hair, a silver septum piercing, and so much eyeliner, it would shock Amy Winehouse herself.

"Fair Henrietta," Peg-Leg Pete whispered, reverence plain as day. "How do you fare, today?"

Ignoring his question, she asked one of her own. "Can I get you something? Macchiato? Cappuccino? Latte? Lobotomy?"

I snorted.

"I don't suppose you have rum?" Pete asked.

She glared at him.

He didn't seem to notice her glare. He was still smiling, borderline delirious with joy as his eyes — actually, *eye*, singular, seeing as the other one was concealed behind a black patch — scanned her face. "You know, lass, I've sailed the seven seas, traipsed lands far and wide across this world, and never seen a beauty like yours."

Hetti's eyes narrowed. *"Far and wide?* Aren't you from Peabody?"

Pete, to his credit, ignored this. "I may be but a poor sea dog, but I swear I'd face down the kraken for a chance to take you on a sunset sail. Savvy?"

"Pass."

Pete's expression crumpled a bit at her instant rejection. "Has another already laid claim to your heart? Tell me the scurvy dog's name! I'll cleave him to the brisket! Let him face me like a man, or walk the plank like a lily-livered coward!"

"Dude." Hetti's eyes flashed up and down, from his drooping eyepatch to the fake wooden leg fashioned over his pants. "I don't want *anything* to do with your plank."

The very picture of heartbreak, Pete glanced at me and shook his head slowly back and forth. "Bloody wenches. Can't live with 'em, can't live without 'em."

Oh no.

Calling any woman a wench was a bad idea. Calling a woman like my barista a wench? That could prove catastrophic.

As predicted, Hetti's throat loosed a low rattle. Fearing she might launch herself across the espresso bar and unleash her deep well of pent-up feminine rage on the pirate, I chose this moment to wade into the conversation.

"What's that you've got there, Pete?" I asked, eyeing the stack of glossy pamphlets in his spindly arms.

"Ah! Right. When our bows last crossed, you said to bring some vouchers by. Half-off admittance at the museum." He shrugged and set them down on the counter. "I'm hoping they're enough to turn the tides. Blimey, business is sinking so fast, we'll soon be fish food."

I took the vouchers, with promises to pass them out to all our future customers, and waved off a dejected Pete as he moped to the exit. With one final longing glance at Hetti, he disappeared.

"You know, you could do worse," I told her when he was gone. "He's a nice guy, if you can get past the whole Jack Sparrow bit. I wonder if he stays in character in bed..."

"Shut up!" she snarled.

"What? I'm genuinely curious." My lips twitched as I attempted to suppress my laughter. "Honestly, Hetti... do you think he screams *'yo-ho-ho'* when he comes?"

On the nearby sofa, the twins both chuckled.

My barista was not as amused. Based on the answering glare she shot at me, I was grateful looks could not, in fact, kill. Because if they could, I'd be on the floor bleeding out.

IT WASN'T until we closed for business that I had a chance to look at Peg-Leg Pete's pamphlets. I'd passed out a handful to our final customers of the day and was stacking the remaining glossy tri-folds back into an orderly pile — I was on counter cleanup while Hetti handled the high top tables — when curiosity tugged at me. I grabbed the top pamphlet and peeked at the contents. They were surprisingly high quality, with pictures of the museum's attractions inside, along with the words WITCH CITY'S ORIGINAL PIRATE MUSEUM in old-timey red font across the front. A small perforated admittance coupon tore away from the bottom section. A full color map of Salem took up the entirety of the back panel. On the location of the museum, there was a bright red X, accompanied by the words *"X marks the spot!"*

I'd nearly set the pamphlet back down on the stack when my hand froze midair. My eyes bored into the map as something deep in the recesses of my brain clicked into place.

X marks the spot.

Not taking my gaze off the map, I reached blindly for a marker in the container by the cash register. Slowly, as though my hand didn't even belong to me, I began to draw them. A series of Xs, scattered all across town. One at the dog park. One at Palmer Cove. One at Gallows Hill. One at Bertram Field. One at the alleyway behind my shop. All the animal sacrifices, dotted randomly across Salem.

But it wasn't so random. Not anymore. Not now that I could see the pattern — one I'd missed before, one I hadn't known to look for. My hand shook a bit as I drew a series of lines to connect the X's, dragging the tip of the marker on a diagonal slant up, then down, then up, then across, until I'd formed the shape of a star. I nearly chewed through my bottom lip as I finished the symbol, looping my pen in a perfect oval, enclosing the shape I'd drawn.

A star within a circle.

A pentagram.

A perfect pentagram, interposed on the city.

Hellfire.

I couldn't believe I hadn't seen it before. Setting down the pen, which I'd begun to grip so hard my knuckles turned white, I traced my fingertip along the star's sectors, coming to rest directly at the center of the pentagram. There was a landmark there, marked in tiny font that made my blood run cold.

Broad Street Cemetery.

I'd been there before, years ago. It wasn't far from the center of town, but it was slightly off the beaten track; not as popular amongst the tourists as The Burying Point where Eliza's body was found, but still historically relevant, since a handful of important Witch Trial era figures were entombed there. The longer I stared at the small green patch on the map, the greater my sense of foreboding. Cold sweat broke out on the back of my neck and a shiver moved down my spine.

There must be a reason this location was at the center of the Heretic's macabre pentagram of sacrifices. Whatever they were planning for Samhain... chances were, it would happen there. I needed to tell Graham ASAP, the minute I saw him. This was a clue. A real, tangible clue, the first we'd had in a while. Maybe the clue we needed to crack the whole case wide open!

I was staring so intently at the map, I didn't hear Hetti approach. When she spoke, she was directly beside me, so near I almost jumped out of my skin.

"What's that?"

"Shit!" My hand flew to my heart. "You scared me!"

The barista's eyes were still locked on the pamphlet. The pentagram I'd sketched out was clearly visible, the dark ink a bold contrast to the colorful map. "What is that, boss?"

"Oh. Um... nothing really. I was just doodling."

"Doodling," she murmured, finally looking at me. Her expression was dubious.

"Um. Yeah." I swallowed hard. "Anyway, you're free to go home for the night. Hunter and Holden are grabbing those boxes of books from the storeroom so I can restock. I can handle the rest of the clean-up."

"Are you still going to your party?"

"Yep, I'm heading straight there after I change into my costume." I paused. "Are you sure you don't want to come? It's going to be fun, I promise."

I'd been trying — and failing — for days to convince Hetti to attend Florence and Desmond's party.

"Pass."

"Suit yourself." I grinned at her, but it felt weak. My head was still spinning. It took effort to keep my eyes from moving to the map again. "Have a good night, Hetti."

"I think I will," she said rather mysteriously. "Goodbye, Gwen."

She took the trash with her when she left — goddess, she really needed a raise — and I headed into the back room. I passed by Hunter and Holden — each carrying a heavy box of books like it weighed no more than a feather — as I went.

"I'm going to change, then we can head out," I informed them. "You know, there's still time for you guys to pull together a costume. There are like three Halloween stores on the way to the townhouse. Oh, I know! Maybe we can get one of those tandem dog suits so you can be Scooby! One of you will be the head, the other the butt..." I trailed off at the frosty looks this suggestion received. "Fine, fine. No costumes for you. No need to scowl at me."

They kept walking.

"Just set those by the bestseller table," I tasked, pausing on the threshold of the storeroom. "If you get the urge to restock in my absence, make sure to put the book on moon phases by the front. It's selling like hotcakes."

They were silent. Apparently, moon phases weren't their thing. But I heard a thud as the boxes hit the floor, and grinned as I saw them beginning to unload the glossy hardcovers.

"Thanks, boys!" I called. "You know, if things don't work out with the whole PI gig, you can work here. My payroll probably isn't competitive with your brother's, but you can't deny, The Gallows is way safer than Gravewatch."

Two low grunts drifted back at me as the twins continued to arrange the books in orderly rows on my display table.

Stifling a giggle, I stepped into the back room and prepared for my transformation into Daphne Blake, girl detective and fashion icon. But even as I changed into my long sleeved purple dress, green neck scarf, lilac headband, and knee-high go-go boots, my thoughts were on the map I'd shoved into my purse for safekeeping. On Broad Street Cemetery. On what would potentially unfold there in ten short days.

And that invisible web of danger around me seemed to tighten all the more.

CHAPTER TWENTY-FIVE

The holy water is supposed to hiss when it hits
your skin, right?
— Gwen Goode, asking for a friend

The streets were a veritable mob scene, more crowded than I'd ever seen them. It was Friday night and the countdown to Halloween had officially begun. I kept between Hunter and Holden, the center of a badass sandwich, as we started walking toward the townhouse, my head whipping back and forth as I took in the utter pandemonium erupting all around me.

The crowd of tourists was so dense, even with the twins glaring at anyone in our immediate path, it took three times as long as usual to wind a path down the pedestrian mall. We passed a family dressed as aliens, their faces obscured by thick green grease paint. A street performer in a scarily convincing Michael Myers costume was collecting tips in exchange for jump-scares. Pennywise, the freakish clown from Steven King's *It*, was taking photographs with squealing teenagers. Freddy Krooner was singing a cover of *Creep* by Radiohead.

Fitting.

Everyone around us seemed to be in costume. It was a blur of rubber masks, colorful face paint, fake vampire teeth, and pointed witch hats. Everything you could think of, from the Addams family to the zombie horde, was out in full force. It was thrilling, if a bit claustrophobic. Spooky music drifted from open shop doors, combining with the swell of chatter into a cacophony of noise. White mist poured from fog machines, adding an eerie effect to the evening. A luminous full moon shone overhead, illuminating what otherwise would've been a very dark night.

Tired of fighting our way through the throngs, we cut down a side alley that led away from the congestion of revelers. Coincidentally, it was the same one I'd been on when I got witchy-roofied by Sally, Agatha, and Eliza weeks ago.

Goddess, was that only weeks ago?

It felt like a lifetime. So much had changed since that night. *I* had changed since that night. I was embracing commitment instead of running from it. And I was falling in love with Graham instead of hating his guts. Though, the verb tense in that latter part was somewhat in question.

Was I falling?

Or had I already fallen?

I was jerked out of my musings when Holden and Hunter jolted to a sudden stop. A hand clamped down on my elbow, halting me in my tracks. I didn't have a chance to ask what was going on — and I didn't need to, as the reason became abruptly clear. Four gargantuan men unfolded from the shadows at the mouth of the alley, blocking our exit to the street. They were all of similar coloring, with bushy red beards and huge, ham-sized fists.

The O'Banion brothers, in the flesh.

Both twins instantly closed rank around me, so close I could feel the heat off their bodies. Tension poured off them in waves, but their expressions were carefully blank.

"We got a problem here?" Hunter asked, eyeing the four men as they approached, coming to a stop about ten feet away.

"Your brother has been sticking his nose in shit that doesn't concern him," Mickey spat, his voice fury-laced. "So, yeah, we got problems. Starting with *her*."

My mouth went totally dry as his narrowed stare shifted to lock on mine. The look in his eyes promised pain. A *lot* of it.

"Your problem is with my brother, not with her," Holden said lowly.

One of the other O'Banion boys stepped up to Mickey's side. "She's his bitch, ain't she?"

My head snapped back like he'd slapped me across the face. Both twins tensed. Either they didn't like him calling me a bitch or they didn't like him getting so close to me. Probably a little bit of both.

"Yeah," Mickey confirmed, still staring at me. "She's fucking Graves. She's also the psychic's boss."

"I'm not her boss!" I snapped without thinking. "I told you before, we have a symbiotic thing going on, like a sea anen—"

"Gwen," Hunter cut me off, flicking out his hand palm-downward in a terse *shut-it* gesture. "Not now."

My lips clamped shut.

"We want the psychic bitch," one of the other O'Banions chimed in, stepping fully out of the shadows. He was even bigger than Mickey and, judging by the scars on his face from a life of bar fights, a good deal meaner. "We know you're protecting her."

"That so?" Holden asked.

Another brother stepped forward. He had a tattoo lacing up the side of his neck and the coldest eyes I'd ever seen. "Mickey made a deal with your brother. He broke that deal. Went his own way. Now, he thinks he can work around us, give back the jewelry Zelda took instead of handing her over like we wanted? And we're just gonna sit by with our thumbs in our asses and... what? Say bygones? All good? Thanks for dicking us over?" He shook his head. "Nah. Fuck that. Fuck you. Fuck your brother." His eyes slid back to mine and a scary light entered them. "And fuck his bitch, too, while I'm at it. That part, I might enjoy."

I shivered.

Holden's jaw clenched.

Hunter's hand on my arm tightened.

The other brother, the scar-faced one, smiled. It was a cruel, evil little smile, the kind that made my skin crawl. "Shane's right. We aren't interested in letting the psychic walk. Not after what she did. Need to teach the cunt a lesson."

The one with the neck tattoo grunted in an agreement. "Forgive and forget is not how we handle things."

"Good thing you're not handling this, then," Hunter said, his voice carefully controlled, revealing none of his emotions.

This retort did not please the brothers.

"Listen up, you fuckwad, 'cause I ain't saying it again." The fourth brother, the biggest of them all, spoke in a deep rumble. "This goes one of two ways. One, you give us the psychic, we deal with her, we don't retaliate against you for butting into our business. Two, you don't do exactly as we say, we break your fingers one by one, take your brother's bitch back to The Banshee, and see how she enjoys a bit of our Irish hospitality."

All the blood left my face. I swayed a bit, but Hunter steadied me.

"I'm thinking we take her regardless," Mickey said, staring at me. "Insurance policy. Your brother gets his bitch back when we get the psychic. Fair trade."

"We'll make sure she's well taken care of," Neck-Tattoo promised, his insinuation unmistakable. "Come on over here, honey. I'll show you what a real man feels like. By the time I'm done, you won't even want to go back to Graves' bed."

Hunter's grip grew painfully tight on my arm. My stomach was a ball of pure lead. I was thankful I'd eaten nothing since my salad at lunch, because it would've come right back up.

"Third way this goes," Holden hissed, leaning forward a bit, eyes locked on Mickey's. "Any of you touch a fucking hair on her head, you've got war with Gravewatch. You want that?"

The brothers glanced at one another. They were smart enough, it seemed, to recognize that this would be a bad thing for them. Unfortunately, they were not smart enough to back off.

"Big words when you're so outnumbered," Neck-Tattoo snarled, stepping closer. "Four against two, tonight."

If I hadn't been so scared, I might've noted my surprise that he knew how to count. As it was, since I was about two seconds away from peeing my purple Mystery Inc tights, I kept silent.

"Like our odds just fine," Hunter noted darkly.

"Come on. Try us," Holden taunted, just as darkly. He sounded like he wanted the O'Banions to do precisely that. He was itching for a fight, I could tell. But he wouldn't throw the first punch — not with me in the mix, at least.

"You give her to us now or you'll regret it later," Scar-Face warned.

"Lot of regrets in my life," Holden said. "Doubt that'll be joining the list, though."

"You Gravewatch boys think your shit don't stink," Neck-Tattoo snarled, clenching his ham-sized fists at his sides. "You don't make the rules around here."

"We run this town." Mickey scowled. "Always have. Always will."

The mammoth one merely glared in silence.

"You guys with the Sharks or the Jets?" Holden sounded amused. "Can't help feeling you're about to break out into a musical number."

"No time to rumble tonight, boys," Hunter chimed in lightly. "Better get home to your mother."

That was it — the straw that broke the camel's back. I had no doubt the O'Banions would've attacked at some point no matter what the twins said or did, but at the mention of their mother, they lost it. All four of them charged in unison. Hunter used the grip on my arm to fling me — literally, like a frisbee — backward, out of range. I sailed through the air, crashing to a breath-stealing halt against the brick alley wall. My purse went flying off my shoulder as I ricocheted, barely managing to catch myself before I fell to the pavement.

"Run, Gwen!" Hunter yelled. He wasn't looking at me — he was busy ducking a punch from Scar-Face, simultaneously aiming a kick at Mickey's crotch. While Mickey crumpled in pain, clutching his balls, Hunter pivoted to deliver a punishing blow to Scar-Face's nose. I heard a muffled crack and saw a dark splatter of blood sail across the brick. Not to be outdone, Holden socked a southpaw to Neck-Tattoo's eye socket. I watched his head snap back with the force of the blow.

Outnumbered or not, the twins were holding their own. In fact, they were kicking ass. They totally would've won... if not for the fourth brother. The big one. Correction: the mammoth one. He was not, I saw belatedly, engaged in the bloodbath. Oh, no. He was stalking my way, his cold eyes intent on my face. When I saw him coming, any hope I'd had about this fight going our way evaporated in less than a heartbeat.

"Damn it, Gwen! *Go!*"

Hunter's voice jolted me into motion. Turning my back on the brawl, I sprinted back the way we came, my go-go boots pounding on the pavement. I could hear Jumbo O'Banion chasing after me, gaining ground with each passing second. Even if I'd had the time to call for help, I couldn't — my purse was lost to me, my phone along with it, sitting uselessly on the pavement somewhere.

My terror mounted to a fever pitch as my wild eyes locked on the mouth of the alley. I could see the throngs of people there, smiling and laughing as they drank in the festivities. If I could only get there, someone would surely help me. I'd be safe. I'd find a phone. I'd call Graham or Detective Hightower. They'd know what to do.

My heart pounded like a battering ram against my ribs as I picked up my pace. I wasn't the fastest runner in the world, especially in heels, but my weekly jogs had built up a decent amount of stamina. The man on my heels might be big, but he wasn't particularly fast. I heard his labored breathing as the distance between me and safety shrank from twenty yards to ten to five.

Jumbo couldn't catch me.

I flew out of the alleyway, into the thick crowd. My momentum was so great, I barreled straight into a cluster of camera-toting tourists with matching shirts that said 'I WENT TO HELL AND ALL I GOT WAS THIS LOUSY T-SHIRT' in bold letters. The impact was like a bowling ball striking stationary pins. Two of them fell backward on their asses, the others wheeled wildly in different directions.

"Hey!" One of the men exclaimed as he caught his balance. "Watch where you're going, lady!"

I didn't even pause to apologize or ensure they were okay. I darted away, losing myself in the crowd, hoping Jumbo couldn't keep track of me in the melee. I didn't dare look back as I moved down the pedestrian mall, weaving past two twelve-foot-tall men on stilts, several guys in the infamous Ghostface mask from *Scream*, and a whole bevy of preteens clad in gold and red Gryffindor uniforms.

I spotted a man in a cop uniform and raced up to him. "Help! Please, you have to help me! I'm being chased!"

After approximately three seconds of staring into his baffled eyes, I realized my mistake. He wasn't a real cop. He was just dressed as one for Halloween.

Hellfire.

"Uh, look—"

"Forget it!" I hissed, glancing back over my shoulder. No sign of Jumbo, but I knew I didn't have long before he reappeared. "Do you have a phone?"

He gave me another baffled look. "Is this some kind of bit?"

Swallowing a scream of frustration, I pivoted on my heels and started running through the crowd again. I was forced to dodge and weave, the street was so thick with people. I tried twice more to ask for help, nearly begging for someone to let me use their cellphone, but people either looked at me like I was a scam-artist attempting to rob them or laughed like it was all part of the Halloween fun. No one took me seriously.

After the third failed attempted at engaging, I chanced a look back and spotted the top of Jumbo's head, jutting up beyond a group of people on a ghost tour.

Shit!

I ducked behind a nearby tree, praying he hadn't seen me. It was dark, I was disoriented, and fear was clouding my judgement. I needed a plan. I needed a safe place to catch my breath. The store was closest. By a small stroke of luck my keys were in the front pocket of my dress, where I'd shoved them after locking up. If I could get there, I could barricade myself inside and call for help. I wasn't far — I spotted Sweet Somethings to my left, one of my favorite places to pop in for an ice cream cone in the summertime. It was only a few blocks from The Gallows.

Pulling a deep breath into my screaming lungs, I ignored the stitch in my side and began to push my way forward once more. I seemed to be moving against the tide of revelers, a minnow swimming upstream against a near-insurmountable current. By the time I rounded the corner and the shop came into view, I was nearly in tears. My spooky-cool window display was dark, the shop shingle swaying lightly in the wind. I raced for it like a port in a storm.

My hand shook as I shoved the key into the lock. I practically flung myself inside, the overhead bells rattling violently as I slammed the door shut immediately behind me. The sound of the deadbolt sliding home was the best thing I'd ever heard in my life.

I didn't flip on the lights — the last thing I wanted was to give Jumbo O'Banion a beacon to follow. The shop was dark and totally silent as I moved deeper inside, but I didn't need light to see. I knew the space like the back of my hand. This was my place. A safe place. My haven, from the time I was small. Nothing could hurt me here.

Someone moved in the shadows behind the espresso bar.

I screamed — a proper, heroine-in-a-slasher-film scream, both blood curdling and ear splitting in nature. Somehow, Jumbo had beaten me here. Somehow, he was inside, waiting for me. Somehow—

Hang on.

The shape in the shadows was way too small to be Jumbo. My scream tapered off as I peered harder, willing my eyes to adjust to the darkness. When they did, I rocked back on my heels, so great was my relief.

"*Hetti*?" I exclaimed, trading my terror for incredulity as recognition blasted through me. "Is that you?"

My barista rounded the counter and sidled toward me in silence. She'd changed out of her goth getup and was wearing a strange back cloak I'd never seen her wear before. I stared at her face for a long beat, wondering why it looked so strange. After a minute, I realized she wasn't wearing any makeup. Not even a stitch. Gone was her heavy eyeliner, her dark lipstick. Her thick silver piercings were missing from their various holes. Even her hair looked darker. No longer vibrant purple, but a deep black shade.

"Hetti?" I repeated weakly.

"Convenient you've come to me," she said oddly, staring at me. "I thought I'd have to track you down, get you away from your party. This is easier."

"W-what?" I blinked. "Listen, there are some seriously bad guys chasing me. Hunter and Holden are in trouble. They might be hurt. We need to call the police, get some help—"

"Oh, no. We can't do that."

I shook my head in confusion. "What do you mean, we can't? We have to. Didn't you hear what I just said? There are dangerous men after me and I need to—"

"I think you should be more concerned with the danger in here," she told me, taking a step closer.

I opened my mouth to ask what the hell that meant, but I never got the chance. Hetti's hand swung up from her side and, when her palm opened, I saw she was clutching a small fistful of familiar shimmery gray powder. Quick as a flash, she leaned forward and blew it straight into my face — delivering my second witchy-roofie in as many months.

Goddess, not again!

My instinctual gasp of shock sucked it up my nasal passages, into my lungs. I stumbled back, catching myself against one of the high top tables, feeling the earth tilt beneath my feet. It had been only a few seconds, but the drug was strong. I was already feeling its lulling effects, my limbs growing heavy, my thoughts clouding over. I managed to steer my eyes in Hetti's direction as my peripheral vision began to close in, black waves encroaching until all I could see was her face.

Her eyeliner-free gaze was more than a little unsettling as she watched me fall to the floor, her eyes filled with a gleeful sort of light that was only half as scary as the words she muttered after I hit the hardwood.

"Hac nocte resurgemus."

My drug-addled brain managed one last task before everything went dark, translating the Latin into English.

Tonight, we shall rise again.

As my consciousness slipped away, I knew somehow my already terrible night had just taken a big, fat turn for the worse.

THE CHANTING WOKE ME.

I came to with a start, gasping awake as air rushed down my throat. My eyelids felt like anvils as I heaved them open, barely capable of getting them to half-mast. A brilliant full moon greeted me, hanging so low in the sky you could almost reach out and take it in your palm. It was bright enough to illuminate the graveyard around me.

Not just any graveyard.

Broad Street Cemetery.

Fear coiled inside my chest, squeezing the air from my lungs. My first sensation was *cold*. I was freezing. It didn't take a rocket scientist to figure out why. I was splayed out on top of a stone crypt, much like the one where I'd found Eliza Proctor's body. And I was totally, completely paralyzed, my limbs unbound but incapable of movement. Somehow, I would've preferred ropes or duct tape. The sensation of utter numbness was more terrifying than any physical restraints.

"You're awake," a disembodied voice said from my left. "Good. It's almost time to begin."

I managed to turn my head a fraction, following the voice. Hetti's voice. Only, she didn't really sound like Hetti. There was a melodious cant to her words, a polished flow that I'd never heard before in all the days we'd spent working side by side. Her real voice, I realized with a painful start. And her real face, without the disguise of heavy makeup and goth gear to obscure it.

Tears prickled at my eyes as I stared at her. Betrayal was burning inside me, a raging inferno in my heart. I tried to speak, but my lips were too numb to get out a single word.

"I assume from the way you're gaping like a fish on dry land that you're trying to ask me something." She stepped a bit closer, away from the circle of cloaked, chanting figures that surrounded my crypt on all sides. "You won't be able to speak or move, not for some time." She glanced up at the moon. "And I'm afraid you don't have much time left, Gwendolyn. The lunar eclipse is only moments away."

My lips parted as I tried again, managing only a faint wheeze. "*Whhhh....*"

"Why?" Hetti's brows arched high on her forehead. Her light brown eyes were full of delight... and a dose of total madness. "You know why, Gwendolyn. You put it together yourself. I saw you, just this afternoon, with that map. Clever girl, aren't you? Nearly spoiled things for us. Couldn't have that — not after six months, slaving away beside you, making dreadful smalltalk, pretending to care about you and your life."

I flinched, a lance of pain shooting through my heart.

Goddess, how could I not have seen her true nature?

It was all a lie. All of it. Every shared laugh, every smile. Every moment I'd spent with this woman was a carefully orchestrated act. I felt supremely foolish. But, beneath the surface, a deep current of devastation was making its way through my system, effective as the paralytic powder I'd inhaled.

"I'll admit, you forced us to move up our timetable a bit." Hetti smiled at me indulgently, as though I was her pet. "Samhain would've been ideal. But the full moon tonight will be suitable enough for the ritual. Coupled with a lunar eclipse and our previous sacrifices, we surely have enough power to proceed."

I forced out another measly whimper. "*Plee....*"

"Please?" She shook her head. "Oh, no, Gwendolyn. I'm afraid the time for bargaining is long over. This plan has been in the making for generations. I will succeed where my mother failed. I will bring our coven back from the banishment your precious *Aunt Colette*—" She spat the words, eyes flashing with spite. "—forced us into. I will drain all remnants of her bloodline to restore our rightful place in Salem. A true force of power, uncontested. As it was always meant to be."

The cloaked Heretics behind her began to chant again, a hushed flow of Latin I wasn't fluent enough to translate.

Hetti paused, brow furrowing as she stared at me. "The Bay Colony Coven has grown old. Not only in age, but in their ideas. They refuse to see the potential unlocked by blood sacrifice. They praise only their precious moon goddess and shun our horned god. They do not understand him, or those of us who choose to follow him. They cannot grasp our loyalties." The glint of madness in her eyes was truly alarming. Her voice was a hushed, fanatical whisper. "It is his dark dominion to which we pay fealty, and his superior malevolence through which we worship. It is through his ruinous grace that tonight, we make our sacrifice and reclaim our stolen birthright."

"*Hac nocte resurgemus,*" the Heretics chanted in unison from all around me, a chilling chorus. "*Hac nocte resurgemus.*"

Reaching into the pocket of her cloak, Hetti pulled out an ornate athamé, much like the one that killed Eliza. My eyes fixed on it, unable to tear away from the blade as it shone in the moonlight.

"We might've left the Bay Colony Coven alone, but their new High Priestess began to cause problems. She was hovering too close, trying to bring you into their circle of protection. We couldn't have that. She left me with no choice." She smiled her crazy smile, spinning the knife playfully in her grip. "I admit, I did find a certain amount of enjoyment in staging her body for you to find."

Hetti killed Eliza.

It all made sense. The pieces fell into place like dominoes inside my mind. She knew my running route. She had access to the weapon that killed her. She was certainly crazy enough to do the deed.

I tried to jerk away as Hetti reached out and patted me on the cheek, but my frozen body barely moved.

"There, there, Gwendolyn. Don't look so distraught. It will all be over soon. You'll be at peace on the other side. And you can take heart in knowing your death was not without purpose. Indeed, you will be the very mechanism by which we rise."

"*Hac nocte resurgemus! Hac nocte resurgemus!*"

With the tip of her index finger, Hetti pushed my temple so my lolling head was facing the night sky once more. I couldn't see her, but I heard the rustle of her cloak as she moved backward to rejoin the other Heretics.

"Tonight, we gather beneath the light of the full moon," she called, her voice high and clear, carrying across the graveyard. "Tonight, we reclaim what was taken from us! Tonight, we—"

"*NOT ON OUR WATCH, YOU WITCH!*"

My head snapped over at the sound of two familiar voices coming from the far side of the graveyard. In disbelief, I watched as Sally and Agatha ran from the shadows, their slight, hunched forms weaving around tombstones. In their hands, they each held a carved wood staff, the kind I imagined a wizard might carry. On their heels, I saw six other dark forms streaking toward us in the darkness, each holding a staff, each cloaked in a similar matching cloak.

The Bay Colony Coven was here.

And they were here to fight.

All hell promptly broke loose. The Heretics charged out to meet them on the field of battle, chanting in Latin as they ran. Paralyzed as I was, I couldn't turn my head to see what was happening as they moved out of sight. All I could do was listen to the sound of pained grunts, the thuds of staffs colliding with flesh, the screams of pain.

"Ag! On your left!"

"I see him, Sal!"

My heart swelled. They'd shown up for me. They were fighting for me. I'd never felt so useless, lying there, unable to do more than twitch the tips of my fingers and wiggle my toes inside my go-go boots. The haze was beginning to lift from my thoughts, my mind clearing a bit more with each passing moment, but my body was still effectively useless.

How long until I could move again?

"This doesn't concern you!" Hetti screeched, her voice lifting above the din. "Begone!"

"You have no power here!" Agatha yelled back in defiance. "You—*Ahh!*"

Her abrupt scream of pain made me jerk upright. I only managed to lift a few inches off the crypt, but it was progress.

"Ag!" Sally screamed. "No!"

I tried desperately to move, but all I could do was lie there, listening as the Bay Colony ladies were slowly overwhelmed by the Heretics. I couldn't see what was happening. Were they alive? Were they unconscious? I thought of Hetti's knife, shining in the moonlight, and heard Agatha's pained scream over and over, a constant replay inside my mind. Tears streamed out my eyes, pooling on the stone beneath my head.

I had never felt so hopeless and weak. Not when I was five, forgotten at school by my mother while she went on a weekend-long bender, which resulted in a short stint at a girls' home on orders of CPS. Not when I was ten, locked out of our trailer all afternoon, forced to take shelter with coked-out neighbors. Not when I was fifteen, awoken by one of the creepy guys Mom brought back to party, his disgusting fingers gliding down my tank top strap. Not when I lost Aunt Colette's light and felt the only solid ground I'd ever walked on crumble into dust.

Not ever.

Silence eventually descended on the graveyard. All I could hear was the thudding of my pulse, a constant roar between my ears, as the Heretics moved back into their circular formation around the crypt. Hetti returned to stare down into my face. Her dark hair was mussed, her cloak torn. There was a dark shiner blooming on her right eye socket.

Good, I thought, glaring up at her. *I hope they gave you hell, you crazy bitch.*

"Now that that minor hiccup has been dealt with," Hetti said conversationally. "We can continue."

Something came over me in that moment. Maybe it was rage. Maybe it was something else — some inner strength I didn't know I possessed, some tiny fragment of the magic that Aunt Colette always told me flowed through my veins.

My golden girl, my little flame, you burn so bright someday you'll set the world on fire.

Fighting the paralysis, I summoned every bit of my strength, infused my arm with all the power I could summon, and reached up. Not for Hetti's smug, victorious face, which was within swinging distance, but for the pendant around my neck. The one Sally gave me.

For protection, she'd said.

At the time, I thought she was being philosophical. But in that instant, I used a far more literal interpretation of her words. My hand closed around the chain and I yanked it free from the confines of my dress. Hetti, too stunned to move, stood there gaping at me as my fist gripped the bone shard. I had no acute control over my movements yet, no real mastery of my fine motor skills, but I aimed in the general direction of her face and jammed upward. The shard made contact with her cheek, the sharp point piercing her soft flesh. I felt no small amount of satisfaction as she screamed and stumbled backward, clawing at her bleeding cheek.

"You bitch!" she shrieked. "You fucking bitch!"

I could hear the Heretics murmuring, closing in from all sides. I used the brief moment of chaos to my advantage, heaving my half-numb body sideways, rolling off the crypt. My body plummeted four feet and hit the earth with a breath-stealing thud. All the air evacuated my lungs in a great whoosh. I sucked in a desperate gulp, knowing I had approximately zero seconds to get away. Never one to squander an opportunity, I started crawling from the crypt, my fingers clawing at the grass as I dragged my dead weight along.

"Don't worry about me, you fools!" Hetti was screeching somewhere behind me. "She's getting away! The eclipse has already begun! We have only a few minutes left for the ritual!"

I crawled faster, aware I wasn't making very much progress, but not about to stop. When a hand fisted in my hair, jerking me up onto my feet, I gasped as pain bolted through me.

"Where do you think you're going?" a low male voice hissed. "We aren't done with you, Gwendolyn Goode."

Several other sets of hands grabbed at my limbs. Before I

knew it, I'd been carried back to the crypt and deposited upon it — this time, they held me down so there was no chance of escape, one Heretic stationed at each appendage, a steely grip around an arm or an ankle. The others moved into position, recreating their circle, chanting their strange Latin spells in an eerie, haunting refrain.

I kept my eyes on the moon, watching the eclipse slowly engulf its glowing surface, shades of deep reddish brown bleeding inward. It was rather beautiful. (In fairness to the moon, it probably would've been more so if it wasn't shepherding in the moment of my death.)

The chanting picked up speed. I didn't try to fight against my captors. Their grips were like steel and my body was so worn out from my previous escape attempt, I knew I couldn't roll off the crypt again even if the opportunity arose. There was a certain sort of acceptance in that knowledge.

I was about to die.

Hetti reappeared, one hand pressing a wad of white cloth to her cheek, which appeared to be bleeding profusely — a sight that gave me no small amount of pleasure — and the other gripping the ornate athamé blade — a sight that instilled within me no small amount of fear. Backlit by the moon, which was now almost fully stained a deep red as the eclipse progressed to totality, she appeared even more deluded than before.

"Brothers and sisters," she called, her formerly smug voice strained by pain. "The moment we have waited for is finally upon us!"

The chanting increased.

The eclipse hit totality, fully encompassing the moon.

It was time.

Hetti looked down at me. Her eyes were brimming with both pain and triumph. "I hope you enjoyed that little show of defiance, Gwendolyn." She lifted the dagger high overhead. "It will be your last."

My eyes fixed on the blade as it sliced down toward my heart. Time seemed to slow down as I watched my death coming at me. They say, when you die, your life flashes before your eyes. That wasn't my experience. I didn't see everything I'd ever been through. I didn't relive the pivotal moments, or replay the highest highs. I didn't see much of anything, really. But I heard something. A deep, rasping voice I'd know anywhere.

Any place.

Any lifetime.

Be it this one or the next. (And, based on current circumstances, it would have to be the next, seeing as I was about to be shuffled off this mortal coil.) I could only hope, as the knife came closer, that reincarnation was real. Because if I got another shot at living, I wasn't going to use it pushing a man like Graham Graves away. I wasn't going to die without telling a man like that — one who pulled out urchin spines and set to rights upended chip displays and wrapped you tight in his arms and rested his forehead on yours and pulled you in close for the best kiss of your life and cooked delicious meals and collected fine art and wanted to fix up your house until it finally felt like a home because he knew you'd never had one — that I loved him beyond measure, beyond limit, beyond reason.

I heard him so clearly, it was like he was there with me in that final moment. And, hearing him, I closed my eyes to block out the horror of Hetti's deathblow, but also to savor the sound.

One last instant of Graham.

One last instant of life.

Not alone, at the end.

Never alone, when I was with him.

"*Gwendolyn!*"

All things considered, it wasn't a bad way to go.

CHAPTER TWENTY-SIX

If at first you don't succeed, try, try again. If at second you don't succeed... take, take a nap.
— Gwen Goode, in need of sleep

First came the shot, then came the scream.

My eyes sprang open in time to see Hetti lurch sideways, thrown off balance as the bullet tore through her shoulder. The knife, which had been headed straight for my heart, fell out of her hand, clattering to the stone by my hipbone.

I blinked, sure I was dead and hallucinating. At least, until I heard Graham's voice shouting my name again, followed by the sound of running footsteps.

He was here.

He came for me.

The Heretics scattered in an instant, releasing my limbs to

run for cover as the Gravewatch men descended on Broad Street Cemetery.

They didn't make it far.

I managed to sit halfway up, my tired muscles protesting as I watched Holden chasing a cloaked figure past a tomb on my right, gun in hand. Hunter wasn't far behind, taking down another Heretic in a full-body tackle any defensive lineman would envy. Sawyer clocked one of them over the head with the butt of his gun as Welles did a wickedly cool leg-sweep maneuver that sent another one of them sprawling ass over elbows across the grass. And then, I couldn't see anything else, because Graham was there, his broad chest filling my whole visual field as his fingers fisted in my hair and he hauled me up against him. He was gripping me so tight it was borderline painful, but I didn't care. Not a hoot. Not an iota. Not at all.

He was here.

I was alive.

We were together.

"Gwen." His voice was rough, almost raw. Ragged with emotions I couldn't put a proper name to.

"I'm okay," I informed his leather jacket, since I was pressed too tight against him to see his expression. The words came out muffled.

He pulled back enough to look down at my face. His beautiful green eyes were narrowed as they moved back and forth, studying me.

"Graham, I'm okay," I repeated.

His mouth was a flat line, no trace of a smile. I wanted to kiss it but I figured that wasn't pertinent at this exact moment in time.

"Scared the shit out of me," he gritted, jaw locked tight. "Thought I was too late."

My hand shook with the effort, but I managed to lift it to his cheek. He had a day's worth of stubble lining his sharp jawline and dark circles beneath his eyes. "Just in time, baby," I whispered. "Now, are you going to kiss me, or what?"

His mouth came down and he finally claimed my mouth with his own. A burning kiss, a desperate kiss, one that said everything he wasn't able to, encompassing all his fear and his need and his love, pouring it into me until I thought my heart might explode from the effort to contain all of it at once.

Only the muffled moan of pain from the ground beside the crypt was enough to break us apart. Graham pulled back from me, turning to glare down at Hetti, who was writhing in pain. The bullet wound to her shoulder was bleeding a lot, but not life threatening.

"He shot me," she wailed, clutching her wound. "He freaking shot me!"

"You tried to *kill me*!" I snapped at her, wishing I was strong enough to do more than glare. She deserved a swift kick in the ass. "You hurt Agatha and Sally!" My eyes flew to Graham. "Oh my god! Are they—"

"They're fine. Unconscious, but breathing steadily. I think they were clocked over the head or dosed with something." His hand cupped my cheek, skimming over my eye socket. "Ambulance is already on its way."

In the distance, I heard the sound of approaching sirens and a wave of relief crashed through me. The Bay Colony Coven would live to hex another day. The Gravewatch boys were tracking down the fleeing Heretics. Eliza's murder had been solved. Hetti was incapacitated. And, best of all, I was still breathing.

My eyes shifted to Graham's. He was staring down at Hetti with distaste but, feeling my gaze, turned his attention to me. He saw me struggling to sit fully upright and instantly moved to help me, his firm hands closing around my waist as my legs swung around to dangle off the edge of the crypt.

"Did you call the police?" I asked, brows lifting.

He nodded. "Hightower is on his way with the full cavalry."

"How did you know? How did you find me?"

"Babe." His lips twitched. "Map in your purse. You led me right to you. Short of using a bat-signal in the sky, couldn't have been better."

I blinked, stunned. (Though, I shouldn't have been. This was Graham, after all. He knew everything.) "Oh."

His lips twitched again. "I was almost back to town when all this went down. Soon as the twins shook the O'Banions, they went to the store. No sign of you, but security cameras picked up your barista here—" He nudged Hetti's side with his steel-toed boot, making her moan. "—dragging you out the back exit, into a van. Doesn't take a PI license to put two and two together. Welles saw what was going on, ran a quick background check. Turns out, your barista isn't who she claims to be. Henrietta Charles is no goth from the Pacific Northwest. She's a local girl with deep ties to a few dark Wiccan groups — so dark, they've been flagged by the Feds for their strange practices in the past. Pose a threat to human life." His eyes moved back to the writhing woman at his feet. "I should've checked her out sooner. That's on me."

"Baby, you couldn't have known."

"It's my job to know, Gwen."

"I hired her — I worked alongside her for six freaking *months* — and I never had a clue who she really was." I sighed, shaking my head. "If you're going to blame yourself, you have to blame me too."

"I do blame you," he said flatly. "Told you before, you have to be more careful about who you hire."

My eyes narrowed. "You know, you're diminishing the happy *my-boyfriend-is-a-hero* glow I've got going on, here."

"Think I'll survive. The *my-boyfriend-saved-my-life* sex later will surely make up for it."

He was not wrong.

The sirens grew so loud, they were wince-inducing. I saw the accompanying strobe of red and blue lights flashing against the crooked tombstones all around us as a dozen squad cars squealed into the parking lot. Graham's men were slowly marching the Heretics back into our line of sight. The cloaked figures' hands were bound behind their backs with cable ties. They looked like sad, broken dolls, staring at the grass despondently.

"She killed Eliza," I whispered, my eyes flickering from Hetti's prone form to Graham's face. "She admitted it."

He nodded. "Figured as much. Hightower will take her — and all her minions — into custody. We'll make sure she's put away for a long time, baby. She won't hurt you again."

It was at this moment, as if conjured, that Caden Hightower arrived on the scene. He ran up to us, gun in hand, chest covered by a bullet proof vest. His bright blue eyes swept the scene, taking in the paramedics hustling toward the incapacitated Bay Colony ladies, the Gravewatch boys standing guard over the Heretics, Hetti writhing on the ground, me sitting on the tomb, and Graham standing at my side, the conquering hero.

"See you've got things pretty well handled, Graves," he muttered, but there was no anger in his tone. "Not sure why I bothered getting this badge when you're going to do my job for me."

"You get the fun part, Hightower." Graham gestured down at Hetti.

Caden grinned, a flash of white teeth in the dark. "True

enough." His bright grin faded as he looked at me. "You okay, Gwen?"

I managed a nod. "I'm fine."

Graham scoffed.

Cade didn't look like he fully believed me, but he nodded. Holstering his gun, he exchanged it for a set of cuffs. Before he knelt to slap them on Hetti's wrists, he met Graham's gaze one last time. There was no humor in his eyes. Not at all. His stare was deadly serious, as were his words.

"You'll take care of her."

It wasn't a question. It was a demand. But Graham answered him anyway.

"You know I will," Graham said, sounding just as deadly serious as Cade. "Not in my nature to let go of something price-less once it's in my hands."

"You're a lucky bastard, you know that?"

Graham shrugged. "Luck's got nothing to do with it, High-tower. Takes work. Takes patience of a goddamned saint. But god knows, it's worth it." He paused. "You'll see what I mean when you meet her."

"Who?" Cade asked lowly.

"Your world," Graham answered.

At that point, done with the conversation whether it was finished or not, he turned his back on the detective. Apparently he had no interest in seeing how it all played out — not with Hetti's arrest, not with his men, not with the paramedics. As soon as his gun was holstered, he lifted me into his arms, one going behind my back, the other sliding beneath my knees. Then, I was cradled against his chest and we were moving — across the dark graveyard, down a short flight of uneven stone steps, to the street where the Bronco was parked. He bleeped the locks and settled me into the passenger seat with so much care, you'd think I was made of glass. He even buckled my seatbelt for me.

When he made to pull back, I laced one of my hands behind his neck and yanked him close, until our foreheads bonked together.

"Graham?"

"Right here, gorgeous."

I sucked in a breath, almost afraid to hope. "It's over, right?"

His fingers slid into the hair by my nape. I almost groaned, it felt so good. His mouth came down to brush mine.

"Yeah, baby. It's over," he whispered against my lips. "No more fear. No more walking on eggshells. No more *existing*." Another lip brush, this one longer, stirring the banked heat inside me to a small blaze. "Time to start *living*."

I kissed him back with as much strength as I could manage — which wasn't much, given my body was still fighting the after-effects of the drugs — until we were both breathing hard, our hands roaming places that weren't exactly appropriate for a crime scene. Several cops were standing by the fence less than a dozen feet away, chattering into their radios as their colleagues loaded Heretics into the back of squad cars.

"Graham?"

"Still here, babe," he whispered against my lips, sounding amused.

"Take me home?"

He kissed me again. "Okay, Gwen. Let's go home."

It was the dead of night when my eyes peeled open. Moonlight was streaming through my window, a shaft of it perfectly illuminating Graham's face in the dark. His eyes were open and they were fixed on me. He looked like he'd been awake a while — which was understandable, given the events of the past week, but still made my brows lift.

"Are you watching me sleep?" I asked, my voice edged with exhaustion.

"Yeah."

"That's a little weird, Graham."

"Not weird at all, in my opinion." His hand slid down my naked side and settled at my hip. "Spent a long time thinking I'd never get to lie here in the dark, you in my arms, breathing deep, feeling safe enough to close those gorgeous eyes of yours. Didn't particularly like the thought of a life of separate bedrooms, but I would've dealt with it if that's what it took to be with you."

My breath hitched.

"Thankfully, you pushed through your fears," he continued. "And, baby, being brave enough to do that? That's a *gift*. One I'm not going to squander. One I'm going to enjoy whenever the fuck I want. That means, yeah, sometimes I'm watching you sleep. You get me?"

My throat was lodged with a lump the size of Texas. Somehow, I managed to mutter, "I get you, Graham."

"Good." His lips found mine, a featherlight brush in the dark. His fingertips dug into my skin as his grip on my hip tightened. "Something else, Gwen."

"What is it, baby?"

"I love you."

I sucked in a breath as my whole world careened to a sudden halt at those three little words. The globe tilted on its axis, the stratosphere spun madly out of sync. "*What?*"

"Know you heard me, but I'll tell you again anyway. I love you, Gwendolyn. I always loved you. Even when you drove me fucking crazy with your bullshit, pushing me away for two goddamn years when we could've been together."

"Um. Excuse me? My *bullshit*? Are you sure you love me? You can't even say it without insulting me at the same time!"

He ignored this snippy retort. "Never been more sure of

anything. I want this. I want you and me, together. Fighting, fucking, laughing, I don't care what we do so long as we do it side by side. I want to build a whole life with you."

"A whole life," I repeated, feeling like I'd been punched in the gut. My pulse kicked up a notch, beginning to pound — an equal mix of joy and panic thrumming through me. When I managed to speak, I could only do it in a whisper. "Together."

"Yeah. You got a problem with that plan?"

"Um..."

"Gwen—" he started, frustration mounting.

"I've never lived like you live," I blurted out. "I might not be any good at it."

"I don't give a fuck if you're good at it," he replied instantly. "So long as you start living."

"I live."

"Baby, you exist. You make it from Point A to Point B." His lips brushed mine again, soothing the defensive hurt that had sprung up inside me as he spoke. "I want you to start *living*. Putting down roots. Not flipping every light switch when you walk out of the room to save on electric, not keeping your thermostat at subzero to avoid utility bills. Not filling your pantry with canned goods and condiment packets as a survival mechanism in case the money runs out."

I flinched in his arms. I couldn't help it — I hadn't even realized he'd noticed my tendency to hoard mini sauce and ketchup packets. (I should have. He was Graham, he noticed *everything*.)

Growing up poor, I'd learned the hard way that starvation was never more than a few meals away. To this day, I could spend hours in the grocery store, running my hands over all the things I'd been deprived of as a kid, filling up my cart with canned goods and frozen pizzas and other non-perishable items that would ensure I'd never go to bed famished, not ever again.

I hardly ever cooked, but my pantry was well-stocked. I had a whole drawer full of ketchup, mustard, and relish, along with myriad soy, duck, and hot sauces, stashed away each time I ordered takeout, just in case I ever fell back on tough times. Hunger was the best condiment in my experience... but I *really* hated plain french fries.

"There's nothing wrong with my sauce packets," I informed him, somewhat embarrassed he'd so easily pegged my food insecurities. "I'm keeping them."

"You're not."

He was so bossy. "*Why?*"

"When I move in, I'm buying bottles," he informed me flatly. "The jumbo-sized ones from Costco that take an age to run out. And, when they do, I'll buy you more."

I blinked. Hard. "But—"

"Not done," he cut me off. "I'm also bringing my fridge from the loft because yours is old and inefficient and doesn't hold half as much shit. While we're on the subject of your kitchen, I plan to renovate it as soon as I'm done with the library. And I plan to actually *cook* in said kitchen, because I'm not living off takeout and wine for the rest of my life."

"You..." I was struggling to process everything he was saying. "You want to cook in my kitchen?"

"Gwen. Are you getting this yet?" His lips twitched as he gazed at me. "I want it *all*, baby. I want to put a ring on your finger. I want to marry you. Not tomorrow, but soon, so brace yourself."

I sucked in another sharp breath.

He kept going. "I want vacations at the beach, you in a bikini, fucking in the sand, sleeping under the stars. I want to teach you to ski in the winters and sail in the summers."

"Skiing is dangerous."

His lips twitched again. "It's also fun as hell."

"So?"

483

"So, everything worthwhile carries some risk. But I'll be right there, step by step, from the bunny slope to the black diamonds."

"*Black diamonds?!*"

"Babe. Do you honestly think I'd let you put yourself in any real danger?"

My eyes narrowed. "You just have an answer for everything, don't you?"

He grinned — *arrogant!* — but when the amusement faded from his expression, it was replaced by something breathtakingly gentle. "Gwen, you have to know... I want more than just vacations and condiment bottles."

I did know that. He'd told me more than once, spelled it out in plain English, as was his way. Still, suddenly, I was trying very hard not to cry. "Um..."

"I want to fix up this house, to make it ours," he carried on. "I want to fill up these rooms with kids, yours and mine. I want to watch you grow old. Gray hair on our heads, a pair of rocking chairs in the back yard. Cranky and wrinkled and unrecognizable and still together. Still in love."

I was losing the battle against tears. "Graham..."

"I want to live by your side, then die in your arms," he whispered. "And when we finally leave this earth, I want matching funeral plots."

Okay, now I was definitely crying. The tears streamed down my face, a free-flowing torrent. He pulled me up against his chest and allowed me to weep into the hollow of his neck. When I'd finally regained a semblance of control over my emotions, I swallowed hard and breathed one word.

"Okay."

"Okay?" His arms tightened. "You're agreeing? You're not going to fight me on this?"

"I'm agreeing," I whispered, voice thick. "But if we must get matching funeral plots, I want mine to say '*I'm with stupid.*'"

He laughed, the sound so full of joy it rocked his whole body.

I craned my neck back to look up into his face. Our gazes tangled instantly, his such a piercing green it took my breath away.

"I love you too, you know," I informed him quietly. "I've loved you since I was ten."

His eyes flared.

"I always loved you," I tacked on, just for the hell of it. "Even when I hated you."

His expression morphed into a hot, possessive look that promised good things in my immediate future. I felt a responding tingle shoot directly between my legs as he leaned down and claimed my mouth in a searing kiss. But not before he'd whispered something that I knew, as long as I lived, I'd never, ever forget.

"I love you, Firecracker. Forever."

EPILOGUE

The door to The Gallows swung open with a tinkle of bells. Everyone tensed in response — from Florence and Desmond, sitting on the espresso bar stools, to Welles, leaning up against the New Age bookshelf, to the twins, planted on the emerald sofa by the window display, to Graham, standing beside me behind the counter, to Detective Hightower, sipping his latte on the other side. (I was no Hetti Charles, but I could work a bit of magic with the espresso machine in a pinch. Everyone was well caffeinated, even without the fancy foam art.)

The atmosphere turned tense because we weren't expecting anyone outside our small circle to come into the shop. We weren't open for business today. We'd been closed all week, in fact, what with my barista turning out to be a criminal mastermind, my psychic and her parrot off to Maine to live with her sister in the backwoods, and my own will to sell mystical curiosities and caffeinated beverages seriously depleted in the wake of my near murder.

I'd spent the week since that fateful night having an obscene amount of sex, letting Graham cook me well-balanced meals, picking out myriad paint samples for the remaining rooms in the house, and letting Agatha and Sally teach me to play canasta. Thus far, I'd lost every round — and a fair bit of my dignity — but gained several pounds in bodyweight thanks to Sally's raspberry cheesecake. (Which was, to put it mildly, orgasmic.)

I'd returned to the shop for the first time today, in hopes of reclaiming my space. One Hetti had tainted with her betrayal. Graham knew I was worried about coming back, so he'd insisted on tagging along. He must've put the word out to the rest of the gang as well because, one by one, they drifted through the door as if by happenstance. None of them bothered to explain why they'd shown up, but they didn't have to. I knew why. It was an undeniable show of support, and it touched me deeply.

My eyes hadn't stopped tingling for thirty straight minutes as I laughed and chatted with my friends, slowly feeling my stress ebb away as they drove off whatever bad memories I'd been harboring. But, as the front door swung suddenly inward, a small modicum of that stress returned.

All chatter ceased. You could've heard a pin drop as a stunning, willowy blonde woman glided into The Gallows. Her outfit was an instant source of envy — a pale white boho-style dress that looked both innocent and sexy at the same time, with a matching set of white lace gloves that covered her hands from wrist to fingertip. Low boots gave her an additional few inches of height, which put her at extremely petite. Maybe five two, tops. Her hair was styled in long, flowing waves that kissed the middle of her back. But it was her eyes that were the showstopper. So light blue, they were almost translucent as they shifted around the shop.

Holden and Hunter sat up straight on the sofa when said eyes glided over them. Welles pushed off the wall entirely when they scanned past him. Detective Hightower's hand froze mid-air, the mug halfway to his mouth as his own intent blue stare collided with the woman's bewitching lighter one. She froze for an almost indiscernible heartbeat when she spotted the badge and gun clipped to his belt but, through what appeared to be sheer force of will, forced her eyes to move on to Graham and me.

"Hello," the stranger murmured uncertainly, pale blonde brows arched. "I'm looking for the owner of this shop."

"That would be me." Smiling, I detached myself from Graham's side and moved around the counter to meet her. (Graham, being Graham, followed close behind.) "Gwendolyn Goode," I offered, extending a hand toward her. "And you are?"

Her eyes finally latched onto me — but not, I noticed, before flashing quickly back to Cade. She hesitated a beat before she reached out to clasp her gloved hand against mine for the briefest of instants.

"Imogen Warner."

"Imogen," I repeated, smiling kindly at her. "Nice to meet you. Is there something I can help you with?"

Her eyes moved to Cade for the third time — *weird* — before shifting back to mine. "I'm..." She swallowed hard, seeming to steel herself. "Well, actually, I was here about the job posting."

"Oh! The backup barista job? That's fabulous! We're closed today but, I assure you, usually it's wall to wall customers in here. Especially this time of year. As it turns out, I'm looking for more than part-time, if you're in need of a full-time gig—"

"No," Imogen cut me off softly. Her light blue eyes were so clear, it was like staring in the shallows of a lake of a summer day. Somehow empty and full at once, both cool and warm at the same time. "Actually... I'm here about... the psychic position?"

The shop air, already tense, went totally electric.

BAD LUCK CHARM

The End

Be on the lookout for AT LAST SIGHT, Book Two in the WITCH CITY SERIES, coming Winter 2023. AT LAST SIGHT will chronicle the love story of clairvoyant Imogen Warner and detective Caden Hightower in another spooky, spicy, opposites-attract romance set in Salem, MA.

PLAYLIST

1. *W.I.T.C.H.* — Devon Cole
2. *Killer* — Valerie Broussard
3. *Freaking Me Out* — Ava Max
4. *She Calls Me Back* — Noah Kahan
5. *Midnight Moon* — Oh Wonder
6. *Willow (moonlit witch version)* — Taylor Swift
7. *Ultraviolence* — Lana Del Rey
8. *Seven Devils* — Florence + The Machine
9. *I Put A Spell On You* — Annie Lennox
10. *Sisters of the Moon* — Fleetwood Mac
11. *Devil Doesn't Bargain* — Alec Benjamin
12. *About You* — The 1975
13. *Romantic Homicide* — d4vd
14. *We Fell in Love in October* — Girl in Red
15. *Halloween* — Phoebe Bridgers
16. *Crystal* — Stevie Nicks

ABOUT THE AUTHOR

JULIE JOHNSON is a New England native and USA Today bestselling author of more than a dozen contemporary romance novels. When she's not writing, Julie can most often be found adding stamps to her passport, drinking too much coffee, striving to conquer her Netflix queue, and  Instagramming pictures of her dog. (Follow her: @author_julie)

She published her debut novel LIKE GRAVITY in August 2013, just before her senior year of college, and she's never looked back. Since, she has published more than a dozen other novels, including the bestselling BOSTON LOVE STORY series, THE GIRL DUET, and THE FORBIDDEN ROYALS TRILOGY. Her books have now been translated into ten different languages and appeared on bestseller lists all over the world, including Der Spiegel, AdWeek, Publishers Weekly, USA Today, and more.

You can find Julie on Facebook or contact her on her website www.juliejohnsonbooks.com. Sometimes, when she can figure out how Twitter works, she tweets from @AuthorJulie. For major book news and updates, subscribe to subscribe to JJ's newsletter.

Connect with Julie:

www.juliejohnsonbooks.com
juliejohnsonbooks@gmail.com

Also by Julie Johnson

THE UNCHARTED DUET:

UNCHARTED

THE FORBIDDEN ROYALS TRILOGY:

SILVER CROWN

GOLDEN THRONE

DIAMOND EMPIRE

THE ANYMORE DUET:

WE DON'T TALK ANYMORE

WE DON'T LIE ANYMORE

Milton Keynes UK
Ingram Content Group UK Ltd.
UKHW021105090823
426580UK00015B/415